D1040334

Acclaim for the novels of Helen A. Rosenburg

High praise for *The Circle of a Promise*...
"Helen Rosburg writes a wonderful feel for history. I enjoy her work tremendously. She's an incredible weaver of historical tales who should not be missed!"

--Heather Graham, NY Times Best-Selling Auther

Four stars for *For Love of Honor*!
"A gripping saga, heavy with historical details. A good read for readers who relish the setting of the French Revolution."

--Romantic Times BOOKclub Magazine

By Honor Bound is compelling! A real page turner!
"A richly developed novel full of well drawn characters and interesting historical details."

--Romantic Times BOOKclub Magazine

Other books by Helen A. Rosburg:

ELLIE AND THE ELVEN KING Medallion Press

THE CIRCLE OF A PROMISE Love Spell/Dorchester
THE CALL OF THE TRUMPET Love Spell/Dorchester

THIS IS THE BOOK OF ARABESQUE Pastime Press
THE SCULPTOR'S LADY Pastime Press

By Honor Bound

HELEN A. ROSBURG

Gold Level

This book is dedicated to
Connie Perry and Leslie Burbank.

Thank you with all my heart.

November 2003

Published by

Medallion Press, Inc.®
225 Seabreeze Avenue
Palm Beach, FL 33480

ISBN 0-9743639-1-X

Printed in the United States of America

For more great books visit **www.medallionpress.com**

ACKNOWLEDGEMENTS

I would like to thank the love of my life, James Rosburg, not only for accompanying me to France in the dead of winter, but for toting all the research materials home.

I would also like to thank my editor, Pam Ficarella. She has a good eye and she cried in all the right parts.

By Honor Bound

Prologue

October 16, 1793

The final few steps were difficult. Though the injury to her leg had been a long time healing, and the pain had lessened greatly, it was still not gone completely. The last stairs to the ground floor had to be taken carefully, and Honneure leaned heavily on her cane. Finally at the bottom, she rested against the wall for a moment to catch her breath and wipe the moisture from her brow. As she did so, the hood of her cape fell back and she immediately stiffened with fear.

A quick glance up and down the narrow street assured Honneure that no one had noticed her. She pulled her hood back up, tucking in stray wisps of pale, wavy hair. The sidewalks usually teemed this time of day. No doubt the crowds had all gone to the square to witness the execution.

A wave of nausea coursed through Honneure's frail form, so strongly it rocked her. She fought to keep down the meager breakfast of bread and tea Dr. Droulet had pressed upon her.

She could not be sick now. She could not. She had to be at the square also. She had to be there, at the end. She could not allow her friend to die alone. No matter how great her own personal danger, the bonds of love could not, would not, be denied.

Honneure squeezed her eyes tightly shut. It was ironic, she thought. So ironic. All of her adult life she had lived for and served her queen. Again and again she had sacrificed her own wants and needs for her sovereign's. She had believed it to be her duty and had been bound by honor to fulfill it. Honor bound. All her life, honor bound. And now?

Honneure shook her head, a humorless smile on the soft curve of her mouth.

Once again she risked all for her queen. Once again she was about to take the chance that she would never again see her beloved Philippe. This time, however, it was not from a sense of duty, but out of love. It was a lesson she should have learned long ago. If she had she might, even now, be in the arms of...

No. She mustn't think that way. There was no going back, only forward. The choices she had made in the past had led her to this moment in the present. She had to take what she had learned and keep moving. For as long, at least, as she was able.

Another swift glance up the street assured Honneure she was virtually alone. Leaning on her cane, she started on her journey. She only prayed she would arrive in time.

The closer she came to the square, the more crowded the streets became. A few people glanced at her curiously. But perhaps it was only because of her limp. Or, because of the dark cloak and hood she held closed at her throat on such a warm, fall day. She recognized no one, and no one recognized her. No one had the slightest clue that she was a fugitive from the revolution. No one could possibly guess that she, too, had been slated to be fodder for the hungry blade of the guillotine.

Nausea churned again in Honneure's stomach. She could almost feel the blood drain from her face. But she did not hesitate. With one leg in rhythm with her sturdy cane, she hobbled onward.

Urgency quickened her lopsided gait, however, when she heard a cry from just ahead.

"She comes! The Widow Capet comes!"

"The Austrian whore!" came another shout. "The whore meets Lady Guillotine!"

Urgency turned to rising panic. Honneure stumbled as someone jostled her shoulder. "Sorry," she mumbled under her breath, although it was not her fault. "Sorry."

An overweight man with grizzled hair scowled at her. "Watch where yer goin'," he growled. Several others around him turned in her direction, all with thunderous frowns riding their brows.

Honneure lowered her gaze and tried to push her way through the mob in the opposite direction. She was going to have to be very, very careful. The mood of the crowd was murderous, indeed.

"There!" a woman's voice screamed. "There she is!"

Honneure felt her bladder weaken. But the woman was not talking about her. Taking a deep breath, she dared to glance up from the littered ground.

All heads were turned to the left. Fathers hoisted little children up on their shoulders so they could see better. Women stood on tiptoes.

Honneure could see nothing. She was only able to hear the creak and groan of the tumbril's wooden wheels as it rolled through the crowded, cobbled square. Emboldened by her growing horror, Honneure elbowed her way through the massed and stinking bodies.

Irritated grunts and rude curses filled her ears. She ignored them. She had but one thought, one purpose. She had to get there in time. Her friend must know she did not die alone.

There was so much pushing and shoving by all that hardly anyone paid any attention to Honneure. Ducking, squeezing sideways, and pushing by turn, she managed to make her way to the front of the crowd. Only a few heads bobbed in front of her. She was able, at last, to see her Queen. Tears immediately rushed to Honneure's eyes.

She sat facing backward, hands tied behind her back. Her posture was rigid, chin held high. The cart rumbled to a halt.

The former Queen had to be helped from the tumbril. Honneure noticed her pretty plum shoes as she slowly climbed the ladder to the scaffold. Her white piqué dress and bonnet were immaculate.

How like her. How very like her. A sob caught in Honneure's throat.

Though she remained erect, Antoinette began to tremble at last. The executioner seized her roughly and forced her to her knees. He tied her to the plank. The guillotine towered above her, blade glinting in the sun.

"You're not alone," Honneure whispered. "Antoinette, dearest friend, you're not alone," she said a little louder. Heads turned in her direction, but she paid them no heed. Pressing closer still to the scaffold, she slipped the hood from her head.

For one brief moment, Antoinette raised her eyes.

"My Queen!" The tortured cry rasped from Honneure's throat. She stretched out her hand, cane clattering to the ground.

The blade fell.

Pandemonium erupted. A thunderous roar, as if from a single, giant throat, burst from the crowd. General cheering followed. A few screams punctuated the tumult as the mob surged forward, crushing a few of its own under its terrible weight. Honneure feared she would be carried along with

4

them, but the few who surrounded her were not moving. They had noticed her when she cried out. Now they stared at her.

Though choking on her tears, Honneure quickly pulled her hood up. It was too late.

"It's that woman, from the Tuileries!" a pock-marked crone cried out. "It's her, the one who escaped!"

"Who? Who is it?" someone asked. A small crowd within the crowd had formed.

Honneure tried to back away, but a hand grasped her skirt.

"The bastard whore!" the scarred woman exclaimed.

Honneure screamed as another pair of hands tore at her, ripping her bodice.

"No!"

"Get her! Don't let her get away!"

Searing pain shot through Honneure's head as someone pulled her hair. She saw a great handful of it come away.

"Leave me alone!"

Hands dragged at her, pulling her down. She was losing footing. A fist connected with her nose and blood splashed.

"No!" Honneure screamed in denial.

But she could not save herself.

She was going to die ...

Chapter One

Winter, 1760

It was cold, as cold as Honneure had ever known it to be in her young life. She was loath to leave the warmth of the kitchen and brave the frigid hallways of the old stone château. She inched closer to the flames leaping and crackling in the hearth.

"Get a move on, child," Cook urged. "Madame will be waiting, and she's in quite a state. I believe there's something wrong with her little dog."

"There's nothing wrong with her dog. She's just heavy with pup," Honneure said as she took a reluctant step away from the fire.

"Be that as it may, you know how she is about her pet. And in the fuss Marguerite's gone and broken a vase or some such thing, and it needs cleaning up. Go on now, off with you. Remember, you're doing this for your mother and you'll want her to be proud. Madame will report to her on your performance, have no doubt."

Mention of her mother was the final prod Honneure needed. She had to fill in adequately for her absent parent, for there was always the fear of losing the coveted position of servant in the château. It was her duty to be loyal, devoted, and hardworking at all times. Without further hesitation the girl hurried from the room.

The shock to her flesh was immediate. Moments later the cold penetrated her plain woolen dress and the chemise beneath. Despite wearing stockings, her shoes were thin, and her toes were numbed at once. It was well and truly winter in the Loire Valley.

Honneure's footsteps echoed hollowly along the stone corridor, then were muffled as she reached the long, ornate carpet outside the master chambers. She knocked on a door at the end of the hall and quickly reclasped her arms across her thin breast.

"*Entrez!*" a voice called from within. Timidly, Honneure entered.

The scene was muted chaos. The mistress, Madame Choiseul, stood in the center of the chamber wringing her hands and murmuring distractedly. Her maidservant knelt in front of the fireplace attempting to calm a small dog who intermittently whined piteously and snapped at the hand trying to stroke it. The remains of a shattered vase were scattered across another red-hued carpet.

"Madame?" Honneure queried softly.

"Oh...oh, yes. The vase." Madame Choiseul waved absently in the direction of the debris. "Marguerite knocked into the table. My little dog...oh, *Mon Dieu!* What have I done? She's far too small...she's going to die!"

Honneure gazed sympathetically at the small animal with the grossly swollen belly. The dog was obviously in labor, frightened and in pain. Broken porcelain forgotten, Honneure went to the hearth and knelt beside Marguerite.

"Not the dog," Madame Choiseul said irritably. "The vase!"

"The dog I can help," Honneure replied without sarcasm. "The vase I cannot."

Madame Choiseul's brows arched over her close-set eyes. She started to speak, appeared to think better of it, then asked,

"Can you really help *mon petit chien?*"

"*Oui,* Madame," Honneure answered confidently, but absently, her concentration already on the small creature. For as long as she could remember, any animal in distress had always commanded her immediate and undivided attention.

"Careful!" Marguerite warned as Honneure extended her hand. "She will bite you."

The dog's lip curled, but Honneure hesitated only a moment. Speaking in a low, soothing voice, eyes averted, her fingers touched the animal's chin with its beard of long, silky hair. The dog growled but did not snap. Honneure's hand gently massaged along the neck to the small, trembling shoulder and, finally, down the back. Her experienced fingers worked in a slow, circular motion down the tiny spine, up again and down. The dog groaned and laid her head on the cushion of her bed.

"What are you doing?" Madame Choiseul hissed. "What have you done? What's wrong with her?"

"Ssssshhh," Honneure soothed, both to dog and mistress. "It's all right now. It's going to be all right now."

A visible contraction rippled across the dog's abdomen, and her head came up. Honneure's fingers continued their caress, and she crooned softly under her breath. The contraction passed, but another soon came. The dog appeared to strain. Her tail curled over her back. Honneure never faltered. Her slow, gentle massage continued through spasm after spasm. Then a final contraction, and the animal bent her body in an effort to lick at something that protruded from the birth canal. A puppy appeared, struggling feebly against its sac.

The little dog licked at the membrane until the puppy's head was clean. It no longer struggled, however, but fell limp and did not appear to breathe. "Have you a linen, please?" Honneure asked. "Quickly."

Marguerite seemed rooted to the spot, her wide-eyed gaze fixed on the lifeless body. It was Madame Choiseul who finally came to her senses.

"Here you are. Here." She thrust a length of peacock blue material in Honneure's direction. "Use this."

Honneure took the item her mistress proffered, picked up the puppy, and rubbed it briskly within the folds of the silk scarf. The bitch whimpered softly, but was distracted at once by another contraction, and within moments a second small form lay by her hind legs. She set about her duty, and the last pup made a healthy mewling sound as it wriggled blindly toward its mother's warm and engorged teats.

"What about the other?" Madame Choiseul inquired anxiously of Honneure. "Is it all right? Is it breathing? It's so still!"

Honneure remained silent. She continued her massage. Abruptly she stopped and held the puppy up, on its back, head unsupported. Nothing. Then, weakly, the tiny animal attempted to lift its head and right itself. It made a sound more feline that canine, and its tail began to rotate. Honneure took a deep breath, smiled, kissed the top of the miniature head and tucked the pup against its mother.

"A miracle!" Madame Choiseul exclaimed. She clasped her hands, and tears glistened at the corners of her eyes. "You've brought it back to life. How can I thank you?"

Now that the drama was over, Honneure was plunged coldly back into reality. "It was nothing...nothing," she muttered, head bent, as she gathered the pieces of broken porcelain. "I'm sorry I interfered. I hope I did not offend."

"Offend? Interfere? Why, you saved that precious little

life!" Madame Choiseul stooped briefly to stroke her pet and admire the two fat pups. She turned back to the child and regarded her as if for the first time. "You are Mathilde's daughter, are you not?"

"*Oui,* Madame," Honneure whispered, horrified to have so much attention turned upon her. A servant's job, as she had been so assiduously taught, was to be invisible.

"Where is your mother, child?"

"Ill, Madame," Honneure breathed, head still bent. "Cook sent me in her place."

"And well done, I might add. You have my thanks for aiding my little dog and her pups. Please tell your mother I pray for her return to good health. She has always been an obedient and willing servant."

No more words would squeeze from her lips, even to thank Madame Choiseul for her kindness. The whole situation was simply too overwhelming.

Honneure dared not look up, but from the corner of her eye saw her mistress turn away finally, back to her pet. With the shards cradled in her apron, she rose and tiptoed quickly from the room.

Praise from her mistress, Madame Choiseul, wife of the king's minister, was heady stuff indeed. To have been able to do what she loved best, to help the little dog, save the life of the pup...

This time Honneure did not feel the cold that clutched at her skin. Her feet barely touched the ground. Something warm and wonderful raced through her veins.

Instead of returning directly to the kitchen, Honneure took a detour to her favorite spot in the château. She ran lightly up the brick-paved, spiraling path to the top of the tower and out into the dreary, freezing afternoon. Her breath plumed about her reddened cheeks as she gazed at the magnificent vista.

Château D'Amboise, since the eleventh century, had dominated the Loire River, the island, and the bridge. Sitting atop the bluff, it was master of all it surveyed. The village spread below like a three-dimensional quilt, varied chimneys thrusting into the air. But it was not the view so much as the history that thrilled her.

Honneure had never known her father. He had died, so her mother had told her, before she was born. There had been only the two of them for all of her eight years, and a life of poverty and toil.

But there had also been evenings and the stub of a candle in a corner of their small, bare room, a few scraps of paper and a bit of charred wood. With these poor tools her mother had taught Honneure to write and to read. She had taught her a bit of geography, the history of the country in which she had been born, and a chronicle of the château that had been their home since Honneure's birth. She rewarded herself now with a stolen moment to revel in the priceless things she had learned.

It filled her with excitement to recall stories of the young Count of Angouleme, Francois, who had spent his adolescence at the château. As King Francis the First, he returned often to the favorite home of his childhood. And it was to Amboise the fabled queen Catherine de Medici fled with the young king Francis II during the plot of March 1560, when Condé, a prince of royal blood and leader of the Huguenot party, intended to seize Francis. A fierce and bloody battle had ensued between the plotters and the royal army. In the end those traitors, who had not been hung or quartered already, had their heads cut off in front of the entire court. Until recently, when Louis XV had given the château to his minister, Choiseul, it had been a prison. Its aura haunted and thrilled her in a way she could not put into words. She treasured the connection it gave her to the world of royalty she could never know. Its characters peopled her dreams and colored a life that would otherwise be only gray.

But Honneure's shivering was not now from excitement, and the mantle of history she so loved could not warm her. It was time to return to the kitchen, her duties, and her ailing mother.

. The thought of her only parent, lying pale and ill on her straw palette tightened a knot of fear in Honneure's abdomen. For the last three winters her mother had had a lingering cough, but it had never incapacitated her. To see her mother helpless frightened the child in a way she could not comprehend, and she found herself running back toward the warmth and light of the kitchen.

* * *

"There you are, miss." Cook, a thin, gray woman whose figure belied her profession, glared at Honneure with mock sternness. "I was beginning to wonder what had become of you."

"I had to clean up this mess." Honneure dumped the debris from her apron into a slop pail. "And Madame's little dog was having her puppies. I... helped."

"Did you now?" The woman smiled. "That was a timely event. You've always had a way with animals, haven't you, little one?"

Honneure ducked her head shyly and shrugged. "I love them," she replied simply, and cleaned up the remains of the leeks and dried apples Cook had been preparing.

"Here now," Cook remonstrated. "You've done enough for one afternoon, and you'll have made your mother proud."

A shadow passed over the woman's features, but the child did not notice. "I've made this broth. Be a good girl and try to get her to take a bit of it. It'll give her some strength."

Honneure murmured her thanks and carefully took the bowl. She walked steadily along the narrow corridor to a series of storage rooms, one of which had been converted to a chamber that served as their tiny home. A small fireplace provided modest warmth and, at the moment, the only light in the windowless room. As Honneure's eyes adjusted to the gloom, she knelt at her mother's side.

"I've brought you something to eat, *ma mère,*" she said softly. "Cook made you some broth."

There was no response. At first Honneure thought her mother was sleeping, but her eyes were open and she moved her head slowly from side to side as if she was in pain. Sweat beaded her brow.

"Mother?"

Still no reply. Mathilde's gaze did not focus on her daughter. She seemed to see something at a distance, beyond the stone walls of their room. The knot in Honneure's stomach tightened.

"How is Mathilde?"

Honneure jumped, startled by Cook's voice. "She's. . ." the child suddenly did not know what to say. Dread, like a lion closing in on its prey, threatened to overtake and overpower her. Tears welled up in her eyes. Angrily, she dashed them away with the back of her hand. "She'll be fine," she declared defiantly. "My mother will be fine."

The kindly woman's initial response was to agree with the child. But to comfort her with false hopes would no longer be a kindness. "Honneure," Cook began, "your mother is very ill. There's a chance she will . . ."

13

"No!" The heat of denial flooded Honneure's face with color. Without realizing she had done so, she covered her ears.

Cook sighed. "Very well, Honneure." She placed the cup and bowl she had carried on the floor near the child and gently pulled Honneure's hands from her head. "But if you are to continue to nurse your mother, you must keep up your own strength. Eat what I've brought you. And sleep. I will check on you both later."

Honneure merely nodded because she could not speak. She took her mother's hand and held it tightly. She did not hear Cook leave.

* * *

"The King!"

Honneure pulled sharply from her reverie and leaned over her mother. Mathilde's eyes widened and briefly brightened, but whether from fever or excitement Honneure could not tell. Or was that fear in her mother's unblinking gaze?

Honneure's own fears resurfaced. What was wrong with her mother? Why did she not seem to recognize her daughter, to hear or understand her? Why did she speak of the King, she who had been a servant all her life?

As if attempting to answer the swirl of questions eddying in Honneure's brain, Mathilde spoke again. "Never tell...never tell." Her voice was no more than a croak. "*Les cerfs... dans le parc... les cerfs.*"

"The deer," Honneure repeated, confused now as well as frightened. "The deer in the park?" What could her mother possibly mean? She took her mother's hand again and smoothed strands of damp hair from her forehead. "Mother, please, tell me what you mean," she begged. "I'm so frightened, Mother. I don't understand. Look at me. Please, look at me! Tell me what you mean!"

Something in her daughter's voice, perhaps the desperate plea of her child, finally penetrated the dying woman's consciousness. With a last great effort of will, Mathilde focused on Honneure, gathered the last of her swiftly ebbing strength, and whispered, "Poor, lost Honneure...my lost *honneur*."

Honneure watched her mother's eyes close once more, and she appeared to sleep. She pulled the rough blanket up over her mother's chest, then turned to the hearth, banked its dying embers, and threw on another piece of wood. She must try to stay awake, she knew, and ensure the fire's meager warmth was not lost. Nothing must disturb her mother's comfort.

The long day, her anxiety, and the fearfully long hours of the night had taken their toll, however. Honneure had meant merely to rest her head on her mother's palette, touching her lightly so she would be instantly aware of the smallest movement and answer her mother's need. But blessed sleep claimed her almost at once. The night deepened, and the darkness, as the fire flickered and died.

Chapter Two

The priest intoned the words of the mass, but they meant nothing to Honneure. She did not understand the Latin and was unfamiliar with the ritual, in spite of the fact Madame Choiseul had brought her to the Saint-Hubert chapel every day since her mother's death. She could not seem to concentrate. She stared either at the flames leaping in the tiny hearth to her right or at the hem of the priest's robe directly in front of her. Occasionally the movement of his hands caught her gaze when he made the sign of the cross. She listened to Madame and Marguerite murmur incomprehensible responses. Her mind drifted off in a haze.

On the left side of the miniature Gothic church, large enough for barely a dozen people, was the only thing Honneure regarded with any thought, the final resting place of a man called Leonardo da Vinci. Her mother had taught her about this great and talented personage, artist, and inventor. Francis I had convinced the great genius of the sixteenth century to come to Amboise in 1516 to end his days at the Court of France. Mathilde had said what honor it had brought to the château. She had received permission to show Honneure the paintings he had brought with him and left behind when he died, pictures of Saint Anne and the Virgin, Saint John the Baptist and Honneure's favorite, the likeness of a woman called Mona Lisa. Mathilde had often said how she would have loved to know such a man, to have talked with him and learned from him. Were they together now? Having both died at the château, were they somehow linked? Did Mathilde get her wish? Was she even now walking and talking with the man she had so admired?

Honneure closed her eyes and tried to hold on to the image. She could not bear to remember her mother as she had last seen her, so pale and cold and still, an alabaster effigy. That was not the mother who had loved her, hugged her, stroked her hair, and tried to teach her all she knew...the mother who was now gone from her forever.

The pain in Honneure's chest was almost unbearable. Her throat ached, and tears burned in her eyes. She clasped her chapped and reddened hands and, still on her knees, rocked slowly back and forth.

"Honneure? The mass is over, child. Come." Madame Choiseul gently assisted Honneure to her feet. "Come back to the château and warm by the fire. Cook will make you some tea."

Honneure obeyed, but stumbled, blinded by her tears. Marguerite pressed a handkerchief into her hand. They stepped outside the church, and the icy wind lifted her long, pale curls. Madame Choiseul guided her across the courtyard with a hand on her shoulder.

"Cook has something to tell you," she continued at length. "She has what I think is some very good news for you."

Honneure did not respond. Since her mother died it was as if the atmosphere had thickened. She could not hear as well, or see. Her body felt weighted, her legs leaden and slow. Sometimes when people talked to her it seemed they spoke in another language. She simply could not grasp what they were saying.

It was like that now. She heard Madame Choiseul, but the

words meant nothing. She trudged at her mistress' side, step after step through the freezing air, neither knowing nor caring where she had been or where she was going. She moved because she had to, but no longer had a purpose. She existed, but did not live. She was alone.

The two women and the child entered the château from the side into what had once been the guard's room, but was now used as a dining chamber. They passed through a short, narrow corridor and entered the kitchen.

"We've returned with your ward, as you see," Madame Choiseul announced needlessly to Cook. "I believe she'll need a cup of tea to take the chill from her bones. Then the two of you can have a nice, little...chat."

Honneure remained oblivious to the meaningful glances the three women shared. Madame Choiseul patted her shoulder. "I'll leave you with Cook now. Be a good girl and mind what she has to tell you."

The mistress and her ever-present servant hurriedly exited the room. They had done their duty as Christian women and, in truth, felt sympathy for the young orphan. She was a comely child, with her fair hair and gray eyes, and had exhibited a lively intelligence prior to her mother's passing. But they were not equipped, nor obliged, to foster a servant's orphan and were just as glad to have found a suitable placement for her.

Cook heard the door to the dining hall close with a resounding thud and sighed deeply. The slamming of the door seemed symbolic. The child's time at Amboise was over. Her mother was gone, and she would likely never again see the only home she had ever known. The door to her past was well and truly closed.

Cook sniffed and dabbed at her eyes with a corner of her apron. She would miss the child, as she would miss the mother. Mathilde had been a strange and mysterious girl who refused to speak of her past, or the father of her child. But Cook had liked her from the first moment she had come to the château, infant still at the breast, begging for work in exchange merely for a place to sleep and something to eat. Cook had taken the chance and importuned the mistress, and had never been sorry. Mathilde had not only been diligent, hard working, and quick-witted, but also graceful and lovely to look at, a ray of sunshine even through all the gray days of winter. And how she had loved that child! Always hugging and kissing her, teaching her in every spare moment.

An audible sob escaped Cook's lips, and Honneure's attention was captured at last. She had never been able to ignore a creature in pain, animal or human, and Cook's distress finally penetrated the layers of her terrible grief. She looked up and tentatively reached out to touch the back of Cook's hand.

"Are...are you all right?"

"Am *I* all right? Oh...child." Cook drew a ragged breath and fought back the urge to sit down and weep. "Of course I'm all right. Here now. Drink your tea. I have something to tell you."

Only a vague curiosity stirred within Honneure's breast. She sipped at the scalding liquid and inhaled the steam rising from its surface.

Cook cleared her throat. "I want you to know the mistress has been very concerned about you. We all have," she added sincerely. "This...this isn't the best place for a child without...well, without a parent."

"But it's where I live," Honneure replied simply.

Cook silently cursed the fates that had put her in this position. "Yes, dear, it has been your home. But with your mother...gone...there's no one here to really look after you. Do you understand?"

Honneure did not understand. Although she hadn't thought about it until this moment, she knew she could look after herself. She would take over her mother's duties, as she had done so frequently of late. She was able to work. She would go on as before. Wouldn't she? Honneure slowly shook her head. "No, I don't understand."

"Oh, dear." Cook sighed. "I'm sorry, child. I'll speak more plainly. You...you're," Cook swallowed. "You're going to leave Amboise."

Thin slivers of fear pierced the armor of Honneure's grief. "Leave Amboise?"

"Madame Choiseul has found a very fine place for you," Cook said quickly. "At a place called Chenonceau. The mistress there is a friend of Madame's and a kindly woman. There's a family who works for her there, in the kitchen and stables. You will live with them and work for Madame Dupin, the mistress of Chenonceau."

Cook smiled as if this was something Honneure should be grateful for. Somewhere deep within her she supposed she should be. But it was not reality. She had never been further than the village of Amboise at the foot of the château. She had known no other home than the small chamber she had shared with her mother. She had known no other world than the one her mother had created for her.

But her mother was gone. Her world had shattered.

Honneure went to a place beyond fear. Even her grief no longer seemed to enwrap her. She felt naked and alone, as if she stood on the edge of a precipice and could not see what lay below. Yet she must jump and trust she would not die on hidden rocks.

"Did you hear me?" Cook asked, worried by the child's

pale, drawn features. "Did you understand, Honneure?"

This time she nodded. She understood very well. She no longer had a mother or a home. She was at the mercy of a world she could barely even comprehend.

For the first time since her mother had died, Honneure prayed. She prayed God would take her too.

* * *

Honneure sat on her palette in the small, chilly room and hugged her pitiful bundle. It contained all her worldly possessions that were not on her back: a change of linen, a cotton smock she wore in summer, and a comb. Her stomach growled with hunger, but she hardly noticed. She had eaten little since the day Cook had informed her of her fate. She attended to her chores, she lay down and slept at night, but cared for nothing. She merely waited.

The wait was nearly over.

Honneure heard footsteps in the corridor. Cook appeared in the doorway.

"They're here," she declared without preamble. "It's time to go, child."

Honneure stood obediently and followed Cook from the room. As they passed through the kitchen, the woman took a shawl from the back of a chair and put it over her shoulders. Moments later they were in the courtyard.

The day was overcast and gray, the clouds seeming to hang just above the château's towers. The smell of snow was in the air. Cook hurried her footsteps as she crossed the courtyard to the waiting wagon.

Honneure noticed the horse first. He was massive, like many cart horses she had seen in the village. But his long winter coat was silky from grooming, and there were no mats in his mane or tail. He appeared plumper than any of the other animals she had ever seen. He bobbed his head as she and Cook approached, dilated his nostrils, and blew two clouds of smoke into the freezing air. His ears pricked forward in a friendly manner, and Honneure couldn't help feeling she had just received a greeting. The shadow of a smile touched the corners of her mouth.

"Honneure, this is Monsieur Mansart," Cook prompted. "He's come to take you to your new home."

The man sitting on the wagon, with large, rough hands loosely holding the reins, gave Honneure a long, slow smile and tipped his woolen cap. His dark hair was thick and curly, she noted, and lightly dusted with gray. His black eyes twinkled under bushy, prominent brows. "Good morning to you, little lady," he said in a voice that seemed to issue from the very center of his barrel chest.

"Good...good morning," Honneure stammered in reply. Without thinking, she dropped a little curtsy.

"Here now, none of that, pretty little miss," the man boomed. "I'm just folks, same as you. Philippe! Where are your manners?"

A head suddenly popped up from the back of the wagon. Thick, black curls lifted in the stirring wind. The resemblance was so strong, Honneure had no doubt the boy belonged to the man. When he grinned, the likeness was startling.

"Hello. Are you my new sister?"

Sister? Feeling warmth that had nothing to do with the temperature, Honneure watched the boy leap over the side of the high wagon. He landed nearly at her feet, grin intact. His eyes were very large and very dark. Their lashes curled nearly to his thick, well defined brows.

"I'm Philippe," he proclaimed as he took her hand and

raised it to his lips with mock courtliness.

"I'm...Honneure."

"I hope so, because we came to collect a girl named Honneure. And you're so beautiful I was hoping it was you we were taking home with us."

Cook tittered. Honneure blushed to the roots of her hair.

"May I take your bundle?" Philippe offered.

Shyly, Honneure handed it to him. "Thank you."

"Thank *you*." He tossed it into the deep straw piled in the bed of the wagon. "And now may I assist you into your coach, mademoiselle?"

Completely disarmed, Honneure took the hand Philippe offered.

"Oh, wait," Cook interjected. "I've not said a proper good-bye." Blinking back tears, she gave Honneure a quick hug. "You're going to be very happy, child. I've no longer any doubt. Bless you," she said under her breath to Philippe. "And God bless you, Monsieur Mansart." Without another word she turned and hurried back inside the château.

Something tightened in Honneure's chest. But she had no time to give it heed, for in the next moment Philippe's hands went about her waist, and she was lifted into the wagon. He jumped in beside her, sat back, and knocked on the bench seat.

"On, Driver," he commanded with feigned authority. "On to my château...on to Chenonceau!"

His father laughed and slapped the horse's rump with the reins. The cart rolled forward.

Now the sensation moved to the pit of Honneure's stomach. It was not fear, however, but something akin to excitement. She stole a glance at the boy next to her.

He was a few years older than she was and as handsome a human being as she had ever laid eyes on. He was also the merriest. She had never met anyone quite like him and found herself hoping he would speak to her again. In the next instant, he obliged.

"So, are you curious?" Philippe asked brightly.

"Curious?" Honneure repeated and felt the color flame in her cheeks yet again. How had he guessed her thoughts? How had he known she wanted to know more about him?

"Yes, curious. About your new home, your new family."

Honneure sighed with relief. "Of...of course I am," she lied. In truth, she had thought of almost nothing in the past weeks. It was as if she had been asleep and had only just awakened. "Of course I want to know."

"Good." Philippe rolled onto his side and propped himself on one elbow. "Because we're a good lot. You'll like us." He grinned. "Are you hungry?"

Honneure started to shake her head, then found herself nodding. Philippe pulled a piece of hard bread from his pocket, broke it, and handed her half. "Can't take a journey like this on an empty stomach."

"How...how far is it?" she inquired timidly.

"We'll be there just after dark. You're not afraid of the dark, are you?"

"No."

"It's a shame though, to arrive at night. Chenonceau is beautiful. Have you ever heard of it?"

Honneure shook her head, bemused. It was a challenge to keep up with the turns Philippe's conversation took.

"It's built right out on the water," Philippe continued. "Over the Cher River, like a bridge. *Maman* says it makes her seasick if she looks out a window for too long. You'll like her, *ma mère.*" The boy abruptly turned serious. "You miss your own mother very much, don't you?"

By Honor Bound

The question took Honneure completely by surprise. Philippe's liveliness and jollity had lifted her spirits, and for a short while she had forgotten her grief. She looked away from him to the passing countryside.

They had left the village behind and Honneure experienced a *frisson* of fear. She had never been so far before. Bare-branched trees lined the rutted road, and woolly cattle grazed on stubble in the now-barren fields. She gazed back toward the distant town and saw the château on the hill, silhouetted against the lowering gray sky. She would probably never see it again.

"Yes," she whispered. "I miss my mother very much."

The lump in her throat was so huge and painful she could neither swallow nor cry. Her eyes glistened with moisture, but the tears would not come. She felt as if she might break.

"It's going to snow soon," Paul Mansart rumbled without turning. "Give the girl a blanket, Philippe. It will not do for the newest member of our family to arrive at her new home with a chill. Your mama will have both our hides."

Honneure remained motionless, staring at the receding château. She felt something go about her shoulders.

"*Maman* will not skin me," Philippe remarked lightly in her ear. "She doesn't know how. Papa is the butcher. She's the cook." He let the silence ride for a moment. "Don't you want to know what I do?"

She wanted nothing but for the pain to go away. Yet she found Philippe's question, and his easy warmth of manner, irresistible. She turned to him slowly. "All right. Tell me. I think you're going to anyway."

"That's the spirit." The grin returned. He chuckled. "I work in the stable. I groom and care for Madame Dupin's horses. Do you like animals?"

The lump in Honneure's throat dissolved. She managed to nod. "I love them."

"Then we will be the best of friends," Philippe replied gaily. "I love nothing more than to be near them, to care for them. Perhaps you'll be able to help me. Would you like that?"

A picture immediately formed in Honneure's mind's eye. She was back at Château D'Amboise, in the stables. Her mother had often allowed her to visit and Charles, the old stableman, had welcomed her company. She recalled the sweet smell of the hay and horses and saw again the ever-dancing dust motes caught in beams of light from the narrow windows. She heard the soft nickers and occasional shrill whinny and felt the warm breath from a velvet muzzle as it thrust into her palm. These were familiar things, and treasured memories, because she had been happy then. Was it truly possible she would know these things and be happy again? She looked up slowly into Philippe's large, liquid eyes.

Seeing the anguished plea in Honneure's gaze, the boy's smile faded. He noticed her eyes were the color of the snow-laden clouds and brimmed with unspilled tears, and his heart went out to her. He could not even imagine losing his own mother, being all alone in the world, or being forced to leave the only home he had ever known. How great her sorrow must be! How great her courage.

A snowflake gently touched Honneure's upturned cheek, but she barely noticed. She was caught once more in the grip of her pain, her grief like a living thing eating away at her heart and growing, growing, until she felt she might burst and die. Or simply float away into the heavy clouds and be no more. The only thing keeping her alive, anchored to the earth, was the look in Philippe's eyes.

By Honor Bound

More flakes fell, dusting Honneure's curls and the blanket around her shoulders. Philippe touched her reddened cheek. The snow had melted from the warmth of her skin and ran like tears. He smoothed away the moisture.

Then her face was against his chest, and his arms were around her, tightly, as she sobbed, and the agony poured from her like a molten river.

And the snow continued to fall from a windless sky, covering them both, on the slow journey to Chenonceau.

Chapter Three

Spring, 1763

"The supply boat is coming!" Jeanne Mansart turned from the kitchen window and wiped her hands on her apron. She nodded to Honneure. "Go on down to the platform, dear, and open the doors. Then get Philippe. I'll be along presently."

Honneure didn't hesitate. Her arm ached from stirring the soup pot in the massive hearth, and rivulets of perspiration ran down her sides and back. The fresh spring breeze off the river would feel wonderful. Thankfully, she put aside the great ladle and hurried from the overly warm room.

As Philippe had told her over three years ago, Chenonceau was built like a bridge, right over the river. Large piers supported the graceful structure, and between two of them was a platform where boats with supplies could draw alongside to unload. Honneure crossed the platform, unlatched the heavy wooden doors, and threw them open.

"Good day to ya!" the boatman called. "I've got the Madam's wines and spices, and I'll be lookin' for some help."

"I'll fetch someone," Honneure replied.

"You're a good girl, Honneure. An' you've grown since I seen you. What are you now? Eighteen? Got a young man yet?"

Honneure blushed and pushed back a wing of wavy blonde hair from her cheek. "Of course I haven't a young man. I'm only eleven, Monsieur Roget. And you know it," she retorted good-naturedly.

"Eleven! *Mon Dieu,* they ripen young in the country, don't they?"

This time Honneure smiled, but declined comment and merely watched as the craft entered the arched space between the two piers. She waited as Roget secured his lines, then sped away to find Philippe.

It was not a short distance to the stable, but Honneure knew the boatman would not thank her for hurrying. He would enjoy his pipe, or a chat with Philippe's father, in the time it took her to find Philippe and return with him. He would most certainly enjoy a piece of one of Madame Mansart's pies. She had plenty of time. Her pace was quick only because she was eager to see Philippe and bask for a few moments in the fragrant coziness of the stable.

From the platform Honneure climbed a short flight of stairs to the main hall and emerged near the front door. She pulled it open slowly, braced against its great weight, and slipped out into the warm spring sunshine.

Honneure now stood in an oval courtyard built atop one of the piers. The sound of the Cher murmured below her. She crossed a narrow bridge to another pier and from there entered the forecourt, a huge rectangle dominated in one corner by the Marques Tower, a former *donjon.* With the river swirling around her, Honneure had the illusion of floating along on a broad-beamed ship. One hand shielding her eyes, she gazed up at the conical roof of the Renaissance style dungeon. As if sensing her regard, a pair of pigeons fluttered skyward and flew off in the direction of the stable. Honneure followed them.

From the forecourt she crossed a final bridge and stepped onto a wide lane. It ran for nearly a mile through dense forest until it reached the main road. To her right sprawled the Diane de Poitiers' gardens, on the edge of which stood the steward's handsome house; to her left and slightly behind, on a curving bank of the Cher, lay the fabulous gardens of Catherine de Medici; ahead and to the left, stretching for almost a quarter of a mile, were the stables and attached residences for the servants. Honneure paused a moment to catch her breath, then continued on her way.

Honneure did not immediately see Philippe upon entering the dim, cool building. But as she looked down the long aisle, several horses raised their heads and perked their ears. The large draft horse who had pulled the wagon that had brought her to Chenonceau whickered. She crossed to his stall and raised her hand to his bewhiskered muzzle.

"You always have a greeting for me, don't you?"

"Honneure?" Philippe emerged from a stall near the end of the aisle. He closed the door, leaned a pitchfork against it, and wiped his brow with a square of linen. "I thought I heard your voice. What are you doing here this time of day?"

"Looking for you."

"This must be my lucky day."

Philippe grinned, and Honneure grinned back. "It's lucky if you feel like unloading Monsieur Roget's boat."

Philippe groaned as he tucked the linen back into his loose, coarse trousers. "I don't suppose you'd like to earn a few muscles by doing that for me, would you?"

"Oh, certainly I would. But then I wouldn't have time to wash the pots and pans or scrub the kitchen floor, and then you'd have to help *me*."

Philippe winked. "*Touché.*" He reached Honneure's side and threw an arm about her shoulders. "Lead on then, fair damsel. My destiny awaits."

Honneure leaned into Philippe and put her arm about his

slender waist. He smelled wonderful, like hay and horses and good, honest sweat, and her heart squeezed as it always did when they were together. Side by side they left the stable and stepped into the bright afternoon.

Honneure had to stretch her legs to match Philippe's long stride. He had grown tall in the years since she had come to live with his family, since she had become his sister. She glanced up at him with adoring eyes, seeing the hay dust that coated his glossy black curls and the moisture that glistened in the hollow of his throat. He was so handsome and so incredibly kind. She loved him dearly, as her own true brother of the flesh, and had since the very beginning, on the journey to Chenonceau.

Honneure often thought of that time. She remembered her arrival at Chenonceau, and her amazement. They had not stopped at the stable as she had thought they would, but continued on to the château. She had not been able to make out its details in the dark. Yet she saw the lights from many windows and was awed by the structure's imposing size. She could not see the river either, but heard the music of its passing as they crossed the bridge from the forecourt to the courtyard. Burning torches cast flickering lights upon the snowy ground. The monumental double doors, a coat of arms on each side, had opened slowly.

"Ah, Paul, you've arrived at last." A handsome, elegantly dressed woman stood in the doorway, framed by light, one hand holding the edges of a shawl together over her breast. "How was your journey?"

"Uneventful, Madame Dupin, as I'd hoped. The treasure we carry is safe."

"Well, come in. Come in where it's warm."

Philippe had not needed to be asked twice. He jumped

from the wagon, then held out his arms to Honneure and helped her down. She was immediately set upon by Madame Dupin.

"Poor child, you must be freezing." She took the shawl from her shoulders and wrapped it about Honneure. "I am Madame Dupin," she added needlessly. Stooping slightly so she might look directly into Honneure's eyes, she said, "And you are Honneure, who has come to be the little daughter of Paul and Jeanne, sister to Philippe. They are my trusted and beloved servants, and I know you will be very happy with them. You have suffered the greatest tragedy a child could ever know, but you are safe now and very welcome in my home. Come. Come and meet the rest of your new family."

Honneure was completely at a loss for words. Never had she experienced such kindness from strangers, nor had she even imagined it might exist. She had thought her life was over. And now this.

The marvels had only just begun.

Steering her gently, Madame Dupin guided Honneure through the doors and into the front hall. Light blazed from what seemed a hundred candles set in silver candelabra. Tapestries lined the walls. The floor was tiled with small reddish squares, each one stamped with a *fleur de lis* crossed by a dagger. Honneure had never seen anything like it.

Followed by Paul and Philippe, Madame Dupin had led Honneure down the corridor to a door near the end. Warmth enveloped her as they stepped across the threshold, and delicious smells. She gazed in wonder at the large kitchen and glowing hearth, teeming baskets of potatoes and onions, sausages and dried herbs hanging from the open joists of the ceiling, an array of highly scrubbed pots and utensils hanging from hooks on the creamy walls. She was overwhelmed.

"Jeanne?" Madame Dupin called. "Are you here? Paul

and Philippe have returned. And they have brought with them the daughter you have always wished for."

"Oh! *Oui*, Madame, I'm coming!" a figure appeared from around a corner.

As long as she lived, Honneure would never forget the moment she met Jeanne Mansart. The woman was the very picture of beneficence and kindliness. A gleaming white apron was tied about her plump midsection. Curling wisps of gray hair, escaped from the chignon at the nape of her neck, framed her round face and apple cheeks. Small blue eyes twinkled brightly. Her welcoming smile seemed to stretch from ear to ear. Then, suddenly, there were tears on her face. She came up to Honneure and knelt, her arms opened wide.

"Oh, you precious, precious, child," she murmured. "My own dear little girl."

Honneure had moved into the circle of the woman's arms and had known, in that instant, she would never know loneliness or fear again.

Nor had she.

Once again, as they approached the château, Honneure gazed up at the boy who had become her brother, her family. In over three years he had never said a harsh word to her. He teased her from time to time, but never maliciously. In fact, she loved his playfulness. His humor, sensitivity, and forthright nature had helped to ease her out of her grief and into the circle of the Mansart family. She truly did think of them now as her own. She even wondered occasionally if Paul was anything like her own father. She hoped so. He was a good man, solid, compassionate, and good humored. And although Jeanne was nothing like her own mother, she loved her deeply as well. There certainly could not be a sweeter woman anywhere on earth. Since Jeanne Mansart had uttered the words, "My own dear little girl," Honneure had been treated that way. She had even adopted their name and proudly called herself Honneure Mansart.

* * *

"Here they are." Roget pushed himself away from the wall and plucked the pipe from his mouth. "Hah, *mon ami,* your son looks more like you every day."

The senior Mansart smiled slowly and gazed proudly at Philippe. "He's a good lad. He'll be a good man."

"And your daughter," Roget added as he climbed down into his boat. "What a beauty, fit for a king, I might say." He winked. "She and the young Duc de Berry are of an age, you know. You should contrive to get her a position at Court. Who knows what might happen."

Standing on the platform, Philippe accepted the barrel Roget handed up to him, hefted it onto his shoulder, and passed it on to his father, who set it inside a storeroom.

"Speaking of the Court," Jeanne Mansart said eagerly, "What news is there?"

Roget grunted as he handed another barrel up to Philippe. "The war with England is over, I suppose you know."

"A war that never should have been waged in the first place," Paul Mansart rumbled. "Thousands of lives lost, and now Canada, India and Dunkirk as well. All because of that woman."

"Now, Paul." Jeanne laid a hand on her husband's arm. "Not in front of the children."

"If you mean me," Honneure interjected, "and if you're talking about Madame du Pompadour, I already know."

All eyes turned in her direction. Jeanne's chin dropped and Paul's eyes widened.

"Madame Dupin tells me about the King sometimes when I help her in the garden," Honneure continued innocently. "She said he has always listened more closely to his mistresses than his ministers."

"Honneure!" Jeanne exclaimed.

Philippe's eyes twinkled with suppressed mirth. "What else has Madame told you about the King and his mis...uh, ministers?"

"Well, things like Monsieur Choiseul attends mass with the latest saucy novel hidden in his missal, and Cardinal Richelieu takes milk baths . . ."

"That will be enough, Honneure!" Color flooded Madame Mansart's cheeks. It heightened when Roget roared with laughter.

"I was right," he choked. "You should send her to Court. She just might keep them all honest."

Paul attempted to hide his smile, but the corners of his mouth quivered. Under his wife's stern glare, he said, "Perhaps, Honneure, you and your mother should see to that soup pot. You wouldn't want to spoil dinner now, would you?"

* * *

"Did I say something wrong?" Honneure asked as her foster mother firmly closed the kitchen door.

"Not wrong, Honneure, just...You shouldn't repeat everything Madame Dupin tells you." Cheeks still flaming, Jeanne turned to the bubbling soup pot herself.

"Do you mean I should repeat some things, but not others?"

"Well...yes."

"But how am I supposed to know the difference?"

Jeanne Mansart sighed deeply, hung her ladle on its hook beside the hearth, and turned slowly to the child she had considered her own since the first moment she had laid eyes on her. She walked around the table and took Honneure's face in her hands.

"Oh, Honneure, my dear, sweet girl, how do I answer you?" She looked into Honneure's storm gray eyes for a long moment. "You've always been so good, so dutiful, and obedient and loving. I could not have asked for a more perfect child. You have never said an unkind word or committed a cruel act, and you have done nothing wrong now."

"But you said . . ."

"I said you shouldn't repeat everything you hear, and you very wisely pointed out to me how difficult it is to know how to choose." Jeanne dropped her hands from Honneure's face and laid them lightly on her shoulders. "You will learn as you grow older, I suppose, as we all do. For now...just be honest, as you always have been."

"You're not angry with me?"

"Oh, Honneure, no, of course not, dearest child. I love you."

"And I love you, *Maman*." Honneure stretched up to kiss her foster mother's cheek. Jeanne hugged her.

"Go now and see if Madame requires anything before dinner."

Honneure walked slowly through the three rooms that comprised the kitchen. She thought about what Jeanne had said to her, but didn't really understand. All that mattered was that her foster mother was not angry with her. She did not think at all about her actual words, the gossip about the King's ministers. Madame Dupin was a frequent visitor at the Court of Louis XV and always brought back wonderful, vivid stories

36

of the lavish lifestyle and colorful characters. Honneure loved the tales, particularly the ones about Choiseul. She recalled his wife, her former mistress, and smiled to herself.

Honneure crossed the corridor into what Madame Dupin called the "green study." She loved the great green tapestry that covered one entire wall. Madame had told her it depicted the discovery of the Americas, their flora and fauna. She let her eyes linger for a moment on the Peruvian silver pheasants, pineapples, orchids, pomegranates, animals, and vegetables she had never even known existed. Reluctantly, she left the room and entered the tiny library.

Madame Dupin sat at her desk composing a letter. She looked up briefly and smiled. "One moment, Honneure. I must finish my thought before it blows away in the breeze."

"*Oui*, Madame." Hands behind her back, Honneure dropped a small curtsy. She gazed over her mistress' shoulder to the window and the gardens beyond, content to wait as long as was necessary. From the library the view of the gardens of Diane de Poitiers was breathtaking.

It was Philippe who had told her about Diane de Poitiers and Catherine de Medici when he had informed her that Chenonceau was widely known as the Château des Dames. Diane, he had whispered to her one evening as they stood on the banks of the Cher feeding swans, had been King Henry II's favorite. He had actually given her Chenonceau as a gift. But when he died, killed in a single-handed combat during a tournament, his widow, Catherine de Medici, forced Diane to give up Chenonceau in exchange for another château. The next day, with their parents' attention turned elsewhere, they had sneaked up to Diane de Poitiers' bedroom. There, on the chimney, Philippe had showed her the initials of Henry II and Catherine de Medici: H and C which, intertwined, could form

37

the D of Diane de Poitiers. She had thought him very clever. And the history of the château began to come alive for her. She had grown to love it, as she had her new family and the mistress they all so willingly served.

Madame looked up from her missive and smiled once again. "You are a patient child. Have you been sent by your mother to see what I require?" When Honneure nodded, she said, "As a matter of fact I should like a glass of sherry." Honneure hesitated, then dropped another curtsy and turned.

"What is it you wish to ask, Honneure?" Madame Dupin inquired perceptively.

"It's...nothing. I don't wish to bother you."

"You never bother me," she replied honestly. "You are curious and intelligent, and I have grown quite fond of our conversations. Now, once again, what is it you wish to ask?"

"Have you ever heard of the...the Duc de Berry?"

"Heard of him?" Madame Dupin snorted. "Of course I've heard of him. Where did you hear his name?"

Honneure dropped her gaze, wondering if she had said something wrong for a second time that day. "Well...Monsieur Roget was . . ."

"Oh, that silly boatman." Madame Dupin waved a hand dismissively. "He is the greatest gossip in France. Tell me what he is saying about the young Duke."

Honneure felt the heat rise from her neck to her cheeks and regretted that she blushed so easily. "Noth...nothing," she stammered. "Just that he and I are...are the same age."

One elegant eyebrow lifted slightly, and a faint smile touched the corners of Madame Dupin's thin mouth. "Yes. Yes, you are very near in age. But there the similarities begin and end, my dear. The Duc de Berry is the eldest living son of Louis, the Dauphin, heir to the throne. The Duke's grandfather is our...illustrious...King, Louis XV."

Honneure's lips formed a small "o."

"Knowing Roget's reputation," Madame Dupin continued, "I am going to assume he made some inappropriate comment about you and a young Prince of France." Seeing Honneure's blush return, she added quickly, "You are indeed a lovely girl, Honneure. You are beautiful and sweet-natured and as bright as a newly minted coin. In short, you are far too good for the likes of any in Louis' Court. Be glad you are who you are and are where you are. You will live a good life. Those who flutter about Louis' throne, like moths around a flame, are doomed. Be thankful you will never know the brightness of that light which consumes all."

With that Madame Dupin turned thoughtfully to the view outside her open windows. When she did not speak again, Honneure realized she was dismissed. She shook her head to clear it of the image her mistress had so vividly painted and hurried from the room. She was indeed lucky, she thought. She did not wish to change anything about her life. She did not aspire to the splendor of a royal Court. She did not even wish to leave Chenonceau.

Ever.

Chapter Four

Summer, 1768

Summer lay across the countryside like a veil of soft gauze. The air was hot and hazy, and everything seemed to move a little more slowly. Even the Cher flowed sleepily between its grassy banks. The swans, necks curved into elegant question marks, glided lazily over the cool, green water, followed by their half-grown cygnets. Weeping willow limbs arched down gracefully to touch the river's shining surface.

Honneure turned from the Cher and started back toward the château. Her basket could not hold another flower. Trudging slowly through the heat of high noon, she made her way through the Catherine de Medici gardens. At the central pool she paused to splash water on her face and neck and on the newly cut stalks, already beginning to wilt. In the eight years she had been at Chenonceau, she could not recall a hotter summer. Shaking moisture from her face, she proceeded to the house.

It took Honneure's eyes a moment to adjust to the dim light of the château's corridor. Grateful for the shade, she quickened her footsteps.

The kitchen appeared empty. Then she heard the sound of a cleaver coming down heavily on the butcher's block. Leaving her basket on the table, she rounded the corner into the area that had become her foster father's domain. He looked up from the bloody carcass and smiled.

"Rabbit for dinner," he remarked.

Honneure tried not to connect the mangled mess on the table with the sleek, adorable animals she loved to watch at dusk when they came out to forage. "It's Philippe's favorite," she said, in an attempt to justify the hare's death.

"Perhaps he'll come home tonight in time to enjoy it."

Honneure's expression immediately brightened. "Do you think he'll be home tonight? Do you?"

Paul shrugged and swung the cleaver again, severing a leg from the trunk. "There's a chance. Your mother figured he'd be back by today or tomorrow. But Austria's a long way away. It's difficult to judge that great a distance. And with a few horses in tow . . ." he shrugged again. "Who knows?"

Honneure turned away as Paul lifted the cleaver a final time. When she heard the chop, she took a wooden bowl and gathered the pieces of rabbit. "I'm going to stew them," she announced, "just as he likes. I have a feeling."

"You and your mother." Paul sluiced water from a ewer over his bloody hands. "She says she has a feeling too."

Honneure tried not to let her hopes fly too high, but it was difficult. She hadn't seen her brother in weeks, since Madame Dupin had dispatched him to Vienna to fetch the precious horses. Over the years he had gone on errands for days at a time, but never this long. She missed him desperately.

When the cast iron pan was hot enough Honneure added a dollop of goose fat and then the rabbit, piece by piece. She turned the parts over once and added a handful of freshly chopped herbs. As the meat browned to her satisfaction, she poured a pitcher of dry red wine over all. Steam curled upward from the pan, and a delicious aroma filled the room.

"Smells *wonderful*." Jeanne put an arm around her

daughter's shoulders. "I just came in to do that, but I'm glad you beat me to it. I think you've become a better cook than I am."

"Never!"

"Well, all right...*almost* as good." She kissed Honneure's cheek. "Shall I make a dandelion salad to go with it?"

Another of Philippe's favorites. The two women exchanged knowing smiles, and Honneure nodded.

"You run along then and arrange your flowers, my dear. I'll take care of the rest of dinner."

Honneure grabbed her basket and fled the kitchen's heat. She had already placed vases with fresh water about the château and had merely to arrange the fragile stems. She began in the chapel, near the front doors, and bowed her head reverently as she placed the flowers gently on the altar. She paused a moment to admire the soaring vaulted ceiling and stained glass windows. To the right of the altar stood a finely carved credence table, and for the hundredth time she read the motto of the husband and wife, Thomas Bohier and Katherine Briconnet, who had built Chenonceau: "*S'il vient a point, me souviendra.*" "If I manage to build Chenonceau, I will be remembered." How correct they had been. It was their coats-of-arms that decorated the front doors.

From the chapel Honneure went to the Louis XIV living room, so named in honor of a visit the late King had made to the château. It was her favorite room and its colors were glorious. Deep pink fabric lined the walls, and the furniture was covered with Aubusson tapestries. She thought of her mother, Mathilde, and how she would have loved the aura of the ornate chamber, where Madame Dupin had entertained such dignitaries and intellectuals as Voltaire, Rousseau, Montesquieu and Diderot. She gazed briefly at the portrait of

Samuel Bernard, her mistress' father, Louis XIV's banker. Though he had left his daughter fabulously wealthy, she had squandered nothing. Her generosity and kindness were legendary. Honneure herself would always be grateful to her.

Honneure's last stop was Madame's bedroom. Near the center of the corridor she pushed open two finely carved oaken doors that revealed the curving staircase. It was always a pleasure to climb the steps and gaze at the coffers decorated with human figures, fruits and flowers. At the curve in the stair was a loggia with a balustrade from which she was able to see the Cher. Late afternoon sun glinted sharply on the somnolent greenish waters and Honneure hurried.

Of the many bedchambers in the château, the one Madame Dupin had chosen for her own was known as the "Five Queens' Bedroom," in memory of Catherine de Medici's two daughters and three daughters-in-law, all of whom had become queens. The coffered ceiling displayed the five different royal coats-of-arms, and the walls were covered with a Flemish tapestry suite that had always fascinated Honneure. Around the walls of the room she could see the siege of Troy and the kidnapping of Helen, Circus games in the Coliseum, and the crowning of King David. She arranged the last of her flowers atop her mistress' desk and on her way out straightened the rich red bed curtains. Her house duties for the day were done.

* * *

The sun was low and at the perfect angle to enter her dormer window in a straight line, filling the tiny room with heat and light. Stripped to her underlinens, Honneure sat on the edge of her narrow bed and pinned the luxuriant masses of honey colored hair atop her head. She poured water from a pitcher into a cracked basin, took a linen cloth and, eyes closed, washed away the day's toil. When she came to her breasts she paused as she always did, still surprised by the changes in her body. It seemed only yesterday she was a thin, wiry, child. Now . . .

Honneure felt the weight of her breasts, not quite sure whether she was pleased or chagrined. In a way she was proud of her new form. But it had its drawbacks, in particular the attention she received from some local young men. And the steward's son, Claud. Honneure shuddered. Thank goodness her brother continued to treat her as he always had.

Philippe.

Something knotted in the pit of her stomach and spread upward into her chest. Even now he might be riding up the long, tree-lined lane to the château. In fact, she fancied she could hear hoofbeats. Moving quickly she pulled on her summer shift of pale blue cotton, slipped into her shoes, and unpinned her hair. There was no time to deal with it. She pulled her fingers through the tangled waves that fell to her waist and ran from the room.

* * *

It had been a dry summer. Dust rose from behind the wagon wheels and hung in the windless air. Philippe felt it settle in yet another layer on his hair and exposed flesh. The white horse he rode had turned a dull dun color, and the two black horses, tied to the back of the wagon, had turned gray. Though the sun was low, the heat had been oppressive all day. The foal that trotted at the white mare's side had begun to lag.

"Stop a moment, Claud," Philippe called to the pudgy lad who drove the cart horse. "This filly can't go much farther."

Claud, son of Madame Dupin's steward, obeyed immediately. He didn't think he could go much farther

44

himself. He was dirty, tired, and sore from sitting in the jolting wagon day after day and silently cursed his father for forcing him to accompany Philippe. He had been indifferent to the sights of Vienna, thought the food uncivilized, if plentiful, and the prostitutes insulting. Thank God the trip was nearly over.

Philippe climbed from the mare and approached the foal slowly. She shied away from him but stayed close to her dam. He stretched out his hand and stroked her neck until she quieted. Rubbing a spot behind her ears, he eased nearer. When he was pressed against her side he put one arm around her chest, the other behind her rump, and lifted her from the ground. She struggled, but only briefly.

"Help me, Claud. I'm going to put her in the back of the wagon."

Together they managed to get the filly into the back of the straw-filled cart. She whinnied for her mother, and the mare nuzzled her reassuringly. To Philippe's relief, the young horse lay down almost at once.

"Let's get going," Philippe urged. "I want to reach Chenonceau before dark."

"You're not the only one," Claud mumbled. He slapped the reins on the cart horse's back and the wagon rumbled forward.

The last few miles were easier. They left the open farmland behind, and the forest deepened as they approached the château. The air was noticeably cooler. Philippe wiped his brow and tried to brush off some of the dust. He shook his head and ran his fingers through his thick, black curls. He was saddleweary and, as fine as the animals were, he was anxious to get home. He missed his own bed, his mother's cooking and, most of all, his sister. Philippe smiled.

He had thought of Honneure often on his trip. She was

such a curious little thing and had such an appreciation for, and love of, history, he wished he had been able to show her Vienna. She had never seen a big city before, and the Austrian capitol was magnificent. She also would have loved the breeding farm where he had picked up Madame Dupin's Lipizzan horses. He himself had never seen anything like it. The sprawling facility had been immaculate, the horses exquisite. He imagined the pleasure he would have describing the sights to her. He could almost see her gray eyes go wide and her lips part as she hung on his every word.

Philippe rubbed the stubble on his chin and chuckled. She had always been such an adoring child. From the beginning she had followed him around like a puppy. Having been an only child for the first twelve years of his life he had feared her near-constant presence would be annoying. But he had discovered just the opposite. As she had emerged from her grief and her personality blossomed, he found her enchanting. Her naïveté, combined with quick wit, intelligence, and down-to-earth honesty, brought a light and laughter into his life he had never known from his loving, but hardworking, solid parents. He loved them dearly, but Honneure was, well...*Honneure*. He had missed her badly. He couldn't wait to see her.

* * *

The sun seemed to rest upon the treetops of Chenonceau's surrounding park. Honneure walked out onto the lane and looked north down the long gravel drive. She could have sworn she heard hoofbeats. She squinted. There was movement...There was!

"Philippe?" she called. "Philippe!"

He heard her voice first and then saw the lissome form,

arms waving, at the top of the drive. Chenonceau, welcoming, rose behind her.

"I'm riding ahead, Claud," Philippe announced needlessly as he put his heels to his horse. The white mare sprang into a gallop.

Was it possible he had grown more handsome in the space of a few weeks? His skin was tanned from days of riding in the sun, and when he grinned at her his perfect teeth seemed even whiter. His wind-tussled curls had grown long and touched the tops of his broad, muscular shoulders. The shadow of a beard crept from his finely chiseled jaw to the high, sharp ridge of his cheekbones. He rode his mount lightly, perfectly balanced, graceful and at ease in the saddle. She loved him.

"Philippe!"

He threw himself from the saddle and into her embrace. She smelled like summer.

His arms went about her waist, and he lifted her from her feet, hugging her tightly. "Little sister...I've missed you!"

"And I've missed you. Now put me down so I can look at you!"

Philippe did as he was bid, holding her at arm's length as they studied one another.

"You've grown prettier, I swear," he said, and pushed a wave of hair from her forehead. With the tip of a finger he traced the natural rose blush of one cheek.

"You're probably right," she replied. "Because you seem to have grown more handsome, too. Or maybe we just look better because we're glad to see each other."

Philippe laughed. "That's certainly true. I've thought of little else than seeing you all the way home from Vienna."

"Oh, really? Only on the way home?" Honneure feigned a pout. "Why not in Vienna? Were there too many other pretty faces to think about?"

"Dozens...hundreds," he teased.

Honneure felt the edges of her smile begin to slip. They always teased one another this way. So why all of a sudden did she feel so strange?

The alien mood was quickly dispelled as Claud pulled up in the wagon. She greeted him, but ignored his mumbled response and the way his small, pale eyes devoured her body.

Gay once more, Honneure helped to put away the horses. Earlier in the day she and Paul had readied stalls for the new arrivals. There was fresh bedding, hay and water. She admired the animals as Claud and Philippe wiped them down and put them away. Honneure herself took care of the filly as the young one did not seem so skittish in her presence. By the time they emerged from the stables, the sun had disappeared below the tree line, and only a rapidly fading halo of light remained.

"Thanks for your help on the trip, Claud," Philippe said, and clapped the stout youth on the back. "Go on home. I'm sure your father is waiting."

"I just hope my *dinner* is waiting," Claud retorted. With a last furtive glance in Honneure's direction, he crossed the lane to his father's house..

"Speaking of dinner, brother dear, I've fixed your favorite."

"Rabbit?"

"Rabbit."

"I'll race you."

It was a favorite game, though she never won. Laughing, golden hair streaming, Honneure chased Philippe into the evening shadows of the towering château.

By Honor Bound

* * *

"So this new breed, you say, is a cross between the Spanish horses and Arabians?"

Philippe nodded at his father across the table. They were in the cozy servants' dining room off the kitchen where it had become their habit, over the years, to dine each evening. "And it's an interesting cross, brilliant really," Philippe continued. "The finest Arab blood was introduced and fused with the local athletic Spanish horses during the Moorish occupation of Spain. Maximillian II brought some of these new Spanish horses to Austria in the sixteenth century and founded a court stud. His brother, Archduke Charles, established a similar stud at Lipizza, near the Adriatic Sea. Hence, the name."

"Lipizzan." Honneure tasted the sound of it. "They certainly are beautiful."

Philippe nodded again. "Strong and versatile, but refined by the more delicate Arab."

"It's about time the Austrians did something constructive," Paul said darkly.

Jeanne reached over and patted her husband's hand. Honneure glanced from one to the other, and then said, "If what Madame Dupin says is true, this alliance with Austria will soon become permanent. The Empress has agreed to the betrothal of her youngest daughter to the Dauphin."

"In my wildest dreams," Paul growled, "I never thought an *Austrian* would become Queen of France."

"She's not the queen yet, dear," Jeanne soothed.

"It won't be long," he retorted. "They say old Louis' new mistress is a lively one, and he's not got much left in him. It won't take long to finish him off."

"According to Madame Dupin," Honneure interjected,

"That's what they said about his last mistress. I wouldn't dig his grave quite yet."

Philippe nearly choked on his wine. Jeanne flashed Honneure a reproving look, but the twinkle in her eyes belied the expression on her face. Paul chose to ignore them all.

"To make matters worse, the Dauphin is only fourteen. When his grandfather dies we'll have a pimply faced boy as King of France."

Despite her foster father's antipathy, Honneure felt sorry for the duke. She recalled her conversation with Madame Dupin five years earlier, when she had not even known who the Duc de Berry was. Barely two years later his father had died spitting blood. Now the boy was no longer a duke, but a prince, the Dauphin, and heir to the throne of France.

"The shadow of kinghood must be a very great burden for someone so young," Honneure said sympathetically. "And it cannot be much easier for his future queen. She's only thirteen and not only contemplating a throne, but marriage."

Paul grunted, but his solemn expression lightened. His foster daughter's generosity of spirit was hard to resist. "I suppose it must be a bit daunting," he conceded.

"Yes, indeed. Poor little thing," Jeanne muttered. "What's her name?"

"Marie, Mother," Philippe replied. "Marie Antoinette."

"And her wedding gift from Madame Dupin will be the horses you brought from Austria. How thoughtful. It will not only remind her of her homeland, but will show honor to her country for their national breed to be chosen as a royal wedding gift."

"Let's just hope the wedding's not too soon. I have a bit of training to do before those horses are ready for royalty."

"Madame Dupin told me they will not wed until the new

Dauphin is sixteen," Honneure said lightly. "So you have two years. Do you think that will be enough time?"

"Two *years*? It shouldn't take me more than two mo . . ." Realization dawned on Philippe's features. "Oh...you . . ."

Philippe's chair clattered over backward as he sprang up. Honneure's scraped the floor as she pushed away from the table in an effort to escape. Paul and Jeanne clasped hands as they watched their children fly, laughing, from the room.

"Some things never change," Paul remarked.

"And pray they never do."

* * *

"I don't want anything to change...ever," Honneure whispered. They sat on the banks of the Cher, backs to a giant plane tree. Moonlight glittered on the water, and cicadas clicked in the velvet darkness.

Philippe turned his gaze to the girl at his side. Her profile was clean and elegant, and he marveled, as he always did, at her simple beauty. "What makes you say a thing like that?" he inquired at length.

"Because I'm so happy." Honneure sighed deeply. "I'm so happy here, Philippe, with you and Mother and Father. Life is perfect. I want it to go on and on this way. Yet . . ."

"Yet, what?" Philippe prompted after a long moment.

"Look at that poor little Austrian Princess. She probably thought her life was just fine the way it was, too. Now, because her mother has decided an alliance with France is desirable, she's engaged to someone she doesn't even know. Everything has changed for her. And who knows if the change will be for the good."

"Becoming Queen of France doesn't sound like such a terrible change to me."

"But you never know, do you, Philippe?" Honneure turned to him and looked deeply into his dark eyes. "You can never know whether the future holds good or ill, can you? That's why I don't want *this* to ever change."

"Honneure . . ."

"Promise me, Philippe. Promise."

The urgency in her tone alarmed him. His head told him to be practical, rational, that he could promise no such thing, no one could. But his heart ruled. "I...promise."

It was foolish, she knew. But she felt better. She leaned on Philippe's shoulder and closed her eyes.

Riding on the river, the night flowed slowly past.

Chapter Five

Fall, 1770

The sky was faultlessly blue. Not a single cloud scudded on the chill, crisp breeze. Red and gold leaves drifted downward from the trees and swirled across the lane. The smell of chimney smoke tickled Honneure's nose. Holding the shawl tightly about her shoulders, she hurried across the bridge into the courtyard and pushed open the heavy door. One of the housemaids was on hands and knees, scrubbing the hall tiles.

"Is Madame Dupin in the library?" Honneure inquired. The girl replied in the affirmative, and Honneure tiptoed carefully across the wet floor. She passed through the "green study" and knocked softly on the open library door.

"Oh, Honneure, come in, my dear." Madame Dupin closed her ledger book and laid it aside. "I've just been going over accounts, catching up. Everything looks in good order. Claud's been doing well on his father's behalf, hasn't he?"

Honneure nodded reluctantly. Since the château's steward had become ill, his son had taken over his duties. It gave Claud an excuse to be around more than usual, and he made her uneasy.

"I was away too long, I fear," Madame Dupin continued. "I missed Chenonceau, and I missed all of you."

"We missed you as well and are happy to have you home again."

"Thank you, dear." Madame Dupin removed her *pince-*

nez and rubbed the bridge of her nose. "I think I shall be home for awhile now. All is well...or as well as it can be...at Court."

Having come to know her mistress well over the years, and having become somewhat of a *confidante*, Honneure knew that if there was something on Madame Dupin's mind, she needed only a gentle prodding to unburden herself.

" 'As well as it can be?' " she repeated. "Do you mean something is amiss?"

"Nothing more than the ordinary." Madame Dupin sighed. "The King's health and will are failing, and this latest mistress, Madame du Barry, takes over more and more control."

"But surely she cannot affect the government."

"Oh, but surely she can," Madame Dupin replied. "Every afternoon, all summer long, du Barry received Louis at the *pavillon* of Luciennes, a gift, as I told you, from her royal lover. And over fruit and a glass of Spanish wine, she would discuss new ways to assert herself at Court. The King allowed her to decide which plays and operas should be given, and at Bordeaux a ship was launched called *The Comtesse du Barry*. She had her Bengali slave, Zamore, baptized, and the Prince de Conti's son – a prince of the blood – stood godfather. I shudder to think what she will want, or where she will meddle, next." Madame Dupin's disgust was evident. She sighed again, deeply.

"That, however, is not what concerns me most at the moment. I worry for the Dauphin's wife."

"Antoinette," Honneure said, using the name by which the young Princess preferred to be called.

"Yes." Madame Dupin nodded. "Antoinette. Such a sweet child. So innocent. But she has managed to make an enemy of du Barry. The witch will make the Princess' life miserable, I fear."

"I'm so sorry to hear it," Honneure replied honestly. "Can't her husband do something to help? He *is* the King's grandson."

"And heir, and he must walk a very fine line. He enjoys an excellent relationship with his grandsire, which is as it should be. He does not wish to compromise that relationship, so he makes his compromise elsewhere. He makes an *appearance* of accepting du Barry."

"But . . ."

"He abhors her. Naturally. Yet what can he do? He can only side with, and comfort, his wife in private, which I pray he does."

"Then their relationship is good?"

Madame Dupin smiled. "As a matter of fact they seem rather fond of one another. Antoinette also gets on well with Louis' brothers, Provence and Artois, which is helpful, and has become quite a friend to his sister, Elisabeth. The King, of course, being fond of pretty young girls, is charmed by her. Yes." Madame Dupin nodded thoughtfully. "She has fit into the family quite well in the scant months since the wedding, and her husband seems to have great affection for her."

"Perhaps du Barry will not be such a problem for her after all."

Madame Dupin's expression turned solemn. "I hope not, but we shall see."

"And in the meantime, there is your gift for the young couple. It should bring them a great deal of pleasure."

"Ah, yes. Philippe believes the horses are ready?"

"Yes, he does. He sent me to ask you if you'd like to see them."

"Now? Why, of course! You should have said something

sooner."

"If I had spoken sooner I would not be so much richer in my knowledge of Court life and the royal family," Honneure replied simply.

Madame Dupin chuckled as she rose and came around her desk. "Your forthright honesty is one of the things I love best about you, Honneure. Come. Let us see how well Philippe has done with his...'project'."

* * *

The two months of training had indeed turned into two years, as Honneure had teased. Madame Dupin had sent Philippe to Vienna to buy two black geldings she had heard about, a matched pair, for the Princess to drive. She had authorized him to select another animal for the future king as a mount. The white mare had caught his eye, as well as the foal at her side. He had seen their potential, not as mounts, however, but driving horses. He had had to wait for the filly to mature before training her, hence the delay in presenting the wedding gift. Honneure thought the horses well worth the wait.

Philippe had been correct. The pair, mother and daughter, were superb. He had hitched them to Madame Dupin's Berlin and driven to the end of the lane. When he saw the two women emerge from the château, he started toward them. Even though she had seem him work the horses many times, Honneure caught her breath.

The pair was not matched, although they would be eventually. The mare was white and the filly mouse gray. White Lipizzans, Philippe had told her, did not achieve their color until they were six to ten years old. But the difference in color did not detract from the magnificence of the duo.

The horses were sturdy and, although not tall, presented a powerful picture. Their heads were shapely, influenced by the Arab blood, with small muzzles and small, alert ears. Their eyes were large and appealing. Their bodies, set off by short, powerful necks, gave an impression of great strength, with well-rounded quarters, heavy shoulders and short, strong legs with well defined tendons and joints. Their tails were carried high and, like their manes, were thick and long. Their carriage bespoke pride in their appearance, and their action was brilliant. Necks arched, chins tucked, they trotted slowly, elegantly, up the lane.

"Philippe was absolutely right," Madame Dupin breathed. "They are incredible together."

Honneure merely smiled. She was so proud of Philippe she thought she might burst.

He sat perfectly erect in the coachman's seat and handled the reins lightly and easily. He maintained constant contact with the horses' mouths, but needed very little pressure to control and guide them. He had a natural touch to which the animals readily responded.

Philippe halted the coach at the entrance to the forecourt, where the women stood.

"Well? What do you think?"

"Bravo. Bravo, Philippe." Madame Dupin clapped. "You've done a brilliant job with these animals. They are indeed a gift fit for a queen."

"Thank you, Madame."

"No, thank *you*, Philippe. I believe these horses will make a sweet girl very happy."

"I'm sorry I do not now have a riding horse for the Dauphin, however."

Madame Dupin shrugged. "It matters not at all. I shall

send the black pair on to Louis. He's not as keen on driving as his wife, so he won't mind she has the more elegant hitch. But he admires horses greatly, and the blacks are beautiful animals. He will be pleased. Now, just tell me how soon you can leave."

Philippe's brow arched slightly. "Leave?"

"Yes, of course. Leave. To deliver the horses to Versailles."

"M...me?" Philippe stammered. "The palace?"

The sun had warmed Honneure, despite the chill breeze. Yet now she felt suddenly cold.

"Why not you, Philippe?" Madame Dupin countered. "You trained the horses, you raised the filly. You know them best."

"But I...I've never...I wouldn't know how to...I mean . . ."

"I do know what you mean," Madame Dupin responded tartly. "But your parents raised you properly. I will even take some credit. Your manners are exemplary, and you are well-spoken. You are also, I might add, a very handsome lad. You cut a fine figure. And you are an outstanding horseman. You will do just fine presenting these horses at the court. You merely need some proper clothes, but that won't take long. Do you think you can be ready to go within two weeks?"

"Uh, yes. Yes, I suppose. I'll be ready."

"Then it's settled." Madame Dupin started back toward the château. She turned briefly and said, "Thank you again, Philippe. You did an excellent job."

He inclined his head in acknowledgment. He did, in truth, know he deserved the praise. He had worked hard and took pride in his accomplishment.

"She's right, Philippe," Honneure said quietly. "You did a wonderful job. The horses are superb."

"Fit for a queen, Madame said. But what about me, little sister? Am *I* fit for a queen?"

It was an effort to smile, but Honneure managed. "You will make Madame Dupin proud in every way."

Philippe grinned back at her. "Thank you, *ma soeur*." He patted the seat beside him. "Would you like a ride back to the stable?"

Honneure shook her head. "*Maman* needs me in the kitchen."

"Very well. I'll see you at dinner." Philippe simply loosened the reins a fraction, clucked, and the pair sprang into a smart trot.

Honneure watched him go. Arms hugged to her breast, she shivered.

* * *

Slowly but surely the weather deteriorated. Steady sunshine had rendered the late autumn days mild, but the clouds of winter were massing. All the trees in the heavily forested park were bare. Dead brown leaves created a spongy carpet on the forest floor. The earth beneath smelled damp and fecund.

The gardeners had labored to plant fall flowers in the de Medici and de Poitiers gardens, and their muted colors provided a bit of relief from the monotony of the gray days. But nothing relieved the growing dread in the pit of Honneure's stomach. She went about her routine as if nothing was wrong. She helped Jeanne sew an appropriate wardrobe for Philippe's journey. She was quieter than usual, more withdrawn, though no one seemed to notice, and she was glad. If they asked her what was wrong, she didn't think she would be able to answer. She didn't know what was wrong.

She would miss Philippe, or course. She always missed him the infrequent times he was away. This time, however, it was more than that. Honneure was frightened.

The day of departure never really dawned. There was a lessening of the darkness. The features of the world appeared, but dimly, cloaked in a foggy mist. No individual clouds existed, just a solid ceiling of gray. It was, Honneure thought, completely fitting.

Almost the entire staff turned out to bid Philippe farewell. Most of them had never left their village before, much less traveled to a royal palace. Philippe was the object of much awe, and not a little envy.

Madame Dupin stood in the forecourt, in front of the modest crowd, with Paul, Jeanne and Honneure by her side. Philippe, dressed in livery, sat in the driver's seat of the Berlin holding the reins and a long carriage whip. The horses stood still, though their impatience showed in the way they bobbed their heads and snorted. The blacks were tied to the rear of the carriage, and one of them pawed the ground anxiously. Madame Dupin's footman, standing on a small platform between the "C" springs at the back of the coach, quieted the horse with a gentle word.

"You are a sight, Philippe Mansart," Madame Dupin declared. "If the Court is not mightily impressed, it will be because they have all been stricken blind."

Honneure silently agreed. Never had he looked so handsome. Part of it was the pride he took in the horses. "Lipizzans are wonderful animals," he had said to her the previous evening. They had stayed up late, long after everyone else had retired, and walked to the stables. "The white mare is exceptional. I hope the Princess takes a sincere interest in this breed of her country. I hope she will consider breeding them, with this mare as her foundation. Her line should be continued."

"You're going to miss her, aren't you?" They had paused at the mare's stall. Seeing Philippe, she nickered and threw her head. Honneure reached through the bars to stroke her cheek. Her startlingly white color glowed faintly in the dim lantern light.

"Yes, I'll miss her," he had replied, sadness in his tone.

"You don't mind leaving her there...returning to Chenonceau...do you?" Honneure was not quite sure why she had asked the question. Or why the response had seemed so terribly, terribly important.

"Of course I don't mind." Philippe had laughed lightly. "I'll be coming back to you, won't I, little sister? I must surely return."

"Oh, I hope so." She had laid her hands on his shoulders then and her head on his chest. "I hope so."

With difficulty, Honneure returned her thoughts to the present. Jeanne had handed a bundle up to her son. "Some bread and cheese and fruit for your journey. Be safe."

"And you be well, Mother...Father."

"Good luck, Son."

Philippe turned to Honneure. The forlorn look in her eyes made him want to climb from the coach and take her in his arms. He was glad they had said their good-byes last night. "*Au revoir, ma soeur.* I'll be home soon. I promise."

She could only nod. The lump in her throat made it impossible to speak.

Philippe lifted his hands, taking hold of his horses and making contact with their mouths. It was all the signal they needed. The Berlin moved forward.

"*Bon voyage,*" Madame Dupin called.

They all stood and watched until the coach had disappeared at the end of the lane. As soon as Madame Dupin turned, the servants dispersed. Claud held the door for his mistress. Only Honneure lingered, staring down the road.

"Don't worry about him, Honneure," said a voice very close to her ear.

She didn't have to look to know who it was. Claud had a somewhat unpleasant odor.

"He really is very talented and good looking. He should cause quite a stir among the...ladies...at Court. He might just have a wonderful time."

Honneure spun to face the overweight young man. "I hope he does," she spat.

"Do you?" Claud smiled slowly. "I wonder."

"What are you getting at, Claud? If you have something to say, say it. I have work to do."

"So do I." He let his eyes roam over Honneure's body. "Especially now that your...*brother* is gone."

Before she could stop him, he reached out and touched her breast. With all the strength she could muster, she slapped his face.

Claud's smile never faltered, but his eyes narrowed. He held a hand to his reddening cheek. "You *will* pay for this, Honneure. As Philippe said...I *promise*."

Chapter Six

Honneure awakened slowly, aware she had slept too long. She was able to make out the features of her tiny room. Dawn approached. She was late.

But it was cold, so cold. And she had grown thin in the months since Philippe had left. This winter seemed the hardest of any in memory. Under her blankets and duvet, Honneure shivered.

She had to rise, however. The sooner she stoked the embers in her small porcelain stove, the sooner she would be warm.

Honneure moved swiftly now. With a shawl clutched about her shoulders, she tended to her fire. In the glow of its modest heat, she drew a woolen dress over her chemise and fumbled at its buttons with numb fingers. She brushed out her long hair, twisted it into a knot at the nape of her neck and pinned it. She had to break a thin skin of ice in her basin to splash water on her face. She was as ready for her day as she could be.

Honneure's footsteps crunched in the snow still on the ground. There were many bare patches, however. It had not snowed in several days. But that would soon change. She could smell the moisture in the air.

Because she was so late, Honneure had not expected to meet anyone on her way into the château. She was surprised, therefore, to see the front door open just as she reached it. Her surprise turned almost instantly to distaste.

"Why, if it isn't Mademoiselle Mansart," Claud drawled in a deceptively sweet tone. He gave Honneure a smile, then slowly let it fade. "You're late," he snapped.

"You're early," she retorted sharply.

The humorless smile returned. "I am often in the château...early. Madame Dupin relies on me more and more these days, since my father died. I doubt she could do without me. Unlike Philippe."

A familiar nausea returned to Honneure's stomach. She turned to go, but Claud's words halted her.

"Your...*brother*...has become quite a favorite of the future Queen, I understand. He'll probably never return...Why should he? The palaces of Versailles, Fontainebleau. All those lovely ladies at Court."

The churning nausea became an acute pain. "I...I have to go," Honneure mumbled. But Claud ignored her.

"How old are you now, Honneure? Nineteen?" he taunted. "And no suitors. You discouraged them for so long, they finally stopped calling."

"Because I want none!" She had not meant to play his game, but the response came before she could bite her tongue.

"No, of course not. There's only one for you, isn't there, Honneure?" Claud shot back. "But he's gone. He obviously doesn't think as much of you as you do of him. And soon you will be so far past marriageable age, *no one* will want you."

Honneure had had enough. Head high, eyes narrowed, she stared at him levelly. "I certainly hope that includes you, Claud. Because your attentions and innuendoes are repugnant to me. I would rather die a slow and painful death than even *consider*, for one moment, marriage with you."

She watched his face redden, darkening his already bad complexion. A vein in his temple visibly throbbed. She gave him a cold, hard smile and turned on her heel. The sputtering sound he made gave her a measure of satisfaction, though she knew it would be worse for her next time.

Come home, Philippe, she silently prayed. *Please come home soon.*

* * *

Jeanne Mansart fussed over Madame Dupin's breakfast tray. When it met her rigid standards, she nodded to Honneure. "You'll have to hurry so it doesn't get too cold. The corridors are icy this morning."

"Icier than you know," Honneure mumbled in reply. She picked up the tray and left the kitchen.

Jeanne and Paul watched her, concern etched into each of their expressions. Jeanne spoke first.

"It seems she grows thinner by the day."

Paul pulled at his chin with a large, roughened hand. "It's bad enough how deeply she misses Philippe. But Claud's advances are becoming burdensome to her as well."

"Claud!" Jeanne spat the name. "I can't understand what Madame sees in him."

"He's made himself invaluable to her."

"He's wormed his way into her affections because he's slimy. Not because he's particularly talented. Worse, she thinks so highly of him she's actually pleaded his case with me for Honneure's hand."

Paul's bushy brows lifted. "I didn't know. How did you reply?"

"Not as I wished to, you can be sure. I simply said I didn't think Honneure would be agreeable to the proposal."

"What are we going to do, Mother?" Paul asked heavily. "I can't stand to watch her grow more unhappy by the day. She was the sunshine in our lives. Now it's gone."

Jeanne glanced sideways at her husband. "Well . . ."

"You've done something already, haven't you?"

"I...I wrote to Philippe," she confessed.

"Jeanne . . ."

"I know, I know," she interrupted. "Being offered a position at the royal stables is a dream come true for him." Jeanne smiled to herself as she recalled that first letter from Philippe. She had expected to see her son, for he was due to return. But a royal messenger called instead, bearing Philippe's missive. In it he informed them that the Princess in particular, loved the new horses and was impressed with their training. She had asked Philippe almost at once to stay on permanently to care for the animals. Though he had been loath to leave his family, it was an opportunity he simply could not ignore.

"But don't worry, Paul," Jeanne continued. "I didn't ask Philippe to come home. I would never do that. So I . . ."

"You what," Paul prompted when his wife hesitated.

"I...I asked Philippe to ask the Princess to find a place for Honneure at Court," she said quickly.

"Jeanne Mansart!" After more than a quarter of a century, Paul knew he shouldn't be surprised, but this was definitely one of his wife's more bold and dramatic moves. She would do anything for her children, but this . . .

"Do you have any idea how hard it is to get a position at Court?" he asked incredulously.

Jeanne shrugged and returned her attention to a lump of dough she had been kneading. "Can't hurt to ask," she replied lightly.

"Lord, woman. You never cease to amaze me."

"I know. It's one of the reasons you love me so much."
She watched her husband turn away out of the corner of her
eye. Paul was right. Probably nothing would come of her
request because nothing *could* come of it. Yet if there was any
way at all to bring Honneure to Versailles, Philippe would find
it. She knew how much he loved and missed Honneure.

And, unlike her husband, she knew much more than that.

* * *

It was so warm in the stables Philippe had begun to sweat
beneath his woolen livery. The heaters for the pampered
horses were all operating at maximum. He could hardly wait to
drive out into the snowy morning. With nimble fingers he
hurried to fix the white mare's harness to the sleigh, marveling
yet again at its workmanship.

"Open the doors!" he finally called to one of the numerous
pageboys who worked in the stables. "We're ready."

With his hands on the lines he moved the mare forward,
but did not get into the sleigh until they were out in the snow-
covered court. Then he hopped into the seat and drove the
horse on smartly. Her caulked hooves were nearly soundless
on the ground.

The vastness and majesty of the Versailles palace struck
Philippe at once, as it always did. He had emerged from the
Large Stables, across the wide court from the Small Stables,
and he smiled, remembering the first time he had seen the
monumental buildings. So massive were the structures he had
thought it was the very palace itself. But the two great
horseshoe-shaped buildings faced the palace, separated from it
by the huge military parade grounds, the *Place d'Armes*.
Taking the central of three broad avenues that converged on the

château, Philippe approached the imposing sprawl that was the Palace of Versailles.

The Ministers' Wings, like two great arms, reached out perpendicularly from the château proper to embrace the broad forecourt. From the forecourt Philippe entered the smaller Royal Court and saw the little Princess and her entourage awaiting him. Philippe slipped the bit in the mare's mouth and held her back while he drove her on. As a result she picked her knees up even higher while she tucked her chin in tighter toward her neck. He knew what an elegant picture she made.

Antoinette clapped her gloved, delicate hands as her personal coachman neared. She adored her white mare, and the handsome, dark-haired young man was quite a sight in the Christmas gift her husband had given her. Her courtiers surrounded the sleigh as Philippe pulled to a halt.

The body of the sleigh was shaped and painted like a true-to-life leopard. Its interior was lined with yellow silk. The red and gold shaft flaps ended in a stunningly carved wolf's head.

Philippe hopped off the coachman's seat, located where the leopard's tail would be, and bowed from the waist. Antoinette acknowledged him with an almost imperceptible nod, blue eyes twinkling merrily, and put her hand on a courtier's proffered palm to climb into the sleigh.

Philippe returned to his seat.

"Be sure to watch closely," she called to the assembled crowd as the mare stepped on.

"I want your opinion on my dear husband's gift."

The mare moved forward at a brisk trot, and Antoinette's Boxer dog, her almost constant companion, loped along behind them.

"Oh, Philippe, I love it," Antoinette said gaily as soon as they were out of earshot. "Was this not the sweetest, most thoughtful gift you could think of?"

Philippe smiled as he responded. Whenever they were alone, the Princess treated him as an equal, not as a servant. At first he had been astounded, for it wasn't how he had expected royalty to behave at all. But the future Queen was one of the most genuine, down-to-earth people he had ever known. They had, in fact, become quite good friends.

"His majesty's gift is indeed thoughtful," Philippe replied. "Costly as well. It speaks loudly of his affection for you."

Antoinette laughed. "Yes, it does, doesn't it. Louis' penury is notorious."

They drove on in silence for a while, circling the great forecourt, the only sound the hiss of iron runners skimming over the snow. Then, suddenly, there was a yip from the Princess' dog.

"Oh, Philippe, stop! Quickly, please! Look and see what he's done to himself."

Philippe halted the mare and jumped to the ground, confident the well-trained animal would not move a muscle. He knelt by the dog and observed him licking his front paw. Gently, he took the animal's foot and examined it.

"What is it, Philippe? What's wrong?"

"He'll be fine," Philippe replied quickly. "His pad's cracked and bleeding from the cold. But he'll need some tending, and he'll be sore for awhile."

"Can he walk back?"

"If you can bear to watch him limp," Philippe responded, tongue-in-cheek.

Despite her concern, Antoinette attempted a smile. "You know me so well," she murmured. "Very well. Pick him up, if you will, and put him in my lap. I'll have one of the stable veterinarians look at him."

Philippe started to do as he was bid, then abruptly stopped, an idea striking him with the force of a blow. Was it possible he might have found a solution to his dilemma?

Philippe agonized, but only for a moment. The situation his mother had described to him in her letter was untenable. The very idea of Claud Maraist with his beloved sister made his blood heat to boiling. He would try anything to get Honneure well away from that obnoxious pig.

"What's the matter, Philippe? Is something wrong?"

"No...no, just . . ."

"Just what, Philippe?"

Philippe lifted the dog in his arms and carried him to the sleigh before he answered. "It's just . . ."

"Is all well?" Madame Campan, Antoinette's chief chambermaid, hurried over to the sleigh, followed by the remainder of the retinue.

"My dog's injured his foot," Antoinette replied shortly. "What were you going to say, Philippe?"

He paused. It was one thing to speak in private with the Princess, quite another in front of her train. But the matter was urgent, and his idea a good one.

"My...my sister is wonderful with animals," he stammered at last. "She has a way with them and has many herbal remedies for their ailments as well. I was just...wishing she was here."

"Is she as beautiful as you are handsome, Philippe?" Rose, one of Antoinette's ladies tittered.

"She's my foster sister," he said with a slight blush. He had not yet gotten used to the way the women flirted with him. "So there is no family resemblance. Therefore, she is by far more beautiful."

"Well said, Philippe." Antoinette smiled appreciatively at

his humor while her ladies giggled. "Your sister resides in your former home, Chenonceau?"

Philippe could not believe his good fortune. Not only was the Princess engaging him in conversation in front of her whole Court, but also her question had given him exactly the wedge he needed to open the door for Honneure a little further.

"Yes, she does, though she was born at Château d'Amboise."

"Indeed?" Antoinette arched her finely drawn brows. Amboise was one of Choiseul's many estates, and Choiseul had been her favorite minister. Not long ago the hated du Barry had managed to have him dismissed and replaced with one of her own minions. As Philippe had hoped, she warmed to the subject of his sister. "And you say she has a way with animals?"

"You need only ask Madame Choiseul, whose favorite pet Honneure saved years ago, when she was only a child."

"Honneure," Antoinette repeated. "What an extraordinary name."

"For an extraordinary woman."

Antoinette smiled as she considered. Her retinue was large enough as it was, and Louis would fuss over the extra expense. He had carefully budgeted the allowance he received as Dauphin, hoping to set a good example for the profligate court, and hated to exceed it. Yet the cost for a woman to care for her pets would be very little. Besides, the du Barry always got whatever she wanted, no matter how outrageous the cost. And she was simply the King's mistress, not a future queen. Antoinette wondered why she shouldn't have what she wanted for a change.

"I have several dogs, all of whom I adore, as you know," the Princess replied at length. "And you obviously adore your sister. For that reason alone, Philippe, I shall create a position for her at Court. I am that fond of you."

"So am I," another pretty young woman murmured, batting long lashes.

But Philippe did not hear. His heart was pounding and the blood roared in his ears. "You...you are serious, Majesty?"

"Oh course, Philippe. You may send for her at once. Now take us back to the palace. I shall tend to my sweet dog in the meantime myself."

Though dazed with disbelief, Philippe responded with alacrity. The sooner he returned the Princess to the palace, the sooner he could write to his mother and Madame Dupin. And the sooner he would see his dearest sister.

* * *

When the snow finally fell, it fell softly, silently, for three days. Bare branches lifted to the gray sky to receive their layers of white. Brown patches on the ground were covered, and rooftops. Smoke curled lazily from chimneys to twine amongst the gently falling flakes. The world turned white.

Honneure stared out the kitchen window. Somewhere deep within her she knew how beautiful it was, but she lacked the emotional energy required to appreciate it. In truth she had energy for very little these days. When she heard her foster mother call to her, she turned slowly.

Jeanne resisted the urge to ask Honneure if she was all right. She would answer in the affirmative, as she always did, though they both knew she was not all right at all.

Madame Dupin had summoned the entire family, however, which was unusual. Jeanne prayed she was right about the reason why. The cure for Honneure's ailment may have arrived.

"Come, dear. Madame wishes to speak with us."

Honneure noticed her foster father standing behind his wife, and her curiosity was sluggishly roused. "All of us?"

"Yes, all of us."

"But, why?"

"Come along and we shall find out."

* * *

Madame Dupin received them in the library, as was usual. Her *pince-nez* were perched on the bridge of her nose, and she glanced up from a letter as they entered the small room. Jeanne was slightly disconcerted to see Claud standing at his mistress' shoulder, but ignored him and stared at the paper in Madame Dupin's hands.

"Thank you for coming so promptly." Madame glanced up at them briefly. "I received several letters by special messenger today. One is for you, from Philippe." She handed the sealed envelope to Jeanne. "I also have one from Philippe. And one from Marie Antoinette, the Dauphine."

Jeanne thought she might faint. She clutched her letter to her breast, afraid to look at either her husband or daughter, afraid even to breathe. As if from far away, she heard Honneure's faint gasp of surprise.

"I will come straight to the point," Madame Dupin continued. "Philippe has written to me that Honneure has been offered a position at Court."

"*Mon Dieu!*"

"My sentiments exactly, Paul," she commented dryly. "The Princess has several dogs of which she is inordinately fond. Apparently Philippe has persuaded her that Honneure is just the person to care for them."

"But...but how can it be true?" Paul stammered.

"It is true. Here is the Princess' letter confirming the offer." Madame lifted a piece of paper, which clearly bore the royal seal. "If Honneure accepts, she will be given a small room in the palace near the Dauphine's chambers, so she will be on call at all times to tend to the royal pets." Madame Dupin turned her gaze at last to Honneure. "This is almost unheard of good fortune, Honneure. What do you say to the offer?"

Despite her initial shock and her longing to see Philippe, Honneure had a ready response. "I could not possibly leave you, Madame, or my family. You have been too good to me. I will not repay your kindness and generosity by abandoning you for a better position."

"You are loyal and honorable to a fault, my dear."

"But wise perhaps," Claud interjected. Ignoring Paul's hard stare and Jeanne's narrowed eyes, he went on. "What if it doesn't work out? The Court is notoriously fickle. What if she spends the next few years caring for the Dauphine's pampered darlings and is then sent packing on a whim? What will become of her? She's almost past marriageable age as it is. If she leaves, she may miss the chance for a good marriage and a normal life."

"It is something to consider." Madame Dupin agreed. "I know Claud, for one, would be happy to make you his wife. That, too, would assure you a secure and excellent future. What have you to say, Honneure?"

Some of the old spark suddenly returned. "If I stay, will I be required to marry Claud?"

This time it was Jeanne's breath that hissed loudly into the silence. Claud's pock-marked face reddened. Madame Dupin looked taken aback.

"Of course not," she replied finally. She glanced over her

shoulder at her portly steward. "I'm sorry, Claud," Madame Dupin said apologetically. "I would not have mentioned it, but you led me to believe Honneure would be agreeable to this union."

Claud looked apoplectic. Honneure smiled grimly. "I would not marry Claud if he was the last man on earth."

Jeanne's hands flew to her mouth, while Paul's jaw dropped. Madame Dupin frowned with displeasure.

"There is no need to be insulting, Honneure," she said sternly. "You need not marry at all, if that is your wish. And you most certainly may remain here with your family. I admire your loyalty. But I would counsel you to think well on this before you give me your final answer."

Honneure started to speak, but changed her mind and merely nodded. She just wanted to be away...away from the library, Madame Dupin, her parents...Claud.

Jeanne curtsied nervously. "Thank...thank you, Madame. We'll talk to Honneure."

They were dismissed.

* * *

"Honneure!" Jeanne whispered as they hurried down the corridor. "I know how you feel about Claud, and I don't blame you, but you didn't have to . . ."

"Stop!" Honneure pressed her hands to her ears. "Please stop!"

Jeanne and Paul exchanged glances, eyes wide with surprise. Surprise turned to shock and dismay when Honneure suddenly bolted. She ran out the front door and away from the château. Jeanne started after her.

"No, let her go," Paul said, a hand on his wife's arm. "She needs time to think, time to be alone." He turned, hearing footsteps behind him, and fixed Claud with an icy stare. "And I'll make sure she remains alone."

Claud clenched his fists to hide the trembling of his hands. It took monumental effort, but he managed to hold his tongue. He would bide his time.

Like a fat, hungry spider, he would bide his time.

* * *

Honneure was not sure how long she had wandered through the white woods. When she became aware once more of her surroundings, she realized she was cold, chilled to the bone. Slender tree trunks all around her dimmed in the fading light.

She was not lost, however. She had only to retrace her footsteps in the snow.

It was full dark by the time she came to the lane. To her left she saw the lights of Claud's house. Honneure shuddered.

That decision, at least, had been an easy one. Arms hugged to her breast, she ran across the lane toward the stable and the family's cozy rooms above it.

Honneure's heart brimmed with love when she entered her room. A candle burned on the small table by her bed. The stove had been lit, and on her bureau were a small pitcher of wine, some bread and cheese and a slice of *saucisson*. Though she wasn't really hungry, she forced herself to eat a piece of bread and cheese. She had grown so thin her clothes fit badly, and she experienced lightheadedness from time to time. Honneure took a sip of wine, removed her shoes and lay down on her bed. Her eyes fluttered closed.

She remembered the night, now seemingly so long ago, when she and Philippe had sat side by side on the banks of the Cher, and she had made him promise nothing would ever change. But too much had changed already.

Philippe was gone. He had promised to return, but had not. Her life had changed in many ways. She could not risk more change. She had been so fortunate to find the Mansart family and come to Chenonceau. If she went to yet another new home, would she be so fortunate? She doubted it.

Honneure also recalled Madame Dupin's words about the Court and the doomed moths that fluttered about its brilliant flame. She believed Madame. She worried about Philippe. Philippe. Would he understand why she couldn't leave? Would he think her mad for turning down such a golden opportunity? Would she ever see him again? Honneure turned on her side and drew up her knees.

She mustn't think such thoughts, they only made her ill. Of course she would see him again. He wasn't a prisoner at Versailles. He had written, in fact, that he would come home for a few days in the spring. That was the thought she must hold on to...seeing Philippe. And Chenonceau, her home, her loving family, Madame Dupin.

But it was Claud who suddenly appeared on the backs of her eyelids. Claud, his face engorged with rage. Claud, who would make her life miserable at every opportunity.

No! Honneure curled into a tighter ball. She mustn't think of him, she mustn't. He was an unpleasant fact of life, that was all. She would ignore him and live her life as she was meant to, caring for her family and serving Madame Dupin. Exhausted, warmed by the bread and wine, she fell into a deep sleep.

* * *

Honneure wasn't sure what had awakened her. The fire in the stove had died, and it was cold in the room. The candle had guttered. She sat up slowly, realizing it must be some time after midnight. She would have to get up, find a new candle, relight the stove, and undress.

She swung her legs over the bed, feeling for her shoes in the darkness.

A hand went over her mouth.

Panic blossomed in her breast and exploded. She was forced backward onto the bed.

"So, you wouldn't marry me if I was the last man on earth?"

Snakelike, the voice hissed into her ear.

Honneure struggled, but weakly. Claud's weight on her frail form was overwhelming. She smelled the stink of his sweat and his sour breath, and nausea rose in her throat.

"Well, the feeling's mutual . . ."

A foul and slimy tongue licked the side of her neck.

". . . but I *will* have what I want."

Honneure felt Claud's pelvis thrust against her. Something hard and obscenely repugnant between his legs drove at her groin. Panic turned to terror. His grip on her mouth was so strong she could not turn her head, and it was becoming difficult to breathe.

Claud's free hand fumbled at her breast, kneading it beneath her woolen dress. Frustrated, he grabbed her collar and ripped away her bodice. His thick lips fastened on her at once.

Honneure could feel herself begin to float away. She wasn't getting enough air.

Abandoning her breast Claud groped at her skirt. He worked it upward until it bunched around her waist and tore at her underlinens.

She was completely exposed. Now she could feel him

fumbling at his trousers.

But it hardly mattered. She was going away, going away where Claud did not exist, nothing existed . . .

The scream could not possibly have been hers. She hadn't even the breath to give it voice.

Yet, it went on...And she could breathe. Great gulps of air filled her lungs. Her body felt weightless. Claud was gone!

The screaming stopped. She struggled to sit up, but arms were suddenly around her, familiar, loving arms.

"Honneure...my baby...Oh, I'm so sorry!"

Honneure hugged her foster mother back and tried to look over her shoulder at the commotion in her doorway.

"No, no, don't look." Jeanne forcibly turned Honneure's head away. She did not want her to see the punishment Claud was about to receive. "It's over now. You're safe... You're safe, baby."

All the fear, the terror, left her in a great, sweeping rush. She was empty, drained. Her arms dropped to her sides. Laying her head on Jeanne's breast, Honneure wept.

Chapter Seven

Early Spring, 1771

Philippe unfolded the note the stableboy had just handed him and quickly scanned the lines. He sighed.

"All right," he said to the lad. "Tell her I'll be there."

The boy ran off, and Philippe returned his attention to the harness he had been polishing. It was already clean and supple, but he had little to do in the afternoons when he had finished exercising the Lipizzans. For nearly a thousand horses, there were almost as many attendants, including equerries, page boys, footmen, coachmen, stable lads, blacksmiths, cartwrights, saddlers, doctors, surgeons, chaplains and musicians. The royal steeds lived almost as well as the royal family, Philippe mused. And while his workload was a great deal lighter than it had been at Chenonceau, it left him with time on his hands. He had never liked being idle.

If Honneure came, however, he could spend much of his free time with her. The prospect cheered him. It seemed he missed her more each day and merely prayed she would accept the Princess' offer. He knew how fiercely loyal she was, and how stubborn. An opportunity that anyone else would jump at in a heartbeat would cause Honneure hours, if not days, of intense deliberation.

But he should learn something soon. It had been nearly three weeks since the messenger had taken the letters to Chenonceau.

In the meantime, there was Olivia.

Holding the shining harness clear of the floor, Philippe stood. The stableboy who had been assigned to assist him with the Lipizzans was at his side in an instant. Philippe handed him the leather trappings and mentally calculated the time.

She had said to meet him in an hour. Half of that time had already passed, and almost all of the rest would be consumed in reaching the rendezvous point she had designated. Philippe ran a hand through his tussled curls and strode from the stable.

There were not only a thousand people who worked in the stables, but also nearly nine thousand who worked in the palace. Nearly twenty-five hundred were housed in the surrounding town, but the rest resided at the palace. The *Grand Commun* boasted a thousand rooms that held fifteen hundred people, and the balance, five thousand, lived within the château itself. As a result the grounds teemed with humanity.

Philippe was immediately lost among the many who hurried on their errands. No one regarded his passing or cared about his destination. It had been a difficult thing to comprehend at first, so different from Chenonceau. Once he had attended to his duties, he had almost complete freedom. In the beginning he had wondered what to do with himself. Then he had realized there were at least as many, if not more, intrigues among the palace servants as the royal Court. Philippe chuckled to himself.

He had learned a great deal since coming to Versailles. He had long known about the King's favorite, of course, Madame du Barry. But he had been shocked to learn of the King's own private brothel. How many women did one man need? He shook his head.

Madame Dupin's stories had prepared him for a measure

of debauchery, but the reality of the Court's excesses had stunned him. He knew he must have appeared wide-eyed at first. The morals of the Court were as loose as the lifestyle and surroundings were lavish. After awhile it no longer surprised him that those who served the Court were morally lax as well. It had proved a temptation he could not hold out against forever.

Because there were so many people entering and leaving the château, no one noticed Philippe in particular. From the Royal Court he climbed the steps to the Marble Court and entered the palace. Cutting through the central block of the château saved him the twenty minutes it would take to walk around the massive wings. He bent his head and quickened his steps, as if bent on some important errand, and exited through the grand, gilded doors to the palace gardens.

To see the vista suddenly stretching away before him was a humbling experience. Philippe had always had a solid opinion of himself, but he felt small and insignificant when gazing down the long view. One vast terrace led to another, each decorated with pools, fountains and elaborate gardens, all leading to the Grand Canal, its ribbon of blue disappearing into the distance. Dense woodland and hunting parks surrounded all, concealing secret gardens and grottoes. Pulse quickening, Philippe hurried to his rendezvous at the Apollo Fountain.

He didn't see her at first. The lure of the beautiful spring day had attracted many to the freshly greening gardens. Then he caught the glint of sunlight on blue-black hair, unmistakable among the powdered wigs and elaborate styles. His blood seemed to heat as it rushed through his veins. He moved in her direction.

Olivia felt him before she saw him. Virility emanated from him like warmth and light from a fire, and she was irresistibly drawn. When she looked up and caught his eye, his fire bloomed within her.

She was on the opposite side of the pool, with the golden Apollo, his chariot and fiery steeds rising from the still waters between them. But Philippe saw only her hourglass figure and lush, pouting mouth. Her dark, slightly uptilted eyes slid away from him in the direction of a woodland path. She moved toward it slowly and Philippe followed.

It had been warm beneath the direct sun, but in the shade of the new-leafed trees Olivia shivered. Resisting the urge to look behind her, she walked farther into the woods. She only stopped when she felt his hand on her shoulder.

"Are you trying to run away?" Philippe laughed softly in Olivia's ear. "I thought you wanted to see me."

Though her heart pounded, she managed to keep her face turned coyly away. "Do you not wish to see *me*?"

"I *wish* to do more than see you." After a brief glance assured him no one else was near, Philippe pressed his lips to a spot just below Olivia's left ear. The musky scent of her flesh stirred him and he pressed more closely against her.

Reluctantly Olivia moved away, eyes still averted. "I have no time today," she said sulkily. "Antoinette requires me to move from the palace into the *Grand Commun*."

"The commune!" Philippe was taken aback. "But why? You've been with her since she first came to France."

Risking a glance, Olivia slid her mahogany eyes in Philippe's direction. "Yes, I've been loyal to her, have I not? I have taken care of her most intimate needs. Yet now I am being displaced."

"Olivia, I...I don't know what to say."

"Don't you?" Olivia pursed her full lips and looked up at him from under lowered lids. "Did you not press your foster sister's case to the Princess?"

"Well, yes," Philippe admitted, totally confused. "And the Dauphine was kind enough to write to my former mistress, Madame Dupin, to ask Honneure to join the royal entourage."

"To care for her dogs, no?"

"No. I mean yes...*Yes*. But what . . ." Philippe paused, realization dawning. "Is she coming? Has the Princess had word?"

Olivia's eyes narrowed. "Would it bring you joy?" she asked in a curiously flat tone. "Have you missed your sister so much?"

Delighted by the prospect of Honneure's arrival, Philippe did not heed Olivia's subtle warning signals. Grinning broadly, he grasped her shoulders and pulled her around to face him.

"You have heard something, haven't you? When is she coming? Tell me!"

Something dark brewed in Olivia's breast. She looked deeply into Philippe's eyes. "She arrives tomorrow, with Madame Dupin," she replied curtly. "She will take over my small chamber. Where *I* used to sleep with the spoiled mongrels."

The venom in Olivia's tone finally pierced the glowing aura of Philippe's happiness. The smile slipped from his mouth. "I...I'm sorry, Olivia. I never meant for this to happen."

"No. You only wanted Honneure. Now you will have her. And what will become of me?"

"Olivia . . ." Philippe let his arms fall from her shoulders and grasped her hands. Enfolding them tightly, he pressed them to his breast and drew her toward him. "Honneure is my *sister*."

"Your foster sister," Olivia corrected.

"With whom I was raised. And who I love as if she were a sibling of blood to me."

"Are you sure?" Olivia leaned forward, her ample bosom now pressed to Philippe's chest, imprisoning their hands. "This love is pure and innocent?"

Her nearness was intoxicating. It took all his self control not to thrust his hips against her.

"I'm sure, Olivia," Philippe managed to whisper. "Just as sure as I am of my feelings for you."

He longed to kiss her, she knew. But she raised her chin only a little, face slightly turned.

"Do you care enough to help me move my things to the *Grand Commun*?"

Philippe was only able to nod.

Olivia smiled, a contented cat's smile. "It might be better, you know, in the commune," she purred. "My chamber is small and spare, but I share it with no one. And with so many people coming and going, who will notice you?"

Her words, as well, inflamed him now. Honneure temporarily forgotten, Philippe freed a hand and raised Olivia's chin with the tip of one finger. She did not resist. As her eyes closed, he lowered his lips to hers.

* * *

Chenonceau's "gallery" stretched from the main body of the château across the Cher to the opposite bank. Built by Catherine de Medici upon a bridge that had spanned the river, it was Honneure's favorite spot. With eighteen arched windows reaching from floor to ceiling, the room was almost always filled with light, even through the gray days of winter. Italian cypress trees flourished in niches between the windows, and two great fireplaces at either end of the gallery warmed the air on the coldest days.

The air was frigid no longer, however. The spring thaw had finally arrived. All the snow had melted, grass was greening, and bulbs had pushed their blossoms up from the cool, dark earth. River ice had broken up and flowed away, and the Cher ran unimpeded between the château's arched piers. Honneure stared at the water and thought it seemed very much like her life...simply flowing away, unable to stop, unaware of a destination, just moving, constantly moving on a predetermined course whose end she could not see.

Honneure sighed and recalled, yet again, the summer night she had sat with Philippe on the riverbank. Foolishly, she had forced him to promise their lives would not change. It was a promise he could not give, and even at the time she had known it deep in her heart. But she had wanted so badly to hang on to her hard-won happiness. Had she tempted fate with her fears of the future? Had she herself brought about the end of an idyllic childhood?

"Everything must have an end," a familiar voice said softly, as if the speaker had heard her very thoughts.

Fighting tears, Honneure did not turn.

"This day will end," Madame Dupin continued. "There will be a period of darkness. But another day *will* begin."

"But will the new day . . ." Honneure had to pause and swallow her tears. "Will the new day be as bright as the ones that have gone before? It is not always so."

"Each day will be what you make of it, Honneure."

"But *you* made my life what it is!" Choking on a sob, Honneure whirled to face her mistress. "You and Mother and Father and Philippe. Even this place, Chenonceau. This is my *home*, my *happiness*. If I leave, how will I ever find it again?"

"'It?'" Madame Dupin's brow furrowed in a stern

expression. "If by 'it' you mean Chenonceau, the château is well known and easy to find. But if by 'it' you mean your happiness, then you are surely lost, Honneure. For the power to find happiness lies within you. If you cannot grasp it, it is no one's fault but your own. And if you find it, it is because of your own personal search."

Too caught up in her fears, Honneure stared at the marble tiled floor and slowly shook her head. "No," she whispered. "There is no happiness outside of Chenonceau."

"You were not happy at Amboise?" Madame Dupin inquired sharply. "The years you spent with your mother were spent in darkness?"

"Oh, no!" Honneure replied quickly. "I didn't mean that. I was very happy with my mother at Amboise."

"And when you left Amboise, did you know how happy you would be with us here? Were you eager to make the journey to your new home?"

"No, no, I . . ." Honneure shook her head vigorously. "I was scared to death. I . . ."

Madame Dupin smiled slowly as she watched the light return to Honneure's eyes as realization dawned. She watched her expression soften, then tighten again with chagrin.

"I...I'm so sorry," Honneure stammered. "I . . ."

"Don't say another word," Madame Dupin said quietly, and touched her fingers to Honneure's lips. "It is *I* who am sorry, Honneure. I should have seen what was happening before my very eyes. I should have been more sensitive to Claud's true character."

"Oh, Madame Dupin, please don't blame yourself!"

"I do not," she replied firmly. "I have regrets, yes, but even those are a waste of time. I do not blame myself, however. Only Claud may have blame. Yet I must still ask your forgiveness and understanding for not banishing Claud immediately from Chenonceau."

Honneure folded her hands in front of her and dropped her gaze. "I...I understand your reasons," she said in a subdued voice.

"He has far too tight a grip on my affairs," Madame Dupin went on as if Honneure had not spoken. "*That* much is my fault. It will take time to extricate myself from his grasp, and for my own safety, I cannot let him know in advance that his days are numbered."

"So I must go instead."

The statement was made simply, without self-pity, and Madame Dupin felt her heart squeeze. "It is not that you must go, dear child, but rather that you cannot stay. Nevertheless, I will make you a promise."

Honneure looked up, feathered brows arched.

"When Claud leaves, if you are unhappy at Versailles, you may always return to Chenonceau."

Tears at once filled Honneure's eyes, and her lip trembled, making it impossible to express her gratitude.

"You do not need to thank me," Madame Dupin said as if again perceiving Honneure's thoughts. "And I do not think you will wish to leave Versailles. You are a beautiful and intelligent woman, Honneure. There can be so much more to life for you than service in a country château. Your curiosity is too strong. I will not always be able to satisfy it with the tales I bring home. You should be able to observe life...history... firsthand, and make of it what you can. There is so much more to life than this château. A great deal more. And I believe it awaits you at Versailles."

Something enigmatic in Madame Dupin's expression and tone gave Honneure pause. "I...I only know that Philippe awaits me at Versailles."

"Yes. Yes, he does," Madame Dupin said slowly. She gazed at Honneure for a long moment, then abruptly smiled and smoothed the front of her blue satin skirt. "*I* shall see him, too," she said brightly. "And you must tell me how I look. *Honestly*."

Madame Dupin had dressed in Court fashion, and an elaborate powdered wig towered over her pale brow. A beribboned hat was pinned atop the mass at a rakish angle that defied gravity, and panniers held her skirt so far out to the sides she would have to turn sideways to walk through a normal door.

Honneure started to say something, but choked on the lie. The choke turned into a giggle.

"Truly horrible, isn't it?" Madame Dupin remarked dryly. "Just thank your lucky stars you don't have to be stuffed into this ridiculous regalia. You look, and undoubtedly are, far more comfortable than I. Turn around and let me see all of you."

Rose-tinted cheeks flushed darker as Honneure did a slow pirouette. Self-consciously she touched the heavy chignon at the nape of her neck. The long, loose curls that framed her face tickled as they brushed against her cheeks.

"You look lovely, Honneure," Madame Dupin pronounced. "The Dauphine's colors suit you."

"I...I can't thank you enough for having this made for me," Honneure said as she fingered the elaborate silver embroidery overlaying the rich, red velvet.

Madame Dupin waved a hand dismissively. "You cannot arrive at the palace from Chenonceau looking like a country girl."

"But I *am* a country girl."

Madame Dupin grew serious again. She stepped forward and took Honneure's face in her hands.

"You are Honneure Mansart," she said in a firm, but barely audible voice. "You are beloved by your parents, myself...and Philippe. Your home is Chenonceau. Your position is to serve the future Queen of France. Everything else is what you make of it. *That* is who you are and who you shall be."

Honneure stared into her mistress' unblinking blue eyes for so long she became lost in the intensity of the gaze. It seemed she could see the river, and the flow of her life, once more. No longer disappearing into a misty and fearful future, however, but winding steadily, and with purpose, toward a destination she herself would determine.

And then they were in each other's arms, and clung for a long moment.

Madame Dupin released Honneure and dashed a tear from her cheek. "Come, dear child. It is time to say our good-byes."

Chapter Eight

May 1771

Trailed by several of Antoinette's ladies, Madame Dupin strolled contentedly arm-in-arm with the Princess through the vast gardens of the Versailles palace. Exiting through the back of the château, they crossed the Water Terrace, flanked on either side by oblong pools. From there they descended two sets of stone stairs to the Latona Fountain. Encircling its four graduated tiers, various fish and figures spit their jets of water into overflowing pools. Heading to the right of the fountain, they followed a path that led into the densely forested parkland. In minutes they reached the Baths of Apollo. Madame Dupin drew in her breath.

"No matter how often I come here, I am always struck by the particular beauty and magnificence of this place," she said in a tone of awe and admiration.

In response, the petite Princess merely squeezed her friend's arm. Together they took in the majesty of the garden.

It was as if they had left the real world behind and entered a fairy kingdom. Varied ivies and climbing plants clung to the stone walls of the man-made grotto. Thick, springy moss covered the ground. Ferns lined the banks of the forest pool, and water bugs skittered across its still, green water. Madame Dupin closed her eyes briefly, then lifted her gaze.

In caves hollowed out of the soaring stone stood the fabulous Apollo sculptures: There was Apollo attended by the lovely Nereids, bathing his feet, pouring water into a basin toward which he languidly stretched his hand; in another niche the horses of Apollo's chariot were being unyoked, and reared away from their attendants in agitation; in a third area the horses were depicted calmly drinking from a pool.

The Princess sighed and leaned her head against her friend's shoulder. "I, too, am overcome by the magic of this place each time I enter." She straightened and uttered a short laugh. "At least I am no longer overwhelmed by the palace itself."

Madame Dupin patted the Princess' hand. "It was a great deal to get used to. I know. I have seen your mother's palace, the Schönbrun."

"The entire château would have fit into one wing of Versailles. It was so simple, so practical, compared to all of this." Antoinette vaguely waved a hand in the direction of the palace. "As was my childhood."

Madame Dupin smiled fondly. "You've often told me how close you were to your brothers and sisters."

"I miss them," Antoinette replied simply. "I miss the carefree days of our childhood." She chuckled softly. "Too carefree, I suppose. Did you know I didn't learn to read until my mother had agreed to my betrothal to Louis?"

"So you've said."

"I worked hard, though it seemed only a game to me. Even when I left for France, it was not reality yet. How could it seem real? Everything the Royal Court does, it seems, is done in excess. Forty-eight, six-horse carriages came to bear me to my betrothed! Nothing was real until . . ." Antoinette knit her brow and her gaze unfocused. "Until we reached an island in the Rhine near Kiehl," she continued softly. "I was taken into a tent, divided in the middle like a bathing tent. All my clothing, even my stockings and vest were removed, and I was handed over to Comtesse de Noailles. Naked, I was required to leave my Austrian ladies behind and step over to the French side of the tent. I left everything behind at that moment. I entered reality." With wide, tear-filled eyes, Antoinette looked at her friend. "I was only fourteen."

"Dear child," Madame Dupin murmured and gently touched the Princess' cheek.

Antoinette shook her head and forced a smile to her lips. "Never mind. I am content now." Once again taking Madame Dupin's arm, she walked along the edge of the pool.

Madame Dupin let the silence drift for a time. Then she stopped, deliberately. Brows arched, she looked Antoinette directly in the eye. "And Madame du Barry?"

The Princess did not respond at once. She looked away.

"She does not know it, but I have seen her rooms. They are filled with porcelain and costly ivories. The furniture is encrusted with ebony and she has a large leather-bound library of...erotica." The Princess blushed. "She rides in the most sumptuous carriage, painted with cupids, hearts and beds of roses. She wants for nothing."

"Oh, yes, she does."

An expression of bafflement settled over the Princess' soft features.

"Your good opinion," Madame Dupin continued.

Antoinette looked away again, sharply. "My disapproval avails me nothing," she said at length, so softly Madame Dupin could barely hear. "Aunt Adelaide, the King's dear sister, encouraged me to express it. And as a result . . ."

" 'As a result,' " Madame Dupin prompted.

Antoinette drew a deep breath. "As a result Madame du Barry had one of my ladies sent away from Court over an imagined slight. She convinced the King to dismiss Choiseul, my friend, and had him replaced with the Duc d'Aiguillon, one of her lovers and opposed to Austria!"

Madame Dupin was taken aback by Antoinette's sudden venom. She rallied quickly and took the Princess' hands in her own.

"Antoinette...Antoinette," she soothed. "I'm so sorry."

"As am I." Antoinette shrugged and appeared to pull herself together. "My husband and even my mother have advised me to at least *appear* accepting of the woman. It is difficult, but I try."

"Of course you do," Madame Dupin said gently. Wisely, she decided to steer the subject away from Madame du Barry. "Speaking of your husband, how is Louis?"

Antoinette's expression softened. "He is well. We often spend an hour or two alone together in the afternoons."

"Oh?"

Although it was only a single word, Madame Dupin and the Princess had become close friends. Antoinette blushed to the roots of her elaborately piled and powdered wig.

"He...he works at his locks, his hobby, while I...while I read or sew," she stammered finally.

"And the nights?"

When Antoinette remained silent, Madame cupped the Princess' chin in her hand and forced her to look up.

"It will happen, my dear," she said under her breath. "When the time is right it will happen. I promise you."

Antoinette smiled though her eyes once again brimmed. "Yes," she whispered. "So I must believe...so I must."

The two friends gazed at each other in silence, then Madame Dupin took Antoinette's arm once more.

"And *I* believe it is time to return to the palace and see

how Honneure fares with your *petits chiens*."

Antoinette's tiny hands flew to her mouth. "I'd nearly forgotten!" she exclaimed with a laugh. "Indeed, let us return at once!"

* * *

Immediately upon her arrival at Versailles, Honneure had been led away by a servant in the Dauphine's livery, while Madame Dupin had gone directly to see Antoinette. The quiet, older woman, who gave her name as Eleonore, had taken Honneure on an abbreviated tour of the château's ground floor so she would be able to orient herself and find her way about the immense palace.

Footsteps echoing in the wide stone corridors, the two women walked for what seemed miles to Honneure. Almost all of the ground floor of the U-shaped structure contained lodging units for the support staff, nearly two-thousand rooms in all. Honneure had wondered aloud where the kitchens were.

"In town," Eleonore had replied succinctly. "Almost everything has been moved to the town. The bakery, wine cellars, fruitery. There is only a room here in the palace to reheat the things brought from the village."

"But...but where do *you* eat?"

"In the *Grand Commun*. You will be taken there later."

The women continued on in silence until they reached a great marble staircase, split in the middle, both sides winding upward and out of sight. Eleonore gestured.

"The King's Staircase," she said briefly. "We will go on to the Queen's."

Honneure already knew that since Louis XV's wife was deceased, the Dauphine occupied these *Petits Appartements*. The royal mistress was housed in chambers nearer to the King.

What she didn't know was how small and frightened she was going to feel.

The Queen's Stair was a duplicate of the King's, though smaller in scale. As they climbed, Honneure was awed by the polychrome marble *revêtement* and illusionistic loggias. The painted people looking down on them seemed more real than she and Eleonore.

Even the beauty and grandeur of Chenonceau had not prepared Honneure for the royal world revealed to her as she climbed to the top of the stair. Niches in the marble-faced walls contained gold medallions supported by bronze cherubs. Huge gold and crystal chandeliers blazed with light. Dumbstruck, Honneure followed Eleonore to the left and down a narrow hallway lined with classical busts. They emerged in a room that took her breath away.

"The Queen's Guardroom," Eleonore said needlessly.

Honneure barely noticed the soldiers standing stiffly at attention. She saw the paintings first, classical in nature and larger than any work of art she had ever seen. There were even paintings on the ceiling and, again, lifelike figures peering down at her as if from a balcony. The walls were faced with designs of red and black marble, white painted doors were decorated with gilt. Numb, she followed Eleonore onward.

The next room, the woman informed her, was the Queen's Antechamber, and it was much like the first. Paintings lined the red velvet walls, and heroic scenes framed in gold drew the eye upward to the golden ceiling and bas-relief carvings. The Salon of Nobles followed, its walls covered with an elaborate brocade. The subjects of the paintings, Honneure guessed, had given the room its name.

Honneure did not think it was possible to see a room more lavish, sumptuous, or elegant than the ones she had already seen, but she was wrong.

"The Queen's Bedroom," Eleonore announced.

The bed, though massive, was dwarfed by the size of the chamber. The walls had been painted white, but very little of it could be seen beneath the intricate gilt decoration. The room itself seemed to be made of gold. The compartmented ceiling boasted even more complex and Byzantine gilt designs. Several chandeliers hung the length of the room. Drapes of heavy golden damask framed floor-to-ceiling windows. Corner reliefs bore the arms of France and Austria.

"She...the Dauphine...she can't possibly actually *live* in these rooms...can she?" Honneure whispered.

Eleonore laughed softly. "Indeed not. These are the reception rooms. Come this way."

Honneure watched Eleonore move aside a heavily embroidered silk hanging to reveal a door. She opened it and motioned for Honneure to follow.

Honneure felt more comfortable almost at once. The series of interior rooms they had entered were smaller and, though exquisitely decorated, felt much more habitable. Walls were painted in gay pastels and light poured in through tall windows. From where she stood, Honneure could see on one side a library, with leather-bound books arrayed on shelves that stretched to the high ceiling. To her left she was able to see a salon filled with delicate furniture and a gilded clavichord.

A tall, stern looking woman approached them from the salon. Though she did not wear the panniers favored by courtiers, neither was she dressed in the livery of the Dauphine's servants.

Eleonore dipped a curtsy in acknowledgment of the woman's superior position, and Honneure followed suit.

"You must be Honneure Mansart," the woman stated in a

surprisingly low voice. "You may go, Eleonore," she said without taking her eyes from Honneure.

Honneure heard the door close quietly behind her as she endured the tall woman's scrutiny.

"I am Madame Campan," she said at length. "The Dauphine's chief chambermaid." She clapped her hands, and a moment later a girl appeared from another room beyond the library.

The girl was quite beautiful, Honneure thought, especially dressed in the colors of the Princess' livery, with her porcelain skin and jet black hair. Her figure was voluptuous, her mouth full and pouting, and Honneure was reminded of an overblown summer rose.

"Olivia, this is Honneure," Madame Campan said. "I will leave it to you to show her to her duties and her chamber."

Though Madame Campan left at once, Olivia did not move or speak. Her catlike eyes regarded Honneure for a long moment, until she began to feel uncomfortable. Honneure attempted a smile.

"I...I'm happy to meet you, Olivia," she managed to stammer.

Olivia remained silent, her dark eyes flicking from the top of Honneure's head to the hem of her full skirt. Suddenly she whirled and motioned to Honneure with the quirk of a finger.

The experience of the grandeur of Versailles had been daunting, yet exhilarating. Its magnificence was thrilling. In spite of the fact that she was a newcomer and knew no one but a brother she wondered if she would even be able to find, Honneure had felt a kind of warm glow within her. Now, however, she felt a chill. Suddenly trepidatious, she followed Olivia through the library.

Beyond the library was a lovely boudoir and adjacent

bathing room that Honneure guessed must be Antoinette's. Olivia opened a small door and gestured for Honneure to precede her.

The first thing Honneure saw in the tiny, sparsely furnished room was the Boxer. He stood in the center of the floor, lips curled in a snarl and hackles raised. Four smaller dogs leapt down from a narrow bed and began to bark furiously.

A brief glance in Olivia's direction confirmed what she suspected. A cruel smile twitched at the corners of the girl's mouth. But Honneure was not afraid of the dogs.

Speaking softly, eyes averted, Honneure crouched. She patted her hand lightly on the parquet floor and coaxed the little dogs to come to her.

The Boxer stopped growling. One small dog stretched its neck, sniffing, then launched itself into Honneure's lap. The other three quickly followed. Though remaining aloof, the Boxer wagged his stubby tail.

Trying to pet all four at once, Honneure looked back at Olivia and smiled. "Will you tell me their names?"

The unpleasant smile had faded, and Honneure was reminded of a spoiled child whose malicious prank had just been foiled. Grudgingly, Olivia pronounced the animals' names and Honneure thanked her.

"I'm merely doing as I was told," Olivia replied coolly. "I've shown you to your room. Those," she pointed at the dogs, "are your duty. If you need to know anything else, ask Madame Campan."

Honneure rose to her feet as Olivia turned to go. "Wait."

Olivia looked slowly back over her shoulder. She did not speak, but merely raised one black, wing-like brow.

"Why do you dislike me?" Honneure inquired evenly.

"We met only moments ago. You don't even know me."

Olivia felt her breath quicken as a disagreeable emotion gathered in her breast. She stared for a long, hard moment at the woman Philippe called his sister.

She was beautiful, lissome, and perfectly proportioned. Streaks of gold highlighted her honey-colored hair. Her remarkable eyes were the color of clouds before a storm. And she was not related to Philippe by blood at all.

"I know *of* you," Olivia said at last. "From Philippe."

The growing unease caused by Olivia's inexplicably chilly manner evaporated. Honneure's heart leaped. "You know Philippe?" she asked eagerly.

"Of course I know Philippe." Olivia felt her smile return unbidden. "I know him very well."

The disquiet returned in an instant. What did that vaguely sinister smile mean? Why did nausea suddenly gnaw at the pit of her stomach? Honneure had no time to find out.

There was a commotion in the outer rooms. Honneure heard voices and a bright, tinkling laugh.

"The Dauphine has returned," Olivia announced shortly, and hurried from the chamber.

* * *

From Madame Dupin's many tales of the Court and its royal inhabitants, Honneure felt she had come to know the Princess at least a little. She had been prepared to meet a sweet, innocent girl some three years younger than herself. She had not at all expected to meet one of the kindest, merriest souls she had ever known.

Introductions were informal with the small dogs barking and leaping about. Madame Dupin smiled fondly as Antoinette laughed, and Madame Campan looked disapproving as

Honneure suspected she usually did. Olivia stood sulkily in a corner of the salon, and for a while Honneure was able to forget about her completely.

"I'm so glad they like you!" Antoinette exclaimed as one little dog after another bounded into her lap, then jumped down and hurled itself at Honneure, who knelt. Even the Boxer, Baron, left his mistress' side briefly to give Honneure a sloppy, but entirely welcome, lick on the cheek. "You do like her, don't you my babies?" The Princess kissed the crown of one tiny head.

"I'm very grateful to you, dear friend," the Dauphine continued. She took Madame Dupin's hand and squeezed it. "Thank you for bringing this lovely girl. My precious pets will be very happy, and therefore so shall I."

"Your happiness is all any of us desire. Though I will miss her, I am glad to share Honneure with Your Majesty," Madame Dupin replied formally, as she always did when they were not alone.

"Even Olivia will be happy, I think." Antoinette glanced in Olivia's direction and flashed a smile. "As conscientious as you were, taking care of my babies was not your favorite task, I fear."

Realization bloomed in Honneure's breast as Olivia murmured a polite, if insincere, reply. She had taken the girl's job, even her sleeping chamber within the royal apartments. No wonder Olivia regarded her so darkly!

Several minutes passed as Antoinette played with her dogs and chatted with Madame Dupin. Then, abruptly, the Princess returned her attention to Honneure.

"Mercy, I nearly forgot. You'll want to see your brother, Philippe, won't you? I am *so* fond of him. I don't believe there is a better horseman in the royal stables."

Honneure ducked her head, flushed with pleasure. "Your Majesty is too kind."

"I am simply honest," she responded lightly. "And the hour is late. You'll be growing hungry, I expect, and anxious to see Philippe. Olivia?"

The dark-haired girl moved swiftly to the Dauphine's side and curtsied.

"Take Honneure to the *Grand Commun*. Madame Campan, please take the dogs."

The meeting was over. Feeling proud and a little giddy, Honneure turned to follow Olivia. Madame Dupin hastily touched her cheek.

"Bless you, my dear," she whispered. "Give my love to Philippe."

Honneure smiled, and hurried in Olivia's wake.

* * *

It was a silent walk back the way Honneure had come a scant hour before. But she was no less awed. The splendor of the huge chambers, fabulous works of art and furnishings was almost overwhelming. Not until they were midway down the grand marble staircase did Honneure remember Olivia, and how she had displaced her. Honneure wanted to say something, but Olivia's rigid back and swift steps didn't seem to invite conversation.

The silence reigned until they had left the château and stood in the Marble Court. Dusk lay softly on the grounds, and the figures moving to and fro were indistinct. Many seemed to be headed toward the *Grand Commun*, a handsome building of stone and brick built within the right angle formed by the north wing of the château and the Ministers' wing. A delicious aroma of roasted meat drifted on the evening air. Honneure paused.

"That smells so good, and I'm so hungry." Unconsciously, she pressed a hand to her empty stomach.

Olivia whirled. "I'm *taking* you to dinner," she snapped.

Honneure recoiled. "I...I'm sorry, Olivia."

The girl merely stared. The elation caused by the wonders of the day rapidly ebbed, and Honneure was suddenly weary...weary, intimidated by Olivia's bristling hostility, and feeling very much alone in a huge and alien place. She wanted only to see Philippe now, to feel his strong and comforting arms around her. But first she had to at least try to make peace with Olivia.

"Olivia, I...I realize you used to take care of the Dauphine's dogs," she began. "And the room was undoubtedly yours as well. I didn't mean to put you out. I'm so sorry if my coming has caused you inconvenience or unhappiness. It certainly wasn't my intention. Please, please accept my apology, and let us be friends."

Olivia's expression remained impassive. "Actually," she said at last, slowly and deliberately, "you may have done me a service. Having a chamber in the Princess' apartments was confining. I shall have a great deal more freedom in the commune. Or, should I say, *Philippe* and I will have more freedom. No one will notice, or care, how much time we spend together."

Honneure felt as if someone had just dealt her a blow. She found it difficult to catch her breath. "You...and Philippe?" she breathed when she was able to find her voice.

Olivia smiled. So. It was as she had suspected...and feared. But she had already wounded Honneure. Now she would move in for the kill.

"Yes. Me and Philippe. Even though you are

his...*sister*...you must admit how handsome he is, how charming. How sexy." Arms crossed over her breast, Olivia hugged her shoulders and shivered as if remembering an embrace. Her eyes were heavy-lidded.

Honneure couldn't respond. She felt numb and sick.

"So, you see, you have actually done us a favor, Honneure," Olivia drawled in a tone dripping poisoned honey. "Now, finally, we have a place where we can be...alone."

Honneure was afraid if she didn't do something, anything, she would be sick. Where was Philippe? She had to see Philippe. She took a staggering step in the direction so many others seemed to be moving in.

Olivia fell in beside her. Honneure didn't look at her. She couldn't. But her presence was there, in the periphery of her vision. Honneure was aware when Olivia abruptly raised her arm.

"Philippe! Here...over here!" she called.

He was coming from the opposite direction, from the stables, no doubt. The coldness within her seemed to thaw a little. He *was* handsome, so incredibly handsome. The ridges of his cheekbones were hard and masculine, his sharp jaw line shadowed by a day's growth of beard. His curling black hair had grown longer and reached to just below his collarbones. His broad chest and narrow hips were emphasized by the tight fitting livery in the Dauphine's colors, and his thighs bulged, straining the red silk hose. Honneure's heart did a somersault.

"Philippe!" Olivia called again.

If she could just see him, talk to him, be near him, surely everything would be all right once more. This horrible sickness would go away.

Philippe heard Olivia's voice. His eyes searched among the hurrying throng. His gaze locked. A broad grin split his features.

He's seen me, Honneure thought. *He's seen me and now everything will be all right.*

But he had seen only Olivia, and she knew it. Picking up the hem of her skirt, the dark-haired girl ran to him. Laughing, Philippe caught her in his arms.

"Kiss me," Olivia hissed. Her right hand tangled in the thick hair at the back of his head. Before he could protest, she pulled his lips down to hers.

The world seemed to spin. The earth tilted beneath Honneure's feet.

All was lost. Philippe was lost. She was lost. She never should have come. She had known it.

By the time Philippe managed to extricate himself from Olivia's embrace, Honneure had disappeared.

Chapter Nine

Olivia awoke to darkness, but she knew it was near dawn. She stretched her cramped limbs slowly and carefully, trying not to wake the man at her side. She reveled in the feeling of her flesh against his and smiled to herself.

Philippe had not had a single thought of Honneure last night, of that Olivia was certain. All he had been aware of was her lips and hands, until they were both naked. And then all he had known was her body. A delicious shiver quivered upward from somewhere deep in her abdomen, and she rolled onto her side, the better to admire her lover.

Philippe lay on his back, one arm flung upward over the pillow. Thick black lashes curled against his cheeks, and long dark curls haloed his head. He snored softly.

There was no denying it. He was the most beautiful man she had ever had in her bed. Simply gazing at him rekindled her desire. His features were sharply drawn, from high, prominent cheekbones to the angular narrowing of his chin. His nose was thin and straight, perhaps a bit too long, but the overall picture was perfection with his generous mouth and full, soft lips. Her gaze wandered downward.

Though tall and lean, driving horses over the years had developed Philippe's chest, shoulders and upper arms to the proportions of a much larger man. A thin line of dark, silken curls ran from the hollow of his throat across the hills and valleys of his muscular definition to a narrow waist and hips, and down . . .

The thin blanket halted Olivia's hungry, visual quest. Unable to resist, she placed the palm of her hand on his flat, hard belly and slipped her fingers under the cover. She encountered a dense mat of coarser hair, and something constricted in her breast. Philippe moaned and rolled away from her.

No longer caring if she woke him, thinking only of the delights of his body, Olivia kissed the smooth, pale skin of Philippe's shoulder and pressed the length of her body against his. He stirred as she caressed his chest and circled the darker flesh of his nipple with the tip of one finger. She gasped when he suddenly caught her hand.

"Don't tell me you want more," he mumbled sleepily.

"Yes, I want more," she whispered. Her tongue darted out to lick his ear lobe. "And more and more. Always. I'll never have enough of you."

Though vaguely disturbed, for no reason he could name, Philippe smiled. Olivia was indeed insatiable and had aroused his exhausted body again and again long into the night. She was skilled in ways he had never experienced, and though she was voracious, he didn't think he could complain. But he did have to set limits. He gripped her hand tighter when she struggled to free it.

"I have to get up," he protested. "The horses are waiting."

"Let them wait." Olivia licked the nape of Philippe's neck.

Philippe hunched his shoulders against the trill of pleasure she sent down his spine. He pushed her hand away, threw his legs over the side of the bed, and rose. Olivia groaned at the sight of his tight, rounded buttocks.

"I can't let them wait," he continued, "and you know it.

Besides, I'm anxious to see if my sister has arrived yet."

Olivia's gaze slid away from Philippe as he pulled on his trousers. Honneure. Always Honneure. With effort she swallowed the bile rising in her throat.

Damn Honneure. Philippe was in her bed now. And he would stay there, she would see to it. Honneure's presence would affect her not at all. Olivia took a deep breath and coyly let the blanket fall away from her naked breasts.

"I...I forgot to tell you last night," she began. "But your sister has, in fact, reached Versailles."

Philippe froze in the act of shrugging his shirt onto his wide shoulders. "What...what did you say?"

"You heard me." Olivia's gaze did not waver. She eyed him levelly, as if defying him to be angry with her.

"Honneure is here, at the palace?" Philippe began to move again. He buttoned his shirt with hasty fingers. "How long has she been here? Why didn't you tell me?"

"She arrived last night," Olivia replied slowly. "And I didn't tell you because...when I am in your arms I can think of nothing but you."

Philippe paused once more and regarded the woman on the bed. Something cold was replacing the warmth that usually infused his veins when he looked at her.

"Where is she now?" he asked finally. "Where is my sister?"

Olivia shrugged lightly, a faint smile at the corners of her sensuous mouth. "How would I know?"

"All right then, Olivia. Where was she last night?"

With a lazy finger, Olivia traced the curve of one breast. But Philippe's gaze did not follow her hand. He stared straight into her eyes. Her smile slipped away.

"In her room, I suppose," she answered flatly. "The one *I*

formerly occupied."

Philippe did not respond. He watched the features of Olivia's face slowly harden, and felt a chill.

"How quickly you seem to have forgotten that your precious *sister* has displaced me," she continued in a low, ominous tone. "You practically begged the Dauphine to find a place for her...and she certainly did. *My* place."

Philippe took an unconscious step backward as Olivia sat up. Her eyes had narrowed to two dark slits.

"So *that* is where she was last night, Philippe. She was in the palace. And then she followed me to the *Commun*. She was with me when you saw me. And took me in your arms."

Slowly, languidly, never taking her eyes from Philippe's, Olivia rose from the bed. The blanket pulled away, and she stood before him naked. She lifted her arms to him. "Hold me again, Philippe. Take me. Now."

Philippe's throat constricted until he thought he might choke. He took another step backward. His gaze flicked briefly over the lush form that had once inflamed him beyond restraint. He felt nothing. Until he looked back into her eyes.

They smoldered. But not, this time, with the embers of desire.

Gaze still locked to Olivia's, Philippe grabbed his livery coat. He reached behind him for the door and opened it. Then he turned on his heel and fled down the hallway. He did not look back.

* * *

Madame Campan allowed herself the luxury of a long, slow sigh. The Dauphine's day was well under way. Prayers had been said, breakfast eaten, and a gown appropriate for the morning hours had been donned. Now the Princess would visit with the King's sisters for an hour. No doubt she would see the King. *Without* the du Barry. The ghost of a smile lightened the corners of Madame Campan's thin mouth.

The little Princess was well on her way to capturing more than just the Prince's heart. The King, always with an eye for a pretty young girl, had taken an immediate liking to Antoinette. The liking had blossomed into sincere affection. Louis joined his sisters every morning as a result, so he might visit with his grandson's wife. His mistress, whose dislike of Antoinette was well known, remained in her apartments. Things were going well. It gave Madame Campan time to turn her thoughts elsewhere. Her eyes slid to a corner of the salon where the new girl plumped cushions on a collection of small dog beds.

For many years, almost all of her adult life, Madame Campan had waited on members of the aristocracy and had quickly worked her way to the upper ranks of service. Taciturn by nature, her reserve had served her well. Much was revealed in her quiet presence, and over the years she had learned to listen, and observe, closely. Little escaped her notice, and she had become wise to the ways of those around her.

As much as she knew about others, they knew little of her. She gave away almost nothing of herself, and her stern countenance did not invite friendships. Almost all who knew her assumed her nature was as severe as her expression. Those she served respected her, and those who answered to her feared her. But a sentimental and caring heart beat within her narrow bosom. She moved quietly in Honneure's direction.

Busy. Just keep busy, Honneure admonished herself as she needlessly realigned the small dog beds. If she kept moving it was easier not to think, not to dwell on the knowledge that Philippe was in love. Their relationship, as she had known it, was lost to her forever. The ache, the pain, was nearly unbearable. She jumped when she felt the gentle hand on her shoulder.

"I think you are done here," Madame Campan said softly. "And I also think you should eat something."

"Oh no, thank you." Honneure shook her head. "I...I'm not hungry."

"No?" Madame Campan arched her finely drawn brows. "You certainly should be. You had no supper."

Honneure glanced sharply at the older woman. How could she have known?

"I saw you leave with Olivia," she replied, answering Honneure's unspoken question. "You came back almost at once."

Honneure could not hold Madame Campan's gaze. Her eyes searched for a safe place to rest.

"Olivia must have said, or done, something to hurt you," Madame Campan remarked shrewdly. When Honneure abruptly glanced back in her direction, she allowed the flicker of a smile to touch her mouth.

"Don't look so surprised, my dear. All who know her are well aware of Olivia's...'personality traits'. If she offended you, I apologize on her behalf. And urge you to forget whatever slight, or subtle cruelty, she inflicted."

It was more than Honneure could bear. Tears rushed to her eyes before she could blink them away. She shook her head, as if to banish the memory, and bravely tried to smile.

"It doesn't matter...really."

But it did, obviously. And it mattered more than Madame Campan had guessed. There was much more going on than she had suspected. If she didn't know better she would think, by the expression on Honneure's pretty face, that the tiff, whatever it was, had involved a man. But that couldn't be. Madame

Dupin had assured them the girl was unattached. There was only her foster brother . . .

Madame Campan drew a deep breath and exhaled it slowly. *So.* She smoothed a pale, errant curl away from Honneure's temple.

"The Dauphine will return at eleven to have her hair done," she began, "and she will want you to bring her dogs to her. At noon she will attend mass and then dine with the Dauphin. Following that she generally returns with the Prince to his apartments to keep him company, if he is not too busy. If he is otherwise engaged, she likes to walk with her dogs...or drive her horses."

The storm that had gathered in Honneure's gray eyes suddenly lightened. Madame Campan continued.

"She has not seen her horses for several days and, I suspect, you have not yet seen your brother."

Honneure's lips formed the word "no" although she could not actually give voice to the lie.

"Then I will recommend to the Princess we send for Philippe this afternoon. It will work out well for all, I should think."

She did not need Honneure's brightly affirmative response to know that she had correctly assessed the situation.

"Now, please have something to eat. There is some lovely fruit and leftover pastries from the Princess' breakfast."

She was, in fact, almost desperately hungry, despite her heartache. The mere prospect of seeing Philippe had reawakened her appetite. In love with Olivia he might be, but he was still her brother. She had missed him. She longed to speak with him, hear the sound of his voice, and feel his arms around her. Those things would not change, Olivia or no Olivia. Heartened, though not free of the burden that still lay on her heart, she accepted Madame Campan's offer.

* * *

All morning Philippe's anger had mounted. For at least the twentieth time he ran over in his mind what Olivia had revealed to him.

Honneure had reached Versailles. She had been with Olivia last night. She had seen when Olivia had thrown herself into his arms. He did not know why the thought disquieted him so much, but it did. Worse, Olivia had not told him of his sister's presence. He did not doubt for a moment that the oversight had been intentional. In spite of her protest, he knew Olivia far too well. Philippe snorted and brushed the mare's already shining coat with renewed vigor.

Olivia's little moues and pouts, her coy and petty deceptions had amused him once. He had been bored and lonely, and she had made him laugh. She had grown more possessive of late, however, and he found less and less humor in her machinations. The delights of her lush body and skilled caresses had bound him to her, however. Again and again he had returned to her. He would not do so again.

With a familiar chill, Philippe recalled the look in Olivia's eyes when she had tried to seduce him back into her bed. She did not love him, but she desired him, and woe to any rival. Obviously she perceived Honneure as a rival. His own sister! Olivia must be mad!

Well, she would not have him to work her wiles on any longer. Some day, some time, there would certainly be another woman in his life. In the meantime, and for all time, he had Honneure. If only he could find a time and place to see her!

"Ah, Philippe, I thought I'd find you here."

Philippe turned toward the familiar voice. The Master of

the Stables was a tall and distinguished man, aristocratic by birth and compassionate by nature. He had a God-given talent with horses, and Philippe respected him.

"It's a safe bet any day you'll find me with my animals."

"The *Princess*' animals," Monsieur Rocard amended mildly. "And she would like to drive her pair this afternoon, as a matter of fact. In an hour. I have no fear you will not be ready as you keep your charges immaculate and constantly at the peak of their athletic ability." He ran an admiring hand over the white mare's muscular shoulder. "I am impressed with this breed, though I was unfamiliar with it until you brought the animals here. You do an excellent job with them, Philippe."

Philippe bowed his head in acknowledgment of the compliment. Praise from the stablemaster was heady stuff indeed. But not nearly as inspiring as the thought of what might transpire in a mere hour's time.

Honneure had come to Versailles to be a member of the Dauphine's household. Whenever the Princess left the palace she was almost always surrounded by the majority of her entourage. Would Honneure be with her this afternoon? Would he finally, actually get to see his beloved sister?

Imagining the sun-gilded highlights in Honneure's hair, the deep, bold gray of her eyes, the tilt of her chin and the smell of summer that always seemed to linger on her skin, he did not even notice Monsieur Rocard depart.

An hour. One hour.

His hands flew.

* * *

"You don't *really* think so!" Antoinette raised her pale, delicate brows with surprise and held the reflection of Madame

Campan's gaze in the mirror. The older woman replied with an almost imperceptible shrug of her thin shoulders.

"My Princess will decide for herself."

"Yes. I certainly shall." Antoinette watched Madame Campan's skilled fingers restore order to the elaborate hairdo that had been created for her some hours before. It seemed a senseless thing to do, considering she was about to drive her horses and bring about even greater chaos to her tresses. But it had given them a few moments to speak privately. The rest of her women chatted among themselves in a corner of the boudoir and had paid no heed to the whispered conversation. She was glad. It was a delicious secret. Especially if it was true. Antoinette smiled conspiratorially at Madame Campan's reflection.

"They don't realize? You're sure?"

"They are as innocent of it as babes," Madame Campan said with quiet certainty.

Antoinette clasped her hands together and raised them to her chin. Her blue eyes sparkled. "An already beautiful day seems suddenly brighter. I find I am quite anxious to see Philippe. Shall we go?"

The instant the Dauphine rose, Honneure's heart began to pound. The Princess' words echoed her own thoughts. She couldn't wait to see Philippe, really see him, not just a glimpse of him as he took another woman in his arms.

A now-familiar nausea rose in Honneure's throat, but she quickly banished it. She was going to see Philippe. Nothing must spoil this moment.

There was a graceful flurry of movement as Antoinette's ladies arranged themselves in her wake. The train of women, courtiers, and a few chosen servants, moved from the *Petits Appartements* into the long series of elaborate and shining reception rooms. Honneure was no less awed by them than she had been the day before, and with delight saw new things she had not noticed earlier. The small dogs pranced ahead of her, tugging at their leashes, while the Boxer walked sedately at her side.

The day was cloudless, almost blindingly bright. Honneure blinked as they stepped out into the Marble Court. It had been cool in the dim corridors of the palace, but the sun warmed her at once. Her heart increased its rhythm yet again.

He had, apparently, waited at the far end of the wide drive until he saw the royal party emerge. As the women moved into a ragged semicircle around the Princess, Honneure saw the distant flick of his long buggy whip. The matched pair of white horses, mother and daughter, started forward as one.

The hours and days and months of work Philippe had put into the Lipizzans was evident. Their trot was slower, more precise, elevated and airy. Their ears pricked sharply, expressively forward. White fire glinted from their coats. They were a living masterpiece. Honneure heard someone near her catch their breath.

"Magnificent. Truly magnificent," someone else murmured.

Yes, they were magnificent. But not nearly as fine as the man who drove them, guided them, worked his magic with those large, strong, oh-so gentle hands. Honneure's heartbeat went from a rapid staccato to nearly stopping in her throat.

He seemed to be more handsome each time she beheld him. The breeze lifted the long, dark curls from his shoulders. Nearer and nearer they came, hoofbeats resounding on the pavement. His brown velvet eyes never wavered from her own. Her breath began to falter.

Madame Campan leaned ever so slightly into the Princess, but she did not seem to notice. The whole of her attention was riveted on the scene unfolding before her.

So skilled were Philippe's hands they seemed to possess knowledge independent of his brain. He continued to guide the horses flawlessly, but his every conscious thought was turned to Honneure. She stood amid a crowd of women, but he saw only her. He moved in the real, waking world, but the reality was as a dream.

How could she have changed so much in a few short months? She seemed taller, but perhaps only because she was thinner. Highlights from the summer before had faded over the winter, but the honey color of her hair had deepened, richened. Smoke and ashes smoldered in the remarkable gray of her eyes. The red and silver of the Dauphine's livery seemed pale and colorless compared to the brightness of her beauty. He had always thought her lovely, but now . . .

He had drawn abreast of his Princess. Familiar with the routine, the horses came to a halt. Philippe came to his senses. He jumped lightly to the ground and bowed before Antoinette. "Majesty," he murmured.

"You never cease to amaze us," the Princess said softly, and exchanged a swift glance with Madame Campan. "Always something new, something surprising, when we thought it couldn't get any better."

"Your majesty is too kind," Philippe replied, misunderstanding just as the Princess had intended. "The horses have the talent, not I."

"You bring it out in them. Just as you inspire the admiration of those around you." Antoinette's eyes flicked lightly over the surrounding ladies, and she noted, as she always did, the way they lavished their admiring attention on Philippe. But there was one whose gaze held more than mere speculative appreciation.

"Although I am anxious, as usual, to have a drive with these glorious creatures," Antoinette continued, "I believe we must pause a moment for something more important."

Philippe's bafflement was evident.

"Your sister," Antoinette prompted. "Has it not been many months since you saw her last?"

It took all of Philippe's considerable willpower not to look in Honneure's direction. Eyes cast respectfully down, he nodded. "Yes, Majesty. Many months."

Antoinette was glad Philippe held his gaze downward. He would wonder at the tears brimming suddenly in her eyes. Surely he would misunderstand. As surely as he misunderstood what he truly felt for Honneure - and she for him. Though the emotion of the moment, what she had witnessed between Philippe and Honneure, caused a painful ache in her throat, the Princess forced a smile to her lips.

"May I suggest, Philippe, since it has been so long, that you take Honneure for a drive instead? I'm sure you will want to hear the news of your parents, and I...I fear the sun is a bit strong for me today."

"Majesty!" Madame Campan was at Antoinette's side in a heartbeat. She put a protective arm about the small, frail shoulders, and the Princess pressed close to her shoulder.

"I am quite well, my dear Campan," Antoinette whispered. "But the two of them need to be alone. And tongues will wag soon enough. Let us not begin the process ourselves, here, today."

"My Princess is wise beyond her years."

Antoinette flashed Madame Campan an enigmatic look. "My own plight is not so dissimilar," she responded under her breath. Then, aloud, "Come, all of you. I shall have to wait for another day, hopefully a less bright one. Mademoiselle du

Bois, take my dogs, if you please. Honneure, I give you leave for the rest of the afternoon. Enjoy it."

Antoinette was surrounded at once by her women, their voices an intertwining babble of concern and distress. They moved away slowly as a single body, the Dauphine uttering reassurances. Other courtiers and a myriad of servants hurried on their various ways across the avenue. Another carriage rolled by. Someone coughed, someone laughed. The murmur of distant voices rose and fell. But nothing, no one in the world existed but Philippe.

Slowly, agonizingly, Honneure raised her eyes.

Chapter Ten

Philippe had always been supremely self-confident. His parents had adored him, and as a child he had been the darling of the entire household, including the mistress herself, Madame Dupin. He had shown an early aptitude for working with horses and had been put into training at once. His talent was readily apparent. He worked hard, achieved much, and continued to earn the admiration, respect and love of all who knew him. Then Honneure had come into his life.

She had enchanted him from the first moment. He would never forget that first glimpse of her, with her sad and frightened gray eyes looking up at him as she stood in the courtyard. Never having known heartache or fear himself, it had been hard to imagine what she must have felt. But he had tried to imagine how devastating it must have been for her to lose her only parent and the only home she had ever known all at once. He had admired her courage, and when her tears had come at last, his heart had gone out to her completely. He had loved her, had tried to surround her with that love as he had been surrounded all his life.

Over the years Philippe had watched Honneure blossom brilliantly. Though she never forgot her mother, Jeanne and Paul had become her true parents of the soul. He had become her brother. He took pride in her achievements, her ready wit and intelligence, her fierce loyalties and her eagerness to learn. She made him laugh often, yet could also bring tears to his eyes with her tender affections. She had been his strength as often as he had been hers. He could never imagine life without her. He could not imagine their relationship ever changing. So what was happening to him now? Why did he feel shaken to his very core?

Versailles and its thousands of inhabitants no longer existed. He was alone with Honneure. She was all he could see, all he was aware of. But something was very, very wrong.

Philippe's heart raced in a way it had never done before. Nor had he ever felt at such a loss, so uncertain of himself, unable even to speak a single word. And it was happening in the presence of Honneure, his sister! What was wrong with him?

"Philippe? Philippe, are you all right?"

He watched her extend an elegant hand to him, touch his arm in a long-familiar gesture. Even through the material of his coat, his flesh burned.

Honneure drew in her breath sharply as Philippe pulled away from her. Pain stabbed through her breast. Was he so deeply in love with Olivia he could not abide another woman's touch, even his sister's? It was more than she could bear, more than she could comprehend. Seeing Philippe in Olivia's arms had shaken her world. Now it had collapsed entirely. With a heartbroken sob, she whirled away from him.

The spell was shattered when Honneure spun on her heel. What had he done, what had he been thinking?

"Honneure, wait...Stop!"

He caught her in three steps, hands pinning her arms. Slowly, gently, he turned her to face him. A bolt of agony seared through him when he saw the tears glistening in her eyes.

"Oh, my God, Honneure," Philippe moaned. "I'm so

sorry. I don't know what I was thinking, I...I was just looking at you and...and . . ."

The tears spilled, staining Honneure's cheeks. "No, I...*I'm* sorry," she whispered brokenly. "I know you want it to be Olivia with you here, now, not me. I . . ."

"Olivia?" Unconsciously, Philippe gave Honneure a little shake. "No, no, not Olivia. I'm so glad to see you, Honneure. What made you think that I would want it to be Olivia?"

He knew before she answered and groaned again. He let go of Honneure's arms and struck his palm to his forehead. "*Damn* that woman. *Damn* her! And *damn* me."

"Philippe!"

"No. I deserve every remonstrance I could possibly heap on myself. And more." Once again Philippe grasped Honneure's arms, this time cradling her elbows in his broad hands. "Listen, forget Olivia. Please. I certainly intend to. It was a terrible mistake. Forgive me, Honneure. Forgive me."

"Forgive you, Philippe?" Honneure slowly shook her head from side to side, confusion reflected in her wide, gray eyes. "Forgive you for what? It's your life, to do with as you please. And with *whom* you please."

"But that's just it, Honneure, don't you see? It's not Olivia I love, it's . . ."

Honneure staggered backward, knees suddenly weak. Philippe let her go, stunned by what he had been about to say.

But it was not possible. Honneure was his sister. He loved her as his *sister*, that was all. That was all it could ever be.

"Honneure, I...I love you...of course. I mean...you're my sister."

Honneure did not respond for a long, long moment. And in that moment a strange knowing seemed to settle upon her, like the folds of a cloak falling about her shoulders, enwrapping and warming her. Words her foster mother had once spoken to her returned in a rush.

"Of all the things I've tried to teach you, dearest child, there is only one thing of true importance. For you may rely on it when all else fails, all knowledge, all logic. And that is your heart, Honneure, your woman's heart. Listen to it when you can trust no other voice. Listen to it, and know it does not lie."

Honneure took a deep breath and smiled into Philippe's eyes. How right Jeanne had been, how wise.

This time when Honneure put her hand on Philippe's arm, she knew he would not flinch away, and he did not.

"Come, Philippe," she said in a voice little more than a whisper. "I've been looking forward to this for a very long time. Let us see how you've fared with the horses."

* * *

Afternoon sunlight streamed into the salon of the *Petites Apartments*. Sitting at the keyboard of her clavichord Antoinette stretched, closed her eyes, and raised her face to the beam of buttery light. "What time is it?" she asked at length.

"Nearly four o'clock," Madame Campan promptly replied.

Antoinette groaned. "The Abbé de Vermond will be here at any moment. His lessons are so *boring*, dear Campan."

"It's only for an hour. Then you have your singing lesson. You always enjoy that."

"Tomorrow it will be the clavichord, singing again the day after, then clavichord . . ." Antoinette sighed deeply. "Do you think he notices? Do you think he cares? Do you think this makes any difference at all?"

Madame Campan glanced up sharply from her needlework. "You are the future Queen of France. You must care even if no one else does." She allowed her expression to soften slightly. "But, yes, in answer to your question. Yes, I think the Dauphin does care."

Hope flickered uncertainly in Antoinette's pale blue eyes. She pursed her rosebud lips. "He *is* kind to me, Campan. And attentive when we are together. I have no complaints on that account. But . . ."

The two women exchanged glances. Though no one else was present at the moment, one could never be certain of one's privacy in a royal palace. And although it was fairly common knowledge that the prince had not yet consummated his marriage, Antoinette spoke of her sadness only to those closest to her, and when she was absolutely certain no one might overhear. The humiliation was simply too great to bear. Suddenly uncomfortably warm, she rose and moved out of the sunlight.

"Open a window, will you, dear Campan? I am not quite used to the warmth of the French springtimes yet."

Madame Campan unlatched the tall double windows and swung them wide.

"Any sign of our sweet Honneure and the handsome Philippe?"

Madame Campan looked down the broad avenue and shook her head. "None."

Antoinette uttered another small sigh. "You were absolutely right about them, dear Campan. Nothing escapes your notice, does it?"

The older woman turned slowly from the window. "Very little," she agreed dryly.

"How long, do you think, before they are able to see what the rest of us do?"

"I believe Honneure already knows. It will be harder for

Philippe. Men's vision is not as clear as women's."

Antoinette laughed gaily. "How right you are, Campan. And how wise." The laughter abruptly died. "They will have time to discover their love at least. *Without* a villainess waiting in the wings to pounce."

"Now, now," Madame Campan admonished gently. "The du Barry can do nothing to truly harm you."

"She can affect the King's opinion of me!" Antoinette flashed, porcelain skin flushing.

"The King is quite fond of you. If his mistress is trying to sway him, she's doing a poor job of it."

"And she sets my husband against me," Antoinette continued as if she had not heard. "Every time that woman slights me, or disagrees with me, Louis sides with her!"

"Openly, yes," Madame Campan agreed. "But only to keep peace with his grandfather."

Antoinette did not reply. She crossed to the window and stared out at the failing afternoon. "As I said before, Honneure and Philippe are luckier than I."

"Perhaps not," Madame Campan replied quietly.

Antoinette looked sharply at the head of her ladies-in-waiting, brows arched. "What do you mean? What possible villainess could there be in *their* romantic tale?"

Madame Campan's response was interrupted by a knock on the door. "That will be the Abbé," she said as she moved across the room. "We will speak later."

* * *

The entire regal, sprawling mass of the palace of Versailles was built upon a hillock in the Galie Valley. The valley itself was surrounded by more hills and punctuated by ponds, heaths and pastures. Immediately surrounding the château and its fabulous gardens were acres upon acres of woods. Traveling along the east-west axis of the grounds, by the side of the Grand Canal and perpendicular to the palace, Honneure was able to more fully grasp the scope and immensity of Versailles. It was almost beyond comprehension. Just the Grand Canal itself defied imagination.

For many years Honneure had listened with avid interest to Madame Dupin's tales of court life and descriptions of the palace. She had a vivid imagination and had thought she had recreated accurate visions of the château and its grounds in her mind's eye. She had not even come close to Versailles' true scale and splendor.

The Grand Canal, made by the hands of man, put the Cher to shame. Driving along the bank of the Canal, she could barely see to the other side, and not simply because of the distance. Boats of every description plied the crystalline waters, from small, gaily painted craft plied by oars, to tall-masted ships. Shaped like a giant cross, the Canal began at the foot of the fabled Apollo fountain and stretched out into the valley.

"It would take hours to drive along the entire shoreline," Philippe had told her. "We'll travel about a quarter of the way, then come back."

Honneure had only been able to nod. The vastness of the grounds had awed her. The panoply surrounding her took her breath away.

Lavishly dressed courtiers on prancing horses trotted past. Richly decorated coaches pulled by as many as eight horses promenaded past them, carriage whips flicking smartly. Various groups of men and women strolled amiably. Amorous couples, armed linked, bent their heads together as they murmured among themselves. Honneure had never felt so small and insignificant. Unconsciously, she leaned into Philippe's shoulder.

"I know how you must feel," he said comfortingly. "I remember how overwhelmed I was my first few days here."

"It's truly unimaginable," Honneure replied. "No one could ever possibly describe this accurately. One must see it to believe it."

They continued on for some time, the white horses maintaining their bold trot, necks arched and ears forward. Honneure noted the many admiring glances cast their way, and her heart swelled with pride. Not only had the animals been scrupulously trained, but Philippe handled them masterfully. It was no wonder the Princess had bid him stay on with her. She must have a very high opinion of him indeed, particularly since she had even granted his wish to have his sister join the royal entourage as well.

Sister.

Honneure became acutely aware of Philippe's nearness, the feel of her arm pressed against his muscular shoulder, but she did not move. She was where she belonged, where she had always belonged. She must no longer think of Philippe as her brother. Just as he, soon, would no longer think of her as his sister. It didn't matter how long it might take. She knew it was only a matter of time; that it had, in fact, already begun. The surety of the knowledge lent her a sense of calm, and she was grateful for it. The realization of her love, her romantic love, for Philippe was so huge it had stunned her, and at the one time in her life when she needed to keep her wits about her more than any other. She must cling to her knowledge, and the peace of it, and perform her duties faithfully. That was first and foremost. All else would come in the fullness of time.

As if sensing her thoughts, Philippe bent to her ear. "We

have been generously given the gift of this time, and I dare not abuse it."

"Nor I, Philippe. The Dauphine has been very, very good to us, and it is my greatest wish to please her. We should return."

The sun approached the crest of the distant hillocks. Shining through a stratum of low, thin clouds, its rosy light burnished the surface of the Canal's waters. The number of boats had diminished, leaving for their places of dockage for the night. As they passed the Apollo fountain, Honneure turned in her seat to admire it for as long as possible, jets of water splashing outward from the hooves of the charging steeds that pulled Apollo in his chariot across the wide pool. Vague regret for their time ended tempered the smile Honneure turned on Philippe.

"Thank you so much, Philippe. Thank you for taking me."

"The pleasure was mine," he responded, surprised by his stiff formality with the girl he had known much of his life. Mere months ago he would have shoved her playfully and patted her behind as she climbed from the coach. Once again he wondered what had come over him, what was wrong. He also wondered at his sudden need to know, exactly, when and where he would see her again.

"I...I'm not privy to the Dauphine's routine. But I usually dine at the *Commun* just after sunset. If...if you're free, I mean. It's where I'll be."

She had never heard Philippe speak so falteringly, so uncertainly. The welcome, numbing calm returned to still her hammering heart. "If I don't see you tonight, Philippe, it will surely be soon." Honneure turned and hurried away without another word.

By Honor Bound

* * *

Not for the first time since her arrival Honneure wondered at the presence of the guards. Scores of people, courtiers and servants alike, came and went through the Royal Apartments with impunity. She decided the guards must be purely for show as they hardly seemed to pay attention to anyone at all. In the beginning she had feared she would feel conspicuous, self-conscious, going to and from the Princess' apartments. Instead she felt happily invisible. She hurried through the gilded bedchamber and slipped behind the door to the *Petits Appartements*.

The anteroom was filled with women, their faces unfamiliar. All eyes turned in her direction, scanned her appearance and dismissed her. The sting was only momentary, however. She was, after all, a servant. The women crowding the foyer were obviously ladies-in-waiting. But whose? Her question was answered almost immediately.

The woman who abruptly flounced through the door from the Dauphine's salon was attractive, though heavily made up. Cleverly drawn brows highlighted lively blue eyes. Her nose was well-formed, her mouth pretty, and her teeth even and white. But an arrogant scowl detracted from the woman's loveliness. There was no doubt at all about who she must be.

The ladies-in-waiting drew aside quickly to make way for their mistress. She ignored them and pivoted on the threshold of the room, satin skirts swishing against the door frame.

"So it's arranged then," she said tartly to someone Honneure could not see. "Olivia shall go with me."

Honneure was unable to hear the words of the reply, but recognized the timbre of Madame Campan's voice. She instinctively pressed herself into the wall as the woman once again started in her direction. Hoping to escape notice, she lowered her eyes. In a cloud of floral perfume, chin held high, the woman marched past her. Her women closed in behind and followed her out the door. Honneure dared to look up.

And found herself staring eye to eye with Olivia.

A slow smile curved on Olivia's generous, seductive lips. "Well, if it isn't little sister, mistress of the mongrels," she mocked. "I certainly hope you find your new position...rewarding. I know that I find it so."

Honneure knew Olivia waited for her to respond, to ask her why. But she did not deign to give her the satisfaction.

"You may think you have usurped my position in the Princess' household," Olivia continued when the silence stretched beyond the limits of her patience. "But you have actually launched me into something far better. Madame du Barry has long noticed my talents and has asked that I join her retinue. I shall be her *personal* servant...not a slave to dogs."

An answering smile touched the corners of Honneure's lips. "I'm glad for you, Olivia. I'm sure you will be much happier. I think you are far more suited to Madame du Barry than to the Dauphine."

Olivia's smile faltered, and tiny lines of doubt appeared between the ebony wings of her brows. Had she been insulted? In a manner very like her new mistress, she drew back her shoulders and lifted her chin. "I *know* I am better suited to serve the Comtesse than an ignorant Austrian upstart!"

Honneure's hand flew to her mouth to muffle the sound of her gasp. Seeing the gloat in Olivia's expression, she regretted the reaction at once.

"Just as I am perfectly suited," Olivia continued in an undertone, "to be Philippe's lover."

Honneure felt the beginning of a chill, but banished it.

She had her secret knowledge now to keep her warm. She merely held Olivia's dark, unblinking gaze and returned her confident smile. It was Olivia who finally turned away, uneasy and unsure why.

Honneure watched her go, walking quickly to the door where she turned to give Honneure a final, withering glance. Honneure did not flinch. Then the door slammed, and Olivia was gone.

"Beware that one."

Honneure jumped, startled, and turned. "Madame Campan! I'm sorry. I didn't hear you."

"I, on the other hand, heard you." Though the smile never reached her mouth, Honneure saw the sparkle in her eyes. "Or perhaps it is Olivia who should beware. You are a clever girl, Honneure, and you have a level head. You will go far and achieve much. Even, eventually, your heart's desire...Philippe."

With that Madame Campan turned and disappeared again into the salon, leaving Honneure alone. She raised tentative fingers to her cheeks and felt dampness there. Tears. Cleansing tears, renewing tears, like the droplets from a baptismal font.

She had been born again, to a new life. She recalled the night when, a year before, she had sat with Philippe at river's edge and had begged him to promise their lives would never change.

Laughing softly, Honneure wiped away her tears.

Chapter Eleven

July 1771

Honneure had to stand on tiptoe to reach the low-hanging branch. Holding on to the heavily leafed bough with her left hand, she used her right to straighten the gauzy muslin draped around the tree. She retied the anchoring bow of pale blue satin and stepped back to admire her handiwork.

The effect was ethereal. Several other nearby trees had been similarly decorated, but with pink or yellow ribbon, and the scene looked as if it might have been taken from the pages of an illustrated fairy story.

"And whose idea was this, yours or the Princess'?"

Honneure turned and gave Philippe a slow smile. "It was a little bit of both, I suppose."

"Well, congratulations to you both. The day is quite a success."

Honneure flushed with pleasure and gazed at the sight surrounding her. The revelers, along with servants, were nearly two hundred strong. Dozens of carpets were strewn across the grass along with baskets and boxes of gourmet delicacies and fine summer wines. Merry groups formed and re-formed as people visited and sampled the ample fare. Laughter mingled with birdsong, the barking of excited dogs, and the occasional whinny of an impatient horse. Honneure glanced at the various coaches and carriages that had ferried the guests to this remote country location.

Antoinette's calèche, drawn by the white mare, stood at the head of the line, footman in attendance. Honneure would never forget how happy and how pretty the Princess had looked driving the mare, her husband galloping along on his own mount beside her. Nor would she soon forget how pleasant it had been to drive with Philippe in the Dauphin's personal favorite coach.

"For I fear it will rain later in the afternoon," he had said to Philippe. "And I would not have my bride get a soaking."

Philippe had been only too happy to oblige the Dauphin and had promptly asked Honneure to accompany him. "Unless, you...you have plans to go with someone else?"

Honneure had smiled to herself as she took her time to respond. She had seen little of Philippe in the past few weeks, purposely. At first she had been too busy settling into her routine as part of the Dauphine's entourage. She had harbored a small, secret fear that he might return to Olivia, but he had not. Her intuition had been correct. Instead, he had spent a great deal of his free time coming around to see if, or when, she might be free. He almost always asked her to join him for meals, but most of the time she was able to dine on the remains of the Prince and Princess' sumptuous meals. She could have declined, certainly, and joined Philippe. Yet she had begun to see the value and advantage in leaving Philippe alone to ponder and look forward to, finally, spending time with her. Perhaps he would sooner come to the realization of *why* he was so eager to see her.

And so she had also hesitated in giving a response to his invitation. It would not hurt for him to think, if only for a moment, she did indeed have an invitation from someone else.

In the end, of course, she had accepted, and had enjoyed immensely their ride out into the country together. Everything, in fact, from the moment she had awakened had gone smoothly. Morning had dawned clear and warm, heavy with the scents of summer. Organization of the event had been flawless, and the party had started out on time and in good form. Now most of the food and wine had been consumed, the day pronounced a success, and it no longer mattered that the Dauphin's prediction would undoubtedly, soon, prove to be correct.

"Those thunderheads look menacing," Philippe said over her shoulder, echoing, as he usually did, her very thoughts. He wore a gauzy shirt, as the Princess had decreed everyone must dress for the day as a peasant or shepherd, and Honneure could see moisture glistening on his skin at the open "V" of his collar.

Trying to ignore both the oppressive humidity and the funny feeling in the pit of her stomach, Honneure shrugged. "The rain held off long enough. The purpose of the day has been accomplished."

"Purpose?" Philippe moved around to face her, a bemused smile on his lips. "This day had a purpose other than a pleasant diversion for the Court?"

Honneure held Philippe's gaze without blinking. "Every day must have purpose," she replied levelly. "Else why the point in rising at all?"

Though she looked completely ingenuous, Philippe had known her long and well. "There's more to this than you're telling me."

Honneure gave another small shrug and glanced up at Philippe from beneath lowered lids. "Perhaps. But at the moment I think we'd best help with the packing."

The afternoon had darkened noticeably. Drivers and footmen readied coaches as guests began to move in their direction. Philippe looked about for the Prince as it was his duty to drive the royal pair in the event of rain.

"I must find the Dauphin," he said at length. "Will you be all right?"

"Of course. Go ahead." Honneure watched him walk away and smiled inwardly. The day had indeed had purpose other than revelry. But had it been accomplished? She let her thoughts stray back to an evening two weeks earlier.

* * *

"Oh, Honneure, I am exhausted!" Antoinette had complained as she collapsed onto the dressing table stool in her boudoir. "Please send for Campan, or Madame Thierry, to help me undress."

"Madame Thierry has gone to put her young son to bed, and I haven't seen Madame Campan for some time. She left on an errand right after you left to join the dancing."

"And what fun it was!" the Princess had exclaimed. "The King has been so kind to hold these soirees every Wednesday just for me."

"He knows how much you love to dance."

"And I do, oh, I do."

"Here, let me help you, Majesty." Antoinette had not protested when Honneure removed her heavy wig and started on the dozens of tiny buttons marching down the back of her gown. In truth, she often preferred Honneure's ministrations to any of the other maids she might have called. They were close in age, of similar, sunny disposition, and had recently begun to enjoy sharing confidences when they were alone. The Princess had not disappointed her that evening.

"The only problem," Antoinette had said eventually, "is that Louis *hates* these galas. He attends for my sake, and for his grandfather's, of course. But I can see how unhappy he is.

He loathes anything formal and is so uncomfortable in the clothes he has to wear. I feel so sorry for him, Honneure. And these evenings are not endearing me to him, I fear. I'm sure he thinks I'm entirely frivolous, but I'm *not*. I love dancing, yes, but like my Louis, I, too, prefer simpler pleasures." Antoinette stood to let Honneure remove the gown.

"I have fourteen brothers and sisters, you know," the Dauphine continued. "And we grew up rather like a bunch of puppies, running around and tumbling over one another in the garden. Mother was very relaxed about our upbringing. She wanted everything to be as natural as possible."

Honneure laughed as she unfastened the belt holding the pannier and laid the cumbersome undergarment aside. "Listening to you talk about your childhood, it's difficult to remember your mother is one of the most powerful monarchs in Europe."

Antoinette smiled sadly. "I miss her very much. But her letters are a great comfort to me, and she always has good advice." The Princess sat back down and closed her eyes as Honneure began brushing her hair. "I wonder," she mused aloud, "what entertainment she might suggest that would appeal to my royal husband's simple tastes."

"*And* have him realize that you really are kindred spirits after all," Honneure added.

Antoinette opened her eyes and studied her reflection for a long moment. "We truly are," she said at last, with a sigh. "But I do grow so weary of waiting for him to discover it."

"As I grow impatient with Philippe."

Antoinette smiled at Honneure's reflection in the mirror. "He *still* has not recognized what is as plain as the nose on his face?"

Honneure laughed softly. "It's his mindset, I think. He's

just so used to thinking of me as his sister, he can't imagine me as anything else."

"And Louis," Antoinette said, abruptly serious, "can't imagine a woman being anything but greedy, grasping, and manipulative." She turned away from the mirror and looked up directly at Honneure. "My husband's parents were very religious, very rigid. You know that, don't you?"

Honneure nodded, grateful to Madame Dupin for all the Court intimacies she had shared over the years. "Yes, I have heard. And I know the Dauphin was taught to shun his grandfather's mistresses, to reject totally those excesses and that way of life."

"Exactly. Louis was brought up to fear and mistrust any but a chaste and Godly woman."

"Which your Majesty is!"

"But how can I show it, Honneure, with this Court being the way it is?" There was desperation in Antoinette's tone. Unshed tears brimmed in her eyes. "How can Louis not think I am frivolous when there is nothing but frivolity all about us? And another evil woman who schemes and exploits an aging King, validating all my husband's fears!"

Honneure's heart went out to the lonely young Princess. She knelt, eye to eye with Antoinette, and gently took her hands. She had never been able to bear anything or anyone in distress.

"We'll think of something. I promise you. We'll think of something very special."

And so they had.

* * *

The day had darkened considerably. Lowering clouds looked swollen and purple, and the wind had dropped. Those who had not left already, hurried to their conveyances as servants rushed to pack up the last of the goods and decorations. Honneure winced as a bolt of lightning crackled brightly against the dark backdrop and looked about anxiously for Philippe. She caught sight of Louis and Antoinette first.

They were running side by side, hand in hand, laughing, toward Antoinette's calèche. The dogs barked at their heels. Honneure watched as Philippe caught up to them.

"My wife has great faith in this animal," Louis called to Philippe as he gestured toward the white mare. "She believes we can outrun the storm. We shall see!"

Honneure watched the Prince assist Antoinette into the vehicle. It was a tight fit for four dogs and two people, particularly when one of them was the size of the Dauphin. Though not yet twenty, he was already inclined to heaviness and was markedly overweight in his upper body and chin. But his blue eyes were bright and intelligent, and his honesty and integrity were evident in every word and action. Honneure could understand Antoinette's fondness for him and her wish to win his affection. She had made a good start and, apparently, had achieved her goal for the day. With a mere shake of the reins, the well-trained mare pranced forward, and Honneure noticed Louis slip a steadying arm about his wife's slender waist.

As she watched the royal pair drive away, Honneure wondered if her own day would end with such success. She recalled Antoinette's words when they had decided at last on a plan of action.

"It will be so romantic, Honneure, such a perfect day. Surely Louis will be able to see me in a different light, away from the pomp and glitter of the Court. Perhaps even Philippe will be able to see through different eyes."

Most of the carriages had departed by the time Philippe returned to her. Thunder rumbled ominously and he cast a worried glance skyward. "We'll have to hurry," he said, and placed a hand in the small of her back to guide her toward the waiting coach.

Honneure slid a quick look at Philippe's patrician profile and thought how familiar it was...and how beloved. How many hundreds of times had she walked beside him like this and admired him? How many times had she looked at him with love brimming in her heart? And when had it changed from sisterly to romantic love?

Or had she been in love with him all along, since the moment she had seen him pop up from the back of his father's wagon?

The wind picked up suddenly, lashing tree branches and sending bits of debris swirling through the air. The carriage horses, a pair of chestnuts Honneure had never seen before, tossed their heads and uttered frightened snorts and whinnies. Honneure noticed Philippe had tied Louis' mount, one of the black Lipizzan geldings, to the back of the coach. He shifted his feet nervously, but was otherwise calm.

"Get inside! Quickly!" Philippe held open the coach door, but Honneure hesitated.

"I'd rather sit with you!"

"No!" Philippe had to shout over the rising sound of the wind. "You'll get soaked."

"I don't care. I want to be with you!"

Philippe warred with precipitate and surprisingly strong emotions. He wanted her to be safe, had always been so protective of her. Yet he also wanted her close. He wanted her beside him, pressed to his shoulder...always.

There was no time to wonder at the sentiments raging

within him. Sentiments, which, he had to admit, had been growing for quite some time. A heart-stopping clap of thunder decided him.

All at once she was in his arms, being lifted. She felt the bench seat with an outstretched hand and slid over to one side when Philippe released her. She pulled long locks of wind-whipped hair from her eyes and clasped her arms to her breast. The wind now had an edge to it, and her thin cotton gown was little protection.

Philippe grabbed the reins before he was even seated. The frightened horses did not need to hear the crack of the whip, and it was all Philippe could do to control them and hold them to a rapid trot. A miniature tornado of leaves and twigs rose abruptly in front of them, and both horses shied to the right.

"Hold on to me!" Philippe yelled as the coach lurched sickeningly.

Honneure didn't need to be told twice. Turning slightly sideways she wrapped both arms around his waist and pressed her face to his shoulder. She felt the first, fat raindrops plop on her arms and head and stain the pale yellow of her skirts.

Philippe no longer held the horses to a trot, but let them break into a gallop. They were a long way from the palace, west and north of the foot of the Grand Canal. Just ahead was a group of buildings, the center of which was the Trianon. Being traditionally the place for illicit royal pleasures, it was situated quite some distance from Versailles.

Philippe groaned. There was no way they could reach the stables before receiving the full brunt of the storm. As if to underscore his thoughts, three consecutive bolts of lightning shattered the sky in front of them. Philippe braced himself for the boom of thunder he knew would follow.

It was more than the terrified horses could bear. The

horse on the right reared straight up while the other bolted sharply left. Philippe tried in vain to control them, but the maddened animals now both bucked and reared. The coach rocked.

Philippe thanked God he had not insisted Honneure ride inside and prepared to push her from the coach. Far better to risk a fall than to be trapped inside and crushed should the carriage overturn. Just when he thought he must drop the reins and push Honneure to safety, the skies opened completely, and rain sluiced down on them like waters from a broken dam.

Honneure was no longer even able to see. She was surrounded and assaulted by a blinding world of water. In mere moments she was drenched to the skin.

The torrential downpour did have one positive effect. The horses were equally blinded and had ceased their mindless plunging. Philippe took advantage of the situation at once.

"Hang on, Honneure," he shouted into her ear. "I'm going to climb down, and I want you to follow!"

She felt him move away, but he never let go of her hand. A minute later he instructed her to climb down. Philippe's strong, muscular arms encircled her waist and he helped her to the ground.

"Stay close. Don't let go of me. I'm going to try and guide the horses toward the buildings around the Trianon!"

Honneure never knew how Philippe was able to do it. His large, steady hands and calm, confident presence soothed the frightened animals, and he was able to guide them through the rain. She didn't even know how he was able to see where he was going. But all of a sudden the wind-driven rain seemed to slacken, and Honneure realized they had come around the corner of a stone building.

"Stay here a moment, don't move."

141

Honneure put out a hand to the nearest horse for the comfort of the touch and waited for Philippe to return. He reappeared leading the black gelding and tied his reins loosely to the carriage shafts. All three animals had put their heads down and, with their tails to the wind, seemed content to wait out the storm now that the worst was over. Once again Philippe took Honneure's hand.

In the lee of the high stone walls, Honneure was able to see the tall ornate doors they approached. Without hesitation Philippe swung them wide and ushered Honneure inside.

"Oh, Philippe!" she gasped. "Where are we? What is this place?"

Philippe glanced around the relatively small, but gracefully styled, high-ceilinged room. "I'm going to guess this is the French Pavilion."

From Madame Dupin's descriptions, Honneure realized Philippe was correct. She gazed about in wonder at the rococo architectural details and furnishings that were attributed to Louis XV's late mistress, Madame de Pompadour. "It's lovely, Philippe," she breathed. "But should we be here?"

Philippe closed the doors and the din of the storm was abruptly muted. "Whether we should or not, I'm certainly glad we are."

Honneure had to agree as she stood, teeth chattering, sodden gown dripping onto the ornately patterned marble floor. She hugged her arms to her breast to try and stop her shivering.

"I'm so sorry, Honneure," Philippe apologized, and moved to her side. He longed to take her in his arms and share his warmth with her, but felt strangely constrained. Instead he rubbed his hands briskly up and down her back.

"Do you...Do you think anyone would mind if we lit a fire?" Honneure inquired as she gamely tried to stop her teeth from clattering together.

"It will only take a moment."

Honneure watched as Philippe hurriedly and expertly laid wood in a small porcelain stove. It wasn't long before flames were leaping and crackling, casting a soft, pale light that nonetheless illuminated the gilt which decorated almost every square inch of the three elegant, connecting rooms. Intimate, very intimate, royal parties were held here, according to Madame Dupin, and Honneure could well imagine. Honneure shivered but not, this time, from cold.

"Come, stand close to the fire," Philippe said as he stripped off his dripping shirt.

Honneure had to briefly close her eyes. He was so incredibly, unimaginably beautiful. She remembered all the summers past when she had come upon him working in the stables, naked from the waist up. She recalled the peculiar feeling of warmth she had experienced and had naively attributed to the mere joy of seeing her beloved brother. The warmth returned, thawing her cold-stiffened limbs and enabling her to move in Philippe's direction.

Smiling, Philippe held out a hand to Honneure. But he felt the smile fade, and his hand dropped slowly to his side.

Something was wrong again. That vague, uneasy feeling had returned. And why, why did he feel this way in the presence of someone so familiar, so beloved?

Lips parted, brow slightly furrowed, Philippe watched Honneure tentatively approach. She had unpinned the ruins of her chignon, and her long, wet hair fell about her shoulders to her waist. Her eyes were the color of the storm that still raged outside their gilded walls, but they held a strange expression he was not able to fathom.

Nor did he seem able to keep his eyes from traveling

downward. Soaked, the thin fabric of her gown clung to her slight frame, accentuating her small but perfectly formed breasts, erect nipples almost seeming to taunt him. She was his sister, he mustn't look at her this way, feel this way . . .

The tumult of the storm outside was replaced by the thundering sound of the blood rushing through Honneure's veins. She could almost feel the throbbing of her arteries as her heart pounded, faster and faster, louder and louder. She no longer felt her feet or the hard marble beneath them. She was no longer even moving of her own accord, but being drawn, inexorably drawn to a destiny over which she had absolutely no control.

He could smell her now, summer, and summer rain, and everything that was good and desirable in the world. And there was no longer any denying it. He wanted her, wanted her more than anything he had ever wanted in his life.

But she was his sister!

Her hands moved without conscious thought. She placed them against Philippe's chest, felt the hard muscle, the pounding of his own heart. Slowly, she lifted her gaze.

Philippe's senses swam. She was too near, too dangerously near. He caught her hands.

"Honneure...please...no." His own voice sounded foreign to him, and he hated to say the words, but he had to, he must! "We can't...can't do this! You...you're . . ."

"*Not* your sister!" The vehemence of the denial startled them both.

Taken aback, Philippe released his grip on Honneure's wrists. His hands dropped, numb, to his sides.

"I am *not* your sister," Honneure whispered this time. Desire so strong it seemed to have a life of its own had taken over her body. She slid her hands upward over the ridges of his collarbone, up either side of his neck. Palms to his cheeks, she captured him.

Philippe groaned, and as the tortured sound escaped and fled, so too did the inhibitions that had held his true emotions in check for so long.

She was not his sister.

She was his love.

Honneure closed her eyes as Philippe lowered his lips toward hers. She felt his arms go around her shoulders. Felt his warm breath against her mouth, his lean form pressed the length of her body. Then, as flesh touched flesh, the world spun away into the vortex of a storm that raged not in the world, but of the soul.

Chapter Twelve

September 1771

It was a perfect fall day, the kind of weather he liked best. There was a chill in the air and a distant scent of smoke. Tattered wisps of clouds scudded across an almost painfully blue sky, and the trees had just begun to turn. Here and there the deep, rich green of the forest was stained with patches of gold and red. It was immensely pleasant to be galloping through the woods on such a day. He would have loved to continue on, see the end of the hunt, but he was just too damn uncomfortable. Reluctantly Louis XV, King of France, reined in his mount. The accompanying huntsmen, his grandson included, slowed as well.

The pain in his joints and resulting infirmity was humiliating. Feeling his color mount along with his irritation, Louis gestured for the other hunters to proceed.

"Go on. Go on, dammit!"

The riders milled uncertainly. Only one detached from the group and rode to the King's side.

"Is anything amiss, Sire?"

Louis frowned at his grandson, the Dauphin, though he was secretly pleased. "There certainly is," he grumbled. "The hunting hounds have gone off without you. How in the hell do you expect to catch up with them?"

"Hard riding, Sire," the younger Louis replied without hesitation. "But not until I'm assured there is nothing wrong

146

with Your Majesty."

"There is nothing wrong unless you fail to bring down that boar."

Louis was torn. It was unlike his grandfather to give up in the midst of his favorite pastime, and he was worried. He was also, however, sensitive. Age had been taking a greater and greater toll on his grandsire lately, and its debilities had become increasingly embarrassing to the proud monarch.

"Very well," he said at length. Raising his arm, he signaled to the other hunters. "We have taken too long in the hunt today," he called. "The King has pressing matters he can no longer ignore. He bids us ride on without him."

Despite his discomfort, Louis smiled to himself as he watched his grandson ride away. He was too serious and straitlaced by far. But he had other qualities that stood him in good stead, among them the ability to rapidly assess a situation and act upon it with authority. Perhaps he would not make such a bad king after all.

With only his servants and most loyal retainers now in attendance, the King allowed himself to slump in the saddle. But he did not linger, though the thought of the long ride home was painful merely to contemplate. Antoinette and some of her more adventuresome ladies, as well as a few wives of the other hunters, liked to follow the hunt and arrive in time for the kill. They would be along presently, and he had no wish for the women to see him in retreat.

With simply a grunt to those accompanying him, Louis pulled his horse off the forest trail, intending to take a shortcut back through the woods. He was only just in time.

The noise of galloping horses and the crashing of vehicles through the forest undergrowth was considerable. Soon he could also hear gay laughter and high-pitched feminine voices.

The King rode deeper into the woods, away from the trail forged by the hunting party, then turned to watch the procession pass.

Antoinette, driving a two-wheeled barouche, was in the lead, just as Louis had supposed she would be. She was a spirited little thing and quite pretty, despite her rather frizzy, red-tinted hair and high forehead. He had done well to arrange the marriage for his grandson. Now, if only the boy would get over his rigid upbringing and whatever onus his overly religious parents had put on him and bed the Prin . . .

The King's train of thought halted abruptly as his eye was caught by the occupant of the second vehicle, also a barouche. Antoinette's Boxer dog sat at her feet while the three smaller ones crowded her lap. She drove her horse with obvious ease and skill, unusual for a servant, which he could tell she was by her livery. It was not the unexpected sight of a female servant so capably driving a horse that captured his interest, however. It was the girl herself.

She was exquisite. Her face was a perfect oval, her features refined and symmetrical. Her smile was unblemished and enchanting. Wisps of pale, wavy hair streamed behind her in the wind. She was the most beautiful thing he had seen in quite some time.

The King's entourage was somewhat surprised to see their monarch recover with such alacrity. They had to spur their animals as he headed back, suddenly and swiftly, in the direction of the Fontainebleau Palace.

* * *

Comtesse du Barry, formerly Jeanne Becu, gazed at her reflection in the ornate Cheval glass and smiled smugly. It never failed to amuse her to recall her past and just how far she had come. Let her detractors say what they might, let the King's sisters go on about her illegitimate birth and years as a prostitute. None of them could alter the fact that she was the King's mistress. She had worked hard to secure the position and worked harder still to maintain it. She deserved everything she had. And more.

The Comtesse, still smiling, fussed at the bodice of her low-cut gown. A dab of silken powder had subtly highlighted the swelling globes straining against the taut, peach satin. A scented handkerchief tucked down into her cleavage gave off the fragrance of summer flowers. Turning her head slowly from side to side, she inspected and admired her make-up. She frowned with irritation when a discreet tapping at her boudoir door interrupted her reverie.

"Yes? Who is it?"

Olivia did not respond. She slipped inside the dressing room and closed the heavy door quietly behind her. With practiced expertise she arranged her features into an expression of sympathetic disappointment.

"I am very sorry to inform Madame that the King has returned early from the hunt."

"What?"

"Even now he rides into the White Horse Courtyard. And it's such a shame. Madame looks lovely."

"*Damn* him!" The Comtesse du Barry turned sharply away from her servant and refocused her attention on the reflection in the mirror. "Am I doomed to die of ennui in this Godforsaken place?"

Olivia remained silent, knowing the Comtesse did not require a response, or even acknowledgment. She often spoke her thoughts aloud merely to hear the sound of her own voice, Olivia knew. She knew many things about Madame du Barry, and the knowledge had served her well. Knowing what would be required next, she approached her mistress and smoothed a nonexistent stray hair back into the elaborate and towering wig.

"Shall I go to the *parterre* for you?" she inquired in an undertone.

Madame du Barry did not answer immediately. There were possibilities to consider.

A young, handsome man, her most recent paramour, awaited her. He was quite a skilled lover, and his ministrations had helped to relieve the relentless boredom of her days at Fontainebleau, where they had come for the King to enjoy the fall hunting. The temptation to join her lover, to go ahead and go to the garden where they planned to "accidentally" meet, was very great.

On the other hand, what if Louis sent for her, and she wasn't there? She had to be very careful when they were in residence at Fontainebleau, for the King still had a roving eye, and there were always many willing and attractive young women around. At home in Versailles she had less to fear because of Louis' own private brothel, a converted hunting lodge he called *Le Parc aux Cerfs*. There he was able to cavort to his heart's content with any number of low-class women who were no threat to her position.

In the end the Comtesse decided it was better to be safe than sorry.

"Madame?" Olivia prompted.

"I suppose you must go in my stead." Madame du Barry uttered a small sound of disgust. "Tell him I...I am unavoidably detained." A slow smile crept onto the Comtesse's prettily curved mouth. "Also tell him I shall make it up to him. Royally."

Olivia smiled dutifully. "I will relay your message. With

pleasure."

Madame du Barry's eyes narrowed as she watched her servant depart. Olivia was clever, and useful. But she would bear watching. They had too much in common for the Comtesse to trust her completely.

There was a flurry of activity among the Comtesse's ladies-in-waiting as she entered her sumptuously decorated salon. She arbitrarily stabbed a beringed finger at several of her ladies.

"The four of you, come with me," she demanded tersely. "I go to wait upon the King."

Madame du Barry's suite of rooms was, by necessity, located close to the King's apartments. She walked briskly along the wide corridor, glancing neither right nor left at the gilt-framed works of the masters. The fragrance of late-blooming flowers drifted on the still air from a variety of gold, silver, and hand-painted porcelain bowls set atop fabulously wrought tables of rare woods and marble. She noticed none of it. She did not hesitate until she had reached the gilded doors of the Royal Suite.

The King's guards, long familiar with the royal favorite, opened the doors without blinking, or even seeming to notice her. The Comtesse sailed into the main salon, casting a jaundiced eye, as she always did, on the peculiar green color which Louis adored and that covered all the room's chairs and benches. Lifting her chin a notch, she looked down her nose at the King's valet, the only person in the room.

"Where is he?" she inquired sharply.

The older man held out his hands as if in supplication. "Gone, Madame, as you see."

"Gone *where*?"

The valet took his time in answering. He liked the

Comtesse as little as she liked him. "I believe he has gone to visit the Dauphine's apartments."

"The Dauphine!" a tic jumped in the Comtesse's cheek as she ground her teeth. "And what could he possibly want with her?"

"I have no idea," the man replied, enjoying the Comtesse's obvious discomfiture. "I only know he has gone to await the Princess' return from the hunt."

Without another word the Comtesse spun on her heel and marched back the way she had come. The Dauphine! She would see about that.

* * *

The 17,000 hectares of forest surrounding the Fontainebleau Palace was so rich in wildlife it virtually guaranteed a successful hunt every time out, and Antoinette loved to follow the hunting party. She enjoyed being outside, away from the palace, having the opportunity to so daringly drive one of her horses and, most of all, to watch and admire her husband. Louis was a strong, powerfully built man who, nonetheless, was an accomplished horseman and huntsman. He almost always brought down his prey, and today would be no exception.

Antoinette and her ladies arrived in time to see the pursued boar brought to bay. The encircling dogs, the King's greyhounds included, barked and howled furiously, dodging this way and that as the exhausted boar made halfhearted charges. The hunters had dismounted and warily approached the scene. The maddened boar made a final lunge.

The man who unfortunately stood in the way was husband to one of Antoinette's ladies. Horrified, she watched the boar's formidable tusks tear a gaping wound in the man's thigh. The man went down with a cry of terror and pain, and pandemonium ensued.

Released at once by their handler, the dogs set upon the boar and began to tear him to pieces. Frightened horses screamed and reared, and amidst a chaos of excited voices, cries and shouts, the victim's wife shrieked and fainted. It was Louis, with Antoinette's aid, who brought about order.

"Someone quiet those horses!" the Dauphin ordered. "Maintenon, bind this man's wound with my scarf. Here. Antoinette, help his wife."

She and Honneure were already on their way. Honneure grabbed the reins of the horse that pulled the woman's calèche and steadied him. Antoinette climbed into the conveyance and helped the slumped woman to a sitting position.

"Someone bring me my salts!"

One of the Dauphine's servants hurried to do her bidding. She opened the vial and held it under the woman's nose, reviving her almost at once.

"Your husband is being tended," she assured the frightened woman as her eyes opened. "Everything is going to be all right. The Dauphin and I will see to it personally."

"Oh, Majesty, you are so kind!" The woman, overcome, raised Antoinette's hand to her lips and kissed it, then laid it momentarily against her cheek.

"There is no need to thank me. I am merely acting as any Christian woman would."

Someone took Honneure's place at the horse's head, and she fell in step behind her mistress, who hurried back to her husband's side.

"Well done, Antoinette," he said to her. "Now we must find one of your ladies who will be willing to take this man back to the palace. He certainly can't ride."

"I will take him," Honneure offered at once. But Antoinette shook her head.

"No. My horse is the swifter. Put him in my barouche."

Louis himself picked the injured man up off the ground. The white scarf binding his leg was already stained heavily with red, and the man's face was as pale as new snow. With great care Louis laid him on the floor of Antoinette's barouche. She climbed into it immediately and shook the reins.

Honneure was hard pressed to catch up with the Dauphine. Silently she thanked Philippe for all the hours he had spent teaching her to drive, and then inwardly winced at the memory. She missed him, desperately, for he had remained at Versailles while it had been her duty to accompany her mistress to Fontainebleau.

But there was little time to mourn. It was all Honneure could do to control her horse as it plunged through the undergrowth. And it took all her skill and concentration to guide him through the close set trees as they fled back toward Fontainebleau. It was as dangerous a thing as she had ever done, and she marveled at the courage of the Princess who drove on ahead, even faster, risking her own life to save a friend.

Trees and foliage sped past so swiftly it was all a dark blur. The wind blew Honneure's hair into tangles, and her arms ached from constantly pulling on the reins to maintain control of her horse. She groaned aloud with relief as the forest at last gave way, and the magnificent facades of Fontainebleau's multiple wings came into view.

Antoinette's horse, winded and exhausted, stumbled and began to falter. Honneure drew even with the Princess.

"Go on ahead!" she called to Honneure. "Call for help!"

A single, swift glance into the Dauphine's barouche told

her she must indeed hurry. Standing like a Roman charioteer, she grabbed the buggy whip and cracked it expertly over her horse's head. The barouche surged forward and, as they entered the far end of the White Horse Courtyard, Honneure started to shout. Figures appeared, like scurrying ants, running toward the commotion.

While King Louis, awed and fascinated, watched from a palace window.

* * *

"Majesty!"

The throng surrounding the King turned in unison. Madame du Barry ignored them all, fixed a pleased smile on her lips and expertly arched a single brow. "What a pleasant surprise to come upon Your Majesty," she purred. "Pray tell what brings you to this wing of the palace?"

"Pray tell what brings *you*?" The King quickly returned his attention to the window. His favorite's petty jealousies and artful games more often amused than annoyed him, but he was not presently in the mood to humor her. Far more interesting things were occurring in the courtyard below him.

The woman driving the barouche so daringly was the one he had admired earlier in the forest. Directly behind her came the Dauphine, urging on a spent and stumbling horse. Even as she drew the animal to a halt her cart was surrounded and a man was lifted from the floor of the vehicle. He appeared to be grievously wounded.

Louis assessed the situation at once. "It seems there's been a hunting accident. Someone send for my surgeon and have the man seen to." As one of the King's courtiers hurried away, he turned from the window. "The Princess, from what I have seen, deserves to be congratulated for her part in this little drama. One of her ladies as well. Let us attend the Dauphine forthwith."

Purposely ignoring his mistress, Louis resumed his journey through the long, light-filled gallery that connected two of Fontainebleau's wings. And as he walked he had to smile to himself. He had been on his way to see his granddaughter-in-law anyway. Now it would be oh-so much more intriguing.

Madame du Barry, a growing storm riding on her brow, followed the King's entourage, footsteps clicking a staccato rhythm on the parquet floor.

* * *

Honneure sat on the edge of her bed in a room similar to the one in Versailles and allowed herself a moment to catch her breath and slow her spinning thoughts. The dogs curled up in their boxes without hesitation, the day's excitement having exhausted them as well. She smiled at them fondly, then closed her eyes and massaged her temples.

If it was not her life, if she was not actually living and experiencing it herself, she would never have believed it possible. Eyes still closed, she let her thoughts drift back to Versailles...and Philippe. Since the day of the storm, since the embrace they had shared, Honneure felt as if she had been living in an enchantment. Versailles itself was the stuff of dreams. Antoinette could not be a more perfect mistress. And now she had her perfect love.

Honneure considered, for a moment, returning to the Princess. But she was being attended to by several of her ladies already. There had been quite a hubbub when the Dauphine had returned to her apartments, gown stained with blood. Assured she would not be needed for awhile, Honneure reclined on her bed. In an instant she was back in Philippe's

156

arms.

Remembering the heat of his body, the feel of his lips as they touched hers, tentatively at first, made her tremble anew. Never, as long as she lived, would she forget that first kiss. It had left them gasping and breathless, full of wonder. For long minutes they had stared at one another as if they had not seen each other for a very long time and needed to quench memory's thirst. Then, slowly, expression full of amazement, Philippe had smiled. She had answered him with a smile of her own.

No words had been spoken, none had been needed. She had laid a palm to his cheek, briefly and gently, as they listened to the rain lessen and finally cease. Then it had been time to leave. She had sat beside him all the way back to the château, a small distance between them on the bench seat, and looked neither right nor left. She had not needed to look at his handsome, beloved features, or at the magnificent grounds surrounding her. She had merely to revel in the warmth of the cocoon that embraced her.

Philippe loved her, had always loved her. But now it was no longer her secret alone.

The following weeks had passed far too quickly. Their moments together had been fleeting, but poignant. Eventually, the time of her departure for Fontainebleau had arrived.

Thanks to Madame Campan's kindness, they had an hour to spend together walking in the gardens the night before the journey. The time had been bittersweet, and Honneure had been unable to stop her tears at the moment of their parting. Philippe had brushed them tenderly away.

"The days will pass swiftly, you'll see," he had said. "And from all I've heard, Fontainebleau is very beautiful. I know you will not regret your time spent there."

"I regret nothing but hours lost I might have spent with you."

"Then do not think of them," he had replied with a grin. "Think only of the hours we will spend together in the future. All the hours of the rest of our lives."

Their kiss had been salty sweet.

"I love you, Honneure. I love you forever."

Raising a hand to her cheek, Honneure realized the memory had brought with it tears of its own. How dearly she loved him and missed him!

But there would be no more time for reminiscence. Honneure jumped to her feet as an urgent knocking sounded at her door.

"You must come at once," plain but sweet Madame Thierry said in a rush. "The King is here. He has asked for *you*!"

Honneure followed Madame Thierry on numb feet, desperately and vainly trying to smooth the windblown curls back into her chignon. The King! What could the King of France possibly want with her?

Honneure's hands shook, and her knees felt weak as she entered Antoinette's salon. The room, though large, could not have held another person. She saw the Dauphine and her ladies off to one side, near the windows, and to her left a group so elegantly clad they could only be the King's own courtiers. Even as she watched they parted, as if of a single mind, and a tall, older, but still handsome man dressed in a huntsman's attire strode forward. His gaze was riveted on hers, and she saw the beginnings of a smile as she dropped into a deep curtsy.

"You ably and bravely assisted the Dauphine, our grand daughter-in-law today," she heard a deep, cultured voice rumble. "I would know your name that I might thank you properly."

Honneure did not dare to look up. "My...my name is Honneure, Majesty," she breathed.

"Honneure," Louis repeated. "An interesting name. And beautiful. It suits you."

She felt a finger under her chin. Gently, she was forced to look up at her sovereign.

"Rise, Honneure. Rise and accept the grateful thanks of the King of France."

She had no choice. Knees still trembling she stood. "Your Majesty does me too great an honor."

The girl was well-spoken, Louis mused. And even lovelier up close. But there was something about her, something that tugged at memory . . .

"Indeed," came another voice from almost behind her.

Honneure turned and recognized Madame du Barry. The hair on the backs of her arms prickled.

"Indeed, the King has done you, a mere servant, great honor," the Comtesse continued. "More than enough for one day, I should think. Majesty?"

Though he did not look at her, he allowed Madame du Barry to take his arm. He gazed thoughtfully at Honneure for another long moment, then turned to leave.

Under the intensity of Madame du Barry's glare, Honneure had dropped her eyes. She was aware of the room emptying only by the shuffling of feet and the soft movement of stirring air. She could not move, could barely breathe for the furious pounding of her heart.

The mighty King of France had deigned to notice her, to speak with her, even to praise her. It was a distinction so great she never even could have imagined it.

So why did hands of icy premonition seem to wrap around her throat?

"Honneure?"

Madame Campan's voice seemed to be coming from very far away. She felt a light touch on her shoulder. Then the room went dark as consciousness spiraled away into a black abyss, and she sank, in a billowing pool of skirts, to the floor.

Chapter Thirteen

November 1771

It was bitterly cold, far too cold for snow although Antoinette wished for it with all her heart. A layer of white would soften the starkness of the bare tree branches and blanket the brown, cold, lifeless ground. Depressed, she turned from her view of the Versailles gardens and stared instead at the flames leaping and dancing in the hearth. It was cozy in her salon, and warm, yet she shivered.

Madame Campan looked up from her needlework. "May I get Madame la Dauphine a shawl?"

Antoinette shook her head.

"A glass of wine perhaps?" Madame Campan persisted.

"You know how little I drink."

"Today might be the very day to change one's habits."

Antoinette favored her lady at last with a glance. "*I* am not the one, I think, who needs to change her habits," she replied in a brittle voice.

The Princess' ladies exchanged nervous glances. Madame Campan laid her embroidery aside and rose somewhat stiffly to her feet. "Fetch the Dauphine a pot of tea," she said to a *femme de chamber* who had brought more fuel for the fire. "Come to the bedchamber, Majesty, and let me massage your shoulders."

Antoinette complied gratefully. Though she knew she should be used to it by now, she sometimes found the royal existence too stifling to bear. To always be surrounded, waited upon, have every word listened to . . .

Madame Campan closed the boudoir door. "We are alone," she said quietly. "You may speak freely of what is on your mind."

"Dear Campan," the Dauphine sighed, love for the older woman filling her heart. "You are always so sensitive, so caring."

"If you will sit I will give you the massage I promised."

Antoinette sank gratefully onto a low-backed, velvet-covered stool. Madame Campan's capable hands began their work.

"Your muscles are in knots," she chided gently.

"Do you wonder why?"

"I wonder only that you do not obey your husband."

Antoinette's eyelids had drifted downward as a flush of warm relief flooded her upper body. Now they flew open again, and the Dauphine sat upright and rigid.

"Campan! What traitorous words do you utter?"

"Simply the truth," she replied evenly. "You steadfastly refuse the Dauphin's advice."

"To speak to that horrid woman?" Antoinette flashed, and thrust to her feet to face her lady-in-waiting. "Yes! Yes, I do ignore his advice. I *will* not dignify her presence in this Court, her hold over the King, by acknowledging her existence!"

"Then there will continue to be a chasm between yourself and your husband, and stiff muscles in your neck."

"But you *know* the things she says about me!"

"If you refer to the incident at Fontainebleau, yes, I do."

"She called me *common*, Campan," the Princess rushed on as if she hadn't heard. "She said it was common of me to take that injured man in my barouche as I did!"

"It wasn't common at all. It was very brave and kind."

"And just the other day when we went out after stag, and I refused to take my party across that poor farmer's fields to arrive in time for the kill...she said it was cowardice, that I was *afraid*."

"You were being thoughtful."

As the Princess spent her vitriol, her shoulders sagged. Pushing them lightly, Madame Campan guided Antoinette back down on the stool and resumed her kneading. "You also behaved quite royally, I would say. That was the generous and courteous act of a true aristocrat."

"Do you think so, dear Campan? Do you really think so?"

"I do not have to think. I know."

Antoinette remained silent for a long moment. "I suppose, Campan," she said at length, "that you would also say it is the act of a true aristocrat to be...polite...to the King's mistress?"

"I believe it would take very little, the smallest gesture, to assuage injured parties, no matter how deserving they may be of their wounds."

Antoinette sighed deeply. "I shall think on it, Campan. This is not something I will be able to do easily. Oh, that feels so much better." Rubbing her neck, the Princess rose once more. "Where are my dogs? I should love to see them before I have to prepare for dinner. I dine tonight with my brother-in-law and his new wife."

"I know, and I am sorry to disappoint, but Honneure has taken your pets for a walk. She is, I think, going to meet Philippe for the first time since our return from Fontainebleau."

A wide smile lit Antoinette's every feature, and she clasped her hands. "Oh, what I wouldn't give to be able to transform myself into one of my little dogs!" she exclaimed. "What a happy reunion this will be. Their love gives me hope, you know, dear Campan. If Philippe was finally able to see, perhaps Louis . . ."

She left the thought unfinished. It was simply too painful to speak aloud any more. Night after night, month after month, she lay alone in her bed. Would Louis ever learn to love her?

"You will win your husband's affection," Madame Campan offered, as if sensing her mistress' thoughts. "You will have a happy ending just as Honneure and Philippe."

Antoinette smiled in assent, but she wasn't so sure she agreed. She wasn't at all certain she believed in happy endings any longer.

* * *

The chill in the air intensified as fall's early sunset stole away the sun's meager warmth. A dry, cold breeze rattled naked tree branches and scudded the last of the season's dead leaves across the frozen ground. Honneure hugged herself, glad of the coat Jeanne had made to match her red and silver livery. She noticed the Boxer had started to shiver, and she knelt to put her arms about his neck.

"I'm sorry, Baron," she murmured. "If Philippe doesn't come soon we'll return to the château." Honneure ruffled the heads of the three small dogs and glanced around at the deepening gloom.

The early night was eerily silent. The knife-edged cold had driven almost everyone indoors, and only those with necessary errands hurried on their way, breath pluming before them. Even the fountains were silent, and thin sheets of ice coated the still pools.

Day's last light glinted off the golden figures of the Apollo fountain, the god and his steeds. Honneure rose and turned slowly, looking for signs of anyone headed in her direction, worried about Philippe. He had never been late for any of their assignations before. They were simply too few and too brief to waste a single precious moment. And this reunion was especially momentous as they had not seen each other in nearly ten weeks. Philippe would never stand her up, or fail to get word to her, unless something had happened to him.

An inner chill shook Honneure. The dogs looked up at her expectantly. She could linger no longer.

With a sick feeling in the pit of her stomach, Honneure bent her head and started back in the direction of the palace. The dogs trotted obediently beside her, silent but for the sounds of their breathing and the tapping of toenails on gravel, until suddenly they began barking. Honneure jerked her head up.

His long stride was recognizable at once. He, too, had had his head down until he heard the small dogs' strident voices. As he looked up he saw her and broke into a trot. She could see the brightness of his smile in the rising moonlight.

Honneure also began to run, the little dogs leaping excitedly and Baron trotting sedately. She dropped the leashes as she raised her arms to Philippe and stepped within the circle of his own.

He buried his face in her hair, the strands cold and silken against his cheek. His arms felt the delicacy of her, the smallness of her bones, the narrowness of her waist. A rush of love nearly overwhelmed him.

"Honneure," Philippe whispered against her ear. "God, I've missed you. I've missed you so."

Nothing had ever felt as wonderful as being in his arms. Nothing. She could never have enough, hold him tight enough, long enough. She wanted to hang on forever, feel his warmth and nearness for eternity. And feel his lips on hers.

Philippe felt her softly gloved hands on his face, tugging him downward. Through half-lidded eyes he saw her lips part in eagerness. Desire rose in him and spread through his limbs like liquid fire, and he brought his lips down to hers and covered them.

Honneure groaned. There had been many stolen kisses during the waning weeks of summer before the sojourn to Fontainebleau. But none had ever been like this. Her knees began to buckle and as he felt her sag against him, Philippe supported her with a firm hand pressed to the small of her back.

Her hips were now pressed to Philippe's. Something thick and hot seemed to form in her abdomen, and she instinctively thrust more tightly against him. Now she felt a hardening there, the maleness of him, the physical proof of his desire for her.

Honneure feared she would faint as her throat threatened to close. Passion filled every part of her body like a living thing struggling to take control of her and give way to the most basic instinct of all. Feeling as if she could no longer breathe, Honneure tore her lips from Philippe's.

"I love you," Honneure breathed raggedly. "Oh, Philippe, I love you so much."

"And I love you." He kissed her again, but quickly. He planted small kisses all over her face, her cheeks, and brow and eyelids. The taste of her, the sweetness, seemed to enter him and permeate his very soul.

Nothing in the world existed but Philippe. Until two small front paws began scratching at the hem of her skirt. Baron gave a polite, but insistent, "woof," and Honneure had to laugh. Hands against Philippe's chest, she pushed away from him.

"I'm sorry, but I can't forget my charges. They're probably freezing to death!"

"No, *I'm* sorry," Philippe apologized in turn. "I was delayed, I couldn't help it."

"I was afraid you weren't coming. I thought something had happened to you."

"Nothing could ever keep me from you, Honneure. Nothing. But I...I received a message I had to deal with."

Something unusual in Philippe's expression sent a little *frisson* of warning along Honneure's nerve endings. "A message?"

Philippe hesitated, recalling the strangeness of it.

He had just shrugged on his coat in preparation to meet Honneure when there was a knock on the door of his spare, cubicle-like room in the stable. He could not have been more surprised to open it and find Olivia standing on the other side. Her smile was familiar. And unpleasant.

"Aren't you going to invite me in?"

"No," he had replied tersely. "Tell me why you've come and be quick about it. I have an errand."

"An errand?" Olivia quirked a brow. "You call a clandestine meeting with your...*lover*...an 'errand?'"

"How did you . . ." Philippe had stopped himself in time. He didn't need to hear it from Olivia. He knew what a small world the immense palace truly was, and how rife with gossip. But it disturbed him to learn that people as insignificant as he and Honneure should be watched as closely as they apparently were. Why, to what purpose? And by whom?

"Tell me what you came for, Olivia," he had demanded harshly. "Or get out of my way."

"Ooooh, what a big, bad boy." Olivia had coyly touched a forefinger to his chest. "I love it when you . . ."

"Don't touch me!" He had grabbed her wrist and pushed her hand away. "And move aside. I'll not waste any more time on you."

Philippe had seen her eyes narrow as he pushed past her,

pulling his door closed behind him. He did not look back as he walked down the narrow corridor, but could feel her stare boring into his back.

"Don't you *dare* walk away from me like that, Philippe Mansart," she had hissed at his retreating back. "I have a message I . . ."

"You know what you can do with it, Olivia," he had called back without turning. He heard her sharply indrawn breath, but ignored her and kept walking. She was vindictive and there would undoubtedly be repercussions, but he didn't care. Honneure had filled his mind then, his every thought.

And she was before him now, and all he *wanted* to think about. Nor did he wish to upset her with mention of Olivia.

"It...It turned out to be nothing," he replied at last. "It was a waste of my time while you were waiting for me in the dark and cold."

"But you're here now." Honneure reached up and smoothed an errant curl from Philippe's pale brow. "You're here, I missed you so terribly, and I'm so very glad to see you."

He couldn't help it. He adored her. Capturing her in his arms once again he drew her against him and found her lips.

The world started to spin. The cold night faded away. All that was left was the heat of her love and desire.

But Philippe had felt her shivering.

"I'm sorry," he said, holding her at arm's length. "It's so damn cold. I should have thought . . ."

"Ssshhh." Honneure laid a gloved hand to his lips. "It doesn't matter. All that matters is that I have seen you, and know you are safe and well."

"I am. And anxious to see you again. Soon. Preferably in the warmth and light of day." Philippe took Honneure's hand, and together they began walking back toward the château

By Honor Bound

"When will you be able to get free?"

Somewhere in the distance a clock chimed. One of the small dogs barked at a group of passersbys and a half-moon rose in the night sky. The couple walked slowly, heads bent together as they planned a future tryst. Too soon they reached the Marble Court. Philippe raised Honneure's hand to his lips.

"Good night," he murmured. "I love you."

"I love you, too."

She moved away from him quickly, reluctant to leave yet anticipating the warmth of the Dauphine's apartments. Nor did she ever want to give the appearance of shirking her duties, which must always come first. Secure in Philippe's love for her, she merely looked forward to the next time she would see him. Honneure turned when she reached the immense palace doors and watched Philippe disappear into the night.

It was difficult, the periods of waiting until she could see him again. But she was patient.

And they had a lifetime together ahead of them.

* * *

The long and boring dinner finally appeared to be coming to an end. Madame du Barry glanced around her with disdain.

Not only was the Comte de Provence's new little wife plain, uninteresting, and totally, disgustingly subservient, but she loathed the room in which she had been forced to dine. The relatively small space of the King's private dining room in the *Appartements Interieurs* hardly seemed befitting of royalty at all. She much preferred the grand and elegant chamber where, although they dined publicly, they at least did so in suitably kingly surroundings. Besides, she rather liked the ceremony of the public meals, when any and all who wished could come and see their monarch sup. It was good for the common people to see how the aristocracy lived. And it was divine to feel the caress of their hungry eyes on her face and form, her fabulous gowns and jewels. With a sigh, the Comtesse cast her gaze on the opposite side of the table.

No doubt about it. There absolutely was a shadow of a mustache on the girl's upper lip. Josephine Louise of Savoy was lucky to have bagged any husband at all. The fact that she had wed one of the King of France's grandsons was positively miraculous. Her family must be powerful indeed. Languidly, she stretched a bejeweled hand toward her glittering crystal wine glass.

"Homely little thing, isn't she?"

The King had leaned close to her to whisper his observation. She could smell the wine on his breath, and it was almost overpowering. Good. It was time to bring up the matter that had annoyed and distracted her all evening. The Comtesse leaned back in her chair until her shoulder nearly touched Louis'.

"My very thoughts, Majesty. And my prayer for your grandson is that it won't take too many attempts to plant a royal seed in that particular field."

The King chuckled, then laughed aloud. All eyes turned in their direction, but the Comtesse ignored them. When she continued to converse with the King in an undertone, the diners drifted back to their own conversations.

Antoinette eyed the pair nervously. She did not like the way du Barry's eyes kept sliding in her direction as she whispered with the King. What new tale was she spinning, what new harm did she concoct?

Lifting her chin a notch, Antoinette turned her attention down the long table. Dozens of candles cast magical, flickering lights on sparkling crystal and silver. White-gloved, white-wigged footmen moved gracefully and unobtrusively to refill glasses or remove an empty plate. A low murmur of conversation hovered over the clink of flatware on porcelain. She glanced at her husband, chatting amiably with Provence's bride, and her heart went out to the girl. She knew what it was like to come to an unfamiliar land and marry a perfect stranger. Her eyes traveled on down the table.

The Comte d'Artois, Louis and Provence's younger brother, was laughing with his sisters, Elizabeth and Clotilde. The King's three, plump sisters, Adelaide, Victoire, and Sophie, sat together across from the nieces and nephew in prim and pointed silence. They occasionally exchanged glances among themselves, but never once turned their attention toward their brother and his much loathed mistress. Antoinette pitied them, for they had gotten on well with the King and had led a relatively happy life until the arrival of du Barry. The King's youngest sister, Louise, had become so demoralized by the situation at Versailles, at its being turned into a virtual brothel, she had entered the Carmelite house in Saint-Denis, one of the poorest and most austere convents. It was widely known she had gone there to pray for the moral conversion of her brother, the King. Antoinette sighed deeply and looked down the table to her left.

Her pale and thin, but utterly jovial brother-in-law, Provence, flashed her a disarming smile.

"Don't look so glum, little sister," he scolded playfully. "Surely amid so much beauty and splendor, you can find some reason to smile."

"I have many reasons to smile," she admonished Provence in turn. "But none of them have anything to do with material possessions."

"Dancing is not material," he responded lightly. "Think of

all the wonderful holiday parties to come. I invite you now to be my partner."

"What about your wife?"

Provence leaned close to Antoinette's ear. "I don't think she knows how," he whispered. "And, besides, there are other moves I would prefer to teach her."

Antoinette could not help laughing, even as the blood rose to her cheeks. Across the table, the Comtesse watched her with a smug and satisfied smile.

"Promise me, Louis," du Barry said to the King without taking her gaze from the Dauphine. "Promise me you will do something about her impertinence."

Louis gulped the last of his wine and set the crystal goblet back on the Belgian lace cloth with an unsteady hand. "Sounds to me like it's only her servant needs punishing."

The Comtesse du Barry briefly considered how gratifying it would be to have revenge not only on Antoinette, but on one of her favorite servants as well. She dared not ask for anything too petty, however. Besides, she had to let Olivia have a little fun.

"No," the Comtesse said at last. "I'm sure it was not the equerry's fault at all, but Antoinette's. I have no doubt she has directed all her servants to ignore requests from any of *my* servants. It is simply another way she has found to snub me and show her self-righteous disapproval." The Comtesse finally turned her heavy-lidded eyes on the King and blinked them slowly. "And I sent my servant merely to ask the equerry permission to borrow that lovely new sleigh of Antoinette's, the one you so admired, that we might have a ride together at first snowfall."

Louis nodded absently, his mind on more fleshly pursuits. But he did make a mental note to have someone have a word with Antoinette. He was tired to death of the trivial squabbling between his mistress and his grandson and heir's wife. Furthermore, their endless skirmishing had polarized his court. Some of his most able and trusted ministers had begun to side with his prissy little grand daughter-in-law, and openly criticized his lifestyle and the drain it put on the nation's treasury. He could not have that any longer. Antoinette must be seen to be in line with all the royal decisions and choices, no matter her personal bent.

It was ironic, however, the King mused. Of all the brides he could have arranged for his grandson, the future King, he had unwittingly chosen one as morally proper and tight-laced as Louis himself. Well, she would simply have to mend her ways. Or at least appear to.

With narrowed eyes, Louis the elder gazed across the table at his pretty, young grand daughter-in-law. Barely sixteen years old and already as prudish as his sisters. Such a pity. But it would change. He would see to it. There would be peace between du Barry and Antoinette.

Chapter Fourteen

Twelve years. Honneure took a deep breath and let it out slowly as she gazed from the Princess' salon onto the cold and snowy scene below her. It was almost impossible to believe that twelve years had passed since the day Paul and Philippe had come to fetch her from Amboise. So much had happened in those years. She had been reared and educated in a beautiful château by a warm and loving family, and had been tutored in the ways of the world by a generous and caring mistress. She had become a servant of the future Queen of France and lived history in its making. She had found the love of her life, who had been before her all along, and was secure and happy in her relationship. She had to be the luckiest woman alive. She only wished she could share her joy with her mistress.

Antoinette looked as forlorn as Honneure had ever seen her. She sat with her smallest, and favorite, dog on her lap and slowly stroked its silken coat while her hairdresser fussed with her elaborate wig. She had already been dressed in her finest day gown. Diamond earrings glittered in her ears. Her highest ranking ladies-in-waiting had dressed in appropriate finery of their own and stood about awkwardly, as ill-at-ease as their mistress. All eyes turned to Madame Campan as she hurriedly entered the room.

"The royal party approaches," she announced without preamble.

By Honor Bound

Antoinette's ladies assembled themselves in two half-circles on either side of the door, ready to fall in behind the Princess as she passed. Honneure crossed to her and held out her arms for the little dog.

"They'll all be waiting for you when you return," she said in an attempt at reassurance.

Antoinette started to lift her pet, then hesitated. "No," she said, as if thinking aloud. "My dogs can accompany me. Why not?" She looked up at Honneure. "You, too. Bring my precious pets, Honneure. There is no reason on earth why they cannot come as well."

Honneure quailed inwardly, remembering her last and, so far her only, face-to-face encounter with the King. She recalled the uncomfortable intensity of his regard and the almost palpable dislike of his mistress. But her duty was to obey, without question, her Princess.

Honneure dipped a curtsy, accepted the small dog and went to fetch the others. She returned in time to take up the rear of the train as it passed from the interior apartments into the formal reception chambers. Their destination was the Salon of Peace, chosen by the King for what he hoped were obvious reasons.

The room was as immense and splendid as the others of the Queen's Apartments. Complex, gilded architectural detail framed ceiling murals depicting classical Greek scenes of heroism. A massive circular, allegorical painting of Louis XIV bestowing peace on Europe hung over the marble fireplace and gave the room its name. Heels clicking on the intricately laid wooden floor, the Dauphine's party moved to the center of the chamber to receive the Court.

The King, his ministers, his grandsons, and all their entourage arrived first. Antoinette gave a small sigh of relief when she saw her husband, and they exchanged brief, fond smiles. Then she drew a great, deep breath.

She could do it, she could. She must. She had promised both her husband and her husband's grandfather, the King. She would speak to the du Barry. She would acknowledge her. How painful could it be?

More footsteps and a cacophony of voices announced the arrival of the Court ladies. Madame du Barry entered the salon first, accompanied by the foreign minister's wife, the Duchesse d'Aiguillon. She was a respectable lady who had been a friend of the late Queen, and Antoinette was rather fond of her. She detested the woman who followed, the Marechale de Mirepoix, known as "the little cat." She treated life as nothing more than a great joke, and Antoinette wondered if du Barry had brought her along as a personal comment on the current proceedings.

Madame du Barry's group came to a halt. The Comtesse looked first at the King, but his attention was elsewhere. Irritated, she glanced pointedly at Antoinette.

The Princess realized she was trembling. Avoiding the Comtesse's gaze, she spoke first to the Duchesse d'Aiguillon. She turned at last to her nemesis and spoke the words she had rehearsed.

"There are a lot of people at Versailles today."

No more than that, but it sufficed. She had acknowledged the du Barry, spoken to her. Officially, the feud was over.

Louis, her husband, looked pleased. The King looked pleased and, certainly, the Comtesse. Antoinette had compromised her morals and principles, but she had done her duty to her husband and her sovereign. Realizing she had been holding her breath, she let it out in a long, slow sigh.

The public spectacle, tantamount to an apology, was over, and the Court ladies retreated. The Comtesse looked back over her shoulder at the King, but he seemed preoccupied, and she moved on. It was the Dauphin who finally broke the silence.

"You look quite lovely, Antoinette," Louis said to his wife in a conciliatory tone. He knew how difficult this had been for her.

"And her Mistress of the Menagerie looks quite lovely as well."

If the floor had opened beneath her feet and she had plunged to her death in a black abyss, Honneure would only have been grateful for the oblivion. She felt every eye in the room upon her as the aging King walked slowly in her direction.

"I remember you," Louis said, and paused in front of the enchantingly beautiful young woman. With a jeweled finger, he tilted her face up that he might look at her more closely. "You were with the Dauphine last fall, when she aided the injured hunter."

Honneure could not speak. Somehow she managed to nod.

Her hair was the color of summer honey, her eyes the color of a summer storm. She reminded him of someone from long, long ago, but he could not place the memory. And it was a shame, because it was a pleasant one.

"Do you know how to dance?" the King inquired abruptly.

"I...I know a few steps," Honneure mumbled.

"Good. I want you to dance for me. Next Wednesday at a fête celebrating the New Year." The King turned to go, then hesitated. He stared at Honneure for a long moment, and smiled. "I will look forward to it."

* * *

Philippe stroked the elegantly curved neck, then ran his

hand over the mare's withers and down her well-muscled shoulder. "You're a beauty," he murmured softly. "Good girl. My good girl."

The mare pushed her muzzle into Philippe's side. Her eyelids grew heavy as he massaged the muscles of her back. But Philippe felt her tense beneath his touch. Watched her head go up and ears prick forward. She whickered.

The huge stables were always full of people coming and going. The mare must sense someone familiar. Philippe's heart beat just a little faster.

Heads turned to see a young woman in the Dauphine's livery hurrying along the clean, wide aisle. But she seemed to notice no one, intent only on her destination. By the time she reached the stalls where the Lipizzans were kept, Philippe had opened the mare's door. Honneure practically fell into his arms.

"Philippe!"

"Honneure...what is it? What's wrong?"

She merely clung to him.

Mindful of the many curious stares, Philippe gently eased Honneure into the stall and closed the door. He held her until he felt the grip of her arms around him loosen. She took a step back and looked up at him.

"Something terrible has happened, Philippe. I must talk to you."

Her eyes were wide and frightened. Even the mare sensed her tension and moved her feet nervously.

"Come, let me take you to my room. We can speak privately."

Honneure hesitated only for a moment, necessity winning over propriety. She nodded and allowed Philippe to guide her to his small room near the animals that were his responsibility.

Honneure's heart squeezed as she glanced about the tiny, windowless, sparsely furnished space. There was a narrow cot, a small trunk for personal possessions he had brought with him from Chenonceau, a peg in the wall for hanging clothes, and a diminutive table pushed into the corner. Letters were spread across its scarred surface, and Honneure recognized the handwriting. Two short steps carried her across the room, and she gazed down at the familiar, beloved scrawl.

"Oh, Philippe, I miss them so," she murmured. She felt Philippe come up behind her, put his strong hands on her upper arms as if to brace her. "I've saved all my letters, too. And the one's from Madame Dupin." Honneure briefly touched the parchment pages with the tip of her index finger, then turned within Philippe's grasp and gazed up at him. "She's so witty, so clever, isn't she? And *Maman* writes as if she was born to it. Reading her letters I'm almost back at Chenonceau. I can see and hear the river, smell the fragrance of the air . . ."

Honneure's throat constricted painfully, and tears rushed to her eyes. When they spilled over Philippe brushed them away.

"Honneure, what's wrong?"

But she couldn't speak. She shook her head.

Seeing the fear in her eyes, the sadness, and feeling helpless to aid her was more than Philippe could bear. Taking her face in his hands, he kissed away the tears that continued to fall, then her eyelids, her chin and cheeks. Eventually his lips found hers.

Honneure could not help but respond. His very presence was enough to make the ground move beneath her feet. When he touched her the world went away.

But she could not let herself forget, not now, not this time. With all the willpower she possessed, Honneure pushed

Philippe away. Hands pressed to his chest, as if to hold him at bay, she swallowed her tears and forced herself to return to the reason she had come.

"Philippe, I...I was with the Dauphine today when she received the Court. The...King . . ." Honneure had to swallow again. "The King took notice of me. He ordered me to a gala on Wednesday. He...he's ordered me to dance for him."

Philippe felt himself grow cold. With the King's notorious reputation, the invitation was certainly not an innocent one.

"Philippe, what am I going to do? You must help me!"

The dread in her voice tore at his heart. "The first thing you must do," he said in a deliberately even tone, "is take a deep breath and try to be calm. Tell me everything, from the beginning."

Honneure complied, including the incident at Fontainebleau.

"Honneure, why didn't you tell me before?"

"It didn't seem important before."

It was important now, however. The King had seen and taken notice of her twice. He had ordered her to appear before him again. And it was particularly significant because he was flaunting his interest in public, in the face of his mistress. Philippe could not doubt the seriousness of the situation. Neither did he want to share the depth of his concern with Honneure.

"Philippe, please," Honneure begged once more. "What are we going to do?"

"There is only one thing *to* do at the moment." Philippe smoothed back the short, fine curling hairs that wisped about Honneure's forehead. "We must not anticipate the worst. We have to take each day, and live it, and deal with a problem if...*if*...it arises."

Honneure looked deeply into Philippe's eyes. She saw her love reflected in them, and returned. She heard the sagacity of his words and tried to hang on to it.

Yet when her thoughts leapt ahead and her imagination carried her back into the King's presence, the fear returned. She laid her head against Philippe's breast and closed her eyes.

"I'm sorry, Philippe," she said in a small voice. "I'm so frightened. I can't help it. What if . . .?"

"Don't say it!" Taking Honneure's arms, Philippe gave her a little shake and forced her to look him in the eye. "Don't even say the words! Nothing has happened, and we're not going to act as if it has, or might. If you must think ahead, think about how beautiful you will look, and how gracefully you'll dance...because you do. Think of how you will impress the Court and please the Dauphine. And how, when it's over, life will go back to just exactly the way it was."

Was he simply trying to allay her fears, or did he truly believe his words? Honneure stared at Philippe unblinking, yet saw only his faith in her, and his love. She wanted to believe him, had to believe him.

But suddenly all she could think of were her musings from only a few hours earlier, when she had counted her blessings and considered herself the luckiest woman alive. She wanted Philippe to tell her that nothing would change, that she would go on being blessed and happy. And then she recalled the night years before when she had asked him to promise the same thing.

All at once Honneure felt very heavy, as if the weight and wisdom of a hundred lifetimes had fallen on her shoulders.

"Sometimes things change for the better," she said at length, her voice almost a whisper. "Sometimes they change for the worse. But change they will, they must. It is the nature of the world. Just promise me one thing, Philippe, please. Promise me you will always love me. Tell me that will never change."

Philippe shook his head, setting long, dark curls astir against his shoulders. "No, Honneure," he said solemnly. "That will never change. That is the one promise I can make that I know will never be broken. I love you. I love you with all my heart and for all time."

"As I love you," she whispered, and laid her head once more against his breast until she could hear the beating of his heart.

It was the one true thing she could hold on to.

Chapter Fifteen

"It is time, Majesty."

The King looked up with bleary eyes at the three men surrounding him, the most powerful ministers of his cabinet. Was it Chancellor de Maupeou who had spoken? The Finance Minister perhaps, Terray? Or had it been D'Aiguillon?

"Did you say something, Emmanuel?" Louis turned slowly in the Foreign Minister's direction.

The three men exchanged glances as the King emptied his goblet and a footman instantly refilled it.

"It was I who spoke, Majesty," Terray repeated. "The gala...you recall. All the guests have arrived. They merely await your Royal Highness."

"Let them wait. This is the third one this week. Am I not allowed a little time to myself?"

Meaningful looks among the trio were traded once again. D'Aiguillon cleared his throat.

"But this one is special, Majesty. It's the one you designated as the official New Year's celebration."

"Ah, yes." The King lifted the goblet to his lips and then set it on a low, handsomely painted table. "We gather tonight in the Hall of Mirrors. People say it's the most beautiful room in the palace."

"And indeed it is, Majesty," Terray quickly agreed.

"Yet barely a hundred years ago it was just a gallery connecting the King's Apartments with the Queen's," Louis continued as if he had not heard his minister. "And until only a few years ago who were you, the three of you?"

The King retrieved his goblet and emptied it. He waved away the footman with the crystal decanter and let his gaze rest on first one minister, then another. He enjoyed their expressions of discomfiture.

"Who were you, after all," he went on, "until my mistress persuaded me that you would be invaluable to me in helping to shape the nation's policies? You all owe your positions to a former prostitute. You know that, don't you? Do you want to know something else?"

All three men shuffled nervously, but no one spoke.

"The Court refers to you as 'the three yellow men.' " Louis chuckled deep in his chest. "You do have rather bilious complexions. I don't know what the Comtesse sees in you. Particularly you, D'Aiguillon."

The Duke could not hold the King's gaze. The other two ministers looked away, as if to disassociate themselves from him. It was common knowledge he was no stranger in the Comtesse's bed. But it was also highly unusual to refer to such matters so forthrightly. The King was in a strange and unpredictable mood, and it made the Duc D'Aiguillon extremely apprehensive. Once again the Duke cleared his throat as if in preparation to speak, but Louis raised a hand to silence him.

"Denials bore me," he said irritably. He picked up his goblet, studied its empty depths and quirked a single brow. The footman moved with alacrity. The King raised his glass.

"To the relief of boredom," he said to no one in particular, and drained his glass. He set it sharply on the table and rose unsteadily to his feet. His ministers moved swiftly to his side.

"I doubt Your Majesty will be bored this evening," Terray

said in a currying tone as the men moved toward the door. "The Hall is positively resplendent. Your Majesty's choice was an excellent one."

Chancellor de Maupeou, who had thus far remained silent, smiled thinly and lightly touched the King's sleeve.

"Do not forget, Majesty," he said unctuously, "that tonight is the night you asked that pretty young woman to dance for you."

Louis halted, swaying slightly, and furrowed his brow in thought.

"The girl with the dogs," de Maupeou prompted. "The pretty little thing with the unusual eyes."

"Unusual eyes," Louis repeated. "Yes. Yes, I do remember. Of course."

The three men sighed almost in unison with relief as the King smiled.

"Perhaps the evening will not be as wasted as I feared," Louis mumbled as if to himself. "Yes, I remember . . ."

* * *

A thousand candles blazed the length of the long hall. They burned from a dozen chandeliers suspended from a vaulted ceiling, its painted segments depicting events from Louis XIV's illustrious reign. They shone from smaller chandeliers perched atop freestanding gilded sculptures of cherubs and classical figures. Dozens of them stood across from each other in long, golden lines, stretching the distance of the elongated chamber. Between each gilded figure on one side of the room stood tall, arched mirrors, reflecting and multiplying the flickering lights. Opposing each mirror across the parquet floor stood a tall, arched window. Beyond the segmented glass panes, snowflakes swirled and danced in and out of the projected candlelight.

At one end of the vast and stunning room, a chamber orchestra patiently awaited its cue. The low babble of a hundred voices wove in and out of the susurration of silk and satin skirts. Crystal beads, gold and silver, glittered on velvet coats of every hue. Precious jewels at ears and throats sparkled with lights from their own inner fires. Laughter and champagne bubbled on pink-tinted lips.

The royal family mingled with the most favored courtiers, the Court's elite. Having few friends yet among the court denizens, Antoinette was content to hover at her husband's side. They moved through the crowd together, nodding and smiling, Louis dropping a few well-chosen words here and there. The Princess saw her favorite brother-in-law, Provence, with his homely, but adoring, wife. The King's sisters were nowhere to be seen, but Antoinette was not surprised. They shunned any function which the du Barry might attend.

The Dauphine cast a quick glance about her, but did not see the Comtesse. Could it be, in light of the latest palace rumor, that she would not attend the night's celebration? A now-familiar unpleasantness returned to the pit of Antoinette's stomach.

Poor Honneure. The Dauphine felt every bit of her fear and distress. It was a terrible situation.

All noise abruptly ceased and all eyes turned to the head of the room. A footman in gilded livery announced the arrival of the King, Louis XV, sovereign of all France. Gentlemen bowed, ladies curtsied. The King, cheeks flushed and eyes reddened, took his place in an elaborately carved gilt and velvet chair. One of the ministers attending him gave a discreet signal, and the music commenced. Antoinette turned away.

He was her husband's grandfather and her King. But he

was also a dissipated old man. His vices were legendary. He hardly made any pretense of running the country any more, but seemed intent instead on distracting himself from the one thing he had in common with his neglected subjects - mortality. His life had become an endless round of parties and merriment and sexual peccadilloes. His mistress, when she was not busy having her sycophants appointed to positions of power, spent her time inventing new ways to rekindle the King's waning interest. And still he cast his greedy and roving eye about for younger and more tender flesh.

"Is something wrong, Antoinette?"

She felt her heart squeeze as Louis covered the hand she had linked through his arm. She looked up at him with as much of a smile as she was able to muster.

"Nothing is wrong, my dear husband. I...I'm merely a little tired, and the dancing hasn't even begun yet."

"The dancing." Louis grunted and absently patted the back of his wife's hand. "The only dancing anyone cares about tonight is the dance your servant will be doing for the King."

"Oh, Louis." Antoinette looked up at her husband with a plea in her wide blue eyes. "Please tell me this isn't going to end as I fear!"

"If your fear is for the girl's virtue, then your fear is not misplaced. And there is nothing you, nor I, nor anyone can do."

Antoinette squeezed her eyes shut. She had tried to tell herself, and assure Honneure, that it was simply a dance, a diversion for the King. When it was over and she had gone her way, he would forget about her.

But it was not to be. It had been naive of her to think otherwise.

"What...what will happen, Louis?" Antoinette whispered.

"What will become of her?"

"She will be ordered to the lodge in the deer park, no doubt," he replied, disapproval rampant in his tone. "She will become just another one of many."

"But, what about the man who loves her? What about her *life*?"

The question was never answered, and a warning glance from her husband precluded any others. Curious ears were beginning to turn in their direction.

And the signal had been given for the formal dancing to commence.

* * *

Earlier the wind had been fitful, but now it roared in earnest. The walls of the great stone stable seemed to shudder as another icy blast tore at its very foundations. Inside the vast building, however, the heat was almost stifling. The royal horses were as pampered as their masters and mistresses, and no expense was spared to keep them safe from winter's rigors. It was almost more than Philippe could bear.

Endlessly pacing the barn aisle in front of the Lipizzans' stalls had raised his already overheated body temperature. Sweat prickled in his armpits and at the small of his back. But it was the least of Philippe's worries.

Tonight was the night. Even now, this moment, she might be dancing before the King. Even now, fate might be conspiring against them.

For, despite his words, Philippe had no illusions about the seriousness of the situation. The King did not idly amuse himself. He was interested in Honneure. And if he wanted her, he would have her.

In spite of the stable's warmth, a chill raised the hairs on the backs of Philippe's arms. And something deeper, darker, far more sinister gnawed at his insides. He raised his hands to his temples and rubbed the flesh there as if aiding the circulation might help to restore memory. What was it Honneure had told him?

It was so long ago. They had still been children, she twelve, perhaps, and he fourteen. They had become fast friends by then, confidants. And she had shared something with him on a day very much like this one.

It had been cold, with blowing snow. Their parents had been elsewhere in the château. He and Honneure had been sitting in the kitchen at the old, scarred table in front of the hearth. Tears had come to her eyes. It had been an important date, an anniversary of some kind . . .

The date of her mother's death! He remembered now.

Without realizing it, Philippe had halted his pacing. He stood stock still in the middle of the aisle. But he still pressed his fingers, hard, to his temples.

He had tried to comfort her. When she leaned her elbows on the table and buried her face in her hands, he had rubbed her back and murmured words of comfort. But she had been inconsolable. Reliving the day of her mother's death, Honneure had also relived her fear and grief and terrible, terrible sense of loss.

"All of a sudden I had nothing. Nothing!" she had cried. The depth of her sorrow had torn at his soul.

"You have your memories," he had replied in a weak attempt to console her.

Honneure had looked up at him then, eyes wide and wet, full of remembered horror...and something else.

"I have more than memories, Philippe," she had whispered in an odd voice. "She *did* leave me something. She left me with a mystery I will never be able to solve."

How intrigued he had been! How anxious to hear her tale and solve the enigma and be a hero in her eyes. But her mother's dying words had left him as cold and baffled as they had left Honneure herself.

"The King!" she had cried.

And "Never tell...never tell!"

Never tell *what*? And what about the King?

"*Les cerfs... dans le parc... les cerfs.*"

The deer...in the park...the deer.

Totally incomprehensible. Then.

Philippe's arms dropped, limp, to his sides. His entire body convulsed with a shudder although sweat streamed from his temples.

Deer in the park...the hunting lodge, *Le Parc aux Cerfs*. The King's private brothel.

Philippe moaned, completely unaware the agonized sound had come from his lips.

"Poor lost Honneure," the woman had breathed at her last. "My lost Honneure?" or "My lost *honneur*?"

Had she lost her honor to the King in his brothel? Did she reclaim it with the birth of her illegitimate daughter and the bestowing of the name?

Philippe licked dry lips with a drier tongue.

Was the King of France Honneure's father?

* * *

The dance was done. The usual rumble of conversation did not immediately continue, however. All attention was fixed on the King.

And the King's attention was fixed on the couple who stood before him. He nodded briefly at his grandson, the

By Honor Bound

Comte d'Artois, by way of acknowledgment. The boy was light on his feet and had partnered well with the girl. Artfully, Artois had allowed the girl to display her grace to the fullest. She was absolutely lovely, and he was pleased, well pleased. And something more.

Memory tugged at the King. It was long ago, another woman. She, too, had danced for him, and he had admired her grace and beauty. He remembered how she had enchanted him and how he had desired her. But he recalled her as only a brief, shining light in his life. Then she had gone, disappeared.

What had happened to her? Where had she gone?

It had been many, many years since he had even thought of her. He might never have recalled her beauty, her elegance, if he had not seen this girl before him now.

How pleasant it would be, how fortunate for him, to be able to relive that long ago love. Louis beckoned to a nearby servant.

"Summon the Dauphine to me," he ordered.

He must speak with her about the future of her servant.

Chapter Sixteen

The wind picked up and the snow fell harder. The storm raged in earnest. Its ferocity was all that had saved her.

Honneure stared at the pale yellow walls of her small room. The Boxer lay on his side in a corner, snoring softly. The three small dogs were in a pile on her bed, watching her sleepily, aware something was wrong. Earlier they had jumped in her lap, but she had gently shooed them away. She hadn't the heart to comfort another creature. She could not comfort herself.

All Philippe's reassurances, all the Dauphine's and Madame Campan's, had been for naught. It had not been just a dance, but an audition. And she had won the part. The King wanted her. He had, in fact, wanted her moved into the lodge that very night.

The storm's teeth had been too sharp, however, its bite too strong. It had held the monster at bay. But what would happen with the dawning of a new, less violent day?

The horror of it was simply too great to imagine. She was nearly numb. Certainly she had no more tears to cry. She had shed them with her mistress and Madame Campan, who had imparted the terrible news.

Following her "performance," Honneure had fled to her room. Not long after she had been summoned into the salon by Madame Campan. The Dauphine had been there, but all her other ladies had been dismissed. It was then she knew that her worst fear was about to be realized. She had not even needed to see the tears on Antoinette's cheeks.

"The King has sent a message," Madame Campan had begun. Honneure could not recall the rest of her words. Her mind had already begun to shut down with the shock of it. She remembered only Madame Campan and the Dauphine's kindness, their sympathy. They had all shared their tears.

But there was nothing anyone could do.

She could run away, of course. But where would she go? She could not return to Chenonceau and bring the King's wrath down on Madame Dupin and her foster parents. What would become of Philippe, who would surely insist on following her? And what of her duty to the Princess? No, she could not leave. It was not an option. Better to suffer her fate and wait for the King to tire of her.

Despair clogged Honneure's breast so thickly it seemed to slow the beating of her heart. Soon, perhaps, it would simply stop. Pain and fear and desperation would kill her. And it would be a blessing. Even for Philippe...*especially* for Philippe.

Though she thought she had cried all her tears, they rose again to her eyes, spilled over, and ran down her cheeks as little rivulets of anguish.

Philippe. What would become of him? What would he do? How would he cope with her loss?

How would she cope with his?

It was unendurable. She could no longer sit in this little room and agonize. She had to see Philippe.

Just one more time.

* * *

Philippe could hear the intensity of the storm through the

thick stone walls. He knew how cold it would be, how it would feel, how difficult it would be to find his way in the darkness and fury of the blizzard.

But it was no longer possible to pace the aisle and wonder and worry. It was late. Surely the ordeal was over by now. What had happened? What had been the King's reaction?

Philippe was still pulling on his coat when he slipped outside through one of the stable's immense double doors. The wind nearly ripped the garment from his back, and he clutched the edges together at his breast. Within moments his gloveless fingers were numb. Snow swirled in his eyes and dusted his shoulders and hair.

Light still shining from the palace was enough of a beacon to steer by. Philippe bent his head and started forward. He had no idea what he was going to do when he reached the château. He didn't even know if he would be allowed to approach the Dauphine's apartments. He only knew he had to try.

The storm buffeted Philippe and played with him like a cat with a ball of twine. He looked up to orient himself and was relieved to see he had almost reached the Forward Court. He was also amazed to see another figure hurrying in his direction. Who else was crazy enough to come out in weather like this? Philippe stopped and shielded his eyes from the blowing snow to get a better look.

The person headed in his direction appeared to be a woman. He watched the slight figure sway and stagger, bent nearly double against the howling wind. What dire emergency could possibly drive her out on a night like this? No doubt she needed aid. Philippe began a brisk walk in her direction. Then his heart skipped a beat, and he broke into a run.

Honneure could scarcely believe it. There he was, as if in answer to a prayer. With a cry, she crossed the final distance between them and flung herself into Philippe's outstretched arms.

"Honneure! Dear God, what are you doing? Where were you going?"

She didn't answer him. Sobs wracked her so violently she could hardly breathe, much less speak.

Philippe felt Honneure sag against him and realized her knees had buckled. In a single smooth motion he swept her into his arms and cast about for the nearest shelter.

It was called the Chapel by the Court of Versailles. To ordinary men it had the dimensions of a cathedral. It would be cold this time of night, but its doors were never locked, and it was shelter from the wind and snow. With Honneure cradled against his chest, Philippe hurried toward its massive doors.

The first thing Honneure became aware of was the cessation of the storm. Then she heard the echo of Philippe's booted feet on marble. She lifted her head from his breast and looked about to see where he had taken her.

They had entered the palace's elegant and soaring chapel. A number of candles flickered in the gloom, and there was just enough dim light to see by. Philippe carried her to an area containing a double row of velvet covered benches and gently set her on her feet. She sank immediately onto the nearest bench.

Words were not needed. The look of misery on Honneure's face told the story. Pain piercing his heart like a dagger's blade, Philippe sank to his knees at her feet.

For a long, aching moment they stared into one another's eyes. Honneure felt the return of her tears.

"Don't cry. Please don't cry anymore." Philippe smoothed the windblown hair from her face, then took her hands and kissed them. "It's not going to happen. I won't let it." He couldn't, and not just because she was the love of his life. With what he feared was the truth about her heritage, she could not possibly become mistress to the King.

"But...but how...what . . ."

"The solution is very simple," Philippe replied, and only wondered why it had taken him so long when the answer was so obvious. He kissed Honneure's hands again. Holding them captured between his own, he pressed them to his heart.

"Marry me, Honneure. I love you so much. I'll never love anyone but you. This is the right thing, you know it. Marry me, please?"

Honneure sat silent, stunned. First there had been the Hall of Mirrors, then the dance, the King's decision. She had experienced her life plunge from the heights to the depths. She was in shock. She could barely comprehend Philippe's words.

"What...what did you say?"

Philippe laughed softly. "I'm asking you to marry me, Honneure. Please, will you marry me? And I'll take you away from here, back to Chenonceau perhaps. Just tell me you'll marry me."

She felt like snow melting. Realization came over her like the warmth of the sun, and she felt herself sinking down, spreading out, returning to the earth, and becoming one with it. Living life's cycle as God and nature had intended it.

Philippe loved her. She loved him also. She adored him. Of course this was the right thing. It had been the right thing all along. They had been destined for one another since the moment of their meeting, on that frigid morning in the courtyard at Amboise. This was the conclusion to the first segment of their lives, and the beginning of the second. This was exactly what had been intended.

"Oh, Philippe...Philippe." This time the tears were tears of happiness. "Yes. Yes, I'll marry you. Oh, yes!"

* * *

Olivia sat in the Comtesse's over-decorated salon and wondered how long it might be before she was summoned. She had no doubt she would be, it was just a matter of time. She let her eyes roam over satin-covered, gilt-encrusted chairs to shelves and delicate tables covered with exotic knickknacks from all over the world. She loved the little elephants, one carved of ebony, the other of ivory, with golden collars and jewel-studded saddles. Boldly, she picked one up to examine it. It was instantly snatched out of her hand.

Zamore, the Comtesse's little Bengali slave, cradled the carving to his chest protectively. "Don't touch mistress' things!" he hissed.

Without hesitation, a tight smile on her lips, Olivia drew back her hand and slapped him. The frightened boy dropped the elephant, and Olivia stooped to retrieve it.

"I'll touch anything I want, you wretched little monkey. Now go away and leave me alone."

Glaring, the boy backed away. "She'll *punish* you!"

Olivia laughed outright. "I doubt it."

The sound of a door opening alerted her and, quick as a cat, she tossed the costly ornament to Zamore. He caught it just as the Comtesse's chief lady-in-waiting entered the room.

"What are you doing?" she snapped. "Put that down at once! You are *never* to touch the Comtesse's belongings without permission."

With a sidelong glance at Olivia, Zamore did as he was told. Olivia gave him a sly, satisfied smile.

"And you," the lady-in-waiting said to Olivia, her disapproval evident. "The Comtesse wishes to see you at once."

Olivia curtsied respectfully to the older woman and then carefully composed her features as she slipped into the adjoining bedchamber.

Madame du Barry lay in her wide, silk covered bed propped up on an impressive array of pillows. Her expression was impassive, but Olivia knew her well.

"How is Madame's headache?" she inquired solicitously.

"'Madame's headache,'" the Comtesse repeated sarcastically, "has served its purpose. I successfully avoided the public humiliation."

"I heard, however, that the ball was breathtaking. They say the Hall of Mirrors was exquisite in the candlelight."

"Do you mock me, Olivia?"

"Oh, no, Madame! Certainly not! I only meant to imply my sympathy for your plight. You were denied the opportunity to spend a most enjoyable evening because...because . . ."

"Go ahead and say it, Olivia," the Comtesse said with a tight smile. "Because the King has an eye for the Dauphine's vapid little dog-walker. Tell me – you who always has an ear pressed to the wall – what was the result of the evening's...entertainment?"

Olivia dropped her chin a notch and looked up at the Comtesse through wide, sympathetic eyes. "I did not see, of course, but I heard . . ."

"Yes, yes, go on." Madame du Barry waved an impatient hand. "What is the outcome?"

It was almost too delicious. Olivia licked her lips, savoring the taste of her rival's defeat. "The King was pleased," she replied at last. "He has ordered Honneure to the lodge."

The Comtesse crossed her arms over her breast and

hugged them as her eyes narrowed. "The old fool," she spat. "He hardly has the wherewithal to take care of *me* any more, much less his stable full of whores."

Wisely, Olivia remained silent. She watched as Madame du Barry threw back her silken coverlet and slid from the high bed. She crossed to her dressing table, sat down and studied her reflection in the mirror with intensity. Stroking her long, slender neck, she slowly turned her head from side to side. Then she turned on her padded boudoir stool and pinned Olivia with a hard stare.

"I have grown tired of the King's dalliances," she said in a dangerous voice. "And more tired still of the young women who throw themselves at him thinking to advance their positions at Court."

The Comtesse paused, recalling the first time, at Fontainebleau, that the King had seen Honneure. She remembered how demure she had been, how shy. How absolutely beautiful. She had not tried to capture the King's attention at all, quite the opposite. Which was far more serious. She was just the sort of sweet, innocent young thing who might rekindle Louis' dying sexual fires. She could not be allowed into the King's bed. This one was too perilously lovely.

"I cannot allow the King to have this girl," Madame du Barry announced with finality.

Olivia's heart sank. She had no chance to win Philippe back unless Honneure was out of the picture. "But...but surely the King will tire of her. Eventually."

"I cannot take the chance. I will not. Not this time."

"Then...then what do you propose?"

"To get rid of her, of course," the Comtesse snarled.

Olivia had to stifle her sigh of relief. "Does

Madame...does Madame have any ideas?"

"Not yet. I don't know enough about her." The Comtesse looked at Olivia and smiled. "That's where you come in, Olivia. You're very good at finding people's weaknesses. And exploiting them."

Had anyone else said such a thing to her, Olivia would have been insulted. Coming from the Comtesse, however, it was a compliment. She returned her mistress' smile, and let it spread into a wide grin. Things were definitely looking up.

"As a matter of fact, I do know something about Honneure. And she has a very great weakness," she replied, thoughts turning to a handsome, dark-haired young man.

"How lovely," Madame du Barry purred. With the tip of her chin, she indicated a chair near the dressing table. "Sit down, Olivia. And tell me all about it."

Chapter Seventeen

The day had dawned with no memory of the night's fury. A perfect, pure and sparkling blanket of white lay atop the world. The wind had died, and the sky was a piercing, cloudless blue. It was the kind of beautiful winter's day that made it possible to wait for spring and kinder temperatures. But Philippe hardly noticed as he drove the leopard sleigh toward the palace and, hopefully, the waiting Princess. His thoughts were in turmoil, and the urgency of time running out pressed down on him like a physical weight. How could everything be so right one minute and wrong the next?

Philippe squinted against the blinding light of sun on snow, but he was not yet close enough to see if Antoinette's entourage had entered the Marble Court. *Please don't let her be late today*, he prayed. He needed to speak to her, to win her to his side and help him to get Honneure to see reason.

The Lipizzan mare trotted on, her coat as pristine as the new-fallen snow. It always gave Philippe such joy to drive her. But there was no gaiety in him today.

Didn't Honneure understand the danger she was in? If she truly loved him, as she had said, and wished to marry him, why wouldn't she listen to him?

To his vast relief, Philippe saw the royal party emerge from the palace as he passed the tip of the northern wing. Fixing a smile to his face, he pulled into the courtyard and halted in front of the Princess' entourage. He stepped down from the coachman's jump seat and bowed to the Dauphine.

Fortunately, it seemed Antoinette, too, was in no mood to waste any time. She took her place in the velvet lined seat with alacrity and bid Philippe to drive on. He did not hesitate. For a few minutes, until they were well away from anyone's earshot, the only sound was the hiss of runners over crisp, new snow.

"Well, Philippe," the Princess sighed at length. "I suppose you'd better tell me what has gone amiss between you and Honneure. This morning, when the two of you came to me and asked for permission to marry, I was overjoyed! It's the perfect solution for everyone. Now, however, Honneure is telling me she cannot go away with you!"

"I apologize deeply to you, Highness, for the trouble you've had to take."

"Nonsense." Antoinette waved a dainty, gloved hand dismissively. "You know how fond I am of both of you. Your happiness matters very much to me. I was devastated last night to learn of the King's decision to send Honneure to *Le Parc aux Cerfs*. You cannot imagine how happy I was to give my permission to you to marry Honneure and take her out of harm's way. But now she says she cannot go, she cannot leave me! She will wed you, happily, joyfully...but she will not leave the palace!"

Philippe briefly closed his eyes. He spoke just loud enough to be heard over the wind rushing in their faces. "Honneure is devoted to Your Majesty."

"But at her own peril?"

"So it seems, Majesty. Ever since she was a little girl, she has felt her loyalties intensely."

"It is an admirable quality, Philippe. Yet this time, I fear, it will not stand her in good stead. Can you not speak to her again, reason with her? Unless she is well away, I'm afraid the

King will have what he wants. And soon. I have put him off for a day or two, saying I must find someone to replace Honneure. But the King is, as you know, an impatient man. He will have what he desires."

"Even if we are wed?"

"Marriage is not viewed as an obstacle to one's desires in this Court," Antoinette replied so quietly Philippe had to strain to hear her. "No, you must take her away, Philippe. At once. And you must convince her yourself. I've done all I can. I have even, as you know, promised to find you another position. But she stands firm on her decision."

There was nothing more to say...except to Honneure. And he was at a loss. She already had her hackles up at his insistence that her devotion was misplaced. The Dauphine had released her, and her place was with him, at his side. Why was she unable to see that?

The temptation rose strongly in Philippe to tell Honneure what he suspected, in fact was almost certain, about her past. Perhaps fear could do what reason could not.

But he couldn't tell her, at least not now, not yet. She had suffered enough trauma and distress in the last few days. He could not add to it a burden of potentially crushing knowledge.

With a heavily burdened soul, Philippe returned the Princess to her party in the courtyard. "Take heart," she said in an undertone as she climbed from the sleigh. "Come to my apartment when you're done. I'll make sure Honneure is there to speak with you."

It was all he could do. He turned the mare back in the direction of the stables and cracked the buggy whip over her flank. She stepped out briskly, long mane lifting from her elegantly curved neck. It took only a few minutes to return to the stables.

There was a great deal of activity, as usual. Philippe did not notice at first the footman making his way in his direction. When he saw him at last, he smiled grimly at the man's nervousness around horses. It was obvious he was from the palace.

"Philippe Mansart?" the footman asked tentatively as he sidestepped the mare.

When Philippe nodded, the man handed him a slip of paper. Philippe thanked him curtly and unfolded the note, which said, "Dearest Philippe, I must see you as soon as possible. Please meet me in the Salon of Hercules. I await you."

The note was not signed and scribbled so hastily he barely recognized the handwriting, but it had to be from Honneure. Had she changed her mind? Is that why she wished to see him now? Hope leaped in Philippe's heart.

It didn't take long to unhitch and rub down the mare, yet it seemed an eternity. The afternoon waned and time was of the essence. Every day, every moment counted now. He hurried from the stable and jogged toward the palace.

It occurred to Philippe, as he entered the first of the courts that funneled visitors into the château, that the Salon of Hercules was an unusual place for Honneure to request a rendezvous. If he was not mistaken, it was part of the greater area that made up the King's suite of apartments. But perhaps that was the reason why. At this time of day, late in the afternoon and before the commencement of evening activities, they would undoubtedly have privacy. Philippe hastened his steps.

He had been correct. After a hurried inquiry, a footman directed him up the King's Staircase.

Philippe hesitated at the top of the royal stair. A few

passing servants eyed him curiously, but no one questioned him, dressed as he was in the Dauphine's livery. He looked to the left, toward the actual living quarters where the majority of the activity seemed to be taking place, and proceeded to the right. He passed through two grand and gilded reception chambers, the Salon of Abundance and Salon of Venus, and came at last to the Salon of Hercules.

The chamber was greater in dimension than the previous two rooms had been and just as ornate. Philippe's eyes were drawn upward to the fantastic ceiling painting of the triumph of Hercules, and he did not notice, at first, the figure standing in a corner of the huge room.

"Philippe. I'm so glad you've come."

The voice was low, seductive, and familiar. And it made his flesh crawl. He halted in mid-stride.

"You." A single word, yet the tone of it fully revealed the depth of his loathing for her. "What are *you* doing here?"

"Why, meeting you, as my note clearly stated," Olivia replied smoothly. She wanted to fly at him and scratch his eyes out. But she would have her revenge, against both of them. Very soon now. "I assume you got my message...that's why you're here?"

"*Your* message." Philippe's hands were clenched into fists.

"Yes, of course. Why, Philippe? Did you simply *assume* the note was from...another?"

He knew he should simply turn and walk out. But a visceral curiosity delayed him.

Olivia took advantage of it. From a cut crystal decanter on a small table she poured two glasses of wine and carried them toward Philippe.

"You can stop right where you are, Olivia."

"But Philippe!" Olivia protested with a smile. "We must toast your good news. We must raise a glass to you and your...future bride."

Philippe felt his blood run cold. "How did you know?" he demanded.

"Oh, Philippe, you know how the palace is. There are no secrets."

Ice continued to creep through his veins. It made it difficult to move. But she was approaching him again, moving closer. He managed to turn away.

"Wait, Philippe. Don't go. We really must celebrate. So much good news in a mere twenty-four hours!" Olivia halted in front of Philippe and smiled up at him. "Your engagement. And Honneure's winning the King's favor . . ."

"Olivia!"

Both heads swiveled toward the door. Madame du Barry frowned at Olivia in mock disapproval.

"I thought this was to be a toast to *good* news. I'm sure your handsome friend doesn't wish to be reminded of any unpleasantness at this particular moment. Neither do I, for that matter." On satin slippered feet, the Comtesse glided toward the pair in the center of the room.

Philippe stood rigid in stunned, awkward silence. What was going on?

Madame du Barry took one of the glasses, the one nearest her, from Olivia and handed it to Philippe. "Take it, please. I insist." When Philippe reluctantly complied, she took the second glass of wine.

"I'm sure you're wondering what this is all about, are you not?" The Comtesse allowed her gaze to caress the equerry from head to foot. He was as divinely good looking as Olivia had said. Perhaps, when this was all over and the rival for the affections of *both* of their lovers had been driven from the palace, she would have a taste of what Olivia found so delicious.

"It is just as Olivia has said," Madame du Barry continued seamlessly. "She, and I, too, would like to toast your happiness. Olivia because she considers you a dear friend, and I...well, I'm certain I don't have to spell out to a man as intelligent as yourself why I would like to see the lovely Honneure happily wed and no longer a temptation to the King."

With a smile on her expertly painted lips, the Comtesse touched Philippe's glass. "To love," she murmured, and drank.

Philippe felt he was caught in the bizarre and complex web of a nightmare from which he could not awaken. This simply could not be happening. But it was. And he wanted it over with as soon as possible. Throwing back his head, he drained the goblet dry.

"I...hardly know how to thank Madame," he said with what he hoped was an air of finality. "It is kind and generous of you to take note of, and care about, the lives of mere servants."

"Oh, I do care," the Comtesse purred. "More than you know."

"Then I thank you again and will take my...take my...leave . . ."

"Olivia? I think you should summon a footman. Your friend doesn't appear...quite himself."

Philippe heard the Comtesse's words, but they seemed to come from very far away, and he couldn't make sense of them. He only knew he had to get away. He turned toward the doorway.

Someone was coming through the door. And he couldn't move his feet. They seemed rooted to the parquet floor. His body, however, had already begun to lean in the direction he wished to go.

The floor came up to meet him, slowly . . .

* * *

Winter's early night was falling, and the setting sun laid sheets of pink and gold atop the fresh snow. Honneure caught her breath as she stood at the window preparing to draw the drapes. The world sparkled, glittered, and almost seemed on fire with color so pale, yet pure, that it hurt the eye.

But cold stung the flesh, and window glass was too thin a barrier against the winter night. Reluctantly, Honneure pulled the heavy silken drapes together and arranged their folds. Behind her Madame Thierry lit the lamps while another servant banked the fire. Madame Campan was in the Princess' boudoir buttoning the gown Antoinette had chosen for the evening. The dogs, walked and fed, were asleep in their beds in a corner of the salon. Her day was almost done.

Where was Philippe?

"Everything is done here," Madame Thierry said. "At least until the Dauphine returns from supper. You may take some time for yourself, if you like."

"Thank you but, no. I think I'll wait here."

"As you wish. I'm going to spend some time with my son. Good evening."

Honneure curtsied in response. Madame Thierry left, as well as the other servant, and the room was suddenly very quiet. Too quiet.

There must be something else to do. Honneure turned, critical eye surveying the room, but everything was perfect. She could find nothing to busy her fingers and occupy her mind. She could avoid reality no longer. And reality was that she had driven Philippe away with her stubborn loyalty and determination.

Honneure clasped her hands and squeezed them together as stinging tears rose to her eyes. Though she tried to stay the memory, it was too new, too fresh. She saw the look in Philippe's gaze as he had proposed, the love and devotion. He would do anything for her; he had proved it. He was willing to give up the best position he could ever possibly have just for love of her, to make and keep her safe. And how had she responded? Honneure winced as the morning's memory assailed her.

Together, hand in hand, she and Philippe had had an audience with the Dauphine. Her delight in their decision to wed had been genuine. She had been saddened, certainly, to hear Philippe say he and Honneure must find a place elsewhere to be out of the King's extensive reach, but had agreed it was necessary. She had even offered to help them find a new position. Honneure blushed as she recalled her response to the generous offer.

She had turned it down flat with protestations that she could never leave the Princess' service. And how could she? Antoinette had been so good to them both. Despite her elevated station, she had been a friend to them. And she had so few friends herself within the Court. How could she possibly desert the Princess?

After having an entire day to reflect on her thoughts, Honneure's mind offered her a ready response. She should leave because it was the only way she would be truly safe from the King. She should leave because she belonged with Philippe. She had known it the instant he had proposed. It was right. Honneure also recalled what the Princess had said to her when Philippe, hurt, had finally left.

"Remember, Honneure, that I came here as a foreign Princess. I thought, when I first arrived, that my loyalties should continue to lie with my mother and my country, Austria. And in the beginning I was correct. By my deportment I represented my country well. Many hard feelings against my country have been softened as a result. Yet, should something go amiss, if, God forbid, relations between France and Austria were to become strained, where should my loyalties be then?"

Honneure had known exactly what the Dauphine was telling her.

"Your...your duty would be to your...your husband."

The Dauphine had nodded slowly, and Honneure had admired such wisdom in one so young. She would make a great Queen one day. Also one day the Dauphin would see what a wonderful wife she had already become.

What kind of a wife will I be? Honneure wondered dismally. She was beginning to fear she would never get the chance to find out.

Where was Philippe? Had she really driven him away?

Honneure was so deep into her thoughts, so entrenched in her anxiety she jumped, startled, when the knock came at the door. She hurried to answer it.

"I have a message for Mademoiselle Honneure Mansart," the young pageboy announced solemnly.

"I am Honneure Mansart."

Wordlessly, he handed her a folded piece of paper, bowed slightly from the waist, and departed. She opened the note. "Before you make any decisions that will affect the rest of your life, come at once to Madame du Barry's chambers." It was signed simply "A Friend."

Honneure crumpled the note and tried to still the hammering of her heart. What was going on?

A sense of dark premonition closed around her shoulders like a heavy cloak. Nothing associated with Madame du Barry would ever come to any good. She should ignore the missive and wait for Philippe. He would come. He would.

Honneure found herself opening the door.

* * *

She had always thought the Queen's Staircase was grand. The King's stair dwarfed it. The sheer size and elegance of it, the splendor of the courtiers traversing it, made her feel as insignificant as an insect. Her apprehension increased and her steps faltered.

What was she doing after all? How could this have anything to do with Philippe? It was probably some scheme Madame du Barry had concocted to further torment the Princess. She should have no part of this whatsoever.

Yet the note had said it pertained to her life, not Antoinette's. It pertained to her decision, and the only decision she was making was about marrying Philippe. Curiosity drove Honneure on as surely as the lash of a whip drove an ox.

Honneure knew, indeed all knew, that the Comtesse's suite of rooms adjoined the King's. She proceeded to the door of the salon and found it ajar. Cautiously, she stepped into the sumptuous chamber.

The room was empty, eerily quiet. Where could everyone be? It was no secret the Comtesse had at least as many servants as the Dauphine. Where had they all gone?

A door on the other side of the salon was also open. Honneure tiptoed across the carpeted floor. Hands braced on the door jamb, she looked into the next room.

It was a short hallway. Several doors opened onto it, and the nearest one was also open. It was almost like an invitation.

Something was wrong, very wrong. Honneure still had seen no sign of a single soul. But the temptation was more than she could bear. She stepped into the hall and crossed to the open door.

It was a small sitting room, prettily decorated in pink and gilt. A floral Aubusson carpet in shades of pink and pale green covered the floor. A dainty, Chinese-style secretary graced one corner of the room. A wide, pillow strewn bench stood in another. A thin, silken shawl of lavender covered two figures reclining on the bench. The fringed ends of the coverlet trailed on the floor.

Honneure must have made a sound when she entered the room, because the person nearest the door stirred and sat up. The shawl fell away from her breasts, and Honneure could see she was naked.

"Honneure." Olivia's uptilted eyes perfectly complimented her feline smile. "What a surprise."

It was not a surprise, not at all. Olivia couldn't possibly look more confident. Honneure didn't have to wonder who lay next to her.

It was her fault. She had driven him away. He had offered her all of his love, everything, but she had attached conditions to hers. He had put her first, above all. She had put duty first. He had turned to Olivia. And she deserved it.

As Honneure slowly backed from the room, Olivia let the coverlet fall away completely. She did not want to look. She knew what she would see.

He was as beautiful unclothed as she had always known he would be. His body was long and lean, and the musculature as perfect as if he had been sculpted. His limbs were akimbo, his long hair falling across a velvet pillow. He appeared to be asleep.

By Honor Bound

In a single instant, Honneure's heart, her life, shattered. She turned and started to run.

Chapter Eighteen

"I've found a larger trunk," Madame Campan told the Princess.

Antoinette looked up from her clavichord. She bestowed a small smile on her chief chambermaid, but her expression remained sad.

"Thank you for taking the time to look, dear Campan."

"A page is bringing it," Madame Campan continued, and brushed her hands together as if she had gotten them dusty. "It's one of Your Majesty's older ones."

"But in good condition, I trust."

"Of course. I also packed in it two or three of the day gowns you no longer wear."

"How thoughtful, Campan!"

"We can't let her leave here with the few things she brought with her," the older woman went on as if she had not heard. "Certainly her livery is no longer useful."

"No," the Dauphine murmured. "I'm afraid not."

"And although she leaves here, she still represents the Court. She was in your employ. She was recommended for her new...*position* . . .by one of Your Majesty's ladies."

"You have done well, Campan," the Princess said gently. "She will be very grateful. I know I am." Antoinette rose from her clavichord bench, crossed to her maid, and took her hands. "You've grown very fond of her. I know how much you'll miss her. So will I."

"She's a lovely, intelligent girl," Madame Campan replied sorrowfully. "Her loyalty to you was unquestioned. You cannot afford to lose people like that."

Antoinette sighed. "I cannot afford to let her stay."

The two woman exchanged glances, no explanations needed. Madame Campan knew everything as she had been with her mistress when the Duc D'Aiguillon had come to her chambers. He had begged the Dauphine's pardon for the intrusion, then went straight to the point.

"I do not know all the details involved in this...situation," he had begun. "Nor do I think I want to as it seems a rather sordid affair. But I do know this much. The King wishes your servant, Honneure Mansart, to proceed at once to the hunting lodge. Particularly since a betrothal, of which he was recently informed, now seems to be broken off. Conversely, the Comtesse wants the girl in question to leave the palace at once, claiming she is involved in a domestic scandal that directly affects her entourage."

At this point, the Duke had had the good grace to look somewhat embarrassed. The yellow cast of his skin actually appeared to redden.

"For the sake of peace in the Court," he had eventually resumed, "I would urge you to send the girl away. The Comtesse bid me tell you she would be in your debt," the Duke had added pointedly.

"Though difficult, it is definitely to your benefit for Honneure to leave us," Madame Campan said at last, bringing both women back to the present. "A respite from the Comtesse's machinations would give Your Majesty time to concentrate on more important matters."

Antoinette knew immediately to what she referred. Her husband would indeed be grateful to have the petty bickering over for once and all. If he saw her hand in it, he would be prouder still. Yet the Princess' conscience bothered her.

"But look where we are sending her, Campan!"

"What choice did you have? Unless Honneure is safely married, there is still the chance the King will pursue her."

Antoinette raised her hands to her cheeks and shook her head. "My friend, dear Madame Dupin, offered to take her back at Chenonceau, but I fear to involve her. Du Barry has taken a dislike to her so great she has even been afraid to appear at Court. And I miss her!"

"Perhaps the Comtesse will relent," Madame Campan said reassuringly. "As the Duke assured us. When Honneure is gone, perhaps Madame Dupin will be able to return."

"Oh, it is all so distressing, Campan!" Antoinette sank heavily into the nearest chair. "And the worst part is...what was Philippe thinking? How could he turn to that odious woman, Olivia, so quickly? He and Honneure would have worked it out! In truth, I'm sure Honneure had already come around to our way of thinking. How did everything go so terribly wrong?"

Madame Campan looked up thoughtfully from under dark, heavy brows. "I believe we should give Philippe, himself, a chance to explain it."

"No!" Antoinette flashed, color rising to her cheeks. "Honneure does not wish to speak to him, and neither do I! His actions spoke loud enough for themselves!"

Madame Campan remained silent, but she wondered. She knew both Honneure and Philippe and had seen them together. She believed in their love. Deep in her heart she could not believe Philippe would have betrayed Honneure like this. But someone who hated her would.

"Think, Majesty, about who is involved in this, and about

who might wish Honneure injury, and have her well away from Versailles."

Antoinette's response was interrupted by the chiming of a mantle clock. She jumped to her feet.

"I haven't time to think, Campan. The Abbé will be here any moment, and I've not finished practicing." The Princess returned to her clavichord and sat down. "But I will tell you this," she added as she ran her fingers over the keys. "I am heartsick about the way this has all turned out. My only consolation is that Honneure will be safe. Happiness in this case is secondary. Honneure will be safe and respectably married. She at least will have a chance to lead a decent life."

Madame Campan silently prayed it would be so.

* * *

Honneure marveled that her clothes and personal belongings were packed so neatly in the trunk. Her fingers were as numb as the rest of her. She could not feel them at all, and how she had managed to manipulate them so well was incomprehensible. She closed the lid of the trunk, locked it, and put the key in her small handbag. It had been incredibly kind of the Princess to give her the things she would need for the start of her new life.

Her new life. Married to a stranger, an old man. A new home in Normandy, on the north coast of France. A new life.

Honneure said the words over and over in her mind hoping she would feel something, anything. But her feelings were dead, she felt nothing, and it was probably a blessing. She remembered the first hours and days after she had found Philippe and Olivia together. She remembered the agonizing, unbearable pain and rivers of tears. She had been grateful when the slow numbing had begun. She could even picture

Philippe in her mind's eye now, his beautiful, naked body stretched beside Olivia, without feeling the dagger of grief reenter her heart. She could face her future with a stranger in a strange place without quaking with fear. Her prayer should probably be that this spiritless half-life never ends.

The distant chiming of the Princess' mantle clock told Honneure it was nearly time. The coach her husband-to-be had sent for her would be arriving soon. She glanced about her small room for the final time.

The bed was neatly made, the dresser empty. Nothing personal, no reminder of her remained. Even the dogs were gone, kindly removed by Madame Thierry. The sight of them had brought tears too easily to her eyes.

No, everything was packed away. It was over, finished. She had left nothing behind.

Nothing.

* * *

The jacket no longer fit tightly across his smooth, hard midsection. There was room to spare. Philippe finished closing the long row of silver buttons and pulled his fingers through his hair. He did not care how he looked. He cared about little. He could not eat, he didn't sleep, although he tried. He prayed for sleep, for relief, however brief, from the relentless, gnawing pain and frustration. But he would not give up. Sooner or later, someone would have to talk to him.

Philippe left his tiny room and strode purposefully into the barn aisle toward the doors. He was going to try again, just as he did every morning and afternoon. He would besiege the Princess for as long as it took until she consented to see him, talk to him. If she would only listen to him, he would convince her, he was certain. The Dauphine was one of the most decent people he had ever known. When he told her the truth, she would recognize it. She would speak to Honneure. Everything would be right again. It was just a matter of time.

The winter chill hit him the moment he stepped through the doors, but he barely felt it. His mind was focused on his errand, the task at hand. He left the huge, comma-shaped building and entered the broad, busy avenue that was the approach to the palace. It was crowded with mounted riders, coaches of all description, and pedestrians. He hardly noticed the nondescript carriage just approaching him.

Philippe paused to let the coach-and-four pass him. As he did, he happened to glance at the vehicle's occupant.

She was dressed in a modest hat and suit, suitable for travel. There was a trunk tied to the roof of the carriage.

"Honneure!"

The horses were moving at a smart trot. When she turned her head, their eyes met for only the fraction of a second. Then she was gone. Philippe broke into a run.

"Honneure!"

She heard him, heard his boots pounding the ground behind them. Heard him call her name, again and again. Heard the ragged sound of his breathing. The sob that caught in his throat. Then....nothing. The carriage rolled on.

Honneure did not look back.

Chapter Nineteen

After a morning of brilliant sun and moderate temperatures, the snow had begun to melt. Dark patches of earth blossomed from beneath a thinning blanket of white. Naked tree branches dripped crystalline beads of water. As the afternoon wore on, however, the sky clouded over, and the elongated droplets became icicles. Once again the world froze.

Madame Campan tugged on the leashes to hurry her charges along. Though the sky was dark, it was too cold to snow. She shivered and pulled the shawl more tightly about her shoulders. At least the wind wasn't blowing, she thought gratefully, and quickened her steps as she entered the Forward Court.

She saw him immediately, although it was a wonder she recognized him. His skin was pale, features haggard. There was dark stubble on his chin, purple bruises beneath his eyes, and his long hair tangled at his shoulders. It looked as if he hadn't eaten or slept in days, and her heart went out to him.

Philippe's dark eyes bored straight into her. There was no way she could pass him without stopping. And she did not feel even the tiniest prick of disloyalty. There was more to the story than had been told, and it was about time someone heard it.

The dogs greeted Philippe joyfully, but he ignored them. He held out his hands imploringly to Madame Campan.

"Please," he begged. "You must help me."

"I intend to," Madame Campan stated flatly. She took one of his outstretched hands. "Come with me."

* * *

Gray. Everything was gray. Barely an hour after they had left Versailles and headed north, the sun had disappeared behind a solid wall of sullen clouds. It was as if all light, all life, remained behind in Versailles, and she was headed into a world, a future, of bleak desolation. It hardly seemed to matter.

The coachman had stopped for the night at an inn along the Paris road. She had eaten her solitary dinner in a corner of the public room near a roaring fire and retired early. She had risen in the dark and was waiting for the coachman when he hitched the horses at dawn. The journey had commenced.

They had traveled all day, skirting Paris. The farther north they went, the darker and colder it became. They passed through villages where the cottages seemed to huddle together against the winter chill, columns of smoke rising uniformly from each chimney. The only sound was that of hoofbeats on hard-packed, frozen ground, and the only sensation was the constant, biting cold.

On the afternoon of the second day, almost twenty-four hours exactly after she had left Versailles, Honneure saw the sea for the first time. The carriage road made a gradual turn to the right, until they were headed nearly due east, and suddenly there it was on her left. It was as gray and somber as the sky. Looking down at a wide, sandy beach, she saw lazy waves breaking in a white foam upon the shore.

They rode beside the water for some time, then turned slightly away, to the southeast, and climbed a hill. Trees lined the road and soon surrounded them completely. The cold and dark seemed to press upon Honneure as if they had weight.

There were no signs of life in the forest, not a squirrel or fox, not even a bird. From somewhere nearby she heard the harsh, cheerless cry of a raven, but the voice was disembodied. The road deteriorated, and Honneure was forced to brace herself with hands pressed to the carriage's interior walls. A misting rain began to fall.

Did the frigid, dismal afternoon seem to be lightening? Honneure turned her attention to the view outside the window.

The forest had been left behind, although trees still bordered the road. But they were trees in orderly rows, small trees, with bare, gnarled branches twisting upward toward the somber sky. On Honneure's right they stretched upward to the crest of the hill; on her left they fell away down to the sea. Apples. They were passing through an apple orchard.

Honneure's pulse quickened slightly. She must be nearing her destination.

"The gentleman's name is Armand Tremblay," Madame Campan had said to her gently. They had been sitting together in the Dauphine's salon. "He is a distant cousin of Madame Thierry. He owns a large and prosperous apple orchard near Honfleur, in Normandy, and he has recently lost his wife. He does not know the details of your plight. Madame Thierry's message to him merely said you wished to live a more quiet life away from Court. He is eager to wed again and readily agreed to his cousin's suggestion. We have been fortunate, indeed, to find such a suitable, respectable placement for you. And so quickly."

Fortunate. Yes. She was fortunate.

Through dull eyes, Honneure watched the orchards give way to a grassy expanse. There had been no snow, or it had melted, and the grass was long and surprisingly green. The road turned upward to the right, and she saw a rock wall. The coach passed through an open wooden gate and the horses slowed.

They were in a farm yard. There was a long, low barn of gray stone with a thatched roof. Across from it was a modest, timbered house, its roof also of thatch. The coachman climbed down from his bench, opened her door, and pulled down the steps. Ducking through the low door, Honneure exited the coach and stepped down onto dark, bare earth. The door to the house opened.

The man's age was impossible to determine, but he was well past middle age. He was thin, almost gaunt, with a pronounced stoop. Thin, gray hair straggled across his head. But he walked steadily toward her. There was an expression that might have been a smile on his thin, pinched lips. His brown eyes were as bright as a sparrow's, and they flicked over her from head to foot. He stopped directly in front of her.

"I am Armand," he said in a surprisingly strong voice. "And you will be Honneure Mansart."

She could only nod.

Again his eyes traveled the length of her body. They lingered for a moment on her bosom and slender waist. Then he turned abruptly to the coachman and waved an age-spotted hand.

"Off with you! Begone! You were paid in advance!"

The coachman scurried to remove Honneure's trunk from the top of the coach and dropped it unceremoniously to the ground. Moments later the horses trotted through the gate and, with a sick, sinking feeling in the pit of her stomach, Honneure watched the coach disappear down the road.

"You'll do," Armand said with a throaty chuckle. This time Honneure had no doubt the man was smiling.

But there was no humor in his expression. The sinking

feeling turned to outright dread.

"Since this is a marriage of convenience," Armand went on, "I find it convenient to get it over with as soon as possible. The ceremony will be tomorrow. You can bring your trunk into the house." Without another word he turned and walked away.

Honneure hesitated a moment, but no one else appeared. There did not seem to be any servants. Armand went inside and closed the door without looking back.

She was caught in a nightmare. This had to be a nightmare.

Picking up one end of the heavy trunk, Honneure began to drag it toward the house.

* * *

The Dauphine raised both hands and pressed them to her mouth. Her blue eyes were wide with horror and distress. Even Madame Campan's expression did not remain undisturbed.

"Philippe, dear God," the Princess breathed. "How horrible. How *could* they?"

"We all know very well how," Madame Campan put in. "The real question is, how do we undo the harm?"

"It's all my fault!" Antoinette cried suddenly. "If only I had listened to you sooner. How can you ever forgive me, Philippe?"

He dropped at once to his knees at the Princess' feet. "Just tell me where she's gone. Lend me a horse. Let me go after her. *Please*."

Antoinette and Madame Campan exchanged quick glances. Anguish etched itself into the Dauphine's delicate features.

"She has gone to Normandy," Madame Campan said at length, softly.

Philippe jumped to his feet and turned to the older woman. "Where? Where in Normandy?"

"Near Honfleur, but . . ."

"Just tell me exactly *where*."

Madame Campan sighed and closed her eyes. How could she tell him?

"She has gone to the farm of a man named Armand Tremblay," she continued finally. "It lies to the west of Honfleur. But wait,...wait, Philippe...Listen to me!"

Philippe paused in his flight toward the salon door.

"Please, understand that we were only trying to protect Honneure. The best way we knew how. She...she has gone to Normandy to...to wed Monsieur Tremblay."

Even his blood seemed to freeze in his veins. "What?"

"I'm so sorry, Philippe!" Antoinette said, finding her voice at last. "But it seemed the only way to keep her safe from the King. And it seemed so ideal. She won't even be a servant anymore, but wife to a respected and wealthy far . . ."

"May I take a horse?"

"Philippe . . ."

"*May I take a horse?*"

Antoinette flinched and Madame Campan started to protest, but the expression of stark desperation in Philippe's dark eyes stayed her. She looked at her mistress, her own gaze beseeching.

The Dauphine nodded. "Of course, Philippe," she replied, composure regained. "Take the swiftest mount in my stable. Take the Lipizzan mare if you wish."

Philippe started to leave, but turned and swiftly crossed to the Princess. Once more he dropped to his knees at her feet.

Though he knew it was not proper, he took her small hands in his own and pressed them briefly to his lips.

"Thank you," he whispered. "Thank you."

"Go with God, Philippe. And ride like the wind."

Chapter Twenty

The weather had not relented. Under glowering skies, Honneure climbed up in the farm wagon and sat next to her husband-to-be. The boy who had appeared earlier that morning to feed Armand's few animals and muck the stalls stood in the yard. He watched them roll through the gate, and then he ducked back into the barn. It was as if he was the only other person in the world beside herself and Armand. When he disappeared, Honneure was alone again with the only other human on earth, a stranger. The man she was about to marry. The nightmare went on and on.

The wagon rumbled and bounced along the rutted road. A few snowflakes fell, but they melted rapidly. Armand did not speak. He did not even look at her. Honneure supposed she should be grateful.

Their evening together had been strained and silent. With curt gestures and a few half-grunted words, he had indicated that she was to make him dinner. She had done so, though she had not joined him at the table. He had not seemed to care.

"You will sleep tonight in that room," Armand had said as she emerged from the kitchen, wiping her hands on a linen cloth, and pointed to one of two doors off the small sitting area.

The room was small and spare, but clean. There were lace curtains at the single window, yellowed but intact. There was a plain, pine dresser with a pitcher and basin, a simple, sturdy chair and a bed. Honneure had lain down without even undressing or opening her trunk. When next she had opened her eyes, a pale light was falling through her window.

"Bread and honey will suffice for today," Armand had informed her when she entered the kitchen. "But don't think you will get off so easily any other morning."

That had been the extent of their conversation up to this moment. When he left the house, she had known he expected her to follow, and she had. She had seen the boy and the horse hitched to the wagon. She had climbed in. Now she was on her way to her wedding.

Honfleur was a seaside village. Several cottages surrounded a protected harbor. Small fishing boats rocked at their moorings. The streets were cobbled, and the wagon bumped noisily and uncomfortably toward the stone church. The horse's shoes rang on the stones with an eerie clang.

At least there were people. Honneure looked down on them as they passed them in the wagon. They were dressed in bulky, winter peasant clothes. Some eyed her with mild curiosity. Most ignored her. A few nodded respectfully at Armand.

The priest in the church appeared to have expected them. A tall, spare, balding man, he greeted Armand with quiet dignity, then turned to Honneure.

"You are the bride, Honneure Mansart."

"Yes, Father." She dropped a small curtsy. The priest smiled at her with genuine warmth, and she felt something within her begin to thaw. A prick of emotion deep within her breast reminded her that she was alive.

"You have come from the court of Versailles, I understand," the priest went on.

Honneure nodded but did not allow her mind, her memory, to go back there. She could not bear to.

"Armand has told me your desire is to lead a simpler life, here in the country."

Again, she nodded. The priest's gaze bore into her, and it took all her willpower not to look away. He knew there was more to her story, a great deal more. He was giving her a chance to tell it.

But she would not. The past was dead and gone. Her future might be grim, but it was hers. It was all she had.

"I do indeed wish to live my life away from the Court," she said, looking the priest straight in the eye. That much, at least, was true.

"You were a servant, were you not?"

"Yes, to the Dauphine," Honneure replied with pride. "She is a kind and generous person. It was with her blessing, and her aid, that I was able to come to Normandy and be...be respectably married."

"And you join in this union with Armand Tremblay of your own free will?"

Honneure glanced at the man beside her. He was old enough to be her grandfather. So, however, was the King. At least this man offered marriage, refuge. What did age matter? It mattered as little as love. It mattered not at all.

The pain of the betrayal, the shock and grief, were still there, stuffed down deep within her. It was a ball of fiery agony that would consume her if she let it. She felt it pushing at her, putting pressure on her throat, making it impossible to speak. She swallowed, took a deep breath, shoved it back down. Honneure licked her dry lips.

"Yes," she answered finally. "It is my voluntary decision to wed Armand Tremblay."

"Very well." The priest nodded solemnly. "Then let us waste no more time."

* * *

Philippe knew the mare would run on until she died beneath him. It was her nature. Long favorites of the Viennese court, Lipizzans were the chosen mounts of officers riding into battle. Their nimbleness and agility enabled them to perform incredible maneuvers, both offensive and defensive. More importantly, their intelligence and loyalty had saved many a rider's life. The mare would do whatever he asked of her. But could he ask her to die?

The wind rushed in Philippe's face, and the ground sped past beneath him. She could go on a lot longer, he knew. Her ancestors had been bred and raised on the Slovenian-Italian border, where the grass of the karst was poor in nutrients, but good for horses' bone structure. The result was a breed prized for its strength and stamina.

But she was winded. Foam flying back from her mouth flecked her withers, and her white hide was dark with sweat. He couldn't ask her for more, he just couldn't.

The mare slowed to a collected canter, then dropped down to a trot. Her head was low, her neck so tired she could no longer hold it up. Philippe pulled her to a walk.

Steam rose in the cold air from her shoulders and flanks. Her sides heaved with the effort to breathe. Her nostrils flared wide and red, and smoke puffed from them rapidly. Philippe halted her and felt her knees try to buckle. He slid quickly from the saddle.

There were on a lonely, tree-lined road deep in the heart of the country. Philippe stroked the mare's streaming neck and looked about him for signs of life. In the distance, to the north, he thought he saw wisps of rising smoke. Honfleur? As the mare's breathing slowed and quieted, he thought he could hear a rushing sound, strange to his ears. He had never seen the sea before, but had heard it described. Was that what he was hearing now? The rush of the sea against the shore?

He was close. But was he in time?

The mare would cool faster if she walked. And he would be moving forward. He could not stop, not now. He had to reach Honneure before it was too late.

* * *

It was over, done. She was Madame Honneure Tremblay.

The priest blessed them. Armand pulled something from his pocket and pressed it into the father's hand. He nodded his thanks. The bridal couple turned, walked down the long aisle and left the church without fanfare. Without joy.

Outside the church Armand turned to her. "I hope you don't expect anything else. Life goes on. We'll go back to the farm."

Of course she didn't expect anything else. What else could there be?

As she climbed back into the wagon, however, Honneure's mind led her to a path she had previously refused to travel. All her thoughts up to now had been on getting away from Versailles, away from the King and Philippe's treachery. Her focus had been on simply getting through the minutes of the day, one by one. All her strength had been given to becoming Armand's wife, the wife of a stranger, an old man. And she had done it. It was time to look to the next test. She couldn't ignore it any longer.

The shaggy, cart horse leaned into the breast collar, and the wagon moved forward. A seagull screeched and a group of them swooped low over the harbor. The odor of dried seaweed and rotting fish hung over the village like a miasma. Honneure looked away from it and down the long road back to the farm.

Her stomach grumbled, reminding her it was growing late. When they returned to the farm she would fix her husband supper from the dwindling supply of dried meat and cheese in his larder. She might have time to unpack her trunk. Then she would bank the fire, take down her hair . . .

Beyond that Honneure's thoughts refused to go. She did not mentally open the door to her husband's bedchamber and look within. She did not want to see what lay beyond the threshold. The hours would pass, night would fall, and she would do what she must. She did not have to dwell on it.

The journey back was passed as silently as the journey out. When they pulled into the yard Honneure half expected to see the boy, but he was nowhere about. She climbed down from the wagon.

"Help me unhitch the horse," Armand commanded.

Honneure's fingers were familiar with the harness. It took only minutes to free the old gelding from the traces.

"Take him into the barn. He'll need hay. The cows, too." With that Armand turned and headed back to the house.

Honneure wasn't sure what she had expected. Nothing, in truth. She had merely tried to keep moving forward. She had become Armand's wife, but what did that mean? She supposed she was finding out.

The barn was low-ceilinged and narrow and smelled of musty straw. Three milk cows were tied to the far wall, a pile of hay was pushed into a corner, and there was a loose box stall for the horse. Honneure led him into the dark enclosure, gave him hay, fresh water and briefly rubbed him down. These were familiar things and she took comfort in them.

The early darkness was fast falling. Inside the house Armand sat at the table by the kitchen hearth.

"Light the lamps and fix us something to eat. In the morning milk the cows. If you don't know how, the boy will teach you. But don't depend on him. Now that you're here I won't be needing him any more."

Her position was clear. But she didn't mind. She had always preferred to keep busy, and she knew the value of labor in soothing the soul. Honneure did as she had been instructed.

It was full dark, but there was a pale light outside the windows. Honneure looked out and saw the clouds had parted to reveal a nearly full moon. Armand followed her gaze.

"We'll not need so many lamps with this light. Put them all out but one. Then bring me that bottle on the shelf."

Honneure was getting used to Armand's near constant directions. Once again she did as she was bid. The bottle, she noted, contained brandy. She put it on the table in front of her husband with one glass. He did not ask her to get another.

The evening wore on. The fire burned down, and the level in the bottle fell. Honneure watched Armand's eyelids grow heavy. She prayed for them to close. Eventually, her prayer was answered. His head fell back against the chair, and he snored throatily.

Was it possible? Was she going to escape the trials of her wedding night?

Hardly daring to hope, Honneure eased out of her chair. On tiptoe she crossed the room and put her hand carefully on the door latch to her bedroom. Holding her breath, she slowly opened the door and slipped inside. Only when she had closed it again did she dare to breathe.

The room was dark, but moonlight illumined its features. Honneure quickly undressed, then let down her hair and brushed its shining lengths until they crackled. She pulled back the covers and slipped between the sheets. She closed her eyes.

Sleep would be impossible, she knew. Every muscle in her body was tensed, waiting. Her ears strained for the slightest sound. He would come to her in time, he must. It was part of the price she had to pay.

Honneure never knew when she crossed sleep's hazy threshold. She only knew that the sound she had dreaded to hear had finally come. Coverlet clutched to her breast, she sat bolt upright in bed.

There it was again. But the sound was at the window, not the door. And there was a figure just beyond the glass. She could see it clearly in the moonlight. Heart hammering, Honneure lowered her legs over the edge of the bed. What new nightmare had been sent to torment her? What new horror was in store?

She wanted to scream, but her throat was paralyzed with terror. If she could just make it to the door . . .

As Honneure rose and sidled past the window, prepared to make a dash, the figure suddenly seemed emboldened. He pressed both hands to the glass. He tapped on it, softly.

Honneure froze.

Something was happening inside of her. The great ball of pain was struggling for release again. Now it pushed against her ribs, making it difficult to breathe.

This wasn't possible. It couldn't be happening.

Honneure took a step toward the window. Another.

She could see his face now. Tears streaked his cheeks. His lips silently formed the sound of her name.

He had come to her. She did not want him, had not ever wanted to see him again. But she could not stop herself from moving toward the window. Could not stop her fingers from opening the latch.

Philippe swung the window wide himself. He braced his

hands on the sill, heaved his body upward.

Then he was standing in the room. Honneure threw herself into his arms.

Their tears mingled as Philippe covered her face with kisses. He kissed her eyes, her brow. His lips retraced and found every spot he had kissed the first time he had kissed her. He heard the sob escape her throat, heard her moan his name.

"Philippe . . ."

"Sssshhhh." Gently, he covered her mouth with his hand. "Keep your voice low, Honneure, but don't be afraid to wake the old man. I watched him through the kitchen window. He woke, took another drink and passed out with his head on the table."

A hundred questions, a thousand words crowded Honneure's tongue, tripping it. "But how...why . . ."

"I'll tell you. I'll tell you everything," Philippe whispered urgently. "First and foremost, I did not betray you, Honneure. I did not. I would not."

"But I saw . . ."

"You saw exactly what Olivia and Madame du Barry wanted you to see."

Honneure listened in stunned silence as Philippe related the tale to her, revealed the deception, and exposed it to the light. And in the light it turned to dust and blew away.

Philippe had not deceived her. He loved her. They had both been duped. Madame du Barry had eliminated a rival. Olivia eliminated her rival *and* had her vengeance. Honneure was gone from the palace, but not with Philippe, not as they had planned. The horror of it rose up like a crushing wave breaking over her head. In a moment she would drown.

"Honneure...Honneure, what's wrong?" Philippe grasped her arms as she sat down, heavily, on the edge of the bed.

"Don't look so stricken! Everything will be all right now. I'll take you away from here. We'll leave in the morning!"

Honneure shook her head slowly from side to side, not in negation of Philippe's words, but in denial of the entire hideous situation.

"If you're worried about the old man," Philippe continued, "Don't be. I'll talk to him, explain to him. He can't keep you here against your will."

The sound that came from her wasn't even human. It frightened him. Though he hadn't eaten in almost twenty-four hours, the weakness in his knees wasn't from hunger. Philippe sank to the ground at Honneure's feet. He took her hands.

"Honneure, what is it?" Philippe whispered. "Tell me."

"Armand and I were married. This morning."

Her eyes were so huge he could get lost in her gaze. He wanted to. He wanted to be lost and never found. He did not want to think his next thought, or experience the agony that was going to accompany it. But the knowledge was relentless.

"You're...married."

Honneure nodded, unblinking. Tears welled. "We drove into Honfleur. There was just the priest," she said in a small voice. "We came back here, and Armand started drinking . . ."

Philippe closed his eyes. Thank God she had married an old man who was fond of the bottle.

"So nothing...nothing happened tonight?" It was more a statement than a question. When Honneure shook her head, he let out a long sigh. "Listen, Honneure, my love. It isn't too late. It *can't* be."

"But, Philippe . . ."

This time it was Philippe who shook his head in denial. "No. He'll let you go. He has to let you go. He'll release you. I'll go to him, talk to him. First thing in the morning!"

Was it possible? Did she dare to let herself hope? Philippe's excitement was contagious. But she was afraid.

"Armand is not...not an easy man, Philippe."

"I'll convince him. We'll be together, my love. Please don't think any other way but that. We belong together, and we will *be* together, Honneure. I promise you."

A tiny spark of hope ignited in her breast. Could it be that her future did not lie at the bottom of a black abyss after all?

"Believe me, my love," Philippe murmured. "Believe."

He kissed the hands he held within his own. He pressed his lips to each knuckle, the back of her hand and then turned it over and kissed her fingers, her palm. He heard her breathing quicken.

The nightmare, perhaps, had ended. But now she was caught in a dream. Philippe was here, in her room. Moonlight streamed through the window as he kissed her hands. It seemed the most natural thing in the world to pull him closer to her.

Philippe felt Honneure pull her hands free. She placed them on either side of his face and gently pulled him nearer. His head pillowed against her breast, and he could hear, feel, her heart beating. Through the thin material of her nightdress, he could feel the warmth of her flesh. His senses swam. He rocked back on his heels to clear his head.

It was her wedding night. Events had gone horribly, terribly wrong, and Honneure found herself wed to the wrong man. But Philippe had come to her. Philippe, her love, her life.

And it was her wedding night.

Honneure rose slowly from the bed. In one smooth, seductive motion she pulled her nightdress over her head. The gauzy material trailed a moment from her fingers and dropped to the floor. She raised her arms and lifted the long, heavy lengths of her hair from her shoulders and then let them fall again. Philippe sucked in his breath.

There was not a more beautiful woman in the world. Everything about her was perfect. Her pink-tipped breasts were full, but not too heavy. Her waist was slender, hips ever so slightly flared. Her legs were straight and shapely. She stood before him with unaffected grace. He rose to his feet.

It never occurred to Honneure to feel shame in her nakedness. There was one love in her life, one husband in her heart. It had always been so. She belonged to Philippe in every way. As he belonged to her.

It was Philippe's turn. She had seen him unclothed once before, when he had laid at Olivia's side. Even in her shock and horror, a part of her brain had registered the beauty and elegance of his form. Her lips parted with desire as he revealed himself again, but so differently this time. So differently.

Philippe unbuttoned his coat and let it fall. His shirt followed. He stood on alternate legs, perfectly balanced, to remove his boots.

Honneure's eyes followed the dark line that began at his throat, down across his muscular chest to his flat belly. She watched him hook his thumbs into his waistband. He was hard already, straining against the taut material. A hot, delicious weakness blossomed in her belly.

Naked and fully erect, Philippe stood before Honneure. She held out her arms.

Her first sensation was the softness of her breasts compressing against his powerful chest. The columns of his thighs pressed to hers. His rigid, pulsing maleness seared a brand into her skin. She closed her eyes to shut the world away and experience pure sensation.

She was his, she was open before him. He had merely to take the cup and drink from it. Philippe tilted Honneure's chin upward and brought his lips down to hers.

She had tasted him before, but never so languidly, so sensuously. She reveled in the feeling of his tongue gliding across hers, searching the secret places of her mouth. She felt the breath from his nostrils blow softly, warmly against the skin between her nose and upper lip. It was so intimate, so arousing. Her hips thrust into his as if of their own accord. Desire became so overwhelming, her entire body and mind were focused on one thing only.

As she melted into his arms, Philippe lifted Honneure and set her gently on the bed. He lay down next to her and cupped a breast in his hand. Her head fell back, her eyes closed and her lips parted. Her breath came in short ragged gasps. She captured his hand and guided it to the warm, moist place between her legs. The heat of her was intense. She moaned as he stroked her. Then it was his turn to groan as she grabbed his member and explored it with her fingertips.

The knowing had only begun, but its completion would have to wait. Nothing could be between them anymore. Not time nor space, air nor moonlight.

Philippe rolled on top of Honneure and entered her, slowly at first. When he felt the resistance he stopped, although it was the hardest thing he had ever done. He stopped and caressed her face and kissed her lips, and suddenly she drove against him. His mouth on hers stifled her cry.

The pain was only momentary. Joy and passion surged through her limbs as she wrapped her arms about his neck, her legs about his hips. Then Philippe began to move, and she rocked against him, and the world went away.

Chapter Twenty-One

It was warmer in the barn than outside, but not by a great deal. The winter clouds were obstinate and refused to be blown away by the rising wind. They wisped and tattered raggedly, allowing the sun to shine through for a few precious minutes, then melded together again. The wind moved them across the sky, but could not scatter them. The temperature fell.

Honneure's hands were numb, but she forced her fingers to work, pulling the cow's teat down and releasing it. To her surprise, the art of milking had come to her easily, and it was a good thing.

The boy had appeared. Dawn had not yet arrived, although there was a lightening of the heavy darkness. He had slipped into the barn just as she finished raking manure into a pile to remove later. His eyes were wide and frightened, and he did not say a word.

"Good morning," she had said to him in what she hoped was a reassuring tone. He had not replied. "Are you here to show me how to milk? I certainly hope so because I haven't a clue."

Still silent, the boy had fetched a stool and a bucket which he placed near one of the cows. Then he came to her and tugged at her hand.

Honneure had followed the boy and obediently sat on the stool as he indicated. Then he crouched down beside her, reached up to pat the cow's flank, and put his small hands on her udder. With what seemed an expert motion, he coaxed a strong stream of milk into the pail. He worked rhythmically until the bucket was almost a third full. He stopped and gazed at her, brows arched.

"Do you want me to try?"

The boy nodded. Honneure had gripped a teat and tried to copy the boy's motion. Nothing happened. She tried again. Nothing. His small, cool hands covered hers and guided her fingers.

Success. Honneure compressed her lips with grim satisfaction. They worked together until the pail was over half full and the udder went dry. The boy stood up and backed away.

"Thank you," Honneure said to him with a smile. "You're a very good teacher. Will you . . ."

The boy turned and ran. He was gone before she could blink.

A great sadness had filled Honneure. The boy was mute, she supposed. But what else he had suffered she could only guess. He certainly didn't seem to want to linger here. She didn't want to speculate on the reason why. She didn't want to know anything more about Armand than she did already. Hopefully, she would not have to.

The last cow was milked. Honneure straightened and pressed a hand to the small of her back. It ached from the unfamiliar position. Then she rose and carried the heavy bucket to the barn door where she set it next to the others. She looked outside.

It was impossible to judge the time by the sun. Its light was once again entirely obscured by clouds. The wind had dropped, defeated, and the army of gray marched in a tight, triumphant formation across the sky above her. Had two hours passed since the dawn?

Honneure's stomach did a somersault.

"I'll come two hours after the sunrise," Philippe had whispered as he hastily pulled on his clothes. She had watched with sinking heart as he had covered the body, the flesh, she cherished. "I don't want to surprise him too early in the morning with this. At least let him have his coffee first."

Philippe had smiled, but she had not been able to smile back. Despite Philippe's reassurances, despite that she knew they were meant for one another and must be together forever, she was afraid. As she had told Philippe earlier, Armand was not an easy man.

Philippe had taken her in his arms a final time in the cold, dark hours before dawn. He had kissed her and smoothed the hair from her face.

"Two hours after sunup, Honneure. Until then, I love you."

Tears had been so thick in her throat, that she had not been able to answer. She had touched her fingers to her lips and stretched them to Philippe as he climbed through the window. For long moments after he had disappeared into the darkness, she had stood shivering in front of the open window. *Come back. Come back, my angel, and take me away with you.*

Honneure recalled her silent prayer as she trudged from the barn to the house. Philippe would return, she had no doubt. It was only a matter of time. But what would happen then? Her stomach gave another unpleasant squeeze as she pushed open the door.

"What took you so long?"

Armand sat in his chair by the hearth. One gnarled hand was wrapped around a cup of coffee she had prepared earlier.

"I...I milked and fed the cows and mucked the barn."

"We need eggs. You need to take a bucket of milk and walk to Widow Maurier's place. She has hens. She'll trade you for the milk."

Fear wrapped its icy fingers around Honneure's heart. "Now? You want me to go now?"

"What else have we got to eat?"

"There's some bread and cheese. I . . ."

"Stale."

"I could toast the bread." Honneure rang her hands, hoping her desperation was not as apparent as if felt. "Then I can fetch the eggs, perhaps a chicken to roast for . . ."

"Have it your way," Armand grunted. "I'm hungry." He drained his cup and thrust it across the table toward Honneure.

Wordlessly, she took it and refilled it. She could feel the rapid beating of her heart all the way up in her throat. *Please come, Philippe. Please come now.*

She was slicing the last of the loaf when she heard the hoofbeats. She tried not to look, but she couldn't help it. Honneure turned to the window.

The white mare was achingly familiar. Philippe rode her easily, gracefully. The gate was open, and he loped through it and into the yard. Honneure cast a sidelong glance at Armand.

"What the hell . . ." Hands braced on the table, he pushed himself stiffly to his feet. "That man is dressed in livery of some sort." Armand looked sharply at Honneure. "What have you got to do with this?"

She could only shake her head helplessly.

"We'll see about this," Armand declared, and marched over to a sideboard in the sitting area. He pulled open a drawer and extracted a pistol.

Honneure caught her breath. Armand fixed her once more

with his cold gaze.

"You're sure you don't want to tell me what you know?"

She couldn't have spoken if her life depended on it. She couldn't take her eyes from the pistol.

"I'll find out for myself then. And woe be to you if I don't like what I hear!"

Trembling all over, arms crossed tightly over her breast, Honneure followed Armand with faltering steps to the door. She saw Philippe dismount and walk toward the house. He stopped halfway up the stone-flagged path and held up his hands defensively.

"Don't shoot, please," Philippe said quickly. "I'm not here to do anyone any harm."

"I'll be the judge of that," Armand said tersely. The gun didn't waver. "State your business."

Philippe's gaze slid away from Armand to rest on Honneure. Only for a moment. But the old man did not miss it.

"So, it's that way, is it?" Something that might pass for a humorless smile touched the corners of the old man's mouth. "You're here on some errand involving my...*wife*?"

Philippe tensed. This was not an auspicious beginning. He would have to be very, very careful.

"I am here about Honneure, yes," he admitted. "But we can talk civilly, without a pistol between us."

Armand snorted. "We can't talk at all. Get back on your horse."

"Monsieur . . ."

Armand cocked the pistol. "*Get back on your horse!*"

The cry escaped her lips before she could stop it. Honneure pressed her hands to her mouth. Eyes fixed on the gun, Philippe slowly backed away.

"I may be old, but I'm not stupid," Armand said in a chill, tight voice. "I never thought that a young, pretty woman would leave the palace of Versailles and come to Normandy to marry someone like me just for the joy of living the country life. There had to be more to it than that. And here it is."

"Monsieur, please, listen," Philippe begged, hands still held palm outward to Armand. "There's been a terrible mistake . . ."

"There certainly has been. And you made it." Armand raised the weapon until it was pointed directly between Philippe's eyes.

"Armand, no!" Honneure darted forward and grabbed her husband's arm. "Stop!"

The old man lowered his arm and looked Honneure in the eye. "You love this man, don't you?"

Armand's gaze challenged her. "I love him with all my heart," she whispered.

The old man turned to Philippe. "And you love this woman."

"She was meant to be my wife."

"But something went wrong, you say."

Philippe nodded slowly. He didn't like the look in the old man's eye, or the half-smile on his thin mouth.

"You'd do anything to have her back, wouldn't you?"

This time Philippe did not bother to respond. Fear held him absolutely still. An instant later his fear was realized.

Honneure was surprised by how swiftly Armand was able to move. Before she knew what was happening, he had his arm around her neck. His forearm was pressed to her windpipe making it difficult to breathe. With his other hand he lifted the pistol to her head. She felt the cold barrel pushed into her temple.

"I don't know who you are, and I don't care," Armand hissed. "But I know what you want, and I *do* care about that."

Philippe had never known such terror, or such helplessness. The old man was a heartless bastard with little to lose. He had no doubt that the spite and bitterness Armand had spent a lifetime cultivating could come to a head right here and now.

"Don't shoot her," Philippe said in a low, soothing tone. "Please...just...don't...shoot."

"I won't. Not if you get on that horse and ride out of here."

Eyes fixed to the hammer of the cocked pistol, Philippe backed away. He felt as if his heart was being torn from his breast.

"And let me make it perfectly clear what will happen if I ever see you anywhere near here again."

Philippe drew even with the mare. He reached up onto her withers and gripped the reins.

"I'll shoot her on the spot," Armand continued. "I'll drop her like a dog. If I have to lose her, at least it won't be to you."

Philippe did not doubt a word the old man said. He climbed into the saddle.

Small, animal-like sounds issued from Honneure's throat. She did not even realize she was making them. This couldn't be happening. It couldn't.

But it was.

She was losing Philippe, descending back into the abyss.

The expression in his gaze, his last glance, would go with her to her grave. She closed her eyes as he turned and rode away.

Armand waited until the rider disappeared down the road and he could no longer hear the sound of hoofbeats. He released his grip on Honneure, and she fell away from him, hands clutching her throat. Her eyes were wide with fright and sorrow.

"You...you *would* kill me, wouldn't you?" Honneure croaked.

Armand studied her a moment. She wasn't hard to look at, although that was not why he had wanted a wife. Those days were over. She looked too skinny, but she was sturdy. And she wasn't afraid to work.

"No," Armand said at length. "No, I don't think I would kill you. You're too valuable to me. But he's not." The old man jerked his head in the direction of the road. "So, if you're thinking to lure him back here and make your escape, think again. It's *him* I'll shoot on the spot, like a dog, if he shows his face around here. And don't think I won't. Nobody'd blame me for killing some young stud nosing around my wife."

Armand started toward the house, then stopped and looked back at Honneure. The smile he gave her made her blood run cold.

"You're mine now. Get used to it. You're here to stay."

Chapter Twenty-Two

May 1772

High, white clouds scudded across a faultlessly blue sky. The sun seemed unusually bright, and Honneure was grateful for the brisk spring breeze. She had adopted the dress of the country, and the material of her simple skirt and blouse was thick and coarse. Though it was still early and cool, her skin was already slick with sweat. She heaved the last of the manure onto the growing pile, stepped back, and scrubbed the back of her hand across her forehead.

Surrounding farmers would be coming soon for their share of this odiferous bounty. They would spread it on their truck gardens and, in return, Armand would be given a share of the eventual harvest. In the meantime, Armand bought what produce they needed in Honfleur. She never accompanied him, she wasn't allowed. She didn't mind. She minded little these days.

Honneure carried the pitchfork back into the barn and set it against the wall. The cows had been turned out to graze, and the barn's only remaining occupant, the old gray gelding, whinnied softly to her. She opened the door to his stall and stroked his ragged, patchy coat.

"You're losing your winter fur, aren't you? I'll bet it itches."

As if in response, the horse rubbed his face against Honneure's side. She laughed. "I hear you. I'll get the brush."

Handfuls of long hair fell away as Honneure vigorously curried the aging animal. When she was finished, he bent his thick neck and looked at her with large, baleful brown eyes. She put down the brush, held out her hand, and he shoved his muzzle into her palm. With her free hand she stroked his long face.

"You're a good boy," Honneure murmured. "Such a good old boy. You're going to miss me when I'm gone. I'm going to miss you, too."

A now-unfamiliar moisture rose to her eyes. It had been months, literally, since she had cried. She had cried all the tears left in her when Philippe had ridden away. She had dried up, literally and figuratively. All that was left in her was cold, hard determination; first to survive; second to reunite with Philippe. And her plan was in motion. Soon, with luck, she would be gone. But she would miss the animals, and worry about them. She doubted they had ever known a moment's kindness until she came.

With regret, Honneure left the stall and pulled the door closed behind her. At the barn door she picked up one of the covered pails of milk and set off across the yard. She would have to hurry now on her next errand.

Spring rains and increased wagon traffic had left the road deeply rutted. Honneure walked along the side, pausing often to shift the milk pail from one hand to the other. She had to admit she was getting tired more easily now. She looked around for the boy, who usually joined her on her walks to the Widow Maurier's farm and helped her carry the milk. But she didn't see him yet. She prayed he had not endured another beating. Or something worse. Honneure sighed, changed hands again, and walked on.

She would miss the boy, too. He had grown very dear to

her. She let her memory meander back to the first time she had seen him again after Philippe's traumatic departure.

Several days had passed, and the weather finally seemed to make up its mind. The wind died away, the gray clouds silently massed anew, and the temperature rose subtly. Snow began to fall, lightly at first, dusting the fence, the roof of the house as well as the roof of the barn. Later, however, it came in earnest. When Honneure had made the coffee and left the house to perform her morning chores, she could barely see past the front path. She could not, in fact, see the front path at all. The snow, when she stepped in it, came up over her ankles.

It had been difficult to open the barn door. She had tugged and tugged, gaining inches at a time, ripping off a fingernail. Suddenly he was there, his little hands under hers, pulling with all his might. The door opened wide enough for them to slip inside, but he looked over his shoulder first, toward the house.

Once inside, Honneure had knelt and put her hands on the boy's thin shoulders. She smoothed a wisp of dirty brown hair back from his pale brow. She was aware of how painfully thin he was.

"Thank you for helping me. Thank you for teaching me to milk the cows. I think we're going to be friends, don't you?"

The boy had nodded solemnly.

"Then will you tell me something? I only want to help you, as you've helped me. Will you tell me if you're afraid of something?" Honneure had asked. "Are you afraid of Monsieur Tremblay?"

The boy shrugged. His eyes would not meet hers.

"Has he ever hurt you? Hit you?"

The boy had shaken his head, but Honneure knew Armand.

"Has he ever yelled at you?" she persisted. "Threatened to tell your parents you're lazy if you didn't move fast enough for him?"

The look of fear in his eyes had been enough. She hadn't needed to feel the hunching of his pitiful shoulders.

"Does Monsieur Tremblay say that to you because he knows you're afraid of your parents? Because he knows *they'll* punish you?"

The boy had tried to twist away from her, but Honneure held him tightly. She had seen mistreated animals before. She knew how to soothe them, heal them. First, however, she had to be sure.

The boy winced when Honneure gently ran her hand down his back. She could count his vertebrae. She could feel the welts.

Sorrow flooded her veins, and her heart swelled with the added burden. Honneure released her grip on the boy's shoulders and folded him into her arms. He was stiff, rigid, his hands braced against her chest, trying to push her away. She held on, murmured in his ear, and gently rocked back and forth. She could feel the tension, the resistance, drain from him. When he relaxed entirely, she picked him up in her arms and held him cradled like an infant.

Slowly, ever so slowly, one scrawny arm had crept around her neck. He turned his face into her breast.

"You're safe here," she had whispered. "You will always be safe here with me."

The minutes had ticked away. Honneure was afraid her arms would no longer be able to hold the child when he looked up at her. He signaled for her to put him down, and she obliged. He quirked a finger for her to bend down to him.

They were eye to eye. The boy had taken her face in his

small, dirty hands and kissed her softly, innocently, on the mouth. He touched his hand to his heart, and then to hers.

Seconds later he had fled, disappearing as swiftly and silently as he had appeared. She hadn't seen him again until days later when she was struggling along the snowy road with her milk pail. He wasn't there one minute, the next he was. He had taken the pail from her and carried it until they had reached the gate to the widow's small farm. He handed the bucket back to her and was gone.

So had their relationship progressed. Over time they had learned to communicate quite effectively with one another. Honneure had learned the boy's name was Henri. He had managed to convey to her that he would do anything to help her, as she had helped him. The temptation had proved too great.

Honneure paused at the side of the road and put the bucket down. She rubbed her hands together and looked around again.

Long rows of apple trees on either side of her were greening, buds swelling on the branches. A cotton-tailed rabbit hopped into view just ahead and nibbled at the roadside grass. But there was no sign of Henri.

A twinge of anxiety triggered a surge of nausea. Honneure clapped a hand over her mouth, but the feeling passed.

Where was he? The favor he had been doing her was a dangerous one. Had he been caught? Honneure's hand slipped into her pocket.

The precious letter was there. Her fingers traced the edges of it. She carried it everywhere with her, afraid to leave it behind at the house. If Armand found it, he would know she had someone meeting the mail rider for her, since she was never able to go to Honfleur herself. Conversely, if she had someone to bring her letters, that person might also be taking them away. And Armand must not find out that she was able to communicate, secretly, with the outside world. He must not know, until it was too late, that she had been able to confide in, and ask for aid from, the one person who could actually help her, save her, return her to her love.

A jay scolded, drawing Honneure's attention back to the moment. It was growing late, but she had almost reached Widow Maurier's farm, and she was not feeling her best at the present. She would wait a little while longer and hope that Henri arrived.

To pass the time, Honneure drew the much-read letter from her pocket. Finding a stump at the side of the road, she sat down and smoothed away the creases in the paper over her bent knees. She read:

"Dearest Honneure,

"How delighted we all were to receive your letter and know you are well. I was so distressed to learn from the Dauphine of your plight and was dubious about its solution, as were your parents when I related it to them. There had been such high hopes for a union between you and Philippe. But perhaps this is best after all. Philippe will retain his very excellent position, you are safe from the King's notorious appetites, and you have actually taken a step up! The Princess has assured us that your husband is of some reputation in Normandy and is quite prosperous as well. Your parents and I are happy for you, especially now that you have reassured us of your health and well-being."

Honneure signed deeply and looked up briefly at the passing clouds. She had hated to deceive her parents and Madame Dupin. She had wanted to pour her heart out to them, tell them the truth, the real circumstances. She had wanted them to know about the deception and tragic misunderstanding that had led to the marriage they all thought so highly of now, a marriage that was simply a continuation of the nightmare.

But just as the Dauphine had exercised caution and restraint in relating details to Madame Dupin, so had Honneure. The first missive had to be bland and innocuous in case Armand intercepted it. She didn't want him to think anything other than she had accepted her fate. With a sigh, she returned to her letter.

"I myself have good news, dear Honneure. Earlier in the year, about the same time you left for Normandy, the Princess made peace (on the surface at least) with the du Barry. One of the results was that I was able to return to Court. I am happy to report that the Princess and I resumed our friendship as if nothing had intervened. It was especially fortunate as only recently there was another unpleasant incident, and I was exceedingly glad to be here to comfort the Dauphine.

"I will not bore you with political details, but of late there has been a strain on French and Austrian relations. As a result there was a witty, but cruel, dispatch floating around that vilified the Dauphine's mother, the Empress. The du Barry got her hands on it and read it aloud at one of her soirees. To add insult to injury, she insinuated to the King that Maria Theresa's letters to her daughter (which the dear child keeps hidden or burns) contained anti-French advice. Nothing could be further from the truth, but the King listened to her. Following up on her victory, the du Barry let it be known that she would call at the Dauphine's apartments.

"I'm sure I need not tell you how our Princess felt about this turn of events! She behaved royally, however, as you would expect. She acquiesced and received the du Barry. She even spoke to her. But the horrid woman was displeased with the Dauphine's tone and expression, apparently. She has said it amounted to a snub! Since then, she has stepped up her verbal attacks on our dear Princess, and the Court is being divided most painfully and embarrassingly. We shall see what happens!

"Certainly I will keep you informed, dear Honneure. I know how devoted to the Dauphine you were, and remain.

"Your parents are in the process of composing a letter to you, but ask me to send their best in the interim.

"All love to you, dearest child."

Madame Dupin's familiar signature scrawled across the bottom of the page. Honneure folded the letter and returned it to her pocket.

Life remained the same at Versailles. Madame du Barry continued her wicked ways. A surge of anger helped Honneure rise to her feet and pick up the pail again.

Would this go on, unchecked, forever? Would that evil woman be able to go on wrecking lives and get away with it?

Honneure had to force herself to remain calm. Blood rushing to her head had caused her a moment's dizziness, and she could afford to rest no longer. She was late. Armand would be waiting for her with his bad temper and needling questions.

There was still no sign of Henri, and Honneure was worried sick about him. He almost never missed an opportunity to walk with her and help her carry the pail. But she was probably just overanxious. The waiting was beginning to tell.

There was no help for it. She had to hurry. Gripping her pail, Honneure hastened up the lane to Widow Maurier's farm.

* * *

The house was built on a gently sloping hillside and was timbered like Armand's, but much smaller. A wooden shed that listed slightly to the right stood behind the house. Chickens went in and out through the open door. Next to the shed was a long row of rabbit hutches, partially filled. There was a patch of vegetable garden, and flowers bordered the path to the front door. A low, stone fence surrounded the whole. Widow Maurier's place was petite, tidy, and entirely welcoming. Honneure always looked forward to the days they needed eggs.

There was no answer to Honneure's knock, and she pushed the front door open an inch or two. A fire burned in the kitchen hearth, but no one sat at the table. The bed in the corner was neatly made. The room was empty. Honneure pulled the door shut, put down her pail and went around the side of the house.

"Madame Maurier?" she called softly.

"Honneure?" a familiar voice replied. "Honneure, come this way...quickly. Help me, please!"

The voice seemed to be coming from beyond the perimeter of the stone wall, somewhere farther up the hillside among the trees.

"Madame Maurier, I don't see you!" Honneure called back. An instant later she saw an arm wave at her from a dense thicket of saplings. Honneure hurried through the back gate and up the hill.

She wasn't sure what she was going to see, some injured animal perhaps. Madame Maurier was as kindhearted as Honneure herself and unable to turn away from a creature in distress. The sight that greeted her eyes, however, was totally unexpected. The shock of it hit her like a physical blow, and Honneure fell to her knees.

"Henri!"

"You know this child?"

"Yes...yes, I know him." Honneure's hands had already gone to work.

The cut over his eye was superficial, but had bled profusely. The other eye was blackening. Honneure's fingers moved cautiously over the boy's ribs. None seemed to be broken. His legs were intact. His right arm, however, was twisted at an unnatural angle.

"The pain of the break is probably what made him lose consciousness," Honneure said, lifting an eyelid to examine Henri's pupil. "Did you just find him here, like this?"

"No, actually." Madame Maurier sat back on her heels, cursing the pain in her knees and hips. "You were late and I was a little worried, so I walked down the road a ways. I saw the child, sort of...crouched...by the side of the road, covered with blood. I called to him, but he ran. He ran all the way up here and then tripped and fell. When I reached him, he was as you see him. "

"Oh, Henri...Henri!" Honneure smoothed the boy's brow and, with the edge of her apron, tried to wipe the blood from his eyes. They opened. "Henri!"

His entire expression was one of relief...until he turned his head and saw Madame Maurier. In spite of his injuries, he tried to scramble away.

"Henri, no...wait." Honneure held the boy gently but firmly. "Madame Maurier is a friend. She'll help you. She helps *me*. Do you understand?"

The boy kept his suspicious gaze fixed on the old woman for a long moment. Then his expression softened. With his good left arm, he reached for Honneure.

"That's my boy," Honneure said soothingly. "Put your

arm around my neck. I'm going to carry you into the house."

The boy immediately tensed.

"It's all right, I promise you. Haven't I told you you would always be safe with me?"

He nodded, and she lifted him. Madame Maurier pushed herself to her feet with a grunt.

"You're safe with me in my house, too, son," the old woman added, a hard edge to her voice. "That bastard stepfather of yours can't touch you here."

Honneure halted and looked sharply at Madame Maurier.

"I thought you said you knew the boy, Honneure."

"I know *him*, nothing else."

"Then come. Come in the house and tend to him, and I'll tell you what I know."

Inside, Madame Maurier draped a clean, white cloth over her bed, and Honneure laid Henri down. "I'm going to have to set his arm," Honneure said needlessly. "He'll probably pass out again when I do."

"Good. Then we'll have our...chat."

Honneure leaned over Henri. "You've broken your arm, dear, and I'm going to have to straighten it. It will hurt very much."

The look in the boy's eyes broke Honneure's heart. It told her the pain she was about to inflict was nothing to him.

"You trust me, don't you, Henri? I'm only trying to help you, to make you better. Is it all right if I do this? "

In response Henri smiled and took her hand. He touched it first to her heart, and then to his. Tears she thought never to shed again rose hot in her eyes.

Honneure gently disengaged her hand, put both on Henri's arm and, with her fingers, gently probed the break.

"Hold his elbow, Madame, please. Tightly," she said

without taking her eyes from the boy's. "I love you, Henri." Holding his gaze, smiling into his eyes, she pulled his arm, hard.

The child passed out again as Honneure had predicted. She worked quickly, splinted the arm with a stick of kindling, and bound it with linen strips Madame Maurier provided. While Honneure cleaned Henri's cut, the old woman made tea and began her tale.

"Life is as bad as it gets for this boy," the old woman said as she measured loose tea into a pot. "His mother, Claudia, had a certain...reputation...and probably doesn't even know who the boy's father is. After he was born they lived pretty much hand to mouth, begging and such. Then Adrien Ducis showed up. There's not a meaner snake slithering on earth than that man. We all thought...hoped...he'd been lost at sea on a fishing boat. But it seems he'd only taken a wrong turn for a while. So he comes back to Honfleur and takes up right away with Claudia. Says he'll give her a roof over her head, decent food. *Respectability*." Madame Maurier nearly spat the word. "But on one condition."

The old woman poured boiling water from a kettle into the teapot. "I suppose you can guess what the condition was."

Honneure straightened from the bed and turned to Madame Maurier. She felt cold all over. "No children," she stated in a flat, emotionless tone.

The widow nodded. "Especially not a *defective* one."

"So how...how does he live?"

"He does chores here and there, earns a little money or a bit of bread. To answer your next question, he sleeps where he can, or in that shack his mother calls a house when Adrien is away fishing. She even feeds him from time to time."

"Then how . . ."

The old woman shrugged. "From what I've heard, Adrie
catches up with the boy every now and then. He knows th
boy sneaks around home when he's away. My thought is he'
like to kill him and be done with it."

Honneure sat down, abruptly, at the widow's table. He
knees felt weak. She wrapped her hands around the steamin
cup placed in front of her.

"I can see how fond you are of him," the widow said in
kindly voice. "And I know now he was waiting for you when
saw him alongside the road." Honneure's look was all th
reply she needed. "Don't feel guilty," she said, coverin
Honneure's hand with her own. "None of this is your fault. H
wasn't beaten because of you. This has been going on sinc
long before you came. If you've befriended him, as I believ
you have, then God will bless you for it."

Honneure looked up at Madame Maurier, but she couldn'
speak. Once again scalding tears had risen to her eyes an
choked her throat. She thought her heart had hardened an
could never be broken again. She had prayed it was so. Ye
now . . .

"Oh...oh no!"

"What is it, Honneure?"

"The time...I forgot all about the time." She pushed bac
from the table and rose. "I've been here far too long. Wil
you...I mean . . ."

"Of course I'll take care of the boy. Don't worry.
Madame Maurier followed Honneure to the door. "Tel
Armand I asked you to stay and help me."

Honneure turned in the doorway. "How can I ever . . ."

"Thank me?" the old woman finished for her. "Just com
back. Soon and often. And don't forget your eggs."

Anne Marie Maurier smoothed back wisps of her snow

white hair and watched Honneure hurry down the path. She
had lived a long life. She had had a long and happy marriage.
She had never had children, but it seemed God was going to
make up for that now. Anne Marie glanced at the sleeping
child on the bed.

He would be the easy one. His story was straightforward.
He was badly damaged, but he was young, and he would heal,
God willing. But this other.

Honneure had disappeared from sight already. Madame
Maurier closed the door and returned to her cup of tea.

The girl's path to Normandy had not been a straight one,
that much was clear. She wondered if Honneure would ever
share the story of its twists and turns with her.

And she wondered when Honneure was going to tell her
she was pregnant.

Chapter Twenty-Three

Honneure had fed the old gray gelding early so he coul)
finish his breakfast before she had to hook him to the wago)
It was Armand's day to drive to Honfleur for supplies. H
hobbled into the yard just as she straightened the long rei)
over the horse's broad back.

Armand stopped next to the wagon and held up a slip (
paper. "You sure you need all this?"

"If you want me to bake you fresh bread," Honneu)
replied evenly. She was learning to deal with the irascible ol
man, hopefully for not much longer. "Otherwise buy thr)
loaves."

"They'll be stale by week's end."

Honneure shrugged. "Suit yourself."

The old man climbed into the wagon without anoth)
word. Honneure knew she would have everything she ha)
asked for. He treated her like a slave, not a wife, it was tru)
but the arrangement suited her. He asked no more from h)
than her labor, and she slept alone in her little room. He di)
not seem to mind her company, but did not solicit h)
conversation. The circumstances were bearable.

Honneure waited until Armand had rattled out of sight i)
the direction of Honfleur. Then she hurried along the road)
the widow's house. She did not bring milk because they di)
not need eggs, but Armand's absence gave her the opportuni)
to visit. She had not seen Madame Maurier or the boy sin)

she had set his arm, three days earlier. She was anxious to know how he fared.

Anne Marie was bent over, one hand on the small of her back, picking dead petals from the flowers along the front walk. She straightened, smiling, when she saw Honneure.

"The boy's fine," she said by way of greeting. "His arm will mend with no ill effect, I think. You did a good job setting the bone."

Honneure took a deep breath. "I was worried. I've only tended to animals before."

"Well, you acquitted yourself ably. There's just one thing," the widow said as she headed toward her front door. "The boy's agitated about something. I can't understand what's upsetting him, but maybe you will."

"I'll try."

Henri had been sitting, knees drawn up, on a palette the widow had prepared for him in a corner of the room. He jumped up when he saw Honneure and ran to her. He held out his splinted arm, smiled, and caressed her cheek.

"You're welcome," Honneure whispered, and briefly, carefully, hugged the boy. She held him at arm's length to inspect the laceration and blackened eye, but his smile slipped away suddenly, and he shook his head.

"What is it, Henri?"

"You see?" the old woman said over her shoulder.

Something was clearly wrong. "Take your time, Henri," Honneure said. "Try to explain to me what's wrong."

The boy jabbed a finger into his chest, and then pointed at the door.

"You want to leave?"

Henri did something totally baffling. He shook his head soberly, and then nodded vigorously. "That's what I don't understand," the widow said. "He doesn't want to leave, but he does."

"I think I understand," Honneure responded. "Henri, you don't want to leave Madame Maurier's house, do you, not for good? But you do want to go somewhere?"

The boy nodded excitedly.

"Where, Henri?" Honneure prompted. "Where do you want to go?"

The boy abruptly sobered again. His gaze dropped from Honneure's face to her skirt pocket. He held out his hand tentatively, brows arched.

"Go ahead, Henri."

The child touched her pocket. His fingers slipped inside. He withdrew the letter she always carried with her. He pointed at it, and then down the road. His eyes widened with fear.

Henri's message was instantly clear to her, and Honneure's stomach plummeted to her feet. She wondered that she hadn't thought of it before, especially with Armand driving to Honfleur today.

"Pull that chair over here, quickly," the old woman said to the child. "Honneure, sit. You're as pale as a ghost."

Honneure sank gratefully onto the wooden chair. Her heart thumped painfully in her chest. Widow Maurier planted both hands firmly on her hips.

"Since the child can't speak, Honneure Tremblay, I expect you're going to be the one to tell me what's going on, aren't you?"

Honneure looked up at the old woman slowly. What was she going to say? How could she begin and, more importantly, how was she going to end?

"Let me make it a little easier for you," Anne Marie continued. "Tell me why the boy is concerned about a letter."

Honneure swallowed. She was going to have to tell the old woman something. And the only thing she had to tell was the truth.

"I...Henri, I mean...he...he mailed a letter for me."

"So your husband wouldn't know."

Honneure nodded.

"Are you expecting a reply?"

Honneure repeated the motion. Her mouth was too dry to speak.

"Was Henri to meet the mail rider for you and bring you the letter when it arrived?" This time Anne Marie didn't need to wait for a response. She knew exactly what was going on. "But the boy is unable to go to Honfleur now, which means Armand might intercept this letter. And when he reads it, as we both know he will, he's going to be very upset indeed, isn't he?"

Honneure could no longer even move her head. She seemed frozen in her chair.

Madame Maurier's hands fell from her hips, and her expression softened with kindness. She took a deep breath. "I don't know who is more injured, you or the boy. At least I can see what his wounds are, so I can help to heal them. But what am I going to do with yours, Honneure? Eh? How can I help you if I don't know what's wrong?"

Honneure felt the story, the truth, rising up in her like a sickness. There would be no cure until she had vomited it out of her. She needed Madame Maurier, a friend, more than anything she had ever needed in her life besides Philippe.

But she was choking on it, strangling on the enormity of it. Tears poured down her cheeks, and her throat worked uselessly.

Madame Maurier turned to Henri. "I can't remember if I

fed the rabbits this morning, child. Will you see whether I have or not? And even if I did, I think they could use a little extra, don't you?"

The boy nodded uncertainly, his gaze on Honneure. Reluctantly, he inched his way out the door. He had hardly closed it behind him when the floodgates were opened.

The old woman held Honneure as she wept...and wept.

* * *

The silence stretched when Honneure had finished her tale. Madame Maurier patted the slender hand she had been holding and stood up slowly. She crossed to the open window and stood listening to the sound of birdsong for a while. How beautiful the world was. And how unfair. She turned back to Honneure, who had remained seated. Her trembling had eased, but she was still as white as a corpse.

"Would you like another cup of tea, dear?"

Honneure shook her head. "No...no, thank you."

The old woman sighed. "The Dauphine of France...the King...Forgive me, Honneure, but it's rather like hearing a fairy story, you must admit."

"I'm telling the truth!"

"Oh, I know you are. I do not doubt you for a moment. It's just...difficult for an old woman like me to take in all at once."

"I'm sorry," Honneure said softly.

Madame Maurier folded her black-clad arms over her shriveled bosom. "No, I'm sorry," she replied slowly. "I'm sorry for everything you've had to suffer. If it hadn't been for the spiteful act of a jealous woman, you'd be married to your Philippe now. Together you would be joyfully anticipating the birth of your child. Instead . . ."

The sentence did not need to be finished. To speak it aloud again was to give it more life and weight than it already had. Honneure forced a smile to her lips.

"Instead," she said, picking up the thread to weave a different cloth, "I will await word from the Dauphine. She will do whatever she can to help me, I know. She is one of the kindest human beings I have ever known."

"So it seems," the old woman replied. Royals were more often a bane than a benefit to common folk. Honneure's story, however, had been entirely believable.

"Since you believe so strongly that the Princess will help you, I myself will go to Honfleur tomorrow. I have a friend there I'll talk to. She can watch for the mail rider, ask for any letters for you. Later, when the boy is better, he can go into town and fetch any mail that's come for you."

Honneure clasped her hands together and held them tightly. "I wish I knew how to thank you," she murmured.

"Thank me when the letter is safely in your hands," Anne Marie replied. "It will be all the thanks I need."

The sun was a little past directly overhead when Honneure had finally started on her way back to the farm. Though she was warm and feeling unwell, she walked quickly. She did not like to provoke Armand any more than she had to. She did not want him to become suspicious. She was too close to her goal.

A flood of inner warmth coursed through Honneure's limbs as she thought of Madame Maurier's many kindnesses. She had found a true friend in the widow. Mingled with the happy anticipation of her escape from Normandy, however, and Armand, was sorrow at the thought of leaving the widow and Henri behind. At least they would have each other.

Honneure smiled to herself as she approached the gate. God really did work in mysterious ways. Even if she had suffered all she had suffered and come all this way, simply to be fate's agent in bringing Anne Marie and Henri together, then it would all have been worthwhile. Just as long as she ended up with Philippe, everything would be worthwhile.

The gate was open, which did not surprise Honneure. She had left it that way. She did not feel the first icicles of fear until she saw the gelding, still hitched, standing in the yard. Honneure halted.

The goods Armand had purchased were still piled in the wagon. The front door stood open. He was waiting for her. She knew it. And she knew why.

Years later Honneure would wonder how she had walked from the yard to the house, how she had actually forced her legs to propel her forward. She would remember everything that happened once she walked through the front door, but not how she got there.

He was sitting in his usual place, in the straight-back chair at the kitchen table, near the hearth. The fire had burned down. Wildflowers she had placed in a ceramic jug were wilting, heads drooping low. Armand smoothed the letter out on the table's surface.

"I've been waiting for you," he said in menacing tone.

Honneure did not speak.

"I've been waiting because I have some news to impart to you. It's from, let me see . . ." Armand glanced briefly at the paper. "It's from a Madame Campan. You know her, I trust?"

Honneure wasn't sure if she had managed to nod or not. The old man continued.

"She says she is writing on behalf of the Dauphine and that she is very sorry, but she has some terrible news. It concerns Philippe. He's the one who was here, isn't he?"

The vessels in her neck seemed to be constricting, cutting

off the blood supply to her brain. Honneure knew she was going to faint, but she struggled against it. She had to hang on, had to know . . .

"Maybe it would be best if I read this part," Armand went on. He picked up the letter. "Where is it...oh, yes. Madame Campan writes, 'Upon Philippe's return from Normandy, there was a tragic accident. He was, apparently, on his way to the Dauphine's apartments to tell us what had transpired between you. Whether it was by her design or not, he ran into Olivia at the head of the Queen's Staircase. According to witnesses, they argued. I talked to someone who said Philippe told Olivia he held her personally responsible for all the misfortunes that have befallen the two of you. In response, Olivia raised her arm to strike Philippe and he, quite naturally, attempted to defend himself. In the ensuing struggle, Olivia lost her balance and fell down the stairs. She did not survive the fall.' "

Honneure saw Armand look up at her. He smiled tightly. Her stomach churned, and her vision seemed to dim.

"I don't know who these people are, but it makes a good story. Would you like to read this next part for yourself?" Armand held up the letter like he might a dead fish. "No? I thought not," he said when Honneure did not respond. "So I'll continue. This is where it gets particularly interesting. Even I, old man that I am, buried up here in the north country, have heard of Madame du Barry. She's the King's mistress, is she not?"

His voice seemed to be coming from farther and farther away. Honneure could no longer even focus on his face.

"'Despite the fact of several witnesses,' this Madame Campan goes on, 'Madame du Barry insisted Philippe pushed Olivia on purpose, as revenge for their "little trick." She was not a witness herself, of course, but we all know her ability to sway the King to her causes. Standing now officially accused of murder, Philippe was forced to flee Versailles. We do not know where he has gone.' "

"My, my, what a shame." Armand folded the letter. "You can read all the sentimental drivel that follows for yourself, if you're so inclined. I'll just paraphrase for you the part that concerns me the most."

Honneure would never know how she found the strength to remain standing. She could no longer feel her hands or feet. The room was tilting oddly.

"Madame Campan advises you, especially since you are *with child*, to remain here, with me. She urges you not to reveal that Philippe is the father of your child." Armand chuckled mirthlessly. "I suppose so I will assume the child is mine and continue to harbor and protect you, call you my *wife*. Give you...and your *bastard*...my name."

At the bottom of the abyss, Honneure saw a tiny light. Its flicker enabled her to keep breathing, to find her voice out of the darkness.

"No...no . . ." she managed to croak. "I'm not worthy...I'll go...I'll . . ."

"No, you're not worthy," Armand snapped. "But you won't be going anywhere. Not only have you nowhere to go, I'll have you hunted down and brought back if you leave."

His words were totally incomprehensible. Honneure simply stared. She did not realize she had started to sway.

Armand grinned. "Just think how impressed my friends will be to discover that I have impregnated my young and beautiful wife." He chuckled again. "Will it be a son, I wonder? A son to follow in my footsteps?"

The chuckle bloomed into cackling laughter. It was the last thing Honneure heard. The darkness that had been trying to close in on her succeeded at last. Gratefully, she embraced it, and sank to the ground.

Chapter Twenty-Four

October 1772

The first sound Honneure heard when she awoke was that of branches rattling against the window. Wind whistled through the eaves. She opened her eyes.

Dawn had barely broken, but the red and golden leaves were so brightly colored she could see them distinctly as they blew past. The yard would be a mess. Honneure let her eyes drift closed again.

The room was cool, but not cold. The moaning of the wind just made it seem colder, she supposed. Still, a hearthfire would be welcome this morning. Honneure wondered if Armand would stir the embers and lay new wood. Sometimes, when she was late abed, he actually lifted a finger or two.

The tapping on the glass was insistent. It was, perhaps, what finally awakened the child. Honneure felt only a flutter at first. She laid her hands on the enormous mound her belly had become.

There...there it was...that sharp little elbow. Honneure felt it move, poking at her palm. Back and forth. The babe was restless today. A rare smile touched Honneure's pale lips. She could get up now. The child was her only reason for living, her sole motive for rising each day.

Honneure maneuvered her legs over the edge of the bed and managed to sit upright. She got to her feet and took her time dressing in the shapeless garment Madame Maurier had made for her. She tied a clean apron below her swollen breasts, wound her long hair into a knot and pinned it at the nape of her neck. She splashed water on her face and gasped at the chill of it. She was ready for her day.

The fire had been started, and Armand gave her an icy glare when she lumbered into the room. Honneure glared right back, and he eventually dropped his gaze. She set about making coffee.

Every move she made was slow and deliberate. Her chores, the activities of her simple life, carried her forward, minute by minute, through each day, from one day to the next. She tried not to think, merely act. She tried not to hate Armand, simply tolerate him. She made meals, tended the house and the animals, and largely ignored her husband. He had learned to speak to her civilly, or not at all. Since the day he had read Madame Campan's letter, she had made it clear she would not suffer his verbal cruelties.

When breakfast was done, Honneure trudged down to the barn. The wind whipped her skirt and tugged wisps of hair from her chignon. Dry leaves blew against her legs. She squeezed through the opening Henri had left for her in the barn door.

She was so late the dirty straw had already been cleaned away, and the boy was milking his second cow. He smiled at her without taking his hands from the teats. The rhythmic sound of milk spurting into a pail was vaguely comforting, and Honneure allowed herself a moment to do nothing but smell the familiar smells of the animals, clean straw, and old timber. Then she gathered an armful of hay and fed the gelding.

When three pails sat in row by the door, the boy came to Honneure, and she bent over to kiss the top of his head. He put both hands on her belly and grinned when he felt movement.

"It won't be long now, Henri."

The boy shook his head, still grinning.

Honneure sighed. "Thank you for your help this morning, as usual. I don't know what I would have done without you these past months."

The boy shook his head, pointed to himself, and then Honneure.

"You thank *me*?" When Henri nodded, Honneure tussled his hair, still streaked with blond from the summer. "You're a sweet boy, Henri, and I love you very much. You know that, don't you?"

In response, Henri winked and Honneure laughed. He was the only one who could make her laugh these days. In an otherwise bleak world, she cherished her relationship with him. And with Anne Marie Maurier.

"Run home now. Tell Widow Maurier I'll be by later for a visit. I think the walk will do me good." Honneure placed her hands on the small of her back and arched her spine. "My back is bothering me a bit today."

A look of concern immediately crossed the boy's fine features.

"Oh, I'm all right. I promise. Go on now. I'll see you later. Maybe I'll bake some of those pastries you love and bring them."

Henri looked hesitant, but eventually left. Honneure watched him slip through the barn door and heard the light patter of his feet as he scampered away. He ran for the joy of it now, not because he was afraid of being seen. Since Armand didn't have to pay the child, he couldn't object to his presence or to the help he lent.

He was such a good boy, Honneure mused, and he had come so far in six months. He had never left Madame

Maurier's since the day he had broken his arm. Their arrangement was entirely suitable to both of them. The widow fed Henri, clothed and housed him, and lavished all her love on him. He adored her in return, took care of all her outdoor chores, and helped with most of the indoor duties. No one ever came seeking him and, on the widow's infrequent trips to Honfleur, she had not even heard that his mother might be looking for him. It was just as well.

Honneure arched her back again and took a deep breath. The pain seemed to be getting worse. She had better keep moving.

It was a pleasant walk to the hillside pasture where she turned the cows loose to graze throughout the day. She used to have to lead them, but now they followed her willingly. She patted each smooth, brown flank as the animals filed past her, heads bent already to the grass.

The wind had died down a little, and the sun was warm on her shoulders. Hands supporting her back, Honneure walked slowly down the hill. She paused on the road.

It was as far back to the farm as to Anne Marie's from here. And not only did her back hurt, but it suddenly felt as if she had a cramp, the kind she used to get just before her time of the month. It was undoubtedly normal, but she would rather check with Anne Marie. Henri would have to have his treat on another day. Honneure started to walk west.

Though most of her days seemed gray, she had to admit the forest was beautiful at this time of the year. The foliage was brilliant, and most of the trees still fully leafed. Red, gold and orange stretched away up the hillside to her left. To her right, fat, red apples crowded the branches of trees marching away in orderly rows. Soon Armand's army of pickers would arrive, and the harvest would begin.

Though it was cool in the shade of the trees, Honneure felt unusually warm. Up ahead on the right was a familiar stump. It had become her place of choice to stop and read her letters from home. With great care, Honneure awkwardly lowered herself onto her seat.

It was bliss to lessen the strain on her aching back and close her eyes for a moment. Honneure recalled her last letter.

It had been from her parents, and all was well. The weather was mild, and the gardens were still in bloom. Honneure let her mind drift back to Chenonceau until she was sitting on the grassy banks of the Cher, watching the green water roll lazily by. The drooping branches of a weeping willow stirred gently in the breeze.

Honneure's heart suddenly ached with homesickness, and she jerked her thoughts back to the present. It did no good to dwell on the Loire valley, her parents, or what might have been. Armand would not let her return to either Versailles or Chenonceau. Philippe was lost to her, to all of them, perhaps forever. Her life was in Normandy. Her life was the child within her.

It was time to go. She couldn't waste any more time. She would have a brief visit with Anne Marie, and then return to the farm and begin her afternoon chores.

But Honneure suddenly found she could not move. The cramp that had been low in her abdomen spread up and outward. Like the stalks of a creeping vine, its tentacles spread across her belly and tightened. Sweat beaded her brow as the pain streaked through her body.

"Oh...no . . ." The words were hardly more than a groan. Honneure panted until the pain receded.

The baby was coming.

A pair of chattering squirrels chased each other up a tree

and frightened a flock of small black birds. They fluttered upward into the sky, so many of them that they looked like ashes rising from a chimney. Like ashes, they scattered in the wind and blew away.

The baby was coming, and she was all alone. Honneure wondered if she would be able to make it to Anne Marie's.

At least she had to try.

* * *

The autumn dusk was magnificent. The wind had died away entirely, and the surrounding trees stood still and stately with the setting sun lighting their colors ablaze. In the distance, the sea roared against the shore. The earth continued to turn toward darkness.

Inside her small house, Madame Maurier signaled for Henri to light the lamps. She took the linen cloth from Honneure's brow, dipped it in the basin of water, wrung it out and replaced it. Honneure did not wake, and Anne Marie was grateful. The girl was exhausted and only had a minute or two now between contractions. The widow sat back and awaited the inevitable.

Honneure's eyelids flew open as the agony gripped her anew.

"Breathe," Madame Maurier instructed quietly. "Just remember to breathe."

It seemed to go on forever. And she was tired, so tired. Her eyes closed again even before the last of the pain had faded. They flew open almost at once.

"Squeeze my hand, go ahead. I won't break."

Tears were forced from Honneure's eyes, a cry from her throat. The widow put her hand on Honneure's belly and felt the contraction diminish. Only a few seconds later, the grossly swollen belly tightened anew.

"I have to look now, Honneure." Madame Maurier gently disengaged her hand from Honneure's. She sat on the end of the bed between the girl's bent legs and lifted the sheet. She heard Honneure groan at the onset of another contraction.

The baby's head had not yet crowned. It would not be long, however. Though she had attended only one human birth, she had assisted in the delivery of many animals. Anne Marie recognized that Honneure fast approached the time when she would want to begin to push. As Honneure grimaced in the throes of another contraction, the widow checked her small bundle of supplies: newly sharpened knife, two lengths of twine, and cloth for swaddling. She was as prepared as she would ever be.

"I...I want to...to push now," Honneure panted.

"Hold on," the widow directed, one hand on Honneure's belly. "Wait for the start of the next one...all right...*push*!"

Honneure's teeth were bared, eyes squeezed tightly shut, face red as she bore down with all her might.

"I see it! Hold on, dear, wait for the next one...go!"

A scream tore from Honneure's throat as the baby's head was delivered.

"Good girl, good girl, Honneure," Anne Marie encouraged as she supported the infant's bloody head. "Just one more now...all right...that's it . . ."

The widow held her breath. Honneure's face screwed up. She pushed.

The baby slithered into the Madame Maurier's waiting hands. A wide grin split her deeply lined face.

"It's a girl, Honneure. You have a daughter. It's a girl!"

The pain had already faded into memory. Something Honneure thought never to feel again bubbled up from somewhere deep inside her. Unbidden, laughter blossomed from her throat.

"A girl? It's a girl?"

"A beautiful babe," Anne Marie pronounced as she deftly cut the cord and swaddled the infant. "A beautiful, beautiful girl just like her mother. Here...here she is."

Honneure's arms reached for the child. Her hands felt the tiny, fragile form. She tucked her in the crook of her arm against her breast. She looked into the blue, blue eyes.

Love, huge and awesome, swelled in Honneure's breast. "My baby," she whispered. She held the tiny hand. Tears of joy streaked her cheeks. "My baby.

"Philippa . . ."

Chapter Twenty-Five

May 1774

To wade in the water, Honneure and Anne Marie had picked up the hems of their skirts and tucked them into their apron sashes. Honneure had laughed at the widow's spindly legs with their fine tracery of spider veins. They both had laughed at Philippa's chubby calves as she toddled along at the edge of the foaming white water. A gusty spring breeze picked up a layer of sand and blew it against them, stinging their flesh and forcing the women to turn their backs. Philippa ran on, unaffected, black curls rioting in the wind. The sound of her laughter trailed in her wake.

"Since that child learned to walk," Anne Marie complained, "I've had to learn to run."

"You love it and you know it," Honneure countered.

"Yes, I do. I love everything about that child," the old woman replied simply. "Most of all, I love what she's done for you."

Eyes still on her daughter, Honneure smiled sadly. "I still miss Philippe. I miss him all the time, think about him all the time."

"You always will, dear," the widow said quietly. "Just as love never dies, neither does the sorrow of losing it. Believe me, I know."

Honneure stopped for a moment. She turned to Anne Marie, took her gnarled hand and pressed it briefly to her cheek. "*I* love you, you know. Philippa and I both do."

Blinking back tears, the old woman smiled. "Oh, I know. I know. And there's my boy, Henri. I'm a lucky woman, a very lucky woman."

The two friends walked on in companionable silence for a while. Then the breeze picked up again, and Honneure shivered.

"It's time to go, I think," she said.

"You won't get any objection from these old bones."

"Philippa! Come here, Philippa...come to Mommy!"

The child turned and grinned, and then continued on her way. Honneure broke into a trot, drew even with the little girl, and scooped her into her arms. Philippa put her arms around her mother's neck and nuzzled her cheek.

"Uvuu, Mummy."

"I love you, too, Philippa." Honneure fought back the tears that threatened her nearly every time she held her daughter like this. She loved her so much the emotion was almost painful. "But it's time to go back to the farm now."

"Nooooo!"

"Yeesssss!"

Madame Maurier caught up with them, and they walked slowly up the beach away from the water. It took several minutes headed slightly uphill to reach the edge of the trees. At the side of the road, they sat to dust the sand from their feet and put their shoes back on. Philippa squirmed and protested, but Honneure prevailed. They had no sooner set on their way again when Honneure heard the steady, brisk clop of hooves coming in their direction.

"This might be Henri," the widow remarked. "At least, I hope it is."

"Are you tired?" Honneure inquired with concern.

Madame Maurier looked aggrieved. "Of course I'm tired. So would you be if you walked five miles in sand at my age." Anne Marie allowed her expression to soften. "Don't worry, my dear. I'm not nearly as old and decrepit as Armand. What happened to him is not going to happen to me."

"Perish the thought!"

"Yes, perish the thought. It's his meanness that got him, you know. That's *not* going to happen to me."

Though what the widow said was probably true, Honneure resisted the urge to chuckle. Armand's state was truly pitiable. His facial features were twisted to one side, his left arm and leg were paralyzed, and he had lost the ability to speak. Most of his time was now spent in bed.

"Well, you're in luck, dear friend," Honneure said, banishing the image of her husband. "Here, indeed, is Henri."

Henri pulled the old gelding to a halt and jumped straight down from the wagon. He appeared excited.

"You look like you have news," Madame Maurier said.

Henri nodded energetically and waved a sealed piece of parchment.

Honneure took the letter Henri held out to her, but did not even glance at it. She had written Madame Dupin a while ago, and this was undoubtedly her response.

"Tell us the news first," Honneure pressed. "You look so excited...tell us!"

Henri shook his head, lips compressed. He had grown tall and had begun to fill out. When he obstinately crossed his arms over his chest, muscles bulged in his upper arms. He shook his head again, pointed at the wagon bench, then the letter.

"Oh, go on, do as he says. Read the letter out loud to us on the way home like you always do." Anne Marie waved a hand impatiently. "Just let me get off my feet."

They all climbed into the wagon, the widow on one side of Henri, Honneure on the other, and Philippa in her lap. With her arms around the child, she finally examined the letter.

"My goodness!" Honneure exclaimed. "This is from the Dauphine!"

Henri grinned and nodded. Anne Marie's eyes widened. Henri stabbed a finger at the letter.

Honneure examined the royal seal, and then slowly broke it. "This is quite an honor. She's only written once before. Usually, Madame Campan . . ."

"Read!" Anne Marie cried.

Honneure complied.

" 'Dear Friend,' " it began. The widow caught her breath, and Henri whistled. A shy, proud smile touched Honneure's lips. She continued.

" 'I know that my dear Campan has written to you from time to time as well as our friend, Madame Dupin, and they have kept you abreast of Court affairs. This time I write myself in fond memory of our friendship, your devoted service, and the "dilemma" we once both shared.' "

" 'Dilemma?' " the widow chirped.

Honneure felt a blush of color rush to her cheeks. "We...we at one time had a...a similar problem. Philippe hadn't realized he...well, that he loved me yet, as I loved him. And...well, the Dauphin hadn't quite realized yet how special his wife was. And . . ."

"Gracious, dear, you don't mean to tell me that the *Dauphine* of France confided her love life to you!"

Honneure felt her cheeks grow even hotter.

"Never mind. Go on. Read."

Honneure took a breath. "'I also want to share my

happiness with you, as you once shared yours with me. I know you must still grieve for the loss of your love, but I pray my news will cheer you. You have always had such a kind and generous heart. So I know you will rejoice when I tell you that Louis and I are happy, truly happy.' "

Honneure paused and took another deep breath. Yes, she did rejoice for the Princess to whom she had been, and was still, devoted.

Henri wiggled his eyebrows suggestively and pursed his lips.

The widow slapped his arm. "Hush. Go on, Honneure."

"'As you undoubtedly know,'" Honneure continued, "'Dear Louis took me to Paris for the first time last June. We drove to Notre Dame through flower-strewn streets and triumphal arches and dined publicly in the concert hall of the Tuileries. Then we walked in the gardens – and they cheered us! So many, many people pressed close, trying to thank my good husband for his many kindnesses to the poor. There was such a great crowd that we remained for three-quarters of an hour without being able to go forward or back. The Dauphin and I several times ordered the guards not to strike anyone, which made a very good impression. Later, when we appeared on the Tuileries balcony, the Duc de Brissac turned to me and said, "Madame, two hundred thousand people have fallen in love with you." I pray it is so. I believe it might be, for Louis seemed to look at me from then on in a different light.'"

They had reached Madame Maurier's gate, and the horse had stopped, but no one seemed to notice. Honneure read on.

" 'When we went in July to Compiegne, Louis adopted the practice of walking through the gardens with me arm-in-arm. Do you know that the practice was copied by the Court? Husbands and wives who hadn't spoken to each other in years were suddenly appearing as cozy as Louis and me! Can you imagine setting such a trend?

" 'Also of note, the du Barry has quite changed her attitude toward me. Knowing how fond I am of jewelry, she arranged to have me shown a pair of earrings, each set with four diamonds and worth 700,000 livres. She said if I liked them, she would ask the King to make a present of them to me. I took great pleasure in telling her I was quite satisfied with the diamonds I already possessed.' "

Honneure chuckled. Finally, the tide had turned.

" 'I must close now, dear friend. Think of me with joy. My thoughts and prayers are with you, as they are with Philippe, wherever he may be.' "

It was signed, simply, "Marie Antoinette."

A hush followed Honneure's reading of the signature. Philippa hiccoughed, and Honneure patted her on the back.

"Well," Anne Marie puffed at length. "That was quite something. A personal letter from the Dauphine of France."

Henri shook his head in forceful denial and began at once to gesture. All eyes turned in his direction, even Philippa's.

Honneure looked confused as she attempted to translate. "This...this is *not* a personal letter?"

Still shaking his head, Henri pointed at the signature on the page.

"It's not Marie Antoinette, the Dauphine?"

Henri nodded slowly. He pointed at the signature again, and then raised his hands as if placing something on his head.

Honneure drew in a sharp breath as realization dawned. "What did you...what did you hear in town, Henri?" she asked in a voice barely above a whisper. "Has the King...has the King...*died*?"

Henri nodded solemnly.

Helen A. Rosburg

"And Marie Antoinette is no longer the Dauphine." Henri continued to nod as Honneure glanced once more at the letter in her hand.

"So this letter is from the...the *Queen* of France . . ."

Chapter Twenty-Six

December 1778

It was the first snowfall of the season. By noon it was nearly as dark as the winter's dusk, and fat, lazy flakes fluttered from the sky. Honneure carefully moved the half of the blanket she was embroidering onto Anne Marie's lap, rose, and crossed to the window. The yard was empty, the barn door still shut. They hadn't returned yet.

"I don't see any sign of them," she said worriedly. "Do you think they're all right?"

The widow didn't even look up from her stitching. "Of course they're all right. Do you think Henri would let anything happen to that little girl?"

"Noooo, but . . ."

"There are no 'buts'. Furthermore, I trust that horse. He'll get them home safely. What does Philippa call him? Oh, yes...*Coozie*. Now how did she ever come up with a name like 'Coozie?' "

Honneure laughed quietly. "I think it's a derivative of 'cozy.' She's told me she thinks he's cozy because of the way he hugs her."

Madame Maurier finally looked up from her stitching. Her eyebrows were twin question marks. "The horse *hugs* her?"

"Well, yes, actually." Honneure smiled to herself as she recalled the scene she had come upon shortly after they had

287

purchased the animal. The old gelding had finally died, and Philippa had been devastated. To console her, Honneure had allowed the girl to pick the horse who would replace him. She had chosen a young, strong, piebald gelding because, she said, he was much more affectionate than Old Gray had been. It had meant nothing to Honneure until she had entered the barn one day and had seen the piebald with his head and neck bent to the side. He was holding Philippa against him, actually pressing her gently into his ribs. "See, Mommy!" she had said. "He's hugging me!" As if to support her, the horse had snorted and tossed his head up and down in the equine equivalent of a nod.

Anne Marie looked skeptical when Honneure related the story to her and returned to her needlework. Honneure left to check on Armand.

He lay just as she had left him that morning after bathing him and changing the linens. He did not appear to have moved an inch. His eyes flickered briefly in her direction and then refocused on the wall in front of him. Honneure sighed and closed the door.

"I'm going to heat some soup. When Henri returns he can sit Armand up and hold him while I try to feed him again. He wouldn't take anything for breakfast. I'm worried about him."

"You can try whatever you like, but I don't think there's anything wrong with him. His refusal to eat is probably just his way of informing you that he doesn't like what you're serving. He's still that ornery, you know. God struck him dumb for the way he treated Henri years ago and left him paralyzed for the way he treated you. But He didn't make him any nicer. He's still the same mean, old codger, and for the life of me I don't see how you can be so kind to him, much less compassionate."

"It's my duty," Honneure replied with quiet dignity and went to the hearth. With a fire tool she pulled the iron arm out, hooked the handle of the soup pot onto it, and pushed it back over the fire. After another quick look out the window, she returned to her seat next to Anne Marie and pulled her half of the embroidery piece back onto her lap.

"The snowfall's growing heavier by the moment, you know."

The widow remained concentrated on her stitching. "They went for a ride. When they've had enough they'll come back."

"What if one of them fell off?"

"Since they're riding double, if one went off they both did."

With a dramatic sigh, Honneure put down her needle. "You're not being helpful."

Anne Marie looked up at last. "Neither are you. You've hardly taken ten stitches since they left."

Honneure frowned at the old woman, but the widow had already dropped her gaze.

"Let's talk about something more positive, shall we?" Anne Marie suggested. "Tell me again about your latest letter from Madame Campan."

Instantly warming to the subject of her beloved Queen, Honneure picked up her needle again. "Antoinette's popularity continues to grow, especially under the present circumstances."

"As well they should," the widow sniffed.

"The King's also," Honneure continued. "The people still haven't forgotten his first great act of generosity upon his accession to the throne."

Anne Marie's brow puckered. "Didn't he and the Queen turn down a traditional gift of money?"

"Yes, *le droit de joyeux avenement*. It's a tax the Parisians would have had to put on coal and wine to raise the money, but Louis and Antoinette waived it. It amounted to over 24 million livres! Then they promptly cut down on their household staffs and even canceled their summer trips to Compiegne to save money."

"I'd be falling down and kissing someone's feet if I were a Parisian," the widow quipped. "If memory serves, the King not only did that, but kicked out all the du Barry's appointees, along with her sorry backside, and put honest ministers in their places."

Honneure nodded soberly. She would never forget how glad she had been to learn that Antoinette, at last, was free from the du Barry's arrogance and cruelties. The Queen herself, shortly after her accession and despite the incredible burden of her new duties, had directed Madame Campan to write to Honneure and inform her of the du Barry's "demise."

"Knowing the tragic impact Madame du Barry has had on your life," Madame Campan had written, "the Queen bid me tell you the woman is gone from the Court. She left with her lover, the Duc d'Aiguillon, for his estate in Ruel. From there she went on to the convent of Pont aux Dames with instructions from the King to see no one, since she knew state secrets. The Duke himself is also now *persona non grata*, as he has been asked by the King to resign."

"Restoration of the Court's integrity was long overdue," Honneure said at length, sadly. "It was no secret to the previous King's subjects that they were being ruled not by him, but by the whims of his succession of mistresses."

"And that we were being taxed," Anne Marie added, an edge of bitterness in her tone, "not to support our country, but to pay for the hussies' gifts!"

Honneure smiled, not at what the widow had said, which was true and very, very unfortunate, but at her spirit. "That era is over, thank goodness. An age of reason has been ushered in.

By Honor Bound

Not only has our new King modified taxes to relieve the burden on the poor and middle class, but also he's trying to curb the excesses of his own nobles. In Madame Campan's latest letter she mentioned an incident to me involving one of Louis' nobles who was deeply in debt. The King ordered him exiled from Versailles until all his creditors had been satisfied. Another, a Prince, had asked Louis for a stay of proceedings against his creditors, a standard practice during the previous reign. But the King replied 'When a man can keep mistresses, he can pay his debts.' "

"Sounds to me like he has it in for any and all mistresses these days."

"Oh, he's always been that way," Honneure replied, diligently plying her needle. "His parents were very moral people, devoted to one another and their children. They were openly and deeply disapproving of the King's lifestyle and profligacy. Louis grew up respecting his grandfather as a monarch, but not as a man."

"According to what you've told me, it was also part of the cause of his hesitancy in trusting and loving his bride."

"I'm sure of it," Honneure said emphatically. "There was also a great deal of anti-Austrian sentiment and people whispering in Louis' ear that Antoinette was nothing more than a spy for her mother, the Empress. She had many more obstacles to overcome than an ordinary bride. But she is extraordinarily kind, loving, and generous. And as moral as her husband. He was able to see that at last."

"Apparently," the widow remarked dryly. "Or we would not be embroidering this baby blanket."

Honneure laughed outright and ran her hand over the soft, pale yellow material. The *fleurs de lis* they stitched were in the Queen's colors, blue and gold.

"As sweet as you've told me the Queen is," Anne Marie continued, "I just hope her husband is as caring. It's one thing to bring justice to a country; quite another to the home."

"Well put. But I can assure you of the King's compassion." Honneure put down her needle for a moment. "Do you remember when the old King died?"

"I do. He died of the small pox."

"Yes. Well, fifty others in the Court came down with the disease, and ten died. Louis decided he should be inoculated, despite the newness of this treatment, and then went into isolation. He ordered that no one should attend him who had not already had small pox and had the humanity to extend the order to the lowest servants."

The widow quirked a brow. "What of the Queen?"

"She had already had a mild form of the disease. She remained with him and attended him herself."

The shadow of a smile touched Anne Marie's mouth. "I'm surprised we weren't embroidering this blanket four years ago."

Honneure returned the smile. "Sometimes these things take longer than others."

"Take yourself, for instance." The old woman knew it was the wrong thing to say before the words had even left her mouth. She pushed the blanket aside and took Honneure's hands.

"Oh, my dear, I'm so sorry," she apologized. "I didn't mean to remind you. How stupid of me."

Honneure shook her head. "No, it's all right...really," she said. But she stared at her lap until she had fought back her tears. She forced a brave smile to her lips and looked Anne Marie straight in the eye.

"We may have only had one night together, but what if we

had never had anything at all? What if I didn't have Philippa?"

"You're a remarkable woman, do you know that, Honneure?" the widow said softly. "Look at what you've accomplished, the life you've built for yourself, despite a tragic series of events and almost overwhelming adversities. And through it all you've maintained your dignity and compassion. You're a wonder to me. I treasure our friendship, and I apologize deeply for hurting you."

Madame Maurier squeezed Honneure's hands, sat back, and picked up her sewing. "Now, enough sentimentality. We have to get to work and finish this before the child is born."

"We'll have to work hard," Honneure agreed, glad of the change of subject. "From what I've heard it could be any day now."

The two women worked for a while in silence, until a gust of wind rattled the windows. Honneure dropped her sewing and stood up.

"That's it. Now I really am worried. Look at how hard it's snowing." She crossed to the window overlooking the yard. To her immense relief, Coozie was just trotting through the gate.

"Look at them, Anne Marie!" Honneure exclaimed. "Just look at them!"

Henri, a tall, strong lad of sixteen sat bareback with Philippa in front of him. The tops of their heads and shoulders were dusted with snow, as was the gelding's broad rump. The children were laughing when suddenly the horse decided to shake off his layer of snow.

Philippa's mouth formed an "O" as she grabbed for Coozie's mane. Henri's arms went around Philippa. A moment later they both lay sprawled on the newly white ground.

Honneure held her breath until she saw her daughter sit up and burst into a fresh spate of giggles. "They're safe and well. I suppose," she added, "I'll check on Armand, then serve the soup. The children will want something hot."

The door to the bedroom creaked slightly as Honneure pushed it open. Armand lay exactly as she had left him. His pale, blue gaze remained fixed on the wall. Honneure walked to the side of the bed.

"Armand, would you like something to eat now? I've made some soup. Armand . . ."

Chapter Twenty-Seven

June 1779

Of the seven summers she had spent in Normandy, this was definitely the most beautiful. Spring had come early and swiftly. Trees had leafed and flowers bloomed. Migrating birds had returned, and the mild temperatures had held. There had been some windy days and some drizzly days, but no typically fierce spring storms. The days simply grew longer and brighter and warmer.

Even the grass seemed thicker and greener, Honneure noted, as the wagon bounced along the rutted road to the widow's farm. The apple trees were certainly well on their way. If the weather continued to hold, it would be a banner harvest this year.

"Look, Mommy. There's the reading room."

Honneure followed the direction of her daughter's pointing finger and saw the weathered stump by the side of the road. She chuckled dutifully at the little joke Philippa had made up so long ago now, it seemed. How many letters had they shared sitting there together, side by side? A twinge of melancholy tugged at Honneure's emotions.

Though she had never seen her grandparents, sitting on that old stump Philippa had come to know them through their letters. She could describe almost every inch of Chenonceau. She even knew the names of the carriage horses Madame Dupin still kept in the barn. But would she ever see the château? Would she ever get to know Paul and Jeanne and experience the love that had helped make Honneure who she was? The love that had helped to bolster her through years of hardship and overwhelming emotional burdens?

There was now, at least, a glimmer of hope in her soul.

Coozie knew the way. Without the slightest touch on the reins, he made the left turn into the widow's drive. He lowered his head as he strained a little harder on the incline. Once inside the gate, he halted.

Anne Marie stood at the front door, smiling and wiping her hands on her apron. Henri pushed past her and trotted to the wagon. Grinning, he held out his arms to Philippa.

Normally the little girl would have leapt, laughing, into the boy's arms. Today she merely sat there until he had lifted her gently to the ground. Honneure had to take a moment to compose herself. This was going to be harder than she had thought.

"Come, Philippa," the widow called cheerily. "I've baked your favorite pie for lunch. Are you hungry?"

The little girl gave an almost imperceptible shrug. She clung tightly to Henri's hand. Anne Marie and Honneure exchanged quick glances over Philippa's head. Honneure climbed down from the wagon.

The house was filled with delicious aromas. "Anne Marie Maurier, you baked more than just a pie, didn't you?" Honneure accused as she stared at the array of foods lined up on the table. "You must have been cooking for days!"

Henri nodded energetically. Philippa's eyes were wide, and her solemn expression appeared to have lightened a little.

"Well, I did want today to be...special." Anne Marie had to struggle to keep her smile from faltering. "And I wanted to be sure we had enough so you'd have plenty to...to take with you."

Once again the women glanced at one another over Philippa's head.

"How thoughtful of you, dear friend." Honneure forced a bright smile. "By the looks of it, we'd be well fed even if we spent a week on the road."

Henri waved his hand to capture their attention, and then shook his head and pointed to his stomach.

"Not with you along, is that what you're saying, Henri?" Honneure inquired. They all laughed when he nodded. "Well, just make sure you have enough for the return trip."

Henri's grin slowly faded. He made a sweeping gesture with his hand and then pointed to his lips and the smile that briefly flickered there.

"Going, you will be happy," Honneure interpreted.

Henri nodded. He made a motion opposite to the first, touched his heart, put a finger to his eye and let it trail down his cheek.

"But coming back," Honneure murmured, "you'll be sad."

Henri nodded slowly. Philippa looked from her mother to Anne Marie. She walked over to Henri and took his hand again.

"I don't want to go," she announced soberly. "If Henri's going to be sad, why do we have to leave? I'm going to be sad, too."

Honneure bit her lip to hide its sudden trembling. "Philippa," she began, but her voice broke.

"Philippa, dear," Anne Marie said smoothly. "Come over here and sit on my lap."

The child did as she was bid. Anne Marie put her arms around her as Philippa laid her head against the widow's narrow breast.

"Do you remember the story your mommy told you, the one about going away?" The little girl nodded reluctantly. "Can you tell the story to me?"

Philippa was still for a long moment, her gray eyes wide and unblinking. Absently, she tugged at the long, thick black curls falling over her shoulder.

"Mommy was just a little older than me," the child began at last. "She had to leave the house where she had lived all her life." Philippa's eyes darted in her mother's direction. "She was very frightened and very sad."

"What else?"

"She was so sad she didn't think she would ever be happy again." Philippa's voice was so small it was barely audible. "She went away to a new home in a wagon with a big, friendly horse."

"And where are you going tomorrow?"

"To a new home."

"How are you going to get there?"

"In a wagon." Philippa squirmed. The smile was trying to emerge.

"In a wagon pulled by what?"

"By a big, friendly horse." It was apparent now she was suppressing the grin.

"And what happened to your mommy when she got where she was going?"

"She was very, very happy." Philippa's small, perfect teeth were revealed at last.

"And what's going to happen to you when you get where you're going?"

Philippa laughed and slipped off the widow's lap. She ran to her mother, threw her arms around Honneure's legs, looked up at her and grinned.

"I'm going to curtsy to the King and Queen and thank them very much."

Honneure smoothed the dark curls, so achingly familiar, from her daughter's face.

"And what are you going to thank the King and Queen for?" Anne Marie pressed.

"For giving us a home," the little girl replied, thoroughly caught up in the game.

"What kind of a home?"

"A *happy* home."

"Yes!" The widow clapped her hands and rose to her feet. Henri joined the clapping, as did Honneure.

"This is the fashion, is it not?" Anne Marie asked. "This...hand clapping...after a performance."

"Indeed, it is," Honneure replied. She stooped to look her daughter in the eye. "And it is another reason why you will love the Queen as much as I do. Would you like to know why?"

"I certainly would," the widow chimed. Henri jabbed a thumb at his chest.

"Well, it used to be that out of respect for the King, one did not clap during royal performances. One evening, however, the Queen – though she was the Dauphine then – enjoyed the dancing of Mademoiselle Heinel so much that she clapped. And went on clapping. She is so gay and merry, so sweet, she infected all around her. Everyone clapped, and went on clapping. And now it is the thing to do after every performance, to show one's approval, even in the presence of the King."

Philippa's eyes were huge. Her rosebud lips formed a perfect "O," a familiar expression. She looked from her mother to Anne Marie and Henri, back to her mother again.

"Mommy?"

"Yes, my darling. What is it?"

"I'm hungry. Can we eat now?"

* * *

It was late. Philippa had long been asleep, curled on the palette she would share with her mother. Henri was in his corner, snoring fitfully. The two women sat close to the hearth, its dying flames their only light.

"It's going to be hard, you know," the widow said, quietly continuing their conversation. "Harder than you think."

"What choice do I have, Anne Marie?"

The widow's only reply was to lower her chin and look up at Honneure from beneath arched brows.

"You know we can't stay here," Honneure replied softly. "Your place simply isn't big enough, and I have...nothing. I couldn't even help to build an extra room on this house."

"With Henri's help we'd manage somehow." When Honneure did not reply, the widow did not press the point. She knew what a sore subject it was, and she silently cursed Armand as she had done nearly every day since his death.

Spiteful to the end, the old man had left nothing to Honneure, not a sou, despite the years she had spent caring for him and his farm. He was as mean in death as he had been in life. He had left everything to an aging sister who, being in failing health herself, had promptly sold everything lock, stock and barrel. Honneure and Philippa had nothing but their clothes. And Coozie, whom they had hidden away from the sales agent, and who would, henceforward, belong to Henri.

Anne Marie felt tears threatening at the corners of her eyes and tried to blink them away. They were a waste of time. Change was the nature of life. And Honneure was, perhaps, doing what was best for her and her child.

"There will certainly be more life for you and Philippa at Court," the old woman said at length. "I myself prefer the quiet country life, but you're young yet. There is so much opportunity, so much for you and Philippa to look forward to."

Honneure let her gaze rest briefly on her sleeping child, and then turned back to the widow. "You will always be family to us. You know that. But I want Philippa to have the chance to know my foster parents, too. And now that Madame du Barry and her entire faction are long gone, there's always the chance . . ."

Honneure left the sentence unfinished. Anne Marie covered her hand with her gnarled fingers.

"Through the years your love for Philippe has never dimmed," the old woman said in a barely audible voice. "If anything, your devotion to his memory has grown. I cannot but imagine that his love is as strong, as unyielding to time, as yours. If it is God's will, you will find each other. You will be together again."

Honneure smiled to hide the trembling of her lip. "I know that if, or when, he is able, he will let our parents know he is safe. Someday he will know about his...his daughter." She glanced once more at Philippa, and then brightened her smile. "And in the meantime, speaking of devotion, there is the Queen."

"Yes, the Queen," Anne Marie repeated, no small amount of awe in her tone. "It amazes me that someone in her position is so...so *normal*, so unassuming."

"She is one of the kindest people I have ever known."

"And over the years, hearing your stories and reading those letters, I have come to believe you. Why, it was only a matter of weeks after you wrote her of your predicament that she replied...*personally*...and said she'd find a place at Court for you."

Honneure flushed with the memory. The Queen had been thrilled, in fact, with the idea of Honneure's return. "Baron has passed on, and two of my little ones," Antoinette had written. "But I have new little friends and know you will think them quite merry. I am as fond of them as I can be and cannot tell you how happy I am to know that you will be returning to care for my dear little ones. I have not as much time for them anymore and spend what free time I can find with my precious daughter. What fun the children will have together when you bring your own treasured child to Court. Did you know that Artois, Louis' brother, has two children now? Louis Antoine, who is only a bit younger than your Philippa, and Charles Ferdinand, who is the age of my Marie Therese. Oh, to hear the sounds of their laughter ringing in these dusty old halls . . ."

"As sad as I am to leave you and Henri," Honneure said at last, "I cannot deny that I long to serve the Dauph...my Queen...again. In many ways I feel almost as if it is my destiny...as if I am bound to her in some way."

"You will forever be bound by your integrity and honor, my dear," the widow replied gently. "Your mother aptly named you."

At that moment Philippa mewed in her sleep, and Honneure was instantly on her feet. "I hate to bring this, our last night, to a close. But I really should lie down with her. Dawn will come all too soon."

"Too soon, indeed." The old woman grunted as she pushed to her feet. "And you'll forgive me if I'll not be welcoming this one with my usual enthusiasm. Come now, let me cover you. You've been a daughter to me, you know."

Honneure merely nodded because she found she was

unable to speak. She stretched out on the palette next to her daughter and closed her eyes while her friend pulled a thin blanket up around her shoulders. In no time at all, the palette's covering was damp with her tears.

* * *

Their good-byes had been said, in large part, the night before. The morning's departure, therefore, was a quiet one. Henri had the horse hitched and the wagon loaded by the time the sun was high enough to banish the dawn's misty damp. Chickens clucked and pecked in the yard while Philippa ran around to the back of the house to say farewell to the rabbits.

"One good thing about your leaving," Anne Marie said as she and Honneure stood next to the wagon. "I'll be able to sell those rabbits again for local stew pots instead of keeping them as pets."

Honneure laughed, in spite of the heaviness weighing down her heart. "But she's named them all. How can you possibly sell a rabbit whose name is Elizabeth to the butcher?"

"Please believe that I will find a way," the widow responded dryly. In her heart, however, she doubted that this particular generation of rabbits would ever leave her farm.

Philippa reappeared, cheeks rosy and hair tangled. Anne Marie bent over, carefully, to hug her.

"Give me a kiss, quickly now," she demanded, not unkindly. "Coozie is eager to be off on his adventure."

"To the Royal Court!" the little girl piped brightly.

"And won't he be the grandest horse there?"

Philippa nodded solemnly, and then threw her arms around the old woman and planted a kiss on her cheek. Anne Marie straightened.

"Put her in the wagon, Henri." The widow turned to face

Honneure. "We've said all that needs to be said. You know you and Philippa will be welcome here, always. Even after I'm gone. Henri loves you two as much as I do."

"I know," Honneure whispered.

"A letter now and then would be welcome."

Honneure simply nodded. It seemed she had not shed all her tears the night before.

"Then off with you. It won't do to keep the Queen of France waiting."

The women hugged briefly, and Honneure climbed up into the wagon. Henri clucked to the horse, and the gelding moved forward.

The old woman stood watching. The month had been dry so far, and dust rose lazily into the still air from beneath the wagon's wheels. Philippa, squeezed between her mother and Henri, turned and waved, a happy smile on her rosebud mouth. In spite of her initial reluctance, she now moved into her future with joy and excitement. It was just as it should be.

Before the wagon went out of sight down the road, Honneure turned. She did not wave, but raised her hand as if in salute. Despite the distance, the two women locked gazes. Then they rounded a bend and were out of sight. Anne Marie sighed, drew a handkerchief from her pocket and blew her nose.

The widow walked slowly back to her house. She only hoped she lived long enough to learn the next chapter of Honneure's story. The girl was special, no doubt about it. Destiny had not finished with her. It had, in fact, probably only begun.

Chapter Twenty-Eight

July 1779

The park-like gardens surrounding the *Petit Trianon* were at the height of their summer glory. Spreading trees shaded rolling, sprawling lawns and small, sparkling lakes. On the grassy verge of one, sunlight glinted on the dome of the Temple of Love. Behind the supporting fluted columns, a marble Cupid bent to carve his bow from Hercules' club. Birds chattered in overhanging branches and endured the scoldings of bold squirrels. It was a perfect summer day.

Inside the small Trianon, the young Queen laughed with her friends and reluctantly noted the length of the shadows outside the salon windows.

"I'm afraid it is time to leave our charming retreat and return to reality," she announced with a moue. "I dine with my dear husband tonight and an old friend who has come to visit, and I must dress accordingly."

"You mean," said Madame Elisabeth, "that you must dress for the friend and the courtiers who will join you. Were you to dine alone with my brother, I doubt you would have to dress at all."

Antoinette's friends, the Duchesse de Polignac and the Princesse de Lamballe, both sensitive souls, reacted with surprised horror. Antoinette, however, laughed and playfully slapped her favorite sister-in-law on the back of her wrist.

"You're too naughty, *ma soeur*."

"If I'm naughty, then you're a scandal," Elisabeth replied with a straight face. "Imagine, at the Royal Court of Versailles, actually being in love with your husband and remaining faithful to him. And you the Queen of France! You could have anyone you want!"

The Princesse de Lamballe, prone to fainting, had turned pale, and Antoinette hurried to reassure her.

"We're only teasing, Marie Therese. Come, a walk in the fresh air will do you good. We'll go by our little theater and see how it's coming along. Monsieur Mique assures me it will be done soon."

The four women left the small, jewel-like building and strolled amiably, arm in arm, through the wooded grounds. As they passed from shadow into a narrow clearing, sunshine highlighted the unusual color of the Queen's simple gown.

"Tell me again what that color is called," the Duchesse de Polignac said. "Didn't the King give it a name?"

"He certainly did!" Antoinette replied with mock pique. "I thought Madame Bertin positively brilliant to come up with this extraordinary color for me. But the first thing Louis said to me when he saw it was, 'My God, Antoinette, that gown is the color of a *puce*.' "

"A flea?!" Marie Therese exclaimed.

"Exactly. And whatever this color used to be called will probably be entirely forgotten over time. My husband has started a trend, and now everyone calls it *puce*."

As the women approached the nearly completed building, workmen stopped and stared in awe. Antoinette smiled at them cheerily.

"Go on," she called gaily. "Don't stop on my account. I long for the completion of this project."

Craftsmen and laborers slowly returned to their duties.

Though the Queen was well known for her easy, friendly nature, it still took many people aback.

"Can we look inside?" Gabrielle, the Duchesse, inquired timidly.

"Why not?" Antoinette replied. "This is *our* theater after all."

Though the interior was not quite finished, it was easy to see that the architect had masterfully designed the limited space. Though small, the stage was as elaborate as any of its grander cousins. Curtains and chairs were in the Queen's colors, and every carving and fixture were exquisite down to the smallest detail.

"My goodness!" Marie Therese's eyes grew wide. "Look at all those seats! How can your Majesty possibly have the courage to perform in front of so many people?"

"In the first place," Antoinette replied, "there aren't that many seats, merely fifty, and I doubt they will ever be completely filled. We're only inviting family and a few favored friends to our little productions. Since Artois will be performing with us there will be his wife, of course, and Monsieur and his wife," she said, referring to the King's other brother, Provence. "The aunts have said they'd like to come, and Clotilde."

"My sister will only come if there's food involved," Elisabeth remarked dryly.

"Ooooh, you do insist on being bad, don't you?"

"You don't care how bad I am," Elisabeth retorted good naturedly, "as long as I'm good on stage."

"You'll be the star, I'm sure. And in the second place," Antoinette continued, returning her attention to Marie Therese, "I will have the courage to perform because I am doing it for my dear Louis. You know how restricted his time has become.

He no longer has time for the real theater. But we will perform at his leisure, and he has merely to walk across the lawn from his home to get here when he chooses. We will be able to put a little entertainment and gaiety back into his life."

"You are so good and kind," the Princess sighed.

"Merely a proper wife to a good and loving husband. Now come. I really must return. I'm anxious to see if my friend has arrived."

As the women walked back toward the palace, Madame Elisabeth wrinkled her nose. "You know," she said, "that theater really is a bit too small."

"Elisabeth!" the Queen exclaimed. "It's not a bit too small for our purposes. Why would you say that?"

"Did you not say Monsieur's and Artois' wives would be attending?"

"Yessss," Antoinette drawled cautiously. She had an idea of what the prankish Elisabeth was about to say.

"Well, then, the theater is obviously too small. Even if we are up on stage, we shall be able to smell the stench."

Marie Therese and Gabrielle had the good grace to blush. Even Antoinette drew a sharp breath and halted abruptly.

"Elisabeth, really," she scolded. "You're going too far. Those poor women simply don't know any better."

"And since they're royalty and supposedly have plentiful water available to them, imagine what the rest of the population must smell like. In my opinion, Piedmont is a country to be avoided at all costs."

"Be kind, Elisabeth. They've been better recently. Didn't you know your brother talked to them? He himself was so offended he informed them, in the nicest way possible, of course, that bodies were for bathing and teeth for brushing."

"One of my brother's greatest acts, so far, as King."

"Oh, Elisabeth, stop now!"

"I shouldn't be surprised, I suppose. Doesn't Louis have *two* tubs, one for bathing and one for rinsing? He doesn't even like to have *soap* left on him, he's so clean."

This time it was Antoinette's turn to blush. And once again, the Princesse de Lamballe appeared likely to faint.

"Enough, Elisabeth," the Queen remonstrated, but a giggle erupted nevertheless.

Hurrying back into the palace, Antoinette was equally unaware of amused smiles...and disapproving frowns.

* * *

The room was narrow, but pleasant, and had a tiny square of window that looked out on the Bosquet of the Queen, a grassy terrace studded with classical statues. There was one wide bed that mother and daughter shared, a cupboard for their clothes, a desk and chair. The single doorway led to a small sitting room they shared with an elderly couple who served one of the King's ministers. Honneure had met them once or twice and found them kindly enough, but distant, and they seemed to spend little time in their quarters. It suited Honneure, for she and Philippa had more room for themselves and the Queen's dogs. There was also a small hearth that would be a luxury come winter, some comfortable if threadbare furniture, and a shelf with an eclectic, but welcome, collection of books.

Standing by the window in their room, Honneure could not help but recall her years with her mother at Amboise. She had adored her mother, and they had been happy, despite the physical poverty of their existence. How much better things were for her and Philippa! How far she had come, from Amboise to Chenonceau, Chenonceau to Versailles. And even though her sojourn in Normandy had begun as a nightmare, she still had treasured memories of her daughter's first years and Henri and Anne Marie. If only she could forget the horror of the day Armand had threatened Philippe and driven him away and out of her life . . .

Honneure shook her head, scattering and banishing the unwelcome memory. Now was the time for a fresh start. She was incredibly blessed by the Queen's friendship and generosity. She had a decent home for her child and food and clothing. Philippa even had friends, for Antoinette had been true to her word. The children of her ladies, and of her most trusted servants, tumbled freely with the royal progeny.

Which was where Philippa was at the moment, and it was high time to collect her. The dogs needed a walk, and there was someone very special Honneure wanted to see. She clapped her hands once and four small bodies roused themselves from various positions about the room.

"Come, little ones," she called, and the four small dogs trotted obediently in the wake of Honneure's swishing blue satin skirt.

It took Honneure several minutes to reach the Queen's Stair, and she hesitated, looking up at the grand ascent. Though she and Philippa had been at Versailles for a little over two weeks, she still did not feel comfortable climbing these steps. Each time she could not help but envision Philippe at the top of the stairs, his argument with Olivia, the woman's fatal fall. The end of all hope.

Picking up her skirts, Honneure trudged upward. She heard the dog's nails skittering on the marble behind her.

There had been a thin, fragile hope in her breast when she first returned to the palace that someone would have word of Philippe, would know if he was safe, or where he had gone. But no one had so much as mentioned his name. It was as if he had never existed. Surely, if someone had word of him, they would have told her. The hope had almost died within her.

Honneure passed quickly through the overwhelmingly ornate and sumptuous reception rooms. In the Queen's bedchamber she opened the hidden door and slipped into the interior apartments. Hearing voices, the dogs bounded ahead of her into the salon, and she called to them to come back to her. Madame Campan appeared in the doorway.

"I'm sorry, Madame," Honneure apologized. "I was just passing through to the nursery stairs."

Madame Campan smiled. "To fetch Philippa? Louis Antoine has grown quite fond of your daughter, you know."

"And she of him. They play together nicely."

"The Queen is pleased. She is also fond of Philippa and grateful her nephew has such a lively and intelligent playfellow."

"The Queen has always been more than gracious. And I'm sorry I must put an end to the children's fun, but it's time for Philippa to help me with the dogs. I assume her Majesty wants to play with them before her evening begins?"

"She does. And she should be returning at any moment now."

"Then I'll hurry."

Madame Campan smiled again, enigmatically this time. "Yes, I believe you do want to hurry."

Honneure's heart leaped and she looked past Madame Campan into the salon. "Is she here?"

"She has gone to her chamber to change out of her traveling clothes, and then she'll be here for an hour or so visiting with the Queen. You have plenty of time."

With murmured thanks, Honneure collected her charges and hurried to the interior staircase. The dark, narrow corridors that connected the King's and Queen's apartments usually made the hair on the backs of her arms stand up, but she paid little heed to the dank passages today. The dogs yapped in excitement as she skipped up the stairs.

* * *

The Queen's informal salon was of a modest size. There were so many people present when Honneure returned with her daughter and the freshly walked dogs that it was difficult to pick out any one person. Her eyes scanned the milling, chattering crowd.

She saw the Queen first, who was the center of attention. Her cheeks were rosy and her eyes bright. Honneure knew how much she loved to be with her friends. Near her stood the Duchess Gabrielle Yolande de Polignac. She was a petite, Raphaelesque beauty with a swan neck and dark, velvety eyes. Honneure knew of the unkind things people said about her - and the Queen - and her hackles bristled. Yes, it was true that the Duchess and her husband were impoverished nobility. It was true that the Queen had the Duke promoted to a more lucrative position so he and his kind, beautiful wife would be able to afford to live at Versailles. But what was wrong with that? The Queen wanted her friend near her. The Duke de Polignac was ably fulfilling his duties as Equerry and earning his pay. Why did the gossip mongers insist on putting the Queen in such a bad light for such a generous and innocent gesture?

Irritated, Honneure let her eyes move on. She was not surprised to see the Princesse de Lamballe on the Queen's other side. The lady was several years older than her friend, but still lovely, pale, slim and sad-eyed, with curling fair hair, her beauty only slightly marred by a prominent nose and large hands. Though she was overly sensitive and prone to vapors, Honneure liked her very much. She was a widow who had remained devoted to her immensely wealthy father-in-law and, despite unkind rumors, Honneure knew why. The great-hearted gentleman had become widely known as "the father of the poor" for his acts of generosity. Always by his side, assisting, his daughter-in-law had become known as "the good angel." To keep such a benignant and loyal person near her, Antoinette had made her a lady-in-waiting, and Honneure was glad.

Honneure's eyes continued to scan the crowd. Her right hand held her daughter's, the left, the dogs' leashes. She did not want to intrude into the room any further than she had to. Moments later she spotted the familiar, beloved features.

The lines in her face were etched a little deeper. There was more white than gray in her hair. But it was the same sweet smile. Honneure's heart brimmed with love.

Madame Dupin made her way through the throng, until she stood facing Honneure and Philippa. Her eyes seemed moist as she gazed at Honneure, and then at the child, who curtsied to her. Madame smiled in return, and then took Honneure briefly, but tightly, into her arms.

"Dear girl," she murmured. "You've only grown more beautiful. And this lovely child . . ." Madame Dupin reached out and gently touched Philippa's shining curls. "She has your eyes. Otherwise she is the spitting image of . . ." She stopped, uncertain whether to continue.

"Of her father?" Honneure finished for her. "Yes, she knows. I tell her all the time." She gazed down at her daughter, proud of the fact she had never given in to Armand. Though the people of Honfleur may well have thought Philippa was his daughter, Honneure had never pretended such a thing to her child, or to her family and friends.

Philippa smiled at her mother, and then looked at the older woman. "You're Madame Dupin, and my papa grew up at your house, didn't he?"

Finding it difficult to speak, Madame Dupin nodded to the child.

"*Maman* told me all about it. Your house is Chenonceau, and it's where *Grandmére* and *Grandpére* still live."

"Yes," Madame Dupin whispered. She cleared her throat. "And we all wish very much that you will come and visit Chenonceau one day. Your grandparents are anxious to see you. They told me to send a hug for you. May I?"

Philippa nodded slowly, her gray eyes wide and solemn. She looked up at Madame Dupin and raised her arms.

Honneure could no longer deny her own tears. This was a moment she had longed for, prayed for. Soon perhaps, she would even be able to make the trip to Chenonceau. She had truly come home.

Madame Dupin straightened and dabbed at her cheeks with a linen handkerchief. "May we take a little walk, dear? I have time before the royal dinner party, and we have so much to discuss."

"Certainly. I'd like that."

They left through the back of the palace to walk through the formal gardens and crossed the Water Terrace, between two large, rectangular pools. Past the pools they entered the *Tapis Vert,* a long, wide avenue of velvety green grass, and approached the Apollo Fountain. Philippa ran ahead with the dogs while the two women talked, heads bent together as they strolled slowly along.

Honneure listened hungrily to tales of her home and news of her foster parents. Though they had been faithful in their letter writing, it was so much better to hear of them first hand.

"They really, really are well and happy?" she asked at a pause in the conversation.

"Oh, yes, my dear. They have aged since you saw them last, just as I have. Wrinkles are time's first erosion, and then gravity takes over and pulls us downward."

Honneure chuckled. "You will never grow old. You're far too young at heart."

"How I wish that were true! But if there is anyone at all in the world whose spirit will keep a person young, it is your foster mother." Madame Dupin grew abruptly serious. "She has carried heavy burdens over these last years, Honneure. Her mother's heart was grievously wounded. Yet she never gave in to despair. And it was she, in fact, who buoyed your foster father and I when our spirits sank."

Honneure dropped her gaze as guilt overtook her emotions. "I'm so sorry," she murmured. "For...for everything."

Madame Dupin tilted Honneure's chin upward and forced her to look her in the eye. "You have nothing to apologize for, Honneure," she said in a firm, but gentle voice. "Nothing that happened was your fault. You...and Philippe...were victims of two cruel and deceptive women."

"But you must have thought so ill of me! I led you to believe I married Armand willingly. Then you find out I'm pregnant with Philippe's child!"

"Honneure...Honneure . . ." Madame Dupin shook her head. "We never thought badly of you, never. Following Philippe's...'accident'...the entire truth came out, and we grieved for you. For both of you. Oh, Honneure." Madame Dupin took her hands. "I'm so sorry if you thought for a single moment you did not have our complete love and support."

"I...I committed a sin against God." Honneure was heedless of the tears streaming down her cheeks. "I was married to Armand, yet I...I . . ."

"Honneure, stop it." Madame Dupin squeezed Honneure's fingers until she winced. "You and Philippe loved each other. You thought your husband would free you to marry Philippe. The only sin committed was by Monsieur Tremblay when he forced you to stay with him. How you endured it I will never know."

"I never...I never believed I wouldn't be with Philippe," Honneure said in a small voice. Tears dripped from her chin to the bodice of her gown. "Then, when I learned what had happened to Philippe, that he was gone, in hiding, I...I didn't want to live. I didn't care about anything. Only his life within me kept me going."

"Oh, dearest child, I'm so terribly, terribly sorry." Madame Dupin released Honneure's hands, put her arms about her and drew her to her breast. "I am sooooo sorry."

"I miss him," Honneure sobbed. "I love him. I love him still, with all my heart. I'll never stop. And I can hardly bear it sometimes, knowing I'll never see him again, never be able to tell him about his daughter . . ."

It was more than Madame Dupin could stand. She had to tell Honneure, she had to. In time she would find out anyway. Better she hear it now, from a friend.

Taking a deep breath, Madame Dupin held Honneure away from her and looked her straight in the eye.

"Honneure, stop, please. There's something I must tell you."

Honneure dashed the tears from her cheeks. The expression on Madame Dupin's face alarmed her. "What is it? What's wrong?"

By Honor Bound

"Honneure, Philippe...Philippe knows . . ."

Chapter Twenty-Nine

August 1779

The weather was stifling, not a breath of air stirred. Honneure stood by the open window of their little room to comb Philippa's hair. She was glad of the plain, muslin gowns the Queen had made popular. Even the colors seemed cool, hers of pale green, Philippa's of sky blue. She tied her daughter's long, thick hair back with a ribbon of darker blue.

"There," she pronounced. "You're perfect."

Philippa looked up at her, eyes wide with concern. "Really? Promise?"

Honneure nodded. "Promise."

Philippa looked at her a moment longer, and then turned and walked slowly into the adjacent sitting room. She climbed into her favorite chair and sat quietly, hands folded. She had been quiet all morning. Quiet, and thoughtful.

Doubt momentarily assailed Honneure. Was she doing the right thing? Was she? Almost everyone thought she was out of her mind, and told her so in no uncertain terms.

Yet she had to do it. She would have no rest, no peace, until she had.

When a knock came at the outer door, Honneure asked Philippa to answer it. She was surprised, and taken aback, when her daughter announced it was Madame Campan. Honneure hurried into the sitting room.

"Madame Campan, what . . ."

"I've come to tell you a coach is waiting."

The older woman's features were expressionless, but there was a hard edge to her tone. Honneure felt herself flush.

"You...you're too kind. You should have sent a page."

"And I would have had I not wanted to urge you, one more time, to reconsider your decision."

The color spread downward to Honneure's neck. "I...I must go," she murmured.

"Think of your child."

"That's exactly who I'm thinking of." Honneure's voice had found its strength.

Madame Campan held Honneure's gaze for a long moment. It did not waver. She let her expression soften.

"Very well," she said at length. "I didn't think you would relent. So, since you are going to go, go with God, Honneure."

To her total astonishment, Madame Campan quickly embraced her. Seconds later she was gone. Honneure took a deep breath and turned to her daughter.

"It's time, Philippa. The Queen has kindly lent us a coach, and we must hurry."

The little girl slid off her chair and approached her mother. She looked up at her, and then took her hand and held it, tightly. Together, side by side, they left the room.

* * *

Everyone, everything, seemed to suffer with the heat. The carriage rolled slowly through the countryside, the coachman unwilling to stress his horses with a faster pace. Dust from the wheels rose lazily in the air, and the only sounds were the clop of hooves on the dry, hard-packed road and the creak of harness. Even the birds had been silenced by the oppressive warmth.

Philippa, fortunately, had fallen asleep. Honneure stared out the window until the dusty green trees passing endlessly by began to blur. Her thoughts drifted, returning to the only place they seemed to be able to go these days.

. She was back on the green with Madame Dupin. In the distance she could hear the splash of the Apollo Fountain. Then Madame Dupin had uttered those fatal words and the world went away.

"Honneure, Philippe...Philippe knows . . ."

Knowledge had flashed through her like a bolt of lightning, electrifying every part of her body. Her nerve endings literally tingled.

Philippe was alive.

Questions had crowded her mind, tumbling over one another. She couldn't speak. Madame Dupin's hands dropped from her shoulders.

"I know how many questions you must have," she said softly. "I'll answer them as best I can."

"Just...just tell me, let me hear it in your own words, that he is alive. And well."

"Indeed he is."

A shudder passed through her. "How long have you known?"

Madame Dupin hesitated. Her gaze slid away from Honneure's to rest for a moment on the fountain's statuary. "For nearly...two years," she admitted at last.

"Two years! Madame Dupin, why didn't you tell me? Didn't you know how desperate I've been to know Philippe's alive?"

"Of course, of course we knew," Madame Dupin replied soothingly. "But your parents and I thought that, under the circumstances, you were better off not...not knowing."

Honneure shook her head, trying to banish the anger that rushed in a pounding fury to her temples. "What circumstances do you mean?" she asked tightly. "A sham of a marriage to a bitter old man? You thought that would be better than for me to know that Philippe was alive so his daughter and I could go to him, be where we belonged?"

Madame Dupin regretted deeply that she had to be the one to break this news to Honneure. She loved her like a daughter. She could not bear to bring her any more pain or suffering than she had already had to endure. But there was no help for it.

"Honneure," she began gently. "There are...other circumstances...that you are unaware of. Your parents and I debated this, whether or not to let you know. And then your husband became ill and eventually died. We knew we shouldn't tell you at that time, with so many other things on your mind."

"But now I'm back, here in Versailles, so you've finally decided to tell me?"

Madame Dupin nodded.

"You said Philippe...Philippe knows about . . ." Honneure's gaze strayed to where Philippa played with the dogs.

Madame Dupin sighed. For the moment, at least, Honneure was ignoring the obvious. "Yes. Yes, he does." She gestured toward the fountain. "Come. Let's sit. I'll tell you everything from the beginning."

They sat side by side on the low stone lip of the fountain. Madame Dupin took one of Honneure's hands and held it in both of her own.

"When the...the accident happened, and Philippe was forced to flee," she began, "the Queen gave him the white Lipizzan mare. Knowing he had been unjustly accused, she wanted to aid him in any way she could. A swift mount would ensure his escape and give him something of value, should he need it, to help him survive.

"Philippe was vague about his first few months in hiding. Your parents managed to get him some money, and he existed for a time. Then he came upon an older gentleman, wealthy, of minor aristocracy, with a lovely farm in the country. He had several horses of which he was very fond, and his stableman had recently passed away. It was the ideal situation for Philippe."

Honneure listened with her entire being, hanging on every one of Madame Dupin's words. She envisioned Philippe happily working at what he loved, and her heart was glad.

"The gentleman admired the white mare," Madame Dupin continued. "Just as I did so many years before, he sent Philippe to Austria to purchase a stallion and a number of mares. Thus began a breeding operation. Philippe was quite successful, and his employer did well selling young horses.

"By this time, however, the King had been dead, and the du Barry banished, for over two years. Philippe decided it was safe enough to come out of hiding. You can imagine our surprise, and joy, when he came riding into Chenonceau one day."

Honneure could see him, riding down the long lane to the château, white horse prancing. His long, curling hair would have blown against his shoulders. Lips parting in a smile would reveal his white, even teeth. His strong, broad hands, sun darkened, would grip the reins skillfully, easily. Her heart thudded in her breast as Madame Dupin described the reunion.

"The first thing he wanted to know, of course, was about you."

"And you...you told him about Philippa? "

"He was shocked at first. Never in my life have I seen such an expression on a man's face. Then he appeared filled with a sorrow so immense it brought tears to your mother's eyes."

Pain shot through Honneure, so intense it was as if she was experiencing the event all over again.

"He...he wanted to come to us, didn't he?" she asked. "But he couldn't because of . . ."

"Because of Armand's threat," Madame Dupin finished when Honneure grew pale and faltered. "Yes, he told us. We were horrified. I thought Paul was going to leave on the spot to go to Normandy and personally throttle your husband." She sighed. "We were relieved, however, I must admit, because we never understood in the first place why Philippe had ridden to Normandy but returned without you. As much as you two loved each other, we could not imagine such a thing."

Honneure closed her eyes. "It was the worse day of my life," she whispered.

Madame Dupin squeezed Honneure's hand in sympathy. Her heart ached, and she dreaded what she must say next.

"Your foster father, at that point, insisted on going to Normandy. Not to strangle Armand, though he still very much wanted to, but to take you and Philippa away with him. He didn't think your husband would shoot a father come to fetch his daughter. He wanted to go to Normandy and bring you back to Philippe."

"But I never heard a word! What...what happened?"

"Philippe had not finished his tale. He asked his father to wait until he had heard everything. And he told us the rest of his story."

Honneure turned her face from the carriage window and stared at the wall straight in front of her. Never, never would she heal from the pain of the wound Madame Dupin, by necessity, had to inflict on her.

Philippe's employer, a kindly man, had had two daughters. One had married well, but the other lived at home still. She was a beautiful girl, and sweet. But her birth had been difficult, and her mother had died. The girl, Suzanne, had never been right. She had a sunny disposition, but had never been able to learn to read or write or figure. At the age of sixteen, some local boys had taken advantage of her, and she had, eventually, given birth to a son. Her father despaired of her ever finding a proper husband. As his health failed, he had turned to the only person in the world he now trusted.

He would leave Philippe everything; the horses, the farm, his money. If he would take care of Suzanne and her son. Forever.

He had not thought he would ever see Honneure again. He did not know he had a daughter. He had loved the old gentleman and was fond of Suzanne and the boy.

Philippe had married.

* * *

An hour earlier, they had turned off the main road. The further into the country they drove, the worse the secondary road became. A particularly severe bump awakened Philippa. She straightened and rubbed her eyes.

"Are we there yet, Mother?"

Honneure returned her attention to the scene outside her window. Woodland had given way to fenced acres of rolling fields. She saw a pair of horses, then another. They were Lipizzans.

"I...I believe we are," Honneure replied in a small voice. She said a silent prayer of thanks that her daughter sat beside her. She did not think she would be able to hold herself together otherwise.

The coachman slowed his horses as they approached a lane intersecting the road. As they made the right turn, Honneure saw a modest stone château standing in the shade of several tall and stately elms. Her heart was so full in her throat she could scarcely breathe.

There were more horses in pastures on either side of the lane. Wheels crunched on gravel as they pulled into a circular drive in front of the house. Bright red geraniums bloomed from pots on either side of the front door. The coach stopped.

Not being royalty, there was no footman, and the driver needed to stay in control of the horses. Honneure opened the door herself and stepped down.

A boy who appeared to be about ten peeked at her from behind the trunk of a tree. He had dark hair and prominent ears. She smiled reassuringly, but he darted away into the house. Honneure didn't move. She didn't think she could. A moment later the door opened again.

The woman, in her mid-twenties, about Honneure's age, was beautiful. Her auburn hair was straight and shining and hung loose around her shoulders. Her features were piquant, her green eyes huge. She smiled uncertainly from the doorway.

Honneure took a few tentative steps forward. "I...I've come to see Philippe Mansart," she said awkwardly.

The woman's face immediately lit up. She nodded happily.

"Is he...here?"

The woman shook her head, still smiling. She moved from the doorway to stand between the potted flowers.

"There. He's there." She pointed to an area behind the

château. "Are you...a friend?"

It was Honneure's turn to nod. She looked toward the small stable the woman had indicated.

"May I? Go there, I mean?"

"Yes. Yes. Go there. See Philippe." The woman's smile was lovely. It never faltered.

Honneure turned back to the carriage and held out her hand to Philippa. The child climbed down and grabbed her mother's fingers. She looked pale.

"Are we going to see him now, Mommy?" she asked softly.

"Yes, Philippa. I think so."

The stable was only a hundred yards away, but it seemed like a hundred miles. Honneure felt the woman's eyes on her until she rounded the corner of the château.

The building was long and low, with a window for every stall. Horses' heads appeared over sills to watch them approach, dark eyes large and curious. Double doors were open, and Honneure and Philippa slowly walked inside. Honneure thought her heart might explode within her breast.

Stall enclosures lined both sides of the aisle until approximately three-quarters of the way down. In the open space between the last stalls and the end of the barn was a muck pile on one side, feed and bedding on the other.

Philippe was forking straw into an orderly mound. He was completely unaware of their presence, and Honneure watched him for several moments. Though the light was too dim to pick out his features, she was able to see his hair, longer now, falling forward over his muscular shoulders. He had stripped off his shirt, and sweat glistened on his enlarged, rolling biceps. She licked her too dry lips.

Nothing had changed. Nothing. He still made her knees

weak, her mouth dry. She was as much in love with him as she had ever been. It would never change. Only the circumstances around them would change.

In her peripheral vision, Honneure saw Philippa looking up at her. She took a step forward, and then another. Her heart raced and her blood thrilled through her veins.

Philippe paused to wipe his brow and heard them, their quiet steps. He turned in their direction and saw their silhouettes, a woman and a girl, backlit by the open doors. Curious, he put aside his pitchfork.

"Hello? Can I help you?"

Honneure didn't reply. She couldn't. Philippa looked up at her again, and then at Philippe. "Papa?" she said softly into the lingering silence.

Philippe froze. Everything within him seemed to stop, the beating of his heart, the flow of his blood, his respiration. "Oh...my...God," he breathed at last.

Philippa let go of her mother's hand. She walked forward steadily until she stood just a few feet in front of her father. She cocked her head to one side, studying him. A smile tugged at the corners of her mouth.

"You look just like Mommy said you would. You look just like me."

Honneure heard a sound that could only be a sob. She moved closer until she could see Philippe's expression. It was agonized. He glanced at her, then back at his daughter. He knelt.

"Philippa?" he whispered.

She nodded. "Mommy named me after you."

"I...I know." He couldn't take his eyes from her. She was beautiful, perfect. She was his daughter. The proof of his love for her mother.

Helen A. Rosburg

Philippe closed his eyes and felt more tears squeeze from beneath his lids. His face was wet with them. He felt his daughter's fingers touch his cheek to brush the tears away.

"Don't cry, Papa," she said gently. "Mommy brought me here because she thought it would make you glad."

He could only nod. Love surged through him, so powerful, so strong and pure, that it rocked him. He captured Philippa's little hand and pressed it to his lips.

"I love you," Philippe whispered.

"I love you, too, Papa," she replied simply. "Even though I didn't meet you until today, Mommy and I have loved you our whole lives."

It was almost more than Philippe could bear. He opened his arms, a prayer on his lips, but Philippa didn't hesitate. She stepped immediately into the circle of his arms.

Honneure saw his shoulders shake as he silently wept against his daughter's shoulder. Nearly blinded by her own tears, she moved forward until she had reached the embracing pair. Crouching, she put her arms around both of them.

A horse whinnied. Sunlight slanting through open windows highlighted dancing dust motes. The world continued to turn as mingled teardrops stained the cool, stone floor.

Chapter Thirty

January 1780

Though it was hardly past noon, the day was as dark as dusk. Angry black and purple clouds warred in the sky, ominous rumblings of thunder announcing each new battle. Honneure glanced out the window of the Queen's interior salon and winced. There were few things she disliked more than winter rainstorms. The weather was cold and gloomy enough as it was. She much preferred snow to the damp depression of winter rain.

A candle guttered, and Honneure fetched a replacement from a cupboard built cleverly into the wall. She took several extras as some of the other candles had burned part way down. Madame Thierry, however, stopped her.

"Remember the economies," she warned. "We're supposed to let candles burn all the way down now."

Honneure nodded. "Thank you for reminding me."

"So many things are changing, it's hard to remember it all."

"Yes, but the changes are necessary," Honneure said loyally. "The King and Queen wish to set the example. The Royal Treasury has made so many cuts in government that the King was able to reduce taxes. He wants his people to know that he and the Queen are doing their parts as well. He does not want to be associated at all with his grandfather's profligate ways."

"We should just be glad, I suppose, that we're not among the household servants who were dismissed. Did you know that over four hundred posts were abolished in the palace alone?"

"What about the King's Hunt? Thirteen *hundred* of those posts were eliminated."

Madame Thierry shook her head and returned her attention to her mending. "We are fortunate, indeed, that the Queen returns the loyalty of us who have been so devoted to her."

"She is a woman deserving of our devotion," Honneure said with feeling. "I only wish her subjects knew her the way we do."

Madame Thierry glanced up from under a raised brow. "I know. But there are always grumblings against people in high places, aren't there? Even royal courtiers, people who should know better, whisper their calumnies about her."

Honneure flushed with a surge of anger. "They seem to be able to twist anything and everything she does. She had Madame Bertin make her more simple gowns, use smaller amounts of material and less expensive materials, and do you know what people say to that?"

"I certainly do," Madame Thierry replied tartly. "They say the only reason she uses the inexpensive material is because it is Austrian made and therefore benefits her country, that she is not selfless, merely conniving."

Honneure could feel the pulse pounding in her neck. Her response, however, was preempted by a low rumble of thunder. She glanced out the window again.

"I'd better check on Philippa and walk the dogs before it starts raining."

"How is she?"

"Better, much better," Honneure said, relief obvious in her tone. "Her stomach seems to have settled, and she's eating a little now."

"It went through the nursery like wildfire, didn't it?"

"Yes, I believe your boy was the only one spared."

"So far." Madame Thierry chuckled. "But I really wouldn't mind if he got just a *little* sick. Then he could pass it on to me. I could stand to lose a kilo or two."

"You look fine to me." Honneure smiled, and touched her friend on the shoulder as she passed. "I'll see you in a little while."

* * *

Honneure entered the sitting room quietly so as not to disturb Philippa if she was sleeping. But one of the Queen's dogs, startled out of a nap, yipped sharply.

"Mommy, is that you?" the child called from their bedroom.

"Yes, my love." Honneure entered the small room. "How are you feeling?"

Philippa pushed herself to a sitting position and rubbed her eyes. "Tired," she said grumpily. "And I missed you."

"Are you hungry?"

Philippa shook her head.

"Maybe later," Honneure said hopefully. "Why don't you lie back down and try to take a little nap? I'll stay with you until you nod off."

"I've been sleeping all morning," Philippa pouted. But she lay back.

"You'll feel better when you wake up next time. I promise." Honneure sat on the edge of her daughter's bed and smoothed strands of dark hair from her forehead. "Just close your eyes and go to sleep."

As Honneure stroked Philippa's brow, she could not help but notice the two small pockmarks. She was fortunate the beautiful little girl had not been scarred more severely. Both of them were. Honneure fingered the marks on her neck. They were fortunate simply to be alive, and she would never, ever forget how frightened she had been when the disease had been initially diagnosed.

It had been near the end of the previous August, in the midst of the unrelenting and oppressive summer heat wave. She had heard there were a few cases of small pox in the town of Versailles and a handful at the palace. A more general and widespread outbreak did not seem likely. Honneure had breathed a sigh of relief when no more victims were reported and everyone afflicted recovered. Then, all of a sudden, Philippa had become ill. In a few days Honneure was down with it as well. How she had cursed herself for not having had the inoculation the King himself was trying to promote.

Philippa stirred briefly as she drifted out of consciousness. Honneure laid her hand atop the child's smaller one.

They were so lucky it was only a mild form of the disease that struck and then retreated. But that would not always be the case. Though she and Philippa were now immune, her foster parents were not. And despite the fact that even Madame Dupin had been inoculated, they refused to take the preventive treatment.

"I'm too old to try anything new," Jeanne had said as they sat at the scarred oaken table in the kitchen of Chenonceau. "I'll take my chances."

It was October. The Court had gone to Fontainebleau, but Philippa and Honneure had still been too weak to return to work and travel as well. The Queen had urged Honneure to take the opportunity to visit her family when she felt well enough. A month later, she had taken her daughter and made the journey home.

The reunion had been bittersweet at first. Jeanne and Paul had been overjoyed to meet their grandchild. But the mere fact of her existence was a reminder of the love Honneure and Philippe had shared - and lost. They had learned, of course, of her visit to Philippe, and it had been almost unbearably painful to describe that day to them. They shared her grief over the tragic timing of events that had conspired to keep them apart still, but had been glad to know he was well and apparently prospering. They asked, awkwardly, about Philippe's wife and her son, but Honneure had had little to relate. Her time with Philippe had been so short, a few stolen moments in the fragrant gloom of the barn. He had spoken briefly with his daughter. He and Honneure had gazed at one another with agonized longing. Neither of them had been able to bear anything more. She and Philippa had left, and she had not seen the woman or the boy again.

Honneure sighed and dashed an errant tear from her cheek. The rest of their visit had been far less emotional. Paul had been eager to learn all he could of the King.

"Is it true he disguised himself and visited the Hotel Dieu unrecognized?" he had asked eagerly, referring to Paris' notorious hospital.

"He did," Honneure had replied. "And he was appalled. He made a tour of the wards and found patients four to a bed three and a half feet wide. When two wanted to sleep, the other two had to get out and lie on the floor. When a patient died, sheets were not changed, even if they had had a contagious disease. Suzanne Necker, wife of the minister of the Treasury, heard of people hustled to the cemetery before they were dead, and now has a morbid fear of premature burial."

Paul and Jeanne had been appropriately horrified. "But the King ordered reforms, didn't he?"

"He issued a decree laying down that at least three hundred patients should have a bed to themselves. Wards were to be established for each category of disease, and separate wards for men and women. To provide extra beds, Louis, Madame Necker, and the Archbishop of Paris put up money for a new hospital in the Saint-Sulpice quarter."

Paul shook his head. "It's hard to believe. From the excesses of the grandfather, to the economies and good sense of the grandson."

Honneure smiled. "He is truly a good man. He reformed the prisons also, you know. He built a place for civil prisoners so they wouldn't have to be confined with criminals. Again, he had sexes separated. He paid for the food and clothing of those who had no private means and founded a prison infirmary run by the Sisters of Charity."

"No wonder you've always written in such glowing terms of the King and Queen," Jeanne said. "The depth of the King's compassion is almost unbelievable."

"I think his most important reform, though, is the one having to do with torture," Honneure had continued, "As you know, an examining magistrate had the right to use physical force in order to get an accused man to confess his supposed crime."

It was Madame Campan who had related the terrible details to her, having heard them from the wife of one of the palace guards. Honneure had recoiled anew as she described to her foster parents the torture, how the prisoner, now tired, haggard, bearded, and vermin-covered after days and perhaps weeks in custody, was seated on a stone stool. His wrists were tied to two iron rings, two and a half feet apart on the wall behind. His feet were attached by long cords to two other rings twelve feet from the wall. The cords were fastened tight and then made even tighter by placing under them a low trestle. After the examining magistrate seized the prisoner's nose, an assistant forced water down his throat from a drinking horn. Up to four quarts were forced down the wretched man's throat; as his body swelled, the cords tightened further still, stretching his limbs in an agony of pain. A surgeon knelt beside him, and if the prisoner's pulse began to fail, ordered him to be carried away and the torture resumed later.

"Louis found this practice barbaric," Honneure went on. "He said he always wondered whether, when the question is applied, it is not the strength of a man's nerves which usually decided whether he is guilty or innocent. He put an end to the torture of accused prisoners, and no longer will any Frenchman be racked."

"Will wonders never cease," Paul had said, arms crossed on the old wooden table. "The King of France, a humanitarian. And to think, we used to sit around this same table and talk about him when he was just a little boy."

Honneure remembered well. She recalled all the tales of the Royal Court Madame Dupin had brought home to her, the stories of the young Duc de Berry and his brothers, the Comte de Provence and the Comte d'Artois, his sisters Clotilde and Elisabeth. In a way, she had grown up with them. Now she knew them as living, breathing people.

From the very first, Honneure's mother had instilled in her a love of history. She remembered a cold winter's day in Amboise, when she had climbed to the tower and looked out over the château and the town below. She loved recalling and reliving the historical details of the past. Now she was actually living history in the making as servant to the Queen of France. Never, in her wildest dreams, would she have imagined such a thing to be possible.

"The wonder to me," Jeanne had said with a chuckle, drawing Honneure from her reverie, "is not that our King is so compassionate, but that my husband has stopped complaining about our Queen. Remember how you used to feel, Paul, about the Dauphin marrying 'that upstart Austrian'?"

Paul's already florid cheeks had deepened another shade. "How was I supposed to know she'd turn out to be so...so...so *nice*?"

Laughter around the table had been interrupted by the arrival of Philippa, who had been playing in the gardens by the Cher. She was a dripping, sodden mess from head to toe.

"Philippa!" Honneure had exclaimed. "What happened to you?"

"I fell in the river," she replied evenly. "But it's not so bad. It's not as cold as the ocean in Normandy." She licked her lips. "And not as salty. I like it."

"Oh, Philippa . . ." Honneure threw her arms around her daughter and hugged her. Philippe was lost to her, and the pain of the loss would never end. But at least she had his child, and the joy of that love was enough to carry her to the end of her days.

A series of thunderclaps drew Honneure sharply away from Chenonceau and back into the present. She glanced down at her daughter, but nature's percussion had not wakened her. Honneure pulled the cover up to the child's shoulders and looked out the window. She would have to hurry to beat the rain. Calling softly to the dogs, she left their small apartment.

* * *

By Honor Bound

The threatening weather had driven almost everyone from the gardens. Thunder rolled on top of itself, and the nearly black sky seemed so low Honneure felt she might reach up and touch it. One of the little dogs was so frightened it would not run with the others, but merely cowered against the hem of her wide, gold-trimmed, blue skirt. Honneure headed briskly back toward the palace.

She was approaching the Water Terrace when her troop of dogs spotted a stray cat. It was unusual, because Louis detested cats and there were few to be seen about the palace. It was also annoying, for the first icy raindrops had begun to fall. Picking up her skirts, Honneure ran after her small charges.

Skirting the edge of one of the pools, the animals ran across the brown, brittle winter lawn of the Bosquet of the Ballroom, over a gravel path and onto the Bosquet of the Queen. There, the cat, back arched and tail abristle, leapt atop a marble pedestal. Standing with her back against the feet of the "Medici Venus," she hissed and spit at her pursuers. Honneure captured the dogs and reattached them to their leashes.

"Bad dogs!" she scolded halfheartedly and tugged them back toward the palace's garden entrance. As she hurried past the trees that bordered the Bosquet's terrace, she saw a small group of people who, oblivious to the weather, were engaged in a heated exchange. Honneure could not help but overhear, and when she realized the topic of the conversation, she slowed her steps.

"The Queen's economies be damned!" a sharp-nosed woman exclaimed. "As if it weren't all for show anyway!"

"I agree," said a man who appeared likely to be her husband. "Everything she saved cutting expenses in the royal household, she threw away again on that pretender de Polignac woman."

"I haven't the faintest idea what you're talking about," blustered a short, round gentleman Honneure recognized as a friend of the Queen's, who had but recently returned from his country estates. "Just what has she 'thrown away' on the Duchesse de Polignac?"

"A million and two hundred thousand livres," the woman nearly crowed. "Four hundred thousand simply to get her out of debts incurred *entertaining* the Queen."

"Justifiable," the portly man retorted. "Since the Queen sponsored her at Court, it is her duty to *fête* her in the royal manner."

"And what about the Queen's duties?" the woman inquired sharply. "Is it her *duty* to supply the duchess' daughter with an eight hundred thousand livre dowry?"

The gentleman's brow wrinkled as his eyebrows rose. "I beg your pardon?"

The woman smiled smugly. "The Duc de Guiche asked for the hand of the Duchess' twelve-year old daughter. As wealthy and well-positioned as he is, he was able to demand an outrageous dowry."

"And get it!" the woman's husband snapped. "Thanks to the Queen. Now what kind of economizing is that? "

Thunder rolled over the gentleman's response. The group looked at the sky and began moving away. Honneure picked up her own steps. The rain was falling faster.

Though she had heard the gossip before, Honneure was deeply upset. She knew, because she had been present when the Duchesse had entreated the Queen, that Antoinette had thought the request excessive. She had put Gabrielle off to consult with her husband and Necker, and they too agreed. In the end, however, the Queen had felt duty-bound to aid her friend as she had "taken up" the Polignacs, and they needed money to meet their new obligations. Although Honneure knew that Antoinette had done it out of a deep sense of friendship, she also knew the Court viewed it otherwise, and it saddened her.

She barely made it to the doors on time. With a great, earsplitting clap of thunder, the skies opened in earnest. Lightning streaked through the black winter sky, and Honneure shuddered.

A thunderstorm in winter was a direful sign.

Chapter Thirty-One

September 1780

The Queen's apartments were in chaos. Traveling boxes were piled willy-nilly, and clothes spilled from open trunks. Maids bustled to and fro, and there was a constant low, rapid chatter as Antoinette's servants talked among themselves. Madame Campan, nerves taut, abruptly clapped her hands. The room fell silent, and all heads turned in her direction.

"More packing and less talking will get the job done more efficiently," she said brusquely. "Time is of the essence. I want everything packed and ready to go within the hour."

Work resumed apace, although frightened glances now replaced nervous prattle. Honneure felt sorry for everyone who lived in fear of the disease currently running rampant through the countryside. Thanks to their bout with the pox last summer, she and Philippa were immune. Most people were not. And this time the disease was virulent; the death toll climbed higher each day.

Which was why, though she herself was also immune, the Queen was hurrying to Fontainebleau where no cases had yet been reported. Because of the unborn child within her, possibly the heir to the kingdom, she must take every possible precaution.

Honneure folded a last handkerchief, tucked it neatly into a corner of the trunk and closed the lid. She wondered what Madame Dupin would do. Having been inoculated, she was safe. Would she return to Chenonceau, her home, where the terrible disease was also spreading like wildfire? Or would she accompany the Queen to Fontainebleau?

A familiar fear blossomed in Honneure's breast and tried to steal through her body. She had been fighting it all day, since she had awakened that morning. When Madame Dupin had arrived, she had said Paul and Jeanne were fine. No one at Chenonceau had yet been stricken. But things had a way of changing quickly. Very quickly.

Another trunk lid thudded closed. Madame Campan directed a quartet of pages to begin taking baggage to the waiting coaches outside. Honneure rose from her kneeling position and brushed the wrinkles from her skirt. Her heart had begun to race, but she had no idea why.

Then she saw Madame Dupin.

She entered the Queen's boudoir where Honneure had been packing. Their gazes locked at once.

Honneure knew. She did not have to be told. It was as if she had been waiting for the news all day. Madame Dupin walked directly over to her and gripped her hands.

"I've had a message from Chenonceau," she began without preamble.

"It...it's my parents, isn't it?"

Madame Dupin nodded. "It's very bad, Honneure. I'm so sorry."

"I must go to them."

"Yes, you must. And I've arranged for you to leave at once. You'll take my coach."

"What about Philippa?"

Honneure had not noticed Madame Thierry standing behind Madame Dupin's shoulder. Now she stepped forward.

"I can take her with me. My son will be glad of her

company on the way to Fontainebleau."

Honneure found herself shaking her head. She and Philippa had not been separated since the day her daughter had been born. She simply couldn't imagine being without her.

Madame Dupin squeezed Honneure's hands. "Think of Philippa, dear. The situation at Chenonceau is no place for a child."

"And think of Louis Antoine," Madame Thierry said, attempting to smile. "The young Duke adores Philippa. I don't think he will go to Fontainebleau without her!"

Honneure was forced to consider reality. Madame Dupin was right about Chenonceau being no place for Philippa in the current crisis. On the other hand, she would be safe and happy with her friends, well looked after by the royal governesses.

"All right," she relented. "Thank you, both of you."

"No thanks are needed," Madame Dupin said gently. "Just hurry on your way. You were already packed for Fontainebleau, weren't you?" When Honneure nodded, Madame Dupin continued. "The driver will take you straight to the château. I've ordered for your parents to be cared for there. You will stay in the house as well." She held up a hand to stay Honneure's protest. "I'll send a page for your luggage. Go now and change into your traveling clothes. And go with my love."

The older woman embraced Honneure quickly, wondering if she should tell her what else she had done. Perhaps not. She had enough on her mind as it was.

Madame Thierry touched her cheek. "Philippa will be fine. I promise you," she whispered.

Fighting back her tears, Honneure hurried from the room.

* * *

By Honor Bound

It had been almost a year ago she had last made the trip. Little had changed, except that it was a little earlier in the season and the trees had not yet attained their full fall splendor. There were only occasional touches of red and gold scattered throughout the passing woodlands.

A stag, startled by the coach, leapt across the road. Honneure wondered how he was able to hold his head up under such a rack of antlers, much less move so gracefully. She tried to think of many things, anything to keep her mind engaged, to keep her thoughts from running ahead to Chenonceau. But it was no use. The stag disappeared on the other side of the road, and her thoughts returned home.

Twenty years had passed, twenty years since she had come to Chenonceau. Her foster parents were no longer young. And in her twenty-eight years she had learned, if nothing else, the hard lesson of change. Everything changed, constantly, inevitably. The more you wanted things to stay the same, the more tightly you held on to the present, and the more bitter your disappointment.

Yet it was difficult not to let her heart lighten just a little with hope when the coach turned down the long, familiar lane. This was home. This was where she had spent the happiest years of her life. Ahead were the gardens where she had come to know the nature and seasons of growing things. The river, where she had spent so many hours contemplating the course and flow of her own life. The barn, and the animals she had loved. The boy she had loved. The man he had become, beloved still, the love of her life...lost.

Fear and heartache crept back into Honneure's emotions. She hugged her arms to her breast as the coach crossed the first of the great piers. With a clatter of hoofbeats and the creaking of harness, the horses halted in front of the elegant stone château.

The front door opened, and Honneure half expected to see Claud. When a young woman in servants' livery appeared, she realized she'd been holding her breath. She opened the door and stepped down from the coach.

The girl was pale, her eyes wide and frightened. She stood to one side as Honneure approached the door, as if afraid she might be contaminated by the slightest touch. And well she might.

"You...you are Mademoiselle Mansart?"

"Yes. And my parents . . ."

"Please," the girl interrupted. "Come inside. They are upstairs, in the d'Estrees' bedroom."

Honneure did not hesitate. She knew the way well and walked briskly down the hall to the stairs. Picking up her skirt, she walked rapidly up the stone steps. In the upstairs corridor she turned and went to the door of the room named for Gabrielle d'Estrees, King Henry IV's favorite and mother to his legitimate son. It was a comfortable room with a huge hearth and four-poster bed. It had been kind of Madame Dupin to install her parents there. Honneure reached for the door latch.

It occurred to her suddenly that the house was very quiet. Too quiet.

Where were the other servants? Wasn't there supposed to be someone caring for her parents?

Honneure listened for a moment longer, ear to the door. Not a sound came from within. All she could hear was the frantic pounding of her own heart. She took a step backward, and then placed her palms against the door, as if she might feel through them what was happening inside the room.

It was then she heard the footsteps. Bootheels on a tile floor. A man's heavy step.

Involuntarily, Honneure took another step backward. She watched the door latch turn, slowly.

The door opened outward. She watched it swing wide. She saw the tall figure stride across the threshold.

Honneure's racing heart burst within her breast.

"Philippe . . ." she whispered, and collapsed into his arms, vision gone dark.

* * *

She was caught in a dream from which she did not ever wish to wake. She was home, at Chenonceau, Le Château aux Dames. Fall had only lightly touched the woodlands, and the trees were still fully leafed. Temperatures were mild but squirrels, alerted by the shortening of the days, scampered frantically to bury their winter stores. Doves called from high atop the dungeon tower. The Cher whispered softly against its banks and swans, their cygnets grown and gone, glided together, side by side, lovers once again.

She did not want to leave the river's edge to return to the château. There was something terrifying inside, something she did not wish to confront. She wanted to stay where she was forever, by the peaceful Cher, with Philippe holding her hand, stroking her brow . . .

"Honneure...Honneure, wake up," he said softly.

She would do anything for him, always. Obediently, she opened her eyes.

His dear, handsome face hovered above her own, inches away. One hand held onto hers, the other lay gently on her forehead. She looked into his eyes, and he did not need to speak.

"They're gone," she said simply, quietly. It was a statement, not a question.

Philippe did not so much as blink. But she knew. The silent communication between them was as it had always been. And the love.

It was so strong it was almost palpable, a thing she might reach out and touch. Time and distance had not dimmed or diminished it. Circumstances had not changed it; tragedy had not scarred it. She lay on the bed, held Philippe's hand, looked into his eyes and knew that nothing, ever, would change what they felt. This was real and eternal, and she clung to it with all of her might.

"When?" Honneure whispered at last, gaze still locked to Philippe's.

"Early this morning. The fever took them quickly. They were spared...the worst of it."

Honneure closed her eyes again. "I came as swiftly as I could."

"I barely made it in time myself."

"You saw them...before . . ."

"They didn't know me, Honneure. They didn't even know I was here."

"They went together. Thank God they went together."

Unable to speak, Philippe nodded. He had loved Honneure all his life, but he had never loved her more than in this moment. He was weak with his love, helpless. He did not know what to do or say. He was powerless.

Honneure felt her grief crowding her, pushing, trying to find a way in and take her over. But she could not let it happen, not yet. There was something that needed to be done first. She wasn't sure what it was, but she sensed it was the most important thing she would do in her life.

Dizziness assailed her when she swung her legs over the edge of the bed, but it passed rapidly. She was afraid Philippe might try to prevent her from rising, but he did not. She pushed to her feet.

"Walk with me. Please."

With a simple gesture, he indicated she should lead the way. Silently, Philippe just behind her, she left the bedchamber, and the château.

* * *

It was late in the afternoon, and the shadows were long. The air had cooled, but the sun was still warm on their shoulders and backs. Wordlessly, Honneure took Philippe's hand, and in the strength of his grip she felt his need of her. She moved a little closer to him until their shoulders touched. She took a deep breath of the clean, fall-scented air.

Honneure let her heart, her instincts, guide her. After crossing the entrance piers she turned to the left, and they entered the de Medici gardens. The autumn planting had been done, and the meticulously cared for beds were rich with the colors of bronze, yellow and a deep, dark, fiery orange. They strolled the paths while the sun sank lower in the sky and did not speak. Honneure did not think a silence had ever been so full.

For almost an hour Honneure retraced the paths of their childhood. Though no word had yet been spoken, she knew they shared the same memories. From time to time they paused, reliving a special moment. Then a glance at one another, and they moved on. They walked down the aisle of the long, low stone barn. There were fewer horses, but the smells were the same, the fragrances of dust and horsehide and straw. It was approaching dusk and a fitful breeze stirred, scraping branches on the roof. They walked outside into the early evening shadows.

From the stables they crossed the lane and entered the woodlands of the park surrounding the estate. They passed the handsome home where Claud and his father had once lived. Honneure wondered if a new steward lived there now. She had seen so few people around the château. It was almost as if they inhabited the world all by themselves.

From the steward's house they walked through the Diane de Poitiers' gardens. The sun had slipped below the horizon, and lack of light had leeched the color from the blooms, but their scent was heady. Honneure let her fingers trail along the tops of a row of blossoms, and their touch was like velvet to her skin. She looked up at Philippe and saw the ghost of a smile touch his lips. They had made many memories here as children, chasing through the winding garden paths. Honneure could almost hear the sound of Jeanne's voice, calling them to come in for supper.

The Cher lay ahead. They could hear its murmur, but they could not yet see it. Drooping willow branches obscured their view. Still hand in hand, they walked down the gentle slope to the water.

The surface of the river was dark. It was the most difficult time of the day to see. The sun was gone, but the night not quite dark. Moon and stars had no light yet to give. Though they stood side by side, Honneure and Philippe could barely see one another. Honneure laid a hand lightly on Philippe's chest.

"Will you sit with me for a while?"

She felt, rather than saw, him nod. She could also feel the tension in him, the grief. With a slight tug on his hand, she sank to the grassy bank, skirts billowing around her.

An owl hooted, and something scurried in the bushes on the opposite side of the river. There was a soft splash as a fish jumped. Then silence.

It was so quiet, Honneure heard Philippe's tears. One leg was bent under him, and she heard the sound of the tears as they fell on the leather of his boot. She raised her hand to his cheek. A painful sob caught in her throat.

Philippe covered Honneure's hand with his own, capturing it and holding against his face. "I...miss them...so much," he groaned brokenly.

The sob escaped her. Her own hot tears gushed from her eyes. "I know," Honneure murmured. "I know."

Her other hand slid around Philippe's neck. She pulled him to her, and he buried his face against her shoulder. His body shook with sobs.

Honneure did not even recognize the agonized moans coming from her as the sound of her own voice.

* * *

Time became lost to them. They held each other and rocked each other, and spent their tears. Night moved on, and a half moon rose in the sky. Night birds called, and a winged, black shape was briefly silhouetted against the stars. They heard the flapping of wings, and then nothing. Honneure brushed the last, lingering tears from her face. Exhausted, she sagged against Philippe.

"There will be many...arrangements to make tomorrow," he said softly, as if to himself. "We should try to get some sleep."

Honneure didn't reply. For a moment she wanted to deny the ending of this time they had together. Then she realized, somewhere deep in her soul, that their time was not over at all. Gracefully, without a word, she rose to her feet.

Philippe unbent his tall frame and stood beside her. Their

fingers twined at once. Walking in step, they headed back in the direction of the château.

Honneure had been given a bedchamber on the first floor. She paused at the door and looked up at Philippe. He returned her gaze unblinking. Moments later, without taking his eyes from hers, he reached around her and turned the door latch.

The room was Diane de Poitiers' bedroom. Two Flemish tapestries of considerable dimension flanked the chamber. Between them stood the massive chimney by the eminent French sculptor Jean Goujon. Honneure stared at the initials of Henry II and his wife, Catherine de Medici: H and C. Intertwined they could form the D of Diane de Poitiers, the King's mistress. Honneure would never forget the day she and Philippe had sneaked into the elegant chamber to see the infamous monogram.

They stood before it, together, again. Moonlight streamed through the tall windows, clearly illuminating the initials.

The bedchamber of Diane de Poitiers, the King's lover. The irony was not lost on Honneure. She turned once more to Philippe.

"I love you," she said simply. "I have always loved you, and I *will* always love you."

Philippe started to speak, but something caught in his throat. Years of futile longing, perhaps. A love so huge it was amazing to him that a mere frail human body could contain it.

It did not matter he could not speak. There were no words anyway to say what he felt. He could only show her. The rightness, or wrongness, of it did not matter either, just as it had not the first time. For this brief time, lovers' time, they were not of the world, but beyond it.

Honneure lifted her face and closed her eyes to receive his kiss. The touch of his lips, the feel of his flesh, and the scent of his breath were exactly as she had imagined them in a thousand dreams. Her very soul quivered with the intensity of her yearning.

Philippe wanted to crush her to him and devour her; but he also did not want the moment to end. He kissed her again, softly, and moved his hands to the buttons at the back of her gown.

It took a long time for Philippe to unfasten the long row of tiny buttons. All the while Honneure was pressed gently against him. His nearness was almost unbearable. She let her fingers trace the contour of his strong jaw, and trail down to the hollow of his throat. She started on the buttons of his shirt.

By the time Honneure's gown had dropped to the floor, Philippe's shirt beside it, they were breathing in short gasps, lips parted. As Philippe removed Honneure's underlinens, he noticed the brightness of her eyes, the glow and glint of her passion. He felt himself swell, and throb, and ache for her.

Philippe had removed his boots. Naked, Honneure knelt to pull his trousers down and away. The sight of his manhood thrilled her in an unnamable way, and she was irresistibly drawn to it. She buried her face in the dark, dense fur surrounding the object of her desire and inhaled his masculine musk. Something shivered in her heart. Philippe groaned and lifted her to her feet.

Honneure and Philippe stared at one another for a long moment. Through their eyes they each entered the other's soul. And in that instant a spiritual bond was forged between them more sure and certain and strong than the necessity of life itself.

Philippe bent his head slowly to his love. He pressed his mouth to hers and felt her hands glide over the muscles of his upper arms, to his shoulders until her fingers laced together behind his neck. He flicked his tongue against her lips, and they parted to receive him. He lifted her then and carried her, cradled against his chest, to the wide bed.

Honneure was in such an ecstasy of loving passion, she was barely aware of being borne to the bed, or laid upon it. She yearned for Philippe so greatly it felt as if her entire body, every cell, every pore, was straining to draw him inward. There was no knowing, no reality, no rational thought until he entered her...and she was whole.

Chapter Thirty-Two

Dawn's light stole slowly over the windowsill. Bright, happy birdsong accompanied it. Honneure lay without moving, eyes closed, for a long time. Philippe had risen earlier, before first light. But not before he had made love to her again. And whispered in her ear, over and over again, the depth of his love for her.

Honneure stretched, as slowly and luxuriously as a cat. Her entire body felt adored and caressed. She did not know what the future held, did not even want to think about. She wanted only to hold onto now, this moment.

Honneure held it for as long as she dared. Reality, however, poked at her uncomfortably.

There were arrangements to be made, although not as many as she had thought. Unbeknownst to her, at the time, Philippe had attended to many of the preparations. While they had been out walking, their parents' bodies had been washed and shrouded by a local woman who was also the community's midwife. Honneure was glad she had not known. They had now only to say their last good-byes and return husband and wife to the earth.

Honneure rose and quickly dressed in the gown she had worn the night before. She brushed her waist-length hair until it crackled, wound it into a chignon, and pinned it at the nape of her neck. She washed and brushed her teeth and pinched her cheeks to add some color. A glance in the mirror had shown her how pale she was - pale and drawn with grief, in spite of the satiation of her soul.

Following memory's path without thinking, Honneure started toward the kitchen. At the threshold, however, she stopped herself.

Jeanne and Paul would not be there. They would never be there again. She did not want to see the empty spaces or change the landscape of her memories. She turned and headed to the front door.

"Mademoiselle Mansart?"

The servant girl from the day before popped her head from the door of the study.

"Yes?"

If anything, the girl looked more frightened than she had previously. She leaned forward, hands braced against the door frame, apparently unwilling to leave the room she was in and enter the corridor.

"Monsieur Mansart had to...had to leave," the girl said in a small, timid voice. "He said to tell you to stay here and wait for him, and he'll...he'll contact you."

A sliver of fear inserted itself into Honneure's heart. "Where did he go?" she demanded sharply. "Do you know? Did he tell you?"

The girl hesitated, then nodded quickly. Her eyes were so wide, Honneure could see a rim of white all the way around the irises.

"He's gone to his home," she said suddenly, in a rush. "There's pox in the countryside. A messenger came this morning...his family . . ."

Honneure did not wait to hear more. She whirled, ran to the front door, tore it open, and dashed out into the sunlight. She looked around desperately, as if she might see Philippe riding away up the lane. But there was no sign of him. He was gone...gone to his family, his wife and stepson. The beautiful, damaged young woman she had seen in the doorway. The innocent child she had borne after an act of savagery.

Honneure's heart went out to them immediately. They were ill and helpless. She had to help them.

And Philippe. She was immune. He was not.

Honneure ran to the stables, calling out before she had even reached the doors. But no one was about. They were either hiding, in fear for their lives, or had fled somewhere they felt was safer. She pulled open the barn doors and hurried inside.

Someone was near. The horses had been fed and watered. She called again, but whoever it was elected to stay out of sight. Honneure jogged down the aisle, looking from side to side for a likely candidate.

The chestnut gelding was the last one on the left. He had sturdy proportions and a kind eye. She led him out of the stall and up the aisle to the tack room.

Her fingers were rusty, and it took several minutes to harness the horse properly. When she had finished, she laid the lines over his back and led him out the doors and over to the carriage house. She knew just what she wanted and, in no time, had him hooked to a light, two-wheeled cabriolet.

Honneure climbed into the vehicle and picked up the buggy whip. It felt good, familiar, in her hand. She jiggled the reins on the gelding's back and clucked to him. He moved forward into a trot, and she guided him onto the lane. When the cabriolet was straight on the road, Honneure raised the whip and cracked it.

The startled horse broke into a gallop. Honneure cracked the whip again, and the gelding extended his neck, ears

flattened. Bumping dangerously through the ruts, they spee(
into the countryside.

* * *

Philippe jumped off his lathered horse at the front door o|
the château that had become his home. As he hurried inside, he
noticed that the red geraniums had dried up and blown away.

"Oh, Monsieur Philippe, I'm so glad you're home!"

Rose, the elderly woman who had cared for Suzanne al|
her life, stood in the entrance hall and rang her age-spotte(
hands. Her plump, normally apple-red cheeks, were as white
as parchment.

"I came as soon as I got your message," Philippe replied,
pulling off his riding gloves. "How are they?"

As Rose shook her head, her tears spilled over. "No|
good, Monsieur, not good." She followed Philippe as he strode
down the hall to the boy's bedroom door. "I heard my Suzanne
call out early this morning, way before dawn, and I went to her
She was burning with fever! And poor little Jacques! I sen|
the stable boy to Chenonceau with the message for you, but he
never returned, so I didn't know . . ."

"I'm here...I'm here now. Don't worry," Philippe said in an
attempt to calm the distraught woman. He threw open the door
to Jacques' bedchamber and crossed the stone floor to the boy's
bed. The bedcovers were in disarray, and the child appeared to
be asleep. There were no telltale blisters as yet, but when
Philippe put his palm to the boy's brow, he was shocked at its
heat.

"Jacques...Jacques, can you hear me? It's Philippe."

The boy's eyelids fluttered open. "Philippe," he muttered
"I...I'm so hot." His eyes closed again.

"I know, I know, Jacques," Philippe replied gently

"We're going to do what we can to make you more comfortable. Try to go back to sleep, all right?"

The child appeared to have drifted off already. Philippe straightened his covers.

"Make sure he has plenty of water," he said to Rose. "When he wakes again, try to make him drink it."

"*Oui*, Monsieur. Yes, but come. Come now and look at my Suzanne."

The woman's tone was so filled with fear Philippe felt his own heart begin to race. He followed Rose to his wife's bedchamber.

Suzanne was much more ill than her son. Philippe knew it the moment he entered the room. The very air smelled of sickness. He looked toward the bed and saw his wife's arms and legs akimbo, the sheets tangled in her sprawled limbs. Her nightdress was pushed up to her hips, and she moved her head feebly from side to side, moaning piteously. His heart spasmed, and he tried to steel himself as he crossed to her side.

"Suzanne?"

"She won't know you, Sir," Rose said. "She doesn't even recognize me. Oh, what are we going to do, Monsieur?"

"Have you called for the doctor?" Philippe asked, knowing even as he did that the question was futile.

"I sent the stable boy there first. But there are so many cases!"

Philippe straightened his wife's gown, noting as he did so the angry red welts beginning to rise on her porcelain skin. Her flesh was even hotter to the touch than her son's. Her eyes were partly open, but all he could see were the whites. He realized that Rose had very good reason to be as afraid as she was.

"What are we going to do, Monsieur Philippe?" the elderly

woman begged anew. "How can we help her?"

"I'm not sure that we can," Philippe replied quietly. "We can only try to make her more comfortable. Fetch a bowl of water and some linens."

"Yes, Monsieur. At once...oh!" Rose halted abruptly in the door. "Who are you?" she demanded.

"My name is Honneure Mansart. I am Philippe's...sister. I'm sorry, but no one answered my knock. I've come to help."

Joy, relief, and terror were immediately at war in Philippe's breast. "Honneure, I...you can't...you shouldn't come near. You . . ."

"I've had the disease." Honneure swept past the old woman. "Philippa and I both had a mild case last summer. We're immune. What about you?"

Philippe hesitated, and then shook his head. Honneure turned to the old woman.

"And you?"

Rose, too, shook her head. Dread was etched into every line of her face.

Honneure sighed. "I'm going to need some help," she admitted.

"Then it will have to be me," Philippe responded promptly.

"Philippe . . ."

"You, of all people," he said in an undertone, "should know I must do my duty. Honor my vows."

She could not gainsay him. All her life she had lived by honor bound.

"All right," she said tartly. Honneure turned to the old woman. "Bring linens and water, please, as Monsieur Philipp asked. But a large basin. Have you any spirits?" she asked Philippe.

"Some...some cognac, I believe."

"I'll need that, too. And what about the boy? Is he this ill?"

"No, not nearly."

"Good. Then we'll go ahead and take care of...of your wife first."

When Honneure had everything she needed, she dismissed the old woman.

"Go and get some rest," she ordered kindly. "Monsieur Philippe and I will take care of them now."

With a single, distressed glance at the bed, Rose hurried from the room. Honneure allowed herself to gaze for a moment into Philippe's eyes.

She had been afraid to see guilt there, but she did not. All she saw reflected there was his love for her. It was all she needed. She got right to work.

"We must try to get her fever down, Philippe. Help me get her night dress off."

When Philippe did not immediately respond, Honneure glanced at him again. There was a flush rising from his neck to his cheeks.

Puzzled, Honneure cocked her head. "What's wrong, Philippe? She's...she's your wife."

"I cared for her," he replied at length, softly, almost apologetically. "I cared for her and the boy, just as I promised her father I would. I did it because I thought you were lost to me, Honneure. But I never loved her. I never...touched her."

Hard on the heels of the relief that flooded her limbs came a sense of almost overwhelming pity. Pity for a sweet, beautiful woman who would never know what Honneure had known.

She banished the thought swiftly and began working the

nightdress up and off of Suzanne's tortured body. Despite his initial reluctance, Philippe was right beside her.

Deftly, gently, Honneure bathed Suzanne in cool water from head to toe. Philippe turned his wife as Honneure worked and, although she groaned from time to time, she never regained consciousness. Honneure could only pray they had eased her discomfort at least a little.

When they had finished, Philippe found a clean nightdress and offered it to Honneure, but she shook her head.

"I'm going to dampen this muslin sheet," she explained, "And wrap her in it instead. In spite of what we've done, she's still on fire, Philippe."

When she had shrouded Suzanne in the wet fabric, Honneure wet a linen square with some of the cognac and applied it to the woman's brow.

"It dries quickly," she said. "And cools the skin."

Philippe could only watch helplessly. Suzanne's lovely face was disfigured by the advancing blisters, and she no longer even seemed to have the energy to toss and turn.

"We've done all we can for her now," Honneure said, laying a hand on Philippe's arm. "Let's take a look at the boy."

To Honneure's relief, the child was not nearly as sick as his mother. She saw no welts as yet, and though his temperature was high, it was not raging. Still, she bathed him too and changed his linens. He was groggy, but able to keep his eyes open, and she gave him some water to drink.

"I'll make some broth," she told Philippe. "He'll be able to take it later. I think he'll be all right."

"I...I can't thank you enough, Honneure. I don't know what to say."

Neither did she. The events of the night before seemed a lifetime away. It was difficult even to comprehend that when she left here she still had to bury their parents. She was filled with an immense sorrow, for Paul and Jeanne, Philippe, Suzanne and a little boy who was probably going to become an orphan. It was all overwhelming, yet she couldn't stop, couldn't rest, couldn't let her guard down. She had to keep going and do all she could to help until the crisis had come to its resolution.

"Say nothing, Philippe," Honneure replied at last, tiredly. "This isn't over yet. I'm going to sit with Suzanne and watch her. I wish you'd try to rest."

"I'll stay with you."

"No, Philippe," she said firmly. "You've been exposed enough. Don't prolong it. Bathe and rest, and if I need you, I'll call you."

He knew the strength in her, the determination. He wished he could tell her he loved her. But it was neither the time nor the place. Without another word, he turned and went to his chamber.

* * *

It was almost, but not quite dark when Philippe opened his eyes. He moved his head on the pillow to see what had awakened him.

She stood by the side of the bed, the fingers of one hand lightly resting on his forearm. Long wisps of hair strayed from her chignon and fell over her slight shoulders. Her features were drawn, and there were dark smudges beneath her eyes.

"I think you should come, Philippe," Honneure whispered hoarsely.

"Suzanne . . ."

Honneure left without answering, and Philippe followed her. The door to his wife's room was open, and Honneure stepped aside to let him precede her. He felt as if he was sleepwalking, moving in slow motion as he approached Suzanne's bed.

Rose sat in a chair at the bedside. One of Suzanne's hands was clasped in both of hers.

"Rose? Rose, how is she?"

But the old woman did not respond. She was calling Suzanne's name softly.

"Suzanne, dearie, it's me, your old Rose. Talk to Rose, my sweet baby. Talk to old Rosie...Suzanne . . ."

Philippe let his chin drop to his chest. He closed his eyes.

He had never loved her, but he had cared for her, deeply. Though she had the body of a woman, she had remained a child, an innocent child. There had never been any harm in her, or malice. She had a kind, open, and loving heart. She had given generously of herself every day of her life and had never asked for anything in return. She had been fiercely devoted to her son and openly adoring of her husband. They would miss her. The world would be a poorer place without her.

* * *

The following day dawned without fanfare. The sky was gray and heavy with clouds. There was no sunrise, merely a banishing of the darkness and a lightening of the ensuing gloom. Philippe thought it was entirely fitting. He turned slowly from the window of the small library.

Honneure watched him warily, as she had all night. He had not grieved, as he had done for their parents, yet seemed weighted down with an almost unbearable burden of sorrow. Even his movements were slower, as if his body had become heavier. His cheeks appeared sunken, and his eyes were dull.

Honneure was nearly ill with worry for him.

"Please, Philippe, please," she begged, as she had done so often in the past few hours. "You have to eat something, get some rest. You'll become sick yourself."

"There's too much to do, Honneure." Philippe sank into a chair behind his desk.

"I told you, I'd do all I can to help."

Philippe stared at her as a mantle clock slowly ticked. The shadow of a smile touched his haggard features.

"I know," he replied finally. "And I appreciate it. But I haven't even asked you yet for the one thing I need the most from you."

"What is it, Philippe? Tell me. I'll do anything, you know that."

But he simply shook his head and looked down at the letter he had written.

"I have to find someone to take this to Suzanne's sister," he said, as if to himself.

"I'll send someone from Chenonceau when I return, if the stable boy hasn't come back."

"Thank you." Philippe glanced up briefly. "I'm sorry I can't go back with you. I'm sorry I can't be with you, with them, when . . ." Philippe swallowed, but was still unable to continue.

Honneure's already wounded heart was bleeding for Philippe. She wanted to go to him, put her arms around him, but could not. Not here, not now, not in this house.

"It's all right," she said instead, voice barely audible. "They would understand...they *do* understand. Your place is here. I...I'll attend to the burial at Chenonceau."

"I have to stay with Jacques," Philippe said as if he hadn't heard Honneure. "I have to tell him about his mother when he's better. I have to stay with him until his aunt comes. Until we bury Suzanne."

Honneure looked away quickly, out the window, blinking back tears. It was amazing to her she had any left to shed. Through blurred vision, she looked past the glass and the branches of an elm to the field beyond. She wished she could see to the future. Wished she did not have to ask this question. But it was impossible not to. She was exhausted, in body and soul, and no longer had the strength to resist.

"And then?" she whispered.

At first she thought he had not heard. The minutes stretched, and the clock ticked their passing.

"Then," Philippe said finally, with a heavy sigh. "Then I will sell the chateau, I suppose, and the horses. I have fulfilled my obligations here."

Honneure realized she was having difficulty breathing. She pulled her gaze from the window and forced herself to look at Philippe.

"But where...where will you go then?"

Philippe's own gaze seemed unfocused. His eyes were directed at a bookshelf on the opposite side of the room, but Honneure did not think for a moment he was really seeing it.

All of a sudden, Philippe shook his head and rubbed his eyes. He drew another deep breath, and the end of it caught on a sob. Honneure saw his face begin to crumple, and tears spring to his eyes. She jumped to her feet.

"Philippe!"

"No!" He, too, rose and held up a restraining hand, palm outward. "Stay where you are, Honneure. If you come any closer I can't...I can't do what needs to be done. I can't say what I need to, ask what I have to ask of you."

Confused, heartbroken and, now, frightened, Honneure

halted in her tracks. "What..."

"Don't say anything, Honneure. Please. I can't go on until I know. I can't do anything. I don't even think I can go on living until I know."

"Oh, God, Philippe," Honneure moaned, hands clasped so tightly her knuckles were white. "What is it? Please...what is it?"

Again, Philippe shook his head as if trying to rid himself of something painful.

"This isn't the time or place, I know, I'm sorry. But I have to know, Honneure. Give me the strength to get through this, please. Tell me, when this is over, that you'll...you'll marry me . . ."

Chapter Thirty-Three

June 1785

Sunlight flooded the royal nursery, and a warm summer breeze wafted through windows opened wide to the fresh summer day. Antoinette cradled her infant son while four year-old Louis Joseph clung to her skirts and looked up at his mother with adoring eyes. The Queen shifted the baby into the crook of one elbow, freeing a hand to smooth the pale strands of little Louis' hair. She looked up as Gabrielle de Polignac approached.

"It's time for his feeding, Majesty. You come with me as well, Louis Joseph. It's time for your *maman* to give your sister her lessons. Come now."

The Queen reluctantly surrendered the tiny Louis Charles to Gabrielle, and Louis Joseph equally reluctantly detached from his mother. Antoinette nodded to Honneure, recently elevated to the position of personal maid, who headed for a distant corner of the large chamber. There, seated at a table built for their youthful proportions, were the three children who had become nearly inseparable: the Queen's daughter, Marie Therese Charlotte, seven; her cousin, Louis Antoine, ten; and Philippa, all of thirteen and achingly lovely. She and Louis Antoine had their heads bent together, as usual, and were giggling over some private joke. Honneure interrupted gently, softly touching the thick, curling hair at the nape of her daughter's neck.

"It's time for your lessons with Marie Therese, my darling."

Philippa and Louis Antoine exchanged chagrined glances.

"I don't know why Aunt Antoinette won't let me have lessons with her, too," the boy pouted.

"It's not that she won't let you," Honneure said quickly. "She would love to have you join Marie Therese and Philippa. But we must all abide by your parents' decision."

"I *hate* my tutor!" Louis Antoine declared.

"No you don't," Honneure soothed. "He's a fine man and an excellent teacher, and you will be very glad of him one day."

Louis Antoine muttered something under his breath as Honneure ushered the girls to the other side of the room, under a sunny window, where Antoinette preferred to give her lessons. She felt sorry for the boy. The Queen was an excellent and patient teacher, far superior to the thin, shy young man engaged by the Comte d'Artois. But there was friction between the Comte and his brother, the King. Artois and Provence both refused to abide by Louis' austerity measures. They spent lavishly and were frequently in debt. To make matters worse, they openly criticized their older brother for his frugality and apparent lack of regal frivolity. It had not made for a pleasant situation and carried over even into the nursery.

Sunlight slanted through the open window like a warm, buttery river. The girls sank to the floor at the Queen's feet, skirts billowing about them. Honneure sat nearby and picked up her embroidery, red roses on white silk, part of a set Antoinette herself was stitching for a group of chairs she'd had made. Honneure loved these peaceful, quiet hours in the nursery. The only part of her day that was better was the moment when she saw her husband again, and he took her into his arms . . .

The nursery door opened abruptly, capturing Honneure's attention immediately. She was surprised to see Madame Campan and dismayed by the expression on the older woman's face. The Queen looked up as Honneure rose to her feet.

"Majesty." Madame Campan dipped a brief curtsy. "I've received news I believe you will wish to hear at once...in private."

Honneure's heart increased its beat. Madame Campan did not ruffle easily.

"Shall I stay here with the . . ."

Antoinette interrupted with a shake of her head. "No, Honneure. Gabrielle will carry on. I want you with me."

Following hasty farewells to her children, Antoinette left the nursery with a sweep of her gauzy skirts. Only the quickness of her step betrayed her anxiety.

* * *

All the ladies-in-waiting present in the interior apartments appeared to be agitated. The Queen dismissed them with a wave of her hand, at the same time motioning Honneure to remain.

"All right, Campan," she said when the salon door had closed behind the last lady. "Tell me what news. Or do I already know? Is there word of *Parlement's* judgment on Rohan?"

Madame Campan nodded slowly, never taking her eyes from the Queen's.

"He has been acquitted, hasn't he?"

Campan's gaze never wavered. "Yes," she replied at length. "He has been acquitted."

Antoinette seemed to sag, and Honneure moved discreetly

nearer. She watched the color drain from the Queen's face while, at the same time, beads of moisture appeared on her brow.

"How can it be? How can this be?" Antoinette murmured, wringing her hands. "His guilt was clear."

"If it is any comfort, Majesty," Madame Campan continued, "Jeanne de La Motte has been condemned. She is to be branded as a thief and imprisoned in the Salpetriere for life."

Antoinette's eyes flashed briefly. "It is not punishment enough," she breathed. "I fear she has tarnished this monarchy to the point where the people will never again be able to see its brightness."

"Majesty!" Honneure gasped before she could stop herself. Even Madame Campan's eyes widened in shock.

"Surely Your Majesty doesn't mean it," she said quickly. "And certainly it isn't true."

"Oh, but it is, Campan."

Honneure stood near enough to the Queen to see she had begun to tremble.

"This...'affair of the diamonds!' " Antoinette spat the phrase. "I turned that necklace down years ago when it was offered to me for purchase. I turned it down again when Louis offered to buy it for me as a gift. The price was ridiculous, and I said so! And I turned it down a third time when Bohmer himself, the jeweler, came to me and told me he'd be ruined if I didn't buy it."

"If I remember correctly," Madame Campan said softly, "Your Majesty told him to break up the necklace and try to sell the diamonds separately."

"If only he had done so." The Queen's voice was barely a whisper. She groped behind her as if feeling for a chair. Gently, Honneure guided her to a seat, and the Queen sank down heavily. When she looked up, unshed tears glistened in her eyes.

"How could anyone think I had changed my mind?" she asked in a tremulous voice. "How could that fool of a man think I had changed my mind when I have always stood so firmly against such profligacy?"

"Because he is just what Your Majesty said, he is...a fool."

Madame Campan shot Honneure a warning look, but she ignored it. Her loyalty to her queen burned fiercely, and she found the injustice nearly intolerable.

"Your Majesty hadn't even spoken to the Cardinal in eight years!" she exclaimed. "You have steadfastly refused to recognize him, precisely because he *is* a pompous, supercilious, egotistical *ass*. And now he has proved it!"

"Honneure!"

"No, no, it's all right, Campan," Antoinette said tiredly. "Honneure is right. His opinion of himself has always been so high that when de La Motte told him that I had relented in my opinion, though I could not acknowledge it publicly, he believed her at once. I'm sure he honestly believed that I was extending my hand to him in friendship, however clandestinely."

"And the letters she sent to him," Honneure pressed on, outraged. "Only an imbecile would have...*could* have believed...the Queen of France would write so intimately to someone she had never even spoken to."

"Nevertheless," Antoinette said sadly, "he believed the forgeries were from me. The Cardinal de Rohan believed I would grant him my public acceptance if he but did me that one favor. If he would only procure the necklace for me. In secret."

Madame Campan snorted uncharacteristically. "The

Cardinal's greatest sin is not stupidity, but gullibility. He fell for de La Motte's scheme as easily as an overripe apple falls from the tree."

"Yes, Campan, he certainly did," Antoinette agreed. "He obtained the necklace from the jeweler in exchange for a payment agreement bearing another forged signature. When he brought it to de La Motte, she gave him still another forgery, a letter from 'the Queen' instructing him to hand over the necklace to the bearer. And so he did. And so Jeanne de La Motte's plot to steal a necklace worth nearly two million livres came to fruition." Antoinette laughed without mirth.

"Do you know what's ironic?" she asked of no one in particular. "She did exactly as I had advised Bohmer to do. She broke up the necklace and sold the stones separately."

"Yes, and it was her undoing," Madame Campan added, a note of satisfaction in her tone.

"Her undoing," the Queen repeated. Her gaze seemed very far away. "And mine . . ."

"Majesty!"

Antoinette shook her head, denying Madame Campan's exclamation. She rose and walked slowly to the window. The tight, frizzy curls that framed her prominent brow moved slightly in the warming breeze. She placed her delicate hands on the sill.

"Don't you see? The people want to believe ill of me. They want to believe the rumors that this was all an intrigue between myself and the Cardinal; that I only pretended to dislike him, the better to conceal our little game; that I did, indeed, want the necklace . . ."

"No, Majesty, no."

This time it was Honneure who shook her head in denial. She came up behind the Queen and touched her gently on the shoulder.

"It's not true, it's simply not true. Just two winters ago, when it was so desperately, bitterly cold, you distributed two hundred and fifty thousand livres from your personal allowance to those hardest hit and allowed the poor to warm themselves and take food in the palace kitchens. And the people built a statue to you out of snow and ice, next to the King's, and wrote on it the rhyme: 'Take your place near our kindly King, Queen, whose beauty surpasses your charms. This frail monument is of snow and ice, but our wishes for you are warmer.' "

"Don't you remember? *I'll* never forget. They can't have changed their opinion so quickly...You are beloved!"

Antoinette turned from the window. "Beloved, yes...by you, dear and faithful friend."

Honneure's heart constricted within her breast as the Queen took her hand and squeezed it.

"But *Parlement* has been traditionally hostile to the monarchy, and this is a great victory for them. By acquitting the Cardinal, *Parlement* has declared that the Queen's private life is not above reproach. In the eyes of the French people, I am compromised. Mark me, Honneure. Things will never be the same again."

"Your Maj . . ."

"No, they will not. And would you like to know what the greatest irony of all is?" Once again, Antoinette smiled humorlessly. Tears had returned to brim at the corners of her light blue eyes.

"The irony," she continued, "is that the necklace was originally made for Madame du Barry. Did you know that? It was made for the du Barry, who liked such gaudy and expensive baubles. But the King died before he could purchase it for her. He died, and she was banished from Court. Yet her greed haunts me still . . ."

The tears spilled over at last, and Antoinette collapsed, weeping, into Honneure's waiting arms.

* * *

In less than an hour, the Queen was in her bed, deeply asleep. She had wept inconsolably until overtaken by exhaustion, and had finally allowed Honneure and Madame Campan to disrobe her and lead her to her boudoir. Honneure had wanted to stay by her, but Madame Campan would not hear of it.

"You have other obligations," she had said, not unkindly. "And a rare opportunity to take some time for yourself. Take advantage of it. I will send word at once if she wakes and asks for you."

And so Honneure found herself hurrying across the Water Terrace toward the Fountain of Apollo. She had left Philippa in the nursery. She and Louis Antoine were always content when they were together. She could return for her daughter later. Honneure knew exactly where she wanted to go and what she wanted to do. It was the best way she knew to rid herself of the premonitory gloom which had settled around her like a pall.

The sun was high overhead, unobscured by clouds, and the magnificent gardens surrounding her were brilliantly in bloom. Yet Honneure felt as if she walked within a shadow. Despite her protestations to her Queen, she was well aware of the mood of the Court and the whisperings in the countryside. The Queen was right.

People were fickle, they loved gossip and they particularly loved to bring the mighty low. Honneure had not wanted to think it could ever happen to someone as sweet, generous and compassionate as Antoinette. But it was happening indeed. Axel de Fersen was a perfect example.

The Queen had met the handsome and dashing Comte de Fersen in June of the previous year. Antoinette had arranged a gay and elaborate party at the Trianon to entertain King Gustavus of Sweden. The Count, one of the King's courtiers, met Antoinette at the gala, and the two became immediate and fast friends. Honneure distinctly remembered the night the Queen had excitedly told her about her new friend, how witty and intelligent he was. Antoinette had been so happy. Her happiness was not to last for long.

Within days rumor reached them that Antoinette was being criticized for throwing too expensive and elaborate a party. The criticism had wounded her deeply, for she had merely done as her husband requested. He had wanted to impress the Swedish king in order to obtain a treaty favorable to France. In that, he had succeeded, and Antoinette had been proud. The cruel censure injured her, but worse was to come. Though she had only seen Axel de Fersen once, at the gala, he was now rumored to be her lover.

Honneure shook her head as she continued on her way. Antoinette's name was constantly being linked to various rakes and dandies. It was ridiculous as there was not a more loyal or devoted wife than Antoinette. Yet Antoinette herself had stated what others hinted at darkly, "Just look at the differences between us, Honneure! Louis is steady, while I am quick. He is reserved, while I am the opposite. He loves books; I loathe reading! He could care less about music; I adore it. His friends are few; mine are many. No wonder people think we must not get along!"

There were other differences as well, Honneure mused, which the Queen had not mentioned. While Antoinette was elegant, majestic, royal in every way, the King was awkward and ungainly. The Queen had remained slim, whereas Louis had become quite portly. These things, too, were talked about...and speculated upon. It was a shame people did not also comment on the positive, the traits the royal couple had in common. For both were great of heart, devoted to their children and their country. Their sense of duty was firm and unwavering. While theirs was not an affair of passion, there was still solid and deep affection. The Queen had been and would continue, without doubt, to be faithful. No one knew better than Honneure, who could account for almost every one of Antoinette's waking hours.

She was not left, however, with a great deal of time to herself, and she treasured the moments she was able to spend in her small, but cozy home. Her footsteps quickened as she approached the Hameau.

The farm on the palace grounds was perfect in every way. Conceived by the Queen, the village boasted eight thatched cottages, a cow barn, stables, dairy, paddocks, and chicken run. There were sheep, goats, Swiss cows, horses, laying hens, and an orchard. Though, once again, the Queen had been criticized and accused of building and running the farm for her own personal amusement, she had actually had it created as an agricultural experiment. So far the experiment was working, and the farm brought in a minimum of six thousand livres a year. One of the reasons for the farm's success was good management, and it was the stable manager Honneure currently sought.

The stables lay at the far end of the small, efficient farm. Just ahead and to the right stood the cottage that had become home. Honneure saw him striding toward the front door, a bucket swinging from one hand.

How many years had it been? And he still made her knees weak. Honneure felt the warmth fill her midsection and spread out to her limbs. She raised a hand in greeting as her lips curved into a smile.

"Honneure! What are you doing home this time of day?"

His broad grin answered hers, and a fresh wave of warmth washed through her. He was definitely, Honneure decided, more handsome than ever. The lines time had carved into his face added character to his mobile features. His hips were still narrow, his waist slim, but his chest seemed larger, shoulders more muscular. A light dusting of snow had touched the thick, dark hair at his temples. Though she never would have thought it possible, she loved him more than ever.

Philippe set down his bucket and walked toward his wife. Merely being in her presence was like being touched by sunlight. She surrounded and filled him in ways he would never be able to express in words. As he reached her she held out her hands, and he took them, drawing her to him. He bent his head to her, and their lips briefly touched.

"This is a rare treat, Wife."

"Mmmmm." Honneure closed her eyes and received just what she wanted...another kiss. "What's in the bucket?"

"Fresh butter and cheese."

"I'll make you and Philippa something wonderful for dinner."

"Where *is* our daughter?"

"I left her in the nursery. You know how she and Louis Antoine love to be together."

There was a quick, hot stab of unnamed fear in Philippe's breast. It was gone as quickly as it had come, but he was still not completely at ease. Honneure was worried about something. He felt the heat of it emanating from her. He took

376

her arm and hooked it through his.

"Come in the house and tell me why you're home early. And why you're so worried."

Honneure glanced up at her husband. He had an uncanny way of sensing her moods, no matter how well she tried to hide them. It had been that way, she supposed, since they were children. She stepped inside the cool, dim cottage ahead of him.

The main room contained everything they needed for their quiet, comfortable life. Utensils of various sizes and shapes hung on the walls around the hearth, much like the kitchen at Chenonceau. Bright curtains hung from the windows. The walls were whitewashed, and a pot of summer flowers sat on the sturdy kitchen table. It was a home filled with warmth and light and happiness. But Honneure shivered as she sank into a chair. Philippe sat at her side.

"Tell me what's wrong," he urged. "Does it have anything to do with the Cardinal de Rohan?"

Honneure's brows arched. "Do you know about the...the acquittal?"

Philippe nodded. "Word spreads quickly. I imagine the Queen is taking this very hard."

"She's distraught."

"As well she might be. People's sentiments seem to lie with the *Parlement*."

Honneure glanced up from her folded hands. "The Queen fears irrevocable damage has been done to the monarchy," she said in a small voice.

The prick of fear returned, but this time Philippe recognized its source. It was a secret he had harbored and protected for over fifteen years. For Honneure's sake, and Philippa's, he must keep it safe still. With the mood building in the country, it became more imperative every day.

"Philippe? Is something wrong?"

He shook his head, more to banish the thought than in denial.

"Nothing's wrong. Especially now that you're here."

Once again Philippe's smile did something to the pit of her stomach. She took his hand, raised it to her lips, and kissed each knuckle.

"I love you," Honneure whispered, and knew she would never be able to tell him how much. Or how much she treasured their life together, the three of them, and how she wanted to go on like this forever.

But the thought itself frightened her. She recalled all the times in her life when she had thought everything was perfect, and how she had prayed nothing would ever change. And it reminded her how fragile the web was they had woven, how easily broken...how transitory happiness.

Honneure rose and pulled Philippe to his feet. She moved directly into his arms and pressed her lips to the hollow part of his throat she so loved. She rubbed her hands over the hard mass of his chest and, with a melting thrill, let her body conform to his.

Her need of him was urgent, demanding, and Philippe's body responded. When her hand moved down his hard, flat abdomen, his manhood rose to meet her. He groaned as she rubbed her hand along his shaft. Bending his knees, he stooped slightly and lifted her into his arms.

Honneure closed her eyes, reveling in the knowledge of the ecstasy and forgetfulness to come.

Chapter Thirty-Four

September 1788

Honneure opened her eyes to pre-dawn darkness. The nip of fall was in the air, and the tiny bedroom was chilly. She snuggled closer to the man sleeping at her side. He rolled over and threw an arm across her breast. Honneure smiled.

Eight years they had been married. Eight years. And the joy of it was still new. She turned her head on the pillow and kissed the tip of her husband's nose.

Philippe's eyes opened slowly. "It's cold," he murmured sleepily. "I'll start the fire."

"You certainly will," Honneure agreed. "But not in the hearth."

She rolled over and faced her husband, letting her fingers trail along the dark line that divided his chest. There were occasional strands of silver, she noticed. She was proud of them. They were a marker of time, a symbol of the years they had spent together. Such precious time. An accumulation of days, each one treasured. Not a single one taken for granted.

Despite the pleasant thoughts, anxiety pricked at Honneure's consciousness. Lately it was like a predator, stalking her, moving in and out of the shadows. Sometimes she was aware of it. Often she was able to ignore it. But it always returned. She closed her eyes and pressed her lips to Philippe's.

The passion between them had never dimmed. At times it

379

was less urgent than others, however, and they loved each other slowly, comfortably. They were a perfect fit and now moved together with the ease of long familiarity, each knowing exactly what the other liked. When Philippe groaned with pleasure, a thrill sparked in Honneure's breast. Her tongue flicked at his mouth, and he drew her in as he rolled on top of her, need mounting, rhythm increasing. She loved the feel of him, every inch of him, every centimeter of his flesh pressed to hers. And the white hot flame bursting between her legs . . ..

* * *

A crackling fire had taken the chill from the air, and the compact house smelled of coffee by the time Philippa stirred herself. The sun was just peeking over the horizon, and a fine mist crept along the ground and swirled about the farm buildings and cottages. An impatient cow lowed, followed quickly by another.

Honneure turned from the window and listened to the sounds of her daughter moving about the loft sleeping area. Moments later she appeared, dressed but disheveled, and climbed down the ladder into the main room.

"Help me with my hair, Mother...please?"

Philippa looked up at Honneure from beneath a fringe of long, thick black lashes. She was so beautiful, and so like her father, it made Honneure's heart ache. She nodded, wordlessly, and took the brush her daughter offered.

It was a morning ritual, brushing, braiding, and pinning her daughter's hair. It was another of the special moments in her life she had come to cherish. But it would not last forever. In barely a month Philippa would be sixteen. It was time to think about marriage and suitable young men her age.

"Ouch! Mother, you're pulling!"

"I'm sorry," Honneure apologized, and tried to concentrate on what she was doing. It was difficult.

Philippa was completely devoted to Louis Antoine, Honneure knew. They had become such fast friends. The child would never willingly leave the young Duke's side, and Honneure certainly understood that kind of devotion. Louis Antoine was precocious, however, despite his younger age, and Honneure could no longer tell herself the relationship was merely platonic. She sighed as she twisted the thick plaits of Philippa's hair.

Unless something changed, there was no doubt what would eventually happen. Honneure had been forced to think about it more and more often of late. She had been forced to examine her innermost feelings. If Louis Antoine and Philippa were to indulge their love, Philippa could never be more than a mistress. Did she want that for her daughter?

No, she did not. Absolutely.

But neither could she deny the strength of a true and honest love. She well knew how rare and precious it was. Moral and religious constraints had not stopped her and Philippe. How could she preach them to her daughter?

The unpleasant turn of her thoughts was interrupted by the touch of her husband's hand on her shoulder, and she turned to him gratefully.

"I'm going to the stables," he said, and kissed her lightly on the brow.

"Have a good day, my love."

Philippe smiled in response and kissed his daughter on the cheek. She hugged him back.

"I love you, Daddy."

"I love you, too."

Tears immediately sprang to Honneure's eyes. She

blinked them away as Philippe strode out the door, and then returned to pinning her daughter's hair. How incredibly blessed they were. Since the day they had wed, it was as if they had always been a family. Philippa had accepted her father and adored him, as if he had raised her since the moment of her birth.

"Thank you, Mother." Philippa explored her hair with her fingers. "Are you ready?"

"I will be in a moment."

Honneure banked the fire and pulled a shawl around her shoulders. Their day was well begun.

* * *

Honneure and Philippa walked side by side through the grand and gilded reception chambers. Dressed in the Queen's livery of blue and gold, no one paid any attention to them. They entered the golden bedchamber and proceeded through the hidden door to the inner apartments. Philippa pecked her mother on the cheek.

"I'll be in the nursery. I'm going to help with Louis Joseph's lessons today."

"I know." Honneure's smile abruptly faded. "How is he?"

Philippa shrugged, an unhappy look on her piquant features. "His back pains him greatly. But he is very brave."

"And you are very kind to be so good to him." Honneure lightly caressed Philippa's cheek. "I'll see you later." She smiled fondly as she watched her daughter continue on to the interior stairs, and moved into the salon.

Madame Campan sat alone, her latest embroidery project draped across her lap. She acknowledged Honneure with the barest tilt of her head.

"Has the Queen gone to the chapel again?"

Madame Campan nodded. "She and her ladies left almost an hour ago."

"She goes more and more often. And now earlier."

"Much of her day is spent in prayer."

Honneure did not respond. There was little to say. Both women well knew the reason for Antoinette's immersion in her faith. She walked on to the Queen's bedchamber to put it in order.

The fateful day had occurred just over a year ago. Honneure would never forget it.

She, Philippe, and Philippa had taken a rare day for themselves and were having a picnic in the gardens not far from the palace. The day was warm, and they sat in the shade of a huge, spreading oak. They had been laughing, happy together. The Princesse de Lamballe's shriek had pierced them like a knife.

"Come...come quickly! Oh, my God!"

The woman came running across the lawn in their direction. Her arms were akimbo, hair streaming.

"Honneure...Honneure!"

All three of them had risen to their feet. Philippe gripped the Princess' arms as she stumbled to a halt.

"Honneure, you must come...at once," she gasped. "Something has happened to the baby!"

"Sophie?" Honneure's blood turned to ice.

But the woman could not respond. Philippe caught her as her eyes rolled up, and she sagged.

"Go on," Philippe urged. "I'll see she gets back to the palace."

Honneure did not need to be told twice. She picked up her skirts and fled, a prayer on her lips.

Sophie Helene was only eleven months old and the apple

of the Queen's eye.

The scene in the nursery was chaos. Several of the Queen's ladies were sobbing, Gabrielle de Polignac chief among them. The Queen herself stood as still and white as a marble statue by the satin draped bassinet. Honneure pushed to her side.

But it was too late. The beautiful infant girl lay dead. There was nothing anyone could do. No cause of death was ever determined. God had simply taken her.

Honneure finished straightening the Queen's chamber and returned to the salon. Madame Campan's hands lay quietly in her lap. Her face was turned to the window, but her gaze was unfocused.

"Do you know why I think she spends more and more time at her devotions?" the older woman said at length, as if no time at all had passed since Honneure had left the room. "She was not even allowed to grieve that poor little baby."

The heat of anger blossomed at once in Honneure's breast. "Nor the King."

Honneure recalled how his ministers had been at him, hounding him even as he tried to grieve in private with the Queen in her chambers. "Disintegrating affairs of state," they had said. France was more important.

"And they criticized my poor Antoinette," Campan continued. "Said she grieved too long for a child who had lived so short a time. When asked why she did not recover, do you know what she replied?"

Madame Campan pulled her gaze from the window at last and looked up at Honneure. Tears shimmered in her eyes.

"She said, 'I grieve because she might have grown up to be my friend.' "

Honneure's heart twisted. Though Antoinette was Queen

of France, surrounded by courtiers and servants and a few professed friends, she was the loneliest woman Honneure had ever known.

"*I* will never desert her," she murmured softly.

"Nor I." Madame Campan sighed. "But dark days are coming." Her eyes fastened once more on the view outside the window. "They began with that horrible affair of the necklace. Public opinion started to turn against her then, and the gaiety, her *joie de vivre*, seemed to leave her. She stopped going to the opera, the comedies . . ."

Campan's voice trailed away. She cleared her throat.

"Then she learned poor Louis Joseph suffered from the Bourbon's hereditary disease," she said, referring to the affliction that had taken the King's older brother when he was but a child. "Then Sophie. And Louise."

Honneure remembered. Antoinette had been extremely fond of the King's aunt, who had devoted her life to the Carmelite order. Her death, so soon after Sophie's, had been a grievous blow.

"Dark days are coming," Madame Campan said again. "The golden era is done."

* * *

Madame Campan's words had remained with Honneure all day. The prediction was dire, but Honneure could not deny the truth of it. Antoinette's life had indeed taken a sad turn. The King's was not much better. France was in turmoil.

Honneure and Philippa hurried homeward together in the failing dusk. The chill air was heavy with the scents of autumn, damp leaves and earth, burning wood. The seasonal fragrances usually cheered her, but now Honneure barely noticed them. All her thoughts were bent on home. And

Philippe.

He awaited them, seated at the table in front of a roaring hearth. In spite of her cloak of gloom, Honneure's heart had lightened when she saw his silhouette through the window. But as she walked in the door, the smile died on her lips.

"Philippe...what's wrong?"

He rose from the table, chair scraping on the stone floor. He indicated the remaining seats, and Honneure and Philippa joined him. Philippa shrugged the shawl from her shoulders, but Honneure kept hers tightly wrapped about her shoulders. An icy river of fear seemed to have replaced the blood in her veins.

"I have disturbing news," Philippe began without preamble. "News so grave the King collapsed upon receiving it."

Philippa's eyes widened. Honneure reached across the table to lay a hand atop her husband's. She was not surprised by his announcement. It seemed she had been waiting all day for another grim reminder that the world, as they had known it, was slowly crumbling.

"He was hunting," Philippe continued, "when he was brought a packet of letters. A short while later one of his huntsmen came upon him. He had dismounted and was sitting with his head in his hands. He was weeping."

Honneure's heart cringed in sympathy. "What could possibly affect him so, Philippe?"

Philippe drew a deep breath. "You know that he disbanded *Parlement* because they would not go along with his reforms for the people."

Both Honneure and Philippa nodded in unison.

"Despite the fact the King was trying to help them, and *Parlement* had blocked his every move, the populace clamored for the body's reinstatement. Though he was loath to do it, there was such an outcry he finally relented. But he believed, he truly believed, that the people didn't really mean it. That they were rebelling for rebellion's sake and would be sorry when *Parlement* reconvened. That they would see what good the King had been trying to do and be remorseful."

"But . . ." Honneure prompted when Philippe hesitated.

"*Parlement* returned in triumph." Philippe shook his head. "There's celebration in the streets. It's a complete rejection of Louis and everything he stands for."

"Oh, Philippe, how horrible." Honneure pressed her palms together and raised her fingers briefly to her lips. "But why? I don't understand. Louis would have lowered taxes, distributed wealth more evenly."

"It's a mob mentality now at work, I fear," Philippe replied. "It's not rational. It's been drummed into them that monarchies are despotic and set against them, and they can't see beyond their own prejudices to recognize what a good and enlightened King is trying to do for them. They want things the way they were. They want *Parlement* back although it will be to their detriment, and beneficial reforms will never pass. They can't see what a brilliant reformer Louis really is. Or was."

"Philippe, don't say that. He hasn't given up. He can't."

"From what I've been hearing, his spirit's been broken. He's apparently resigned to the fact that he must reap what his grandfather sowed."

Honneure remained silent as fear clutched at her heart. She knew her husband well. So well that she could see in his eyes there was more. He had something else to say, though he did not wish to.

"Go on, Philippe," Honneure whispered at last. "Say what

you must."

Philippe held his wife's gaze. He knew what her response would be. He also knew he had to try. It was his duty as the head of the family to try and protect them.

"The King's acceptance of his defeat will further weaken the crown. There's already upheaval in the country. I fear worse. Much worse."

Honneure had already begun to shake her head slowly from side to side. "No . . ."

"Listen to me, Honneure," Philippe pressed on. "It may no longer be safe to remain at Versailles. I have the money from...from Suzanne's father. And the horses I've bred from the Queen's gift of the Lipizzan mare. We have enough to buy our own place, start over, away from the storm I fear is on its . . ."

"No!"

Philippa's chair tumbled over backward as she leapt to her feet. Her parents stared at her in shocked surprise.

"I won't go...I can't!"

"Philippa . . ." Honneure rose and extended a hand to her daughter, but Philippa backed away from her.

"No, leave me alone," she cried. "You don't understand. I can't leave Louis Antoine...I love him...he loves me! I won't go!"

Honneure raised a hand and pressed it over her heart. So. It was as she had suspected. She was surprised only by the timing. She had not expected it so soon. She opened her mouth to speak, but Philippe was quicker, both in word and action.

In one smooth, swift motion, Philippe rounded the corner of the table and grabbed his daughter's wrist. Thunder rode on his brow.

"Have you lain with him?"

Honneure gasped in horror. Philippa's mouth fell open.

"Have you?" Philippe demanded. "I asked you a question. Answer me!"

Philippa seemed to regain her senses. She shook her head.

"No," she whispered hoarsely. "No . . ."

Philippe crumpled before Honneure's eyes. His chin dropped to his chest, his shoulders slumped, and his knees bent. She was afraid he was going to fall and started toward him.

But Philippa had returned to life. She pulled her wrist from her father's grip, and Honneure could see her fists were clenched. Her dark eyes flashed fire.

"But you can't stop me," she exclaimed suddenly. "You can't stop *us*. We . . ."

Philippa's head snapped sideways with the force of her father's blow. The reddened print of his palm was almost immediately visible on her cheek.

Honneure's hands flew to her mouth. The whites of Philippa's eyes were visible all the way around the dilated pupils.

"You'll never see him again!" Philippe roared. "Do you understand? I'll lock you up if I have to, but you will *never see him again*!"

Utter silence followed the outburst. Then, abruptly, Philippa burst into hysterical tears and fled up the ladder to the loft. Honneure started after her, but Philippe grabbed her hand.

"Leave her," he ordered. "Come with me."

It was not happening. It was not possible. She did not know this person Philippe had become. Numb and docile, Honneure followed her husband out of the house and into the cold night air. He walked around the side of the cottage, away from neighboring windows, and stopped. Honneure stared at him.

Philippe's sanity returned as his terror abated. Guilt assailed him, and he reached for his wife. She shrank from him, and he groaned.

"You don't understand," he said brokenly.

"You're right," Honneure whispered. "I don't."

Philippe pressed his fingers to his eyes, and then scrubbed his face with his broad, strong hands. He felt sick to his stomach.

How could he tell her?

Honneure had begun to tremble. She was cold. Inside and out.

"Tell me, Philippe," she said in a flat, emotionless voice. "Tell me what I don't understand."

He had known this time would come. Eventually. In his heart he had prayed it would not. But he had known.

"Do you...do you remember the night you were ordered to dance for the King, Louis' grandfather?" he began in a voice foreign to even his ears. "I was so afraid for you, Honneure. And not just because of the King's intentions. There was something else. Something from the past, something you'd told me when we were children. It was haunting me. Making me ill, literally, with fear, though I didn't know why. Then it came to me."

She was caught up entirely in his tale. She did not resist when he again reached for her hands. Having captured her, Philippe drew her closer to him. She looked up at him and became lost in the torment of his gaze.

"When your mother died," he continued, "you told me of her cryptic words. It had always bothered you, a puzzle you could not solve. A last message from your mother you could not decipher. And neither could I, Honneure. I could never help you. Not until that night when I put it all together at last."

It had been a day of shocks. Honneure had a feeling she was about to receive the greatest one of all. She turned her face away, as if expecting the same blow Philippe had delivered to their daughter.

"She spoke of the King," he went on, relentlessly. It had to be said now, all of it. The secret was too dangerous to reveal; too dangerous to keep. "Why? Why would she speak of him on her deathbed?"

Honneure closed her eyes.

" 'Never tell,' she said. Never tell what?"

She began to shake her head.

" '*Les cerfs... dans le parc.*' What sense does that make, Honneure? What sense does it make unless she meant...*Le Parc aux Cerfs?*"

The King's brothel.

"Noooo . . ."

" 'My poor lost Honneure...my lost *honneur*.' Her lost *honor*."

Tears streaked her face, steaming in the night air.

"No," she breathed again. But she knew, in her soul, it was true.

"Don't you see, my love?" Philippe's voice was agonized. His own cheeks were wet. He clung to his wife as if he might save her from drowning. "Louis XV was Louis Antoine's great-grandfather. And Philippa's grandfather...your father . . ."

Chapter Thirty-Five

June 1789

It was one of the saddest days of her life. Honneure stood to one side of the church, near the back, and touched a handkerchief to her tearstained cheeks. At the front of the church were two rows of monks chanting the Office of the Dead. Between them lay a small white coffin.

Louis Joseph, Dauphin of France, had succumbed to the disease known as the "King's evil." Over the years his spine had twisted until one hip was higher than the other, and his vertebrae protruded pitifully. The past few weeks he had remained bedridden in enormous pain.

An audible sob escaped Honneure's throat. He had been an exceptionally sweet child, and so intelligent. He had born his pain stoically and had gently comforted the parents whose only wish was to comfort him. He had been heir not only to the throne, however, but also to a hereditary and fatal disease.

Now he lay in his coffin, with his crown and gold spurs.

The Queen was being supported by two of her ladies-in-waiting. The King's head was bowed, his face wet with tears. Gabrielle de Polignac had a handkerchief pressed to her lips trying to muffle the sounds of her grief, and the Princesse de Lamballe was prostrate.

Two of her children dead, a son and a daughter. Honneure did not know how the Queen was able to bear her burden. She missed Philippa so acutely she could hardly stand it, even though she knew she would see her daughter again. Antoinette would only see her babies again in heaven.

Honneure raised her eyes to the light falling through the high, clerestory windows and whispered a silent prayer of her own.

Life was so tenuous, happiness so frail and fleeting. She was watching her Queen's life collapse before her eyes. The very fabric of France seemed to be disintegrating. What was going to happen to the King and Queen, the country? What was going to happen to her own family? What was going to become of them all?

Honneure had not thought anything could be worse than the night Philippa had declared her love for the young Duc d'Angouleme, and Philippe had revealed his long held secret. It appeared her own life, and her family's, had just fallen apart. The world had rocked beneath her feet.

At first she had wanted to deny it was true. But it answered too many questions, solved too many little mysteries. There were other comments her mother had made, her occasional bitterness and, most revealing, her attitude toward the King. A man she could not possibly know personally, yet loathed.

So Honneure had not been able to deny it and had been forced to look at herself, and her mother, in a whole new way. Having been told merely that her father had died prior to her birth, she had been free to imagine anything she wished about him. And her fertile imagination had conjured many things. But never a King. Certainly not the handsome, but dissipated and corrupt King Louis XV. The man who had wanted to make her one of his concubines. Her father.

Honneure shuddered.

He had desired her mother. Had he seen something in her

that reminded him of Mathilde?

She would never know. Perhaps it was a blessing. The knowledge of her parentage alone certainly carried a heavy enough load of curses.

Philippa and Louis Antoine had been separated. Forever. The kindly Madame Dupin had been their savior once again and had taken Philippa in as she had once taken Honneure. Philippa was at Chenonceau and would never return to Versailles.

It had been a compromise upon which she and Philippe were finally able to settle. Philippa was sent out of harm's way, but she and Philippe would remain with their sovereigns. She was bound to her Queen. She could not leave her, and Philippe had understood, despite the added danger they now faced.

Fate itself seemed to be conspiring against the beleaguered monarchy. A bizarre and violent hailstorm the previous summer had ruined wheat crops. Bread was scarce and prices out of reach for the ordinary man. A trade agreement with England brought into France cheaper, but well-made goods, and many Frenchmen found themselves out of work. Not only were they suffering from English competition, however, but from a drying up of Court spending. By supporting the *Parlement* in its insistent demands for cuts in royal spending, the tradespeople of Paris were really cutting their own economic throats. A prime example was the Queen's dressmaker, Rose Bertin, who had recently gone bankrupt. Yet all blame fell upon the crown, of course. Anyone of royal blood was openly despised.

And her father was the man who had, ultimately, brought France to her knees. If her secret was ever to become public... The service had ended, and the pathetic little coffin was being borne up the aisle. Due to the tenor of the times, Louis Joseph, former Dauphin of France, would be buried inexpensively at Saint-Denis.

When the sad procession had passed, Honneure fell in behind the mourners and left the church. It did not seem the sun should be shining so brightly.

* * *

The summer's day was nearing its end when Honneure returned to the palace. The King and Queen had already retired to their apartments, but Honneure had stayed behind to retrieve the Queen's personal effects from the royal coach. She cried quietly as she picked up a handkerchief bearing the royal monogram. It was soaked with the Queen's tears.

Honneure walked slowly up the Queen's Staircase. She felt drained, exhausted. She barely noticed the splendor of the surroundings that had always so enchanted her. Her very eyelids felt heavy. But her senses became more alert as she made her way through the reception chambers.

The formal rooms were unusually crowded. Many faces she had not seen before. Others Honneure recognized as attendants of several of the royal ministers. Her curiosity turned to anxiety when she reached the Queen's bedchamber and saw the crowd, many of them courtiers of the King.

Hers had long been a familiar face at the Versailles Palace, and Honneure passed into the interior apartments unimpeded. She was not surprised to see the throng within.

The King's attendants stood shoulder to shoulder with the Queen's ladies-in-waiting in the modest foyer. From within the salon she heard a voice, loud and demanding. Her hackles went up at once. Who could possibly be speaking to the King and Queen in such a way on this, of all days? Pressed against the wall, Honneure made her way into the salon unnoticed.

The King and Queen sat side by side. Though her bearing was regal, Honneure could see the lines of grief etched into Antoinette's delicate features. Louis had his fingers pressed to his temples as if he was in pain. One of the King's ministers stood in front of the royal couple, a frown on his bloated features. Louis shook his head.

"No, I cannot," he said lugubriously. "I will not."

"You must, Highness," the man insisted. "It will be political suicide to let the States General convene without you."

Louis merely shook his head.

"The militants of that body are already proclaiming that they represent the whole nation," the minister went on heatedly. "This notion will be strengthened by your absence. The monarchy *must* be present during the re-formation of the government, or government will re-form without it!"

"No! Dammit, no!"

Louis came to life all of a sudden and slammed his palm down on the arm of his chair so forcefully his jowls quivered. "You will not do this to me again! The first time we lost a child, you did not allow me time to mourn. You will not do so again. I am a father before I am a King!"

The minister seemed inclined to continue the argument, despite the force and emotion of the King's reply. But Honneure did not wish to be present for it. She knew how it would end. Louis was, indeed, a broken man. The crown was certainly in danger of falling, and the thought struck terror into her heart. As quickly and quietly as possible, Honneure melted into the crowd and left the Queen's apartments.

* * *

The early evening was still warm, but dark enough that Honneure had expected to see a lamp lit in the cottage. The house was dark, however. Philippe did not appear to be home. Honneure hurried on toward the stables.

She saw him before he saw her, and she paused for a moment to watch him. He had been out riding Snow Queen, great-granddaughter of the original Lipizzan mare, and was just returning. A rising moon, full and round, cast a silver sheen on the animal's white flanks as she pranced in a high trot toward the stable. Honneure stood in shadow and, although she knew Philippe had not seen her yet, the mare was aware of her presence. Her ears pricked forward, and she nickered softly. Honneure smiled in the darkness, forgetting for a moment her fears.

Honneure had been present at Snow Queen's birth. With her skilled hands, she had helped to deliver the tiny, premature foal. She had concocted, mixed and administered the added nutrients the foal had needed to grow strong and healthy. They had formed a bond as solid as the one between horse and trainer.

Philippe recognized the mare's greeting as the special one she used for Honneure, and his eyes probed the shadows. He halted the mare and slid from the saddle as his wife stepped toward him.

"I'm sorry I didn't see you." Philippe smiled. "But Snow Queen knew you were there." He slapped the mare's shoulder affectionately, and then drew his wife into his arms. "How was it?" he inquired with concern.

"Very, very sad," Honneure replied, knowing he referred to the young Prince's funeral. "But there was worse to come."

Philippe did not respond at once, but continued to hold his wife against his breast. Every day, it seemed, there were new and evil tidings. For just one moment he wanted to hold the woman he adored and make the world go away.

Honneure remained silent until her husband released her and held her at arm's length. He sighed deeply.

"All right. Tell me what could be worse than the death of a child."

"Nothing," Honneure responded quickly. "But the King's grief has apparently overwhelmed him."

Philippe sighed again and dropped his hands from Honneure's shoulders.

"I was afraid of that. He's not going to attend the States General, is he?"

"No," Honneure replied in a small voice. "I heard one of his minister's tell him, in so many words, that if he didn't take control he would lose his authority."

"His minister was correct."

Snow Queen nudged Philippe's back, and he stroked her neck.

"You know it's time to go, don't you?" he said to the mare.

"Philippe!"

"I only meant to the barn. Don't worry."

Honneure dropped her gaze guiltily. She knew her insistence on remaining with the Queen at Versailles was endangering them. Only last night Philippe had told her he feared the country was on the brink of revolt. Suddenly fearful again, she looked back up at him.

"Do you really think there'll be a revolution, Philippe?"

"If the King doesn't take control, the country will move on without him. When they do, they'll realize they don't need him. He will be deposed. Or worse. And the nation will be torn in two."

Honneure shivered and hugged her arms to her breast.

"I'm frightened, Philippe," she whispered. "I'm so frightened."

He did not tell her that he was frightened as well. He simply took her into his arms again.

"As long as I am alive, my love, you have nothing to fear," Philippe murmured into his wife's pale, summer scented hair. "As long as I live, no harm will come to you . . ."

Chapter Thirty-Six

October 5, 1789

The day was unusually warm for October. Summer seemed to cling, reluctant to leave. Fall had been held at bay, and there was not yet any color in the trees. It was undoubtedly pleasant, but Honneure knew sharper weather was right around the corner. It was going to change, suddenly, and then would come the winter storms. She wondered if she would ever see another summer at Versailles.

Honneure put the thought out of her mind and tried to enjoy her surroundings as she strolled along through the gardens of the Trianon behind her Queen and Madame Dupin, who had come for a brief visit. It had been wonderful to hear news of Philippa, who was apparently doing well. It had been less agreeable to see the silent plea in Madame Dupin's gaze. Her plea to the Queen, however, was not silent at all.

The two women had been walking arm in arm, but now Antoinette stopped and shook her head in response to something her friend had said.

"Please, be reasonable, my dear," Madame Dupin continued. "Your husband was wise enough to send Artois and his family, and the Polignacs, out of the country. They are safe and so should you and the children be."

Antoinette dropped her friend's arm and looked her in the eye. "You know I cannot leave my husband," she stated simply.

Honneure knew what an effort the Queen was making to hide her emotions. She would never forget the night of July 16th. Antoinette had been in tears at saying farewell to her most loyal friend. Not for the Trianon Theater this time, Gabrielle had disguised herself as a chambermaid to escape the country. The two women knew they would probably never see each other again.

"And you know," Madame Dupin pressed, tearing Honneure from her memory, "That calumnies are being spread about you in the newspapers."

Antoinette shrugged and gave a small laugh in an attempt to make light of it.

"The tales are ridiculous. If I had taken all the lovers they are saying I did, I would be too exhausted to get out of bed. Why, they're even saying the Duc de Coigny is the father of my first child! How could anyone possibly believe such lies?"

"I don't know," Madame Dupin responded quietly, her expression grim. "But they do. And you are in danger, dear friend. Grave danger. The country has gone mad. Did you not have warning enough with the storming of the Bastille?"

Antoinette paled, and her smile faltered, but she quickly regained control of herself. Once again she linked her arm through Madame Dupin's and resumed their stroll.

"Though I have been accused, through all the long years of my marriage to Louis, of interfering in politics and directing his decisions, particularly in favor of Austria, nothing could be farther from the truth. You know it well enough. Louis is the sole voice of the crown, and I trust him. At this very moment he is out shooting, and my only concern is that he bag enough for supper. Despite defections, we still have many mouths to feed!"

It was Madame Dupin's turn to shake her head. She

started to speak, but Antoinette interrupted her.

"Look." The Queen waved a hand in the direction of the little stream that fed the pond of the Hameau. "Here is another of my concerns. Do you see how low the water level is?"

"I do," Madame Dupin replied sharply. "Furthermore, I know why it is low. And so do you, though you will unquestionably continue to deny it."

Both Honneure and the Queen stared at Madame Dupin in shocked silence.

"There is a drought," the older woman went on, a tone of near desperation in her voice. "There is a drought and, although the price of a loaf has dropped to twelve sous, the new harvest is slow in coming through the water mills. Bread is still scarce in Paris and of poor quality. The people must eat, dearest friend. And to whom do you think they will turn if they cannot? Whom do you think they will blame?"

"The ones they have blamed all along," Antoinette replied at length, her voice nearly a whisper. "The ones they blame for everything."

"Yes!" Madame Dupin grasped her friend's hands. "And in a world gone mad, who knows what they will do?"

Madame Dupin's very real fears finally seemed to have communicated to the Queen. Her eyes widened, and her lower lip appeared to quiver.

"You don't...you don't think they would come here, to Versailles...do you?"

"I think there is absolutely no guessing what they will do. Which is exactly what makes them so dangerous! Antoinette, please, dearest friend...I am leaving in an hour for Chenonceau. Come with me. Come with me, and let us find a way to get you and the children out of the country from there!"

Honneure saw the Queen's moment of indecision. She

saw her waver before giving her final refusal. Mere hours later, Honneure would curse herself for not taking advantage of that moment - for not falling on her knees and begging Antoinette to leave with Madame Dupin. It was a regret that would remain with her for the rest of her life.

* * *

Madame Dupin had departed, as she said she would, within an hour from their stroll through the gardens. Though the Queen had put on a brave face, it had been a difficult farewell. Honneure had been torn as well.

"Know that I keep Philippa well and safe," Madame Dupin had said to her in parting. "But also know that she depends upon her mother and father for her happiness. And that you and Philippe are always welcome at Chenonceau."

Honneure had not known what to reply, besides her gratitude. She would not leave her Queen. Standing near Antoinette, they had watched Madame Dupin's carriage depart, and then retired to the palace to await the King's return from the hunt.

Louis returned just before three. Antoinette met him in the Royal Court, delighted with his twenty and a half brace.

"We shall be well fed tonight, indeed!" she declared. Honneure and the assembled courtiers watched her plant a fond kiss on her husband's cheek when he had dismounted from his horse.

It was so normal, such a domestic scene, that Honneure was almost able to forget Madame Dupin's dire words and the fear they had engendered. Minutes later the brief moment of happiness was snatched away.

A breathless messenger appeared and handed a note to the King. Honneure, slightly behind the Queen, saw him open it.

"It's from Saint-Priest," he said, referring to his Minister of the Household. Louis' brow furrowed as he scanned the lines. "He says the people are asking for bread." The King crumpled the note and smiled thinly. "Of course they are. And if I had any, I would give it to them. They would not have to ask."

Honneure watched her Queen smile loyally at her husband's good-natured attempt at levity. He rewarded her with a pat on the cheek.

"Sire!"

The crowd parted as a second messenger arrived. He was mounted, and his horse looked hard-ridden. The man leapt from the saddle and threw himself at his monarch's feet.

"Sire, a mob approaches," he exclaimed. Still on his knees, he looked up at the King. "But I beg you not to be afraid. They are only women!"

Louis bestowed a kindly smile on his messenger. "I have never been afraid in my life." He turned from the man to one of his courtiers. "Summon my ministers. I am calling a Cabinet."

It was well the King appeared so fearless, Honneure thought, recalling yet again Madame Dupin's warning. She herself had never been so frightened in her life.

* * *

The summer-like dusk fell softly. Honneure hovered in a corner of the Queen's salon waiting, along with several of the Queen's ladies, for further word of the approaching mob. Minutes earlier the Queen had been informed of the Cabinet's resolution.

One minister, Necker, had proposed to grant whatever the crowd should demand. Another, Saint-Priest, suggested the

King place himself at the head of his troops and defend the Sevres Bridge. Still others recommended he retire, swiftly, with his family to a loyal province. Typically, Louis chose neither the hero's nor the coward's course. He had elected to wait quietly for the crowd. His bodyguard had been instructed, on no account, to open fire.

Honneure had watched Antoinette closely as she received the news. Her bearing remained regal. She did not betray her innermost thoughts by so much as the blink of an eye.

Honneure admired her courage. But at least she knew where her husband was and what he was thinking. Honneure's own stomach churned with anxiety over Philippe.

Where was he? Had he learned of the imminent confrontation? Was he in a place of safety? More importantly, would he remain there...or seek to secure the safety of his wife?

Honneure clasped her hands and chewed at the inside of her lip. She longed to feel his arms around her, longed to press her face against his broad, strong chest and let his soothing caress take away her fears. She wanted to smell the familiar, heady scent of him and hear the sound of his voice, his lips against her ear.

But her place was with the Queen. She could only pray that Philippe would trust to her safety in the palace, and see to his own.

* * *

Madame Campan came with the announcement that the Paris mob had reached Versailles and entered the Forward Court.

"We should be able to see them from the King's Dining Room," Antoinette replied calmly. "Ladies?"

It was simply a walk from the Queen's Apartments to the

King's. So why did she feel as if she was going to an execution? Honneure realized she had begun to tremble.

The royal assembly lined up at the dining room window. Honneure, at the back, stood on tiptoe to see over the heads of those in front of her.

There appeared to be, literally, thousands. And they were not just women. Men now swelled the ranks, though the women stood out with their red cottons and white caps. They were armed with scythes, pitchforks, pikes, muskets, and daggers. They shouted that they would tear the Queen to pieces to make the cockades.

Antoinette blanched and took a step away from the window.

"Come, Majesty," Madame Campan urged. "There is no need to remain here and listen to this."

The Queen shook her head. "No. I must stay. What are they doing now?"

"They appear to be entering the Assembly," one of the ladies-in-waiting replied.

"To make their demands, no doubt," Antoinette said. She appeared to have recovered her composure. "Let us pray they are more reasonable than their design for cockades."

* * *

Darkness had fallen. The Queen had dismissed most of her ladies to join their own families and had taken up her vigil, waiting for the King, in one of her formal reception chambers, the Queen's Antechamber. It had always been one of Honneure's favorite rooms with its deep burgundy wall coverings and Louis XIV marble revetments and brocades. The Queen herself had had the wood moldings remodeled.

"I am so sorry, Honneure, that you and Philippe do not

reside within the palace," Antoinette remarked softly, breaking the silence within the lofty ceilinged room.

Honneure arched her brows. "Majesty?"

"You could be with him now, as I'm sure you must desire."

"My place is with you, Majesty."

"As things remain, however," Antoinette continued as if she had not heard, "I fear it is far too dangerous for you to try and leave the palace."

Honneure did not respond. Her mouth had gone dry from fear, and her tongue felt swollen. It was, indeed, too dangerous to attempt to leave.

The head of the Assembly had chosen twelve of the Parisian mob army to meet with the King in the Salle de Conseil. The remainder roved the palace grounds. For all Honneure knew, they had invaded the Hameau. She closed her eyes and murmured a prayer for her husband's safety.

Seconds later her reverie was interrupted by the entrance of the King. Antoinette rose to meet him, and he took her hands in his.

"What's happening, Louis? Tell us, please."

The King seemed overwhelmed with emotion. He cleared his throat.

"There were twelve of them," he began. "Their spokesman was a mere girl, a pretty child, a flower seller from the Palais Royal. When I asked her what she wanted, she replied simply, 'Bread. We want bread.' "

"And you replied?"

"I replied that she knew my heart. I would order all the bread in Versailles to be collected and given to the people."

"Oh, Louis!"

"The poor girl fell to the floor. When she was revived she

begged to kiss my hand, but I told her she deserved better than that. I embraced her."

"My dear, dear husband," Antoinette crooned, and touched his florid cheek.

"Do you know what happened?" It was obvious the King fought tears. "When she returned to the crowd to tell them what had transpired, she found herself in danger of her life for her conversion to the Court. The crowd threatened to strangle her with her own garters."

Antoinette's indrawn breath was audible in the ensuing silence.

"They seem to have gone mad, Antoinette. There is no reasoning with them."

As if to underscore the King's statement, several shots sounded in the courtyard.

Antoinette cried out and flung herself into her husband's arms.

"Oh, Louis, what now? What's happening now?"

"I shall find out," he replied, gently disengaging himself from his wife's embrace. Without another word, he turned and strode from the room.

* * *

It was almost two in the morning. Most of the candles in the Queen's Antechamber had guttered and gone out. The Queen was pale and trembling, and the King looked haggard. Madame Campan had fallen asleep sitting in her chair, but Honneure remained wide awake, her thoughts in turmoil.

In every town of France a citizen militia had been organized, answerable to the Assembly, known as the National Guard. The Versailles guard was hostile to, and jealous of, the King's troops, and had welcomed the Parisian horde. Earlier in the evening they had provoked a clash with the King's bodyguard, and shots had been fired. The incident had died down, but with the Parisian women bivouacked outside the gates, everyone in the palace had become a virtual prisoner. The Parisian guard, twenty thousand strong, had been summoned, and it was news of their arrival they now awaited.

Honneure strained to hear the sound of footsteps, every nerve in her body strung so tightly she seemed to hum. If only she knew what had become of Philippe! She could be strong for herself, for her Queen; but her fears for her husband were nearly disabling. She had to know if he was well and safe!

Despite her anticipation, Honneure jumped, startled, when the long-awaited footsteps sounded at last. The King straightened in his chair.

"Majesty." The attendant bowed low. "General La Fayette, of the Parisian Guard."

A tall and distinguished gentleman swept into the room. He approached the King and dropped to one knee.

"Rise, La Fayette," Louis said at once. "And give us your assurances."

"We are twenty thousand strong, Your Majesty," the general replied. "And it is our duty to protect the palace and its inhabitants."

"You give me your word, personally, the royal family is safe?"

"You have my word, Majesty."

Louis sighed. "Return to your troops. With my thanks."

As soon as the door had closed behind the general, Louis turned to his wife.

"Try and get some sleep, my dear. For tonight, at least, you are safe."

* * *

In spite of La Fayette's and the King's reassurances, Honneure's fears were not eased. Worry for both the Queen and Philippe tormented her. She had declined the offer of a place to sleep in Madame Campan's chamber, choosing instead to sit in the Queen's interior salon, outside the door to her boudoir. The night had fallen quiet at last, but she did not trust the silence.

There was utter madness afoot in the land. If she had not been living the history herself, she would not have believed it. Paris housewives marching on the palace of Versailles, imprisoning the King and Queen! It was beyond the limits of imagination.

Yet it had happened. And because it had, Honneure was able to imagine even worse. She had not long to wait.

The cry went up at five-thirty, just before dawn.

One of Antoinette's ladies-in-waiting, who had remained in the Antechamber, suddenly flew into the salon.

"Save the Queen!" she screamed. "Save the Queen!"

"What?" Honneure grabbed the hysterical woman's shoulders and gave her a shake. "What are you saying? What has happened?"

"Treachery!" the woman cried. "One of the women surrounding the palace was given a key to a locked gate, and they are inside! They have killed and cut off the heads of two guards...and they are headed for the Queen's Apartments!"

Honneure did not wait to hear more. She ran from the salon back toward the Antechamber. She was greeted by two other ladies running toward her. For their lives.

She could hear the crowd now. They had reached the door to the Antechamber and were pounding on it. Honneure could clearly hear their enraged chant.

"Death to the whore! Death to the whore!"

The door began to splinter.

Honneure turned and fled. At the very moment she locked the door to the interior apartments behind her, she heard the women break through to the Antechamber. She rushed into the boudoir.

Antoinette, alerted by her ladies, stood in her shift and petticoat, stockings in hand.

"Come! Come quickly!" Honneure ordered. "There's no time to dress. Hurry!"

Honneure grabbed the Queen's hand and pulled her through the door to the corridor connecting with the King's chambers. As they locked it behind them, they heard the women raging in the Queen's bedchamber. It sounded as if they were tearing it to pieces. Honneure could even hear the sound of saber slashes rending silk. She tugged at the Queen again.

"Louis!"

Honneure sagged with relief. The King and his personal guard had come to find them. Minutes later they were joined by their children and the royal governess, Madame Tourzel.

"Follow us, Antoinette," the King said. "We'll go to a safer place. And trust in La Fayette."

* * *

The King's faith had been well placed, Honneure thought. The general had quickly cleared the palace of assailants and restored a modicum of order. The royal family, Honneure, and the three ladies-in-waiting had been able to come out of hiding. But the crowd had gathered in the Marble Courtyard and was clamoring for the King.

"I do not know how long I can hold them, Majesty," La Fayette said.

"Then I shall give them what they want," the King replied.

"Louis, no!"

The King did not reply, but smiled sadly at his wife. There were great purple pouches beneath his eyes. He turned away and walked to the balcony overlooking the courtyard.

A resounding cry went up from the horde below. The King held up his hands, but the noise did not abate. It grew louder still and soon coalesced into an intelligible chant.

"The Queen! The Queen!"

The King turned slowly and looked at his wife. Honneure watched in horror as Antoinette began to move toward him.

"Majesty, please...no!" Honneure stepped in front of the Queen. "Forgive me, but I cannot allow you to do this."

"I belong at my husband's side," Antoinette said quietly. "You, of all people, so loyal and devoted, should understand this."

Honneure had no response. She watched in agonized silence as the Queen, in her yellow striped dressing gown, hair in disarray, stepped onto the balcony.

Honneure followed, standing as close behind her sovereign as she dared. She gasped as she saw the muskets leveled at the Queen.

Antoinette did not flinch. Instead she drew a breath and straightened her already rigid back.

The roar of the crowd subsided, and then came back, full-throated and overwhelming.

"Long live the Queen!"

The Queen's courage had turned the tide. Honneure felt tears prick at her eyelids. Then another shout rang out.

"The King to Paris!"

The crowd took up the cry. "The King to Paris! The King to Paris!"

"Oh, no," Honneure whispered. "No . . ."

* * *

Honneure had not thought she could experience greater sadness than she had at the funeral of poor little Louis Joseph. But as she watched the royal family being bundled into the coach, she thought her heart might break.

Following the people's demand for the King to go to Paris, Louis had retired from the balcony to confer with his ministers. They had almost all been of a single mind. Flight was now out of the question, and appeasing the mob seemed the only way to avoid further bloodshed. The King had returned to the balcony.

"Friends!" he had called out. "I shall go to Paris...with all I hold most dear. My wife and children. I trust to the love and protection of my good subjects!"

And so the royal family had hastily packed. Honneure had personally seen to the Queen's trunk and, when she had done, quietly approached Antoinette.

"I have your Majesty's wardrobe in order," Honneure had said. "With your permission, I would like to hurry home to tell Philippe I am leaving and pack some items of my own."

Honneure had silently prayed the Queen would allow her to briefly return to the cottage. She just had to see Philippe before she left and know he was safe. She wanted to hold him in her arms one more time, for she did not know when she would see him again. But Antoinette had been firm.

"No, Honneure. I am only allowed to take one servant with me, and Madame Campan, as chief of my servants, owns that position. You have other obligations as well. Go to

Philippe. And if I am able, I will send for you."

The news had stunned Honneure. She had devoted her life to the Queen. She could not imagine being left behind. Yet she had no choice. And, in truth, a part of her soul rejoiced.

Philippe...she would not have to leave her beloved husband.

But her heart cringed as the time of departure neared. At one twenty-five, avoiding the bloodstained staircase where the guards had been murdered, Louis and his family went down to his waiting carriage.

Honneure tried to stay near Antoinette and her children, but it was difficult. They were surrounded by their bodyguard, who was having trouble pushing through the large and disorderly crowd. The carriage was encircled, and the National Guard stood ready at the head of the procession.

The fishwives of Paris had helped themselves to the Versailles trees and brandished branches trimmed with ribbons. Others waved flags; some wore grenadier bearskins and shouldered muskets. Those too drunk to stand sat astride the guns. Loaves of bread were impaled on bayonets, and carts of flour were being drawn by the King's finest horses. At the rear of this assemblage came carriages carrying the few remaining courtiers, retainers, and belongings.

As they neared the coaches, Honneure was forced farther and farther behind. The King climbed in his carriage and turned to a trusted officer.

"Try to save my beloved Versailles for me," he said quietly.

Then he was inside, seated beside Antoinette. Also with them was Marie Therese, eleven; Louis Charles, four; Louis' sister, Elisabeth, and Madame Tourzel. The coach started forward, and soldiers and fishwives surged around it, firing guns and chanting songs. Honneure heard someone shout threats at the Queen. The scene was chaos.

Honneure tried to hold her place and watch the procession recede, but the rowdy crowd jostled her until she nearly lost her footing. She withdrew closer to the palace, until she was actually pressed up against its walls. They were warm, she noticed, from the afternoon sun. A sound above her caught Honneure's attention.

Even as she looked upward, she saw shutters being closed in a window. The sound echoed, over and over and over, as doors and windows throughout the palace were closed and locked.

The crowd had thinned, all following the royal procession, intent on the journey back to Paris. Though she was dressed in the Queen's colors, no one paid Honneure any attention. With her heart in her throat, she picked up her skirts and started to run.

* * *

It was quite a distance to the Hameau, and Honneure had to pause several times to catch her breath. Each time she did, her anxiety deepened. There were signs everywhere that the mob had traipsed through the gardens. Occasionally there was evidence of wanton destruction. Had they gone as far as the Hameau?

Only growing fear enabled Honneure's exhausted body to keep moving. It seemed the crowd had, indeed, reached the little farm. A small herd of sheep, released from their pen, bleated in alarm and shied away from her. Where was their shepherd? Where was anyone?

"Philippe? Philippe . . ."

It was a miracle Honneure was able to force the breath from her tortured lungs to call her husband's name. But there was no response. Terror increasing, she ran on to their cottage.

The front door stood ajar. A clay vase lay shattered on the doorstep. Honneure pushed the door wide and stepped inside.

The kitchen table was overturned. Clothes were strewn everywhere. She knew before she called that the house was empty.

Philippe was gone.

Chapter Thirty-Seven

January 1792

The dream was the same, always the same. Even asleep Honneure knew it was her recurring dream. Yet she could not escape the terror of it. She was running, running through the Versailles gardens, past the Trianon, trying to reach the cottage. But her legs were so tired, and the ground beneath her feet seemed to have turned into molasses so that it was nearly impossible to pick them up and move them. And she had to hurry, hurry before the mob came and took Philippe away. She had to reach the Hameau before they came upon her beloved husband and killed him . . .

Honneure awoke with a start and sat bolt upright in bed. Though the small room was icy, sweat stood out on her brow. Her waist-length hair was tangled about her shoulders and upper arms from constant tossing and turning. She cast her gaze wildly about the shabby, rented room.

"Philippe!"

He stood up from the stove he had been trying to light, and revealed himself to his wife.

"I'm here," he replied gently.

Philippe was well aware of Honneure's fears. Since the day the King had been removed from Versailles, though it had been nearly three years earlier, she suffered from nightmares and unexplained attacks of anxiety. He understood how afraid she had been when she returned to the cottage and had found him gone. On top of everything else that day, she had thought she had lost her husband.

Philippe had, in fact, been searching for Honneure. Knowing of the King's removal to Paris, he had feared Honneure had accompanied the royal family. He was out searching, trying to ascertain whether she had gone, or remained behind, when she had come to the cottage. She had found it in disarray because he had started a frenzy of packing when he thought he might have to quickly follow her. When he finally returned to the cottage and found her, she had been nearly hysterical. She had never been quite the same since.

Something profound had changed in Philippe that day as well. He had always been secretly afraid that Honneure's devotion to her duty superseded her love for him. But it did not, and he had seen it clearly that day. Loyalty and devotion were the very core of her nature. Her great sense of integrity did not allow her to show, in any way, even the slightest waver in her devotion to her duty. What was in her heart, however, was another matter. And what was in her heart was a fiercely passionate, undying love for her husband.

Overwhelmed with love himself, Philippe crossed the bare floor to his shivering wife and sat on the edge of the bed. Taking her chin in his hand, he tenderly kissed her mouth.

"I'm sorry I gave you a start," he apologized. "I wanted the room to be a little warmer for you when you woke."

"You are always thinking of me," Honneure sighed, and stroked the stubble on his unshaved cheek. "I am the luckiest woman in the world."

"Then it is appropriate that you are married to the luckiest man."

Philippe kissed her again and tried to smooth the tangles from the masses of her hair.

"Never mind that," Honneure said. "I have a brush. But Snow Queen has no way to fetch her own breakfast."

"I hate to leave you."

"And I hate to see you go. But I'll keep busy today."

"Oh?" Philippe paused in his shaving preparations. "And just what's on your agenda for today?"

"I thought I'd write a letter to Philippa, and then visit the Queen." Honneure endured Philippe's sharp glance. "I'll be careful, I promise."

"Honneure . . ."

"I know, I know. But she so treasures the little luxuries I'm able to bring her."

"Luxuries you should be keeping for yourself," Philippe reminded her.

Honneure glanced away guiltily. Philippe worked so hard for what little they had. Times had changed so drastically it was not safe to be perceived as having money, even a little. Philippe had hidden away their nest egg, therefore, and had taken the lowly job of cabby to support them on a daily basis - to appear as "one of the people."

"The people." Honneure shuddered. The people of Paris barely resembled human beings any longer, as far as she was concerned. She recalled the first terrible days following their arrival in the city.

Everyone of even decent appearance seemed to be suspect. Had they worn their livery, the Queen's colors, they would have been torn to pieces on sight. It was difficult enough just having the Lipizzan mare, a horse of such obviously noble and aristocratic lineage. Philippe had been forced to tell a series of lies, painting himself as a thief and a criminal, entitled to take what he had needed from someone who had more. He had been accepted at once as a comrade and patriot among the locals in the rundown neighborhood where they had found a room to let. Thus accepted, they had begun their succession of days in a world of topsy-turvy values, Philippe as a cabby, Honneure attempting to continue her service to the Queen.

Honneure bent to pull on her woolen stockings and noticed a new hole. She could certainly use another pair, one to wear while she was darning the other. But the winter was a brutal one, and poor little Marie Therese, imprisoned along with her parents, needed them more. Stockings, soap, hair pins; little things had come to mean so much to the royal family.

Honneure straightened and hurriedly pulled on her dress as Philippe finished his ablutions. He moved behind her to fasten the long row of buttons on her plain, black shift, and then wrapped his arms around her and rested his chin on her shoulder.

"Promise me again you'll be careful, my love."

"I am always careful, Philippe," Honneure replied. "There are always six guards outside the Queen's room these days, and at least half of the staff are spies for one side or the other, the Assembly or the Jacobins."

A familiar anger sparked to life in Honneure's breast, warming her. She turned within Philippe's embrace to face him.

"I just don't understand!" she exclaimed. "I'll never understand. Why can't they see how good the King and Queen are? Why must they torment them like this?"

It was a question that could never be answered, and Honneure knew it. Reason and sanity no longer existed in France. She buried her face in her husband's chest, but she refused to cry. Enough useless tears had been shed.

Husband and wife shared one more lingering kiss, and Philippe left to begin his day of driving. Honneure stood in the doorway and listened to his steps descending the narrow wooden stairs. A door creaked open, and then shut. Honneure sighed.

Another gray, cold day for her husband, fingers stiff and freezing as they gripped the harness reins. And for what? A few sous only, barely enough to keep them alive and Snow Queen fed. Enough to keep them going one more day, so that Honneure might trudge to the Tuileries with her scraps of gifts for the Queen she had once served in splendor. How much was Philippe willing to suffer for her, and for how much longer?

Honneure closed the door to the hallway and leaned her head for a moment against the unpainted wood. She was tired, so tired. And so full of doubts. With an effort she straightened, squared her shoulders, and turned from the door. She had to get through her day, a step at a time, just as Philippe did.

The room was still cold, and she pulled on a pair of gloves from which the ends of the fingers had been cut. She fetched pen, ink, and paper from her small box of treasures and sat at the scarred table with its rickety legs. It had been a while since she had written to Philippa, and she was anxious to feel in contact with her again.

But it was hard to get started. Weekly, the madness seemed to spread. She wanted to chronicle the times for her daughter, yet did not want to alarm her. It was becoming more and more difficult to choose her words. Honneure put down her pen and placed her head in her hands.

The first letters to Philippa and Madame Dupin had not been so hard. It had not seemed so terrible for Louis and Antoinette in the beginning. When the King and Queen had first been brought to the Tuileries, they had still enjoyed relative freedom. They had, for instance, been allowed to spend the summer months at their château in St. Cloud. During the rest of the year in Paris, Antoinette had been free to spend her time trying to improve the welfare of the people, and she visited hospitals, asylums and orphanages. Louis had worked almost constantly with the Assembly, trying to conciliate them and bring an end to the civil unrest.

After a time it appeared they had succeeded, and a constitutional monarchy was formed. The King lost most, but not all, of his powers and retained his crown. It appeared that peace, and a semblance of political sanity, was on the horizon.

But another faction was at work, Jacobin extremists, people who wanted not only to abolish the crown altogether, no matter how weakened it had become, but who also wanted to abolish any kind of power at all that was not held by themselves. As a result, the unthinkable had happened.

Honneure rose from her seat and crossed to the stove to warm her hands. Whenever she thought of those horrible days, a chill went through her.

A new kind of thinking had swept France, self-serving to the extremists who were its proponents. Man, being a natural being, did not need to look to the supernatural, to God, to take care of him, they said. He needed only the state. The Jacobins wanted to make patriotism not only a new religion, but the only religion. To that effect, church properties had been seized and nationalized, the clergy reviled. Effigies of the Pope burned in the streets.

A new clergy had risen from the ashes, but it owed its loyalty to the state, La Patrie, not to the Holy See in Rome. The King had abided, and compromised, much. And while he publicly acknowledged the new order, privately he would not surrender his traditional Catholic worship. Refusing to attend Easter services led by a new, schismatic priest, he and his family had tried to leave for St. Cloud and their own priest.

Honneure shivered until her teeth started to chatter. She wrapped a second shawl around her shoulders and briskly rubbed her arms.

A mob had prevented Louis from leaving the Tuileries, to worship as he chose. He and his family were, well and truly, prisoners of the people. Their freedom was only an illusion, and the writing was on the wall. If they wished to survive, they would have to escape.

Warmth from the small stove had crept into Honneure's chilled flesh, and her shivering stopped. She was no longer able to feel the chill air in any event, for her memory had carried her back to the day she had almost lost Philippe.

With the help of a man who had become a loyal friend, Axel de Fersen, a flight to Varennes was planned. Late on the appointed evening, the children were first smuggled out of the Tuileries palace. Later, avoiding servants known to be spies, the King and Queen followed. Axel de Fersen himself actually drove them away from the Tuileries in a hired carriage. Hours later they rendezvoused with the larger berlin Fersen had purchased to carry the entire royal family to safety, Louis' sister, Elisabeth, and Madame Tourzel included. Fersen had handed over the reins to the driver who would continue the journey out of Paris and to the relative safety of Varennes. The driver was supposed to have been Philippe.

Tears, unnoticed, streamed down Honneure's cheeks. They were tears of gratitude and prayerful thanks.

A sudden and disabling stomach ailment had made it impossible for Philippe to drive the King's Berlin. Another driver, loyal to the crown, had been found at the last minute.

He had been a good man, and Honneure mourned him. When the royal family had been recaptured and returned to Paris, he had not survived the wrath of the people.

Philippe had undertaken the mission out of loyalty to his wife first, his King and Queen second. Though frightened because of the journey's obvious dangers, Honneure had been proud of him. Nothing, she had thought, nothing could, or should, come before one's duty. It was how she had always lived her life. Loyalty was the paramount virtue. It had been, she thought, her mother's unspoken legacy to her. Remain loyal to those you serve, devoted to duty, and you will survive. You will have food and warmth, and a place to sleep.

Then she had almost lost Philippe, and it was the second time the ground had rocked beneath her. The change within her had begun the day she had returned to the cottage and found it empty. The change, it seemed, was now complete. And it was what enabled her to live in a world where goodness and kindness were now scorned. She had a new tool for survival.

The chiming from a distant clock tower brought Honneure abruptly back to the present, and she re-seated herself at the table. More time had passed than she realized. The Queen would be expecting her soon. She picked up her quill, her mind completely changed about what she would write to her daughter. She only wondered that it had taken her so long to realize the metamorphosis she had undergone.

* * *

"Dearest Daughter," Honneure began. Her pen flew as her excitement increased.

"I have spent hours this morning agonizing over what I would write to you. During the past many months I have, as you know, tried to document events here in Paris for you. We

424

are living history in the making. It is not for me to judge the rightness or wrongness of events. Those who come after us will have to decide for themselves when they read of these times. One thing I can say with certainty, however, is that I am glad you are not here. To have you, too, facing danger would be more than I could bear. Which brings me to the point of this letter.

"Do you know how much I love you, dearest Philippa? Though I have always tried to be a good mother, and a good wife to your father, I fear I have not properly shown, or expressed to you, how very much I love you both. And it is the very danger and insanity of these times that have made me realize that you and your father really do come first in my life, and that I may not have let either of you know it. I hope I can now remedy that.

"Knowing who my father was, and how perilous it would be should our secret be revealed, still I followed the Queen to Paris. I thought it was my duty to continue to serve her, no matter the personal risks. As you, and certainly your father, know, devotion to duty has been the cornerstone of my life. Duty always came first.

"I continue to live by this ideal and suspect I always will. My error has not been in believing that loyalty comes first, but in who comes first in my loyalties. These dark and dangerous days in Paris, however, have helped me to understand my priorities. And my first priority is my family. Nearly losing Philippe, missing all the precious days I might have been spending with you, have made me realize, finally, that our lives as a family are more important than my service to the King and Queen.

"This has been a difficult decision for me to make because, no matter my illegitimate birth, the King is family, too. Although, for obvious reasons, the world must never know, we are still cousins. It will be hard to leave my Queen, and the King, behind. Yet I can no longer deny that it is time to flee Paris. We must be reunited. We have spent too much time apart already.

"I have not even told your father yet of my decision. It only came to me this morning as I pondered what to write to you. I anticipate the joy with which your father will receive this news when he returns tonight, and my day is considerably brightened already. Hopefully, it will not take us long to leave the city, and we will see you soon, my darling. Until then I remain,

"Your devoted Mother
"Honneure Mansart"

* * *

The population of Paris had swelled to nearly three-quarters of a million, and the narrow streets were crowded and dirty. To make matters worse, it had snowed a few days earlier, and Honneure was forced to wade through filthy slush. The sky was gray and overcast, and the damp cold seemed to eat right into her bones. Yet she smiled as she trudged in the direction of the Tuileries château.

In the basket she carried with the Queen's small gifts lay her letter to Philippa. On the way home she would post it. Soon she and Philippe would be on their way home to Chenonceau. The mere thought filled her with an almost inexpressible joy. She felt liberated, freed from bonds she had not even known had bound her for so long. There was more than just a revolution in France. There had been a revolution in her soul.

Honneure emerged from the dismal, labyrinthine streets to

the wide boulevard that ran along the Seine, and she quickened her step. Ahead lay the Tuileries, a dark sixteenth century palace that, until the King's arrival, had been uninhabited since 1665. The steep-roofed, three-story, gray stone château was uncomfortable in the extreme, freezing in winter, stifling in summer. Its furniture was stiff and old-fashioned and its windows small. The accommodations were only one of many indignities the royal family was being forced to endure. But at least they were together.

Honneure had a whole new sense of just how important that fact was. The hardships of imprisonment might be many, but there were blessings, too. With little else to distract them and few duties to attend to, the King and Queen were able to spend most of their days with their children. The Queen continued to tutor them, and their father had the time now to play with them. As long as they were allowed to remain together, life was endurable. And soon, Honneure told herself, their confinement must be ended. The situation could not go on indefinitely. Even if Louis was deposed, it was not the worst thing that could happen. At least he would have his freedom...and his family.

The guards at the gate stopped Honneure, as usual, though she was a frequent and familiar visitor. She swiftly produced the blue pass she had been issued that enabled her to visit the Queen. Moments later, she entered the dim, drafty corridors of the château. And was stopped again.

"Your pass, please."

Honneure's eyes narrowed as she regarded the thin, gray woman who had confronted her. She wore the uniform of the Jacobins, the tricolor cockade hat, and a perpetual sneer. It was well known the woman spied on the Queen and enjoyed throwing her weight around. As in the present situation.

Biting her tongue, Honneure reached into her basket to retrieve her pass. Almost every time she ran into Honneure, the woman asked her to produce it, although she knew Honneure never could have gotten into the palace without it. Petty harassment apparently amused her.

Honneure's fingers groped in her basket and eventually found what she sought. Irritated, she snatched it out of the basket. She did not realize she had also caught a corner of her letter, and she did not see it flutter to the ground.

The Jacobin woman waited until Honneure had disappeared down the corridor. Then she bent and picked up the envelope. A queer, hungry smile stretched her pale lips as she tore open the paper and began to read.

Life had never been easy. The narrow, filthy back streets of Paris were all she had ever known. She had suffered grinding poverty as a child and could never even remember a time when she had not been hungry. She had fared little better as an adult and toiled daily to buy enough to eat, simply to be able to get up and do it again the following day. There had never been any hope in her life, any color in her gray sky, until the Revolution.

Now everything was changing. The oppressed were changing places with the oppressors. The heads of the aristocracy were rolling in the streets, and their blood flowed in the gutters. Those who had known only privilege would now find it a privilege merely to exist.

Still smiling, the woman carefully refolded the letter.

She had always thought there was something intrinsically wrong with Honneure Mansart. Her beauty itself was an affront. Her carriage and bearing were too haughty by far.

The woman nodded slowly to herself as she tucked the envelope into her threadbare bodice. She had been right all

along. There was something wrong with Mademoiselle
Mansart. She was tainted by royal blood.

It would be spilled.

Chapter Thirty-Eight

The guards outside the door to the King and Queen's chambers eyed Honneure suspiciously, as they always did. More than one did so with a wicked leer and caressing glance. She ignored them and waited patiently while the locks, one by one, were undone. It was ironic, she thought. Locks had once been Louis' hobby. Designing and building them had helped him pass many happy hours. Now the very instruments he had loved held him prisoner...locks...and his own sense of honor.

The outer door opened, and Honneure proceeded into a dim and dank corridor. At a second, inner door, she again halted and waited for the unlocking procedure.

There had been a time, not long ago, when Louis could have abdicated in favor of his son. Louis Charles, however, was only six years old. The Duc d'Orleans, now known as Egalité, would have ruled on the boy's behalf as regent. But the Duke was weak and ineffectual, and Louis' integrity would not allow him to surrender his realm to the rule of such a man. There would have been safety in the King's abdication, for him and his family. But no honor.

A premonition seemed to hold Honneure in its grip as she hurried down the last dim and chilly hall. The Queen, too, might have fled earlier to safety with her children, but her sense of honor and duty had bound her to her husband, the King.

Was it too late for them? Had their decisions, however

noble, condemned them?

Had Honneure's loyalty to the Queen condemned her as well?

No. Honneure shook her head. She could not think such a thing. It was not too late for her. It wasn't. She had come to her senses in time. Soon she would be back at Chenonceau with her husband and daughter, and dear Madame Dupin. She would be back where she belonged. The Queen, in fact, had been urging her to do so for some time. There was little she could do for Antoinette anymore, aside from these small favors. It was well and truly time to leave.

Honneure at last entered the first chamber of the modest suite of rooms that housed the King and his family. The stone walls were bare and cold. A worn carpet covered most of the floor. There were several straight-backed chairs and a desk, all occupied.

The Queen looked up from an open book that lay on the desk. Her brow had been furrowed in thought, but it smoothed, and a smile lit her lips when she recognized Honneure.

"What a pleasant surprise," she remarked brightly. "It is well past your usual hour, and I was afraid you weren't going to come."

"I'm so sorry. I know it's almost your lunch time. I won't stay long."

"Nonsense."

The King rose from the seat he had taken between his two children and his sister, Elisabeth. He was dressed simply in black silk trousers and a waistcoat in a gold color known as "the Queen's hair." No longer allowed to ride, or take much exercise at all, he had grown heavy, with prominent jowls. But his blue eyes were still merry, despite his circumstances. Honneure dropped a deep curtsy, amazed as usual by the monarch's warmth and informality. The King raised her to her feet with a simple touch under her chin.

"We are always happy to see you," Louis continued. "And to enjoy your far too generous gifts."

Honneure blushed and ducked her head. "They're nothing, really."

"Oh, yes they are!"

Young Louis Charles jumped up from his chair and ran to Honneure's side. His long, chestnut hair was in disarray, and his eyes were wide and eager.

"Have you brought something for my sister?"

Honneure touched the Prince's head and smiled down at him with genuine affection. He adored his older sister and always thought of her first.

"Of course I have. But first let me show you what I have for you." Honneure's fingers searched within her basket and withdrew a few sheets of writing paper.

"Thank you...thank you!" the boy exclaimed. "Now I have something to write my lessons on."

"I thank you as well," Louis said, and nodded somberly.

"I'm just glad I was able to find some," Honneure replied. "Literature and education seem to have little importance these days, and what paper there is all seems to go into the presses of the scandal and hate mongers."

The Queen's indrawn breath was audible, and Honneure was instantly sorry. The shock of events over the last three years had turned her hair white, and her nerves were always dangerously on edge. Honneure had not meant to cause her any additional anxiety and apologized.

"Show us what you've brought for Marie Therese," Antoinette said, wisely changing the subject.

"Yes...what have you brought for my sister?"

Honneure crossed to where the child had remained seated. Marie Therese Charlotte was a serious little girl, and it was always difficult to coax a smile to her lips. Honneure reached into her basket once again and produced a pair of warm woolen stockings.

Marie Therese accepted them with a sober expression, but Honneure, who had known her almost all her life, could tell she was pleased.

"Thank you very much," the child said.

"You are quite welcome." Honneure turned to the Queen and handed her a small package of soap. "This is for you and Princess Elisabeth. I'm sorry there isn't more. These were the only luxuries I could find this week."

"Dearest friend," Antoinette said as she took the small packet. Tears glittered in her eyes. "These gifts, given with a loving heart, are more precious than gold and gems. Don't you know that?"

Honneure could only nod. Soon she would have to tell the Queen she would no longer be able to come. Although she knew Antoinette would be glad for her and would tell her she was doing the right thing, it was still terribly difficult. She knew how keenly Antoinette felt the defection of her friends, people who had once sworn their love and loyalty and had now turned their backs. The Queen treasured her few remaining friends, a handful of devoted servants included.

But it was time to go. Honneure could no longer deny it. As if to reassure herself, she reached into her basket to touch the letter.

"Honneure? Are you all right?"

Concerned by Honneure's sudden paleness, Antoinette pushed back her chair and rose to her feet. The King touched Honneure's elbow.

"Do you feel ill, my dear? You don't look well at all."

"I...I'm fine." Honneure managed to shake her head. "But I've...forgotten something. I really must go."

"Of course. Leave at once if you must. Don't let us detain you." The Queen's brow furrowed once again.

Honneure tried to utter the proper words of farewell, but her tongue seemed to have cleaved to the roof of her mouth. Her stomach seemed on the verge of rebellion. Dipping a hasty curtsy, she groped behind her for the door handle.

Seconds later, she was fleeing down the long, dark corridor.

* * *

The trees that marched along the banks of the Seine were bare. They seemed to pass far, far too slowly as Honneure ran along the river path. And although she felt she was barely moving, her heart threatened to explode within her breast.

She had backtracked to the palace entrance so carefully. She had not found the letter.

Had she merely thought she had put it in her basket? Did it lie safely at home?

But the thought, the image, was not true. Honneure's memory replayed the morning's events, and she saw in her mind's eye exactly where she had placed the letter.

Honneure could no longer feel her feet hitting the ground. Pure terror raced through her veins with a numbing poison.

If someone had found that letter, she was doomed.

Heedless of the carriage traffic, Honneure veered off the path and ran across the busy boulevard. The gray walls of the city closed around her.

Philippe...let me find you...just let me find you . . .

She no longer had any hope she had left the damning

missive at home. She knew in her heart what had happened, what had become of it. Remembered pulling the pass from the basket a second time.

Just let me see you one more time, Philippe, my beloved... Honneure knew she would only be able to draw a few more ragged breaths before she could go on no longer. Her legs were already starting to fail her as she rounded the last corner onto the dim and dirty street where they lived.

Panic burst at once in her breast, and Honneure stumbled to her knees.

They were outside her building, their tricolor hats bright in the shadowy light of the narrow street. Even as she watched, someone leaned out the open window of their small room. He shouted, and though Honneure could not hear the words she knew he informed his colleagues of her absence.

Honneure rose slowly to her feet, heart thudding against her ribs. They hadn't seen her yet. Perhaps she could simply turn and walk away. It was near the time of day Philippe returned Snow Queen briefly to her rented stall for a cup of oats. If he was there . . .

One hand pressed to the cold, gray stone of the corner building, Honneure began to back away from the men midway down the block. She never took her eyes from them. She held her breath as they turned and looked in her direction. And good sense fled before the crushing wave of terror.

Honneure whirled and started to run.

She heard their shout. She knew her fatal error. With the last of her strength, she fled toward the rundown stable.

* * *

Philippe, too, heard the shouts, and the hair on the back of his neck rose immediately. In these dark days, voices raised in anger and alarm all too often meant death or imprisonment to some unlucky victim. The Jacobin extremists, in their reign of terror, literally chased down some of their luckless prey on the city streets. And *La Lanterne*, their guillotine, was perpetually hungry. Not wishing to witness another of their foul roundups, Philippe pulled on the white mare's reins and slowed the coach in preparation to turn it around. He was not fast enough.

It was a woman, he noted. Her mean, black skirts were clutched in her hands, the better to run, and her long disheveled hair streamed out behind her. Her eyes were wide with terror. They were staring right at him. Philippe's heart thudded to an abrupt halt, and his flesh and blood turned to ice.

"Philippe!"

Her cry tore through him, an ax blade splitting his chest. He was propelled into action.

Tears sprang to Honneure's eyes when she realized her final prayer would be answered. If she could just stay on her feet, just keep going for a few more steps, she would feel his arms around her one more time. She saw him jump from the coach to the curb, saw him sprint toward her . . .

Rude hands grabbed at Honneure's shoulders. As she was pulled backed, she stretched out her hands.

"*Philippe . . .*"

He touched her fingertips, grasped her hands. With all the strength in him, he pulled her into his arms, held her against his heart.

Then a bright, white light blossomed in his brain, and he knew no more.

Chapter Thirty-Nine

August 1792

Though it was barely noon, the small cafe was packed with men and a few coarse looking women. The stink of stale wine and sweaty bodies filled Philippe's nostrils, and smoke burned his eyes. He made a show of drinking the sour red wine he held clutched in his hand, but his throat threatened to close each time he raised the glass to his lips. He longed to push his chair back, leave the crowded, noisy table, and breathe the relatively fresh air of the Paris street. But he didn't dare. He'd come too far. They trusted him now; he was one of them. He was learning the things he needed to know. He coughed, nearly choking, as the man next to him clapped him sharply on the back.

"Isn't that right, Philippe?"

He turned to his neighbor, who grinned at him through the sprouting stubble of a gray beard.

"You know I always agree with you, Luc," Philippe replied, though he had long ago stopped listening. Luc was a member of the Jacobin Club, a rabble-rouser, and one of his favorite pastimes was exhorting a crowd while drinking seemingly endless quantities of red wine.

Luc laughed. "You're a smart man!" He turned to the others at the table and some of the men who had left their seats and stood near, the better to hear him.

"Philippe knows. He's with us," Luc continued.

"Robespierre, Danton, Marat, Desmoulins...our leaders have finally issued the call to arms. Heed them! Join us!"

"Call to arms...bah." An old man, long white hair disheveled, grunted rudely. "Robespierre and his ilk have been stirring up trouble in the press all along. They've blackened the King. And the Queen. But that's all they've a mind to do. They've done their job."

"Not by half." Luc's eyes had narrowed, nearly lost in the wrinkles of his heavily lined face, and his tone was menacing. But the old man seemed not to notice.

"The King's gone along with the Assembly, given 'em everything they wanted," he went on. "And he's in prison to boot, though he's committed no crime. So what do your...*leaders*...plan to do?"

Philippe could almost feel Luc bristle next to him. Hate came off of him in nearly palpable waves.

"Execute the criminal," he replied in a tone so low and deadly that the men around him stiffened. Even the old man appeared to visibly lose some bluster. Nevertheless, he arched his shaggy brow.

"Criminal?" he repeated.

"Yes, criminal!" Luc slammed his roughened palm on the crude, stained table. "Is counter-revolution not a crime? Are counter-revolutionaries not criminals?"

The old man looked taken aback. But he was not done yet.

"And just how is the King a counter-revolutionary?"

Luc sat back, a smug smile on his sun-darkened features, and crossed his arms. "Did the King not veto the Assembly's decree?"

"To punish and exile priests not loyal to the state, you mean?"

Luc nodded slowly. "His action is contrary to the will of the people, to the revolution that is cleansing France. Therefore he is a counter-revolutionary. He has committed *treason*!"

Once more Luc's beefy fist came down on the table, rattling glasses. Philippe could not help but wince. Fear roiled the wine in his stomach.

In the months since Honneure's arrest and imprisonment, Philippe had tried his best to ally himself with the extremists. If he knew what they were planning, if they trusted him, he might have a chance to rescue his wife. He had not realized the task would be so difficult, so terrifying.

The city indeed seemed to have gone insane; madness gripped the people. The streets ran red with blood, and still they were not satisfied. It had soon become clear to Philippe that they did not merely wish to depose the King, but murder him, and all his family...legitimate and illegitimate alike.

Philippe rubbed the scar above his left temple, his permanent reminder of the day the terrorists had seized Honneure. It had become like a talisman to him. He rubbed it, and then nudged the man next to him.

"This...call to arms," he began. "Tell me more. Is there a plan?"

Luc quaffed the contents of his glass and set it down heavily. He wiped his lips with the back of his hand and grinned.

"We've got a plan all right," he crowed. "If the Assembly won't take care of the criminal they're harboring, then the rest of us will. We're going after the cringing lion in his den...the Tuileries!"

Only with great effort of will did Philippe manage to control the expression on his face. "The...Tuileries . . ."

Luc appeared briefly puzzled by Philippe's reaction. Then the grin split his face anew.

"That's right...I'd forgotten! You'll want to be right there with us when we go after Louis and his Austrian whore. You'll want to be right there with us for your vengeance, won't you? You'll want to put the head of your lyin', bastard wife on the pike yourself! Imagine keepin' a secret like that from you all those years...one of the old Louis' bastard whelp!"

The surge of emotion that coursed through Philippe was so powerful it was debilitating, and it was the only thing that kept him from ripping Luc's own head from his shoulders. Carefully, slowly, he reminded himself that the only way he might hope to save his wife was to appear to be on the side of her jailors.

"You're absolutely right," he said between clenched teeth. "I want to be the one to...take her myself."

Once again Luc clapped Philippe smartly on the back. "You'll have your chance, boy. Tomorrow, if all goes right."

"And will we be...armed?"

"Hah! Will we be armed? Fifty thousand arms from the arsenal are being distributed first thing in the morning. And we have federal troops that have come over to our side as well."

Philippe had to fight to control a shudder. It appeared the end was very, very near, and it was going to be far worse than he had ever imagined. The mob, savage and bloodthirsty, had become impatient. They were going to take what they wanted with their own hands.

And if Philippe was to be able to take what he wanted, he had to be with them. Every step of the way.

* * *

Honneure lay absolutely still on her hard, narrow bed.

There was a single, small window in the airless room, but it did not open. Hot August sunlight poured through the glass and made the temperature of the tiny, bare chamber nearly unendurable. Honneure could only abide it by remaining completely motionless. She lived almost entirely inside her mind. It was how she had learned to survive.

With her eyes closed, she walked through the gardens of Chenonceau and along the grassy banks of the Cher. She dangled her feet in the cooling waters. She placed her palms on the cool, stone walls of the château. She felt a stirring breeze lift the hair from her shoulders. She was refreshed. But she was alone. Always alone.

It was too painful to people her dreams with memories of those she loved. She was alone.

She had been alone since the day they had taken her.

There had been questions first, of course. She had denied nothing. There was no point. They had the letter.

What they did not have was Philippa. In a hurry because she had been late to visit the Queen, she had decided to address her letter when she posted it. In spite of their threats and their petty tortures, she had not given it to them. Nor had she given them Philippe.

He did not know the truth, she had told them. She had kept it from him all those years. And all the while she had prayed he had told them the same thing.

Please, save yourself, my darling.

It had been her prayer, over and over and over.

Perhaps God had answered her. There was no sign of him. She had not heard of his imprisonment.

Please, let him be with Philippa at Chenonceau.

This was her new prayer. She had none for herself. She did not expect to live.

The France she had known was dead. The King and Queen soon would be. She had no reason to disbelieve her jailors. At least she had seen her sovereigns one last time.

They had wanted to humiliate her. The King and Queen as well. She had been shoved into their chamber, her letter read aloud.

The royal couple had maintained their dignity, as always. Cousin to a servant? Not by the slightest word or gesture did they give anything away.

But she had seen sympathy in Antoinette's gaze, and deep, deep sadness.

Then she had been taken to this room. She had a bed and a chamber pot. Simple meals were brought to her regularly by a young man who was obviously simple. Because she didn't eat, they had sent a doctor to examine her. He was a kindly old man, and he urged her to eat, to save her strength. But for what? So she could better mount the steps to the guillotine?

Honneure turned her thoughts away from the inevitable and returned to Chenonceau. The flow of the Cher carried her away.

* * *

It seemed a little cooler. The light must be gone, the day faded. But Honneure still did not open her eyes. Earlier she had heard the door open and had assumed it was her dinner. She wasn't hungry. The vague aroma that drifted to her nostrils sickened her. She wanted to go back to Chenonceau. She set out on her way.

A soft touch on her forearm drew her back. She resisted the temptation to open her eyes.

"Honneure?" the soft voice whispered.

It was the doctor. She pictured him, thin, with a bird-like

face, glasses perched on the end of his nose.

"Honneure, open your eyes, please. I want to know you hear and understand me."

"I hear you."

"Open your eyes, Honneure."

He carried the stub of a candle, and it flickered gently in the darkness. Shadows played on his gaunt features. She saw the slight hump on his back and his perpetually hunched shoulders.

"Thank you, my dear. I haven't much time. I simply came to urge you, once again, to eat."

It seemed so pointless, so senseless. Then she saw his gaze flicker toward the partially open door.

"Eat, my dear. You'll need your strength." Dr. Droulet patted the back of Honneure's hand. His voice dropped to a whisper. "There's rumor of trouble. If the château is attacked, you might have a chance of escape." The doctor coughed and raised his voice again. "I'll try to look in on you tomorrow. Good night, child."

Honneure watched him shuffle to the door. It opened wide, and she saw her jailor beyond the threshold. The door closed again, and locked. She shut her eyes.

Tomorrow.

She didn't dare to hope. But neither could she live without it.

Slowly, painfully, she roused herself from her stupor and sat up.

* * *

It was true. Everything Luc had said was true. It was a nightmare.

At five in the morning a provisional government had been

installed. Danton himself arrested the Commander of the National Guard and replaced him with a friend. The mob had been armed. The Place Vendôme had been filled with a crowd carrying human heads on pikes. And now they swarmed through the streets toward the Tuileries. The insurrection had begun.

Philippe felt himself being swept away and carried along by the mob. He wasn't sure how he had come by the musket gripped in his hands. He only knew he had to be there when they stormed the château. He had to be at the forefront. He had to be the first to find her.

It was nearly eight o'clock. The sun was already bright and hot. Not a breeze stirred, and the leaves on the trees were limp and still. Even their shade did not seem to cool. Sweat poured from Philippe as a crowd nearly twenty thousand strong surged around him. They pressed against the gates of the Tuileries.

Standing near the front, Philippe saw a young man emerge from the palace. He strode boldly across the courtyard, and his back was rigidly erect. But Philippe could see the fear in his eyes, the pallor of his cheeks. He ignored the shouts of the mob.

"Do your duty bravely!" he ordered the National Guardsmen who stood at their posts. "You are in service to the King! It is your obligation to protect the royal family!"

In response, the Guardsmen ostentatiously unloaded their guns. Whoops of approbation rose from the crowd. The young man whirled and, at a brisk pace, returned to the palace. A muttering, like the stirrings of an angry sea, rolled through the insurrectionists as the minutes passed. Philippe counted the seconds with every beat of his heart.

After what seemed an eternity, the palace doors opened

once again. A dozen Swiss grenadiers appeared. They surrounded the royal family. A cry, almost as if from one, giant throat, went up from the mob.

The crowd pressed forward. Philippe felt himself thrust against the iron bars of the huge gates. He was in grave danger of being crushed.

But a hush fell over the crowd. They watched in apparently baffled silence as the King, his family, and their escort walked across a leaf-strewn path to the Riding School, where the National Assembly was housed.

"The King takes refuge with the Assembly!" someone shouted.

Philippe felt the stirring in the sea around him again. But the mob seemed indecisive. The King and his entourage disappeared inside the National Assembly building.

Philippe found himself torn as well. If they did not attack, Honneure would be safe. But she would also still be imprisoned. He would have no chance to save her. Pressed to the fence, he listened to the increasingly angry rumblings of the people. Then some of the nine hundred gendarmes and National Guardsmen left their posts. They unlocked the gates and drew them open. The mob was invited in.

Chaos erupted.

Philippe would never be quite sure what had happened, or why. The King and his family had left the Tuileries. There was no reason to attack. Yet, suddenly, the twelve cannon brought up by the crowd began to fire. A group of armed Parisians charged the palace, shooting at the red-uniformed Swiss.

In self-defense the grenadiers fired back. Two of the attackers fell, blood blossoming from their chests.

But the Swiss were doomed by a shortage of ammunition

and overwhelmed by vastly superior numbers. Most of them died at their posts.

Philippe had no time to register shock at the carnage taking place before his very eyes. He was being carried along with the assailants as they entered the palace. They went wild, raging all around him in a frenzy of destruction.

Chandeliers and looking-glasses were smashed. Fires were set, and smoke began to swirl through broken windows. Looters carried away plates, carpets, and bottles of wine. Terrified servants fled in panic, only to be caught and massacred in cold blood. Some were impaled on pikes, some mutilated obscenely. Using his musket as a club, Philippe fought his way through the nightmare of turmoil and bloodshed and found a staircase.

She had to be in one of the upstairs rooms. He had to find her. Panic was a live bird fluttering in his throat, making it difficult to breathe.

He made it to the top of the stairs. Others knocked into him. A tall, bald, and muscular man, bloodlust in his eye, pushed past him and kicked open the nearest door. A woman screamed and clutched a child to her. The man dispatched the little boy with a single blow, breaking his neck. As he sagged to the floor like a ragdoll, the attacker picked up the woman and carried her across the floor. With a mighty heave he threw her through the window.

Sickened, dizzy with terror, Philippe staggered down the hallway.

He had to find Honneure . . .

* * *

She had lain awake all night. Perhaps because the food lay so uneasily in her shrunken stomach. Perhaps because a spark of hope had been fanned to life in her breast and warmed her. However unwanted, the small flame burned within her, and life returned. She lay wide-awake and listened to the distant sounds of the city night.

At what she judged to be about midnight, she heard a tocsin sound. What did the alarm mean? Could there possibly be truth in Dr. Droulet's words after all?

Quiet followed. Still Honneure lay in the darkness, senses alert. She watched the bare walls of her chamber lighten with the coming of the dawn. She heard movement in the corridor.

No one came with her breakfast, however. Somewhat past the hour when it usually arrived, she sat up and swung her legs over the edge of her thin mattress.

Then she heard it.

It was like the coming of a far-off storm. There was a rumbling, as of thunder, but so faint one could not be certain of its origin or meaning. The tips of her fingers began to tingle.

Within minutes individual voices could be heard, shouts and cries. A mob approached!

Honneure rose and in two steps had reached her tiny window. But it was impossible to see anything. Just the leaves of the trees reaching up to the second story. She gripped the edge of the sill and turned her head, the better to hear.

A roar went up. Were they attacking? Would she indeed have an opportunity to escape?

The crowd fell silent again. Honneure's heart raced. What was happening?

Honneure jumped back from the window as a cannon shot roared into the silence. The storm was overhead now, and it broke, thunder rolling in deafening booms. She put her hands to her ears.

Honneure heard the shots nevertheless. And the sounds of

breaking glass. Screams. Terrible, agonized screams. The smell of smoke and gunpowder drifted to her nostrils. Panic bloomed, white hot, in her breast.

A mob was attacking the palace. The inhabitants were being massacred. They were coming, and she was locked in her room. There would be no chance of escape. Only through death.

Honneure heard the sound of wood splintering, a door being shattered. It was very close.

A terrified scream. More breaking glass.

Heavy footsteps. Someone kicking at her door. It surrendered within moments, and she stood face to face with a tall, muscle-bound man, breathing heavily. Blood stained his hands.

A strange calm overtook Honneure. This was the end. She did not even bother to back away as he approached. She looked up into his dark eyes, glazed and maddened.

"Oh, no you don't!"

Her attacker whirled, surprise etched into his crazed features. The small, thin, and graying woman gestured at him with her pike staff.

"Out of my way...this one's mine!"

It was the woman who had found her letter. The author of all her torment, all her misery. The spark of warmth fanned into a blaze. Honneure's fists clenched at her sides. She didn't even notice the tall man leave.

"So...we meet again." The older woman's eyes narrowed. "Only you're not so high and mighty this time, are you?" She raised her pike menacingly. "Thought you were better than the rest of us, didn't ye, with your *royal* blood?"

Honneure took an involuntary step backward as the woman took one forward.

"But you're nothing better than a King's bastard. Your mother was no better than a King's whore." The woman cackled and shook her weapon.

Honneure jumped and felt the wall at her back. The woman took another step toward her.

"You've run out of room now, haven't you? You've nowhere to go. You're just like the rest of them now, aren't you...*doomed*!"

The evil smile slipped suddenly from the woman's face, and her thin mouth twisted into a snarl. She tipped her pike downward, its point aimed toward Honneure's heart.

There was nowhere to run, it was true. She had come to the end. Absurdly, she recalled something Madame Dupin had said to her many years before.

"Be glad you are who you are, and are where you are...Those who flutter about Louis' throne, like moths around a flame, are doomed. Be thankful you will never know the brightness of that light which consumes all."

Honneure nearly laughed aloud. How right she had been. How horribly, prophetically correct.

Something snapped in Honneure in that moment. Perhaps it was the last struggle of the instinct within her to survive. Perhaps it was simply anger, anger at her fate, the insanity that had brought her to it. Or merely her own stubborn blindness. But she suddenly did not want to be the helpless moth, wings already on fire.

Honneure's initial assault took the older woman completely by surprise. She had not for a moment expected her cornered prisoner to grab the weapon pointed at her heart. She felt the wooden shaft slip a few inches between her fingers.

Honneure almost managed to wrest the pike from the woman's grip. Almost, but not quite. She did have her off balance, however. As the woman pulled back on the weapon, attempting to wrest it from Honneure's grip, Honneure shoved. Off balance, the woman staggered backward. It was all the advantage Honneure needed.

The tables had turned too quickly. The older woman was not quite able to comprehend the fact that there were hands around her neck, squeezing. She was finding it difficult to breathe. And she continued to stumble backward. In a moment she would lose her footing altogether. This couldn't be happening! Panicked, she took a renewed grip on her weapon and thrust it at her assailant.

The pain nearly overwhelmed her. Something stabbed at her groin, close to the top of her thigh. Honneure's chokehold momentarily loosened, and as it did the woman pushed on her weapon with a new burst of strength. Honneure felt a searing agony slide down her leg almost to her knee. The sound of material ripping came to her ears over the ragged, sobbing breath of both women.

She was weakening. And if she lost the battle, she would lose her life. She would never see Philippe again.

Philippe . . .

The woman knew she had injured her opponent, seriously. But she had not killed her. And the fingers were tightening once again. Her vision was growing dim. Her lungs threatened to burst. She dropped her pike and clutched at the hands throttling the life from her body.

Honneure heard the weapon clatter to the stone floor. But she was tired, so tired. She could barely hang on. Her knees buckled.

There was no more light, no more breath. In a final desperate attempt to save her life, the older woman let go of the hands around her neck and shoved her attacker with all her failing strength. The last thing she knew was the sensation of falling forward.

Honneure surrendered. There was nothing left in her. She was dizzy and light-headed. The room around her had become a blur. She fell beneath her assailant. The pain, and all the horror, drifted away . . .

* * *

The terrible screams had abated. All around him were the dead and dying. The massacre was coming to an end. But Philippe was more desperate than he had ever been in his life. He couldn't find her.

Where was Honneure!?

At the end of the long corridor, Philippe whirled and started back the way he had come. At each doorway he stopped and peered within. Ruined paintings, broken glass, shattered furniture, blood, and tortured, mutilated bodies. But none hers.

Where was Honneure?

He had almost made it back to the head of the stairs. There was a room on the left, one he could not remember having seen before. Philippe dashed through the doorway.

A thin, gray-haired woman lay sprawled on the floor, a broken pike beside her. A large, shimmering pool of blood spread out from beneath her. It was more than Philippe could stand finally. He could not bear to look closer. Retching, he fled from the room.

Chapter Forty

October, 1793

It was a perfect autumn morning. The air was cool but not chilly, the sunshine a balm. Honneure tipped the pitcher over the windowbox and watered the geraniums, still summer bright. As she did, she gazed out over the gabled rooftops and chimneys of the city and thought, idly, of how pretty it looked. In certain places, and from the right perspective, Paris was a beautiful place. How well it masked the sickness within!

Honneure turned from the window to the cheery room that had become her world. Leaning heavily on her cane, she limped forward to refill her pitcher. There were several more plants to be watered, and the canary had to be cleaned and fed. She moved slowly, but it didn't matter. These simple chores were all she had to do, day in and day out. She also kept the modest apartment clean and cooked for the doctor. She did everything she could to make his life easy and pleasant. But she would never be able to fully repay him.

The sound of footsteps on the wooden stair alerted Honneure, and she turned the heat up under the coffee. She limped to the door and opened it.

Dr. Droulet, his slight form bent, but still spry, entered the apartment and kissed Honneure fondly on the cheek.

"Good morning, dear girl," he said, and handed her a long, thin loaf of bread. "You were asleep when I left this morning. How are you feeling?"

"I'm just fine, and you should have awakened me." Honneure took the loaf, still warm from the oven, and laid it on the cutting board.

"For what reason? You need your rest. You're still healing."

"It's been over a year. I'm healed."

Dr. Droulet accepted the plate of buttered bread Honneure offered him. "You nearly died, Honneure. You were unconscious for almost a month. Even the very young do not recover swiftly from wounds as grievous as yours."

Honneure placed a cup of coffee in front of the doctor, and then slowly, carefully, eased herself into the chair opposite him at the table. Her right leg, stiff, stuck out awkwardly.

"I only recovered at all because of you," she said at length.

The doctor grunted. "I'm just lucky I found you."

Honneure reached across the table and patted the doctor's hand.

"No, *I'm* lucky," she whispered. Tears had thickened the sound of her voice, and she cleared her throat. She sat back and smoothed the clean, white apron over her lap. "Is there any news this morning?" Honneure inquired lightly.

Dr. Droulet looked up from under shaggy, gray brows as he sipped his coffee. He put down his cup.

"No. No news. Not yet at least."

Honneure studied her fingernails. "It can't be much longer though, can it?"

"I doubt it."

"Because it's a foregone conclusion, isn't it?"

"Oh, Honneure." Dr. Droulet sighed deeply. He rose and walked around the small table to lay his hands on Honneure's shoulders. "Yes," he admitted finally. "I'm afraid it is."

"She will follow the King to the guillotine."

Dr. Droulet did not reply. The main reason Honneure healed so slowly was her depression. He did not like her to dwell on things that only caused her pain. He didn't want her to continue to live in the past. She had to start thinking about her future. Or she would not have one.

"Honneure . . ." the doctor began.

"Tell me again," she interrupted. "You saw him. You saw him arrive in a coach. He maintained his dignity, didn't he?"

Dr. Droulet sighed again. "Yes, Honneure," he replied tiredly. "He maintained his dignity to the very end."

"And his innocence."

The doctor nodded.

"He was innocent, you know. He was never a counter-revolutionary, like they said. He only wanted to help his subjects. And they murdered him for it."

"Honneure . . ."

"They will murder the Queen, too. They can't allow her to live. This trial is only a sham."

"Honneure, stop. Stop it now." Dr. Droulet gently squeezed Honneure's shoulders. "I want you to think about yourself for a change. I want you to write a letter."

Honneure shook her head.

"Yes, Honneure," the doctor persisted. "It's time you wrote that letter. It's time you let your family know you're still alive."

Honneure shook her head more vigorously. "No."

"I have someone very trustworthy who will carry the letter to Chenonceau. No one will know. No one will connect you with Madame Dupin or your daughter. They'll be safe. They'll . . ."

"No. I can't take the chance. No letters." Honneure's

voice was brittle with fear.

Dr. Droulet returned to his chair and sat down. He reached across the table and took Honneure's hands.

"What about your husband?" he inquired softly. "Wouldn't it ease your mind to know whether or not he was safe?"

Honneure pulled her hands from the doctor's grip and folded them in her lap. "He's only safe if he stays far, far away from me," she replied tightly. "All of them, Madame Dupin, Philippe, Philippa...all of them are far better off forgetting all about me."

He would have said more, but it was evident Honneure's mind remained firm. She pushed back from the table and stiffly rose. She picked up his empty plate and carried it to the wash basin. Her rigid back remained turned to him as she attended to her chores.

The doctor did not bother her again. There would be sorrow and devastation enough to come in the next few days.

* * *

The Revolutionary Tribunal had finished with their questions. Thin and gaunt, hair now completely white, Antoinette rose unsteadily to her feet. Leaving the courtroom, she leaned on the arm of her counsel, Chauveau-Lagarde. She was exhausted and soul-weary. But she held her head erect as she walked down the aisle between rows of spectators. The faintest of smiles touched her lips.

During the worst moment of the trial, when she was accused of having committed unnatural acts with her son, seven year-old Louis Charles, she did not respond. When asked why she did not reply, she had risen from her chair, emotion at last overcoming her. Antoinette recalled her words perfectly, "If I have not answered, it was because Nature refuses to answer such a charge against a mother." Then she had turned to the spectators and appealed to all the mothers in the room.

A murmur of sympathy had run through the crowd. There had even been a few shouts of approval. The courtroom had to be called to order. Living in a nightmare that would not end, it was one tiny spark of light. Antoinette clung to it.

Chauveau-Lagarde led his client to a small room where they would await the verdict. He helped Antoinette into a seat, and she smiled at him gratefully.

"You have been very kind to me, my friend," she said quietly. "I hope you know how deeply I appreciate it."

The young man flushed. "I do know," he replied modestly. "I only wish I was able to do more."

"What more could you do? Their minds are already made up."

Chauveau-Lagarde averted his eyes. There was no denying it. Having no evidence, they had twisted the truth beyond all recognition. Even their questions to the former Queen contained lies. There was no way she could acquit herself.

"Do you know one of the more remarkable features of this trial?" Antoinette continued. "Almost every charge originated, years before, in the slander and calumny of Versailles. Our beloved Versailles . . ."

Antoinette's gaze seemed very far away. She drew a deep breath.

"We were so happy then. We didn't think anything could hurt us, not really. Not until the affair with the necklace." Antoinette smiled ruefully. "That was the beginning of the end, you know. I knew it even then."

"Madame . . ."

"What I did not know, " she went on as if she had not heard her counsel, "was how even the Trianon would be turned against me. I had it built for dear Louis, you know. He was so busy, so devoted to governing his subjects and attending to business, he had no time for entertainment. So I brought the entertainment to him. Now I am accused of gross overspending and profligacy." Antoinette uttered a short laugh.

"They accused me of influencing my husband," she went on. "They said I made use of his weak character to carry out many evil deeds. But I told them, didn't I, monsieur? I told them I knew no one of such character as they described."

Chauveau-Lagarde ducked his head to hide his sudden emotion. He had never known anyone so noble, kind, or gracious. He had not meant to love her, but he did. There would never be another like her.

A knock at the door brought both occupants of the small room to attention. But Chauveau-Lagarde hesitated.

"Go ahead, dear friend, answer it," Antoinette urged. "My fate was sealed long ago. Let us hear their condemnation and be done with it.

* * *

Honneure opened her eyes slowly, unsure what had awakened her. The gentle knocking was repeated. She pushed herself up on her elbows, surprised to see the sun so bright already. She had slept late again.

"Yes?" she called.

"Honneure, it's Dr. Droulet. I must speak with you."

"Of course! Come in."

The doctor entered the room and sat on the edge of the bed. "I went out to get the bread this morning," he began.

"And you heard," Honneure finished.

He nodded. "Even now the crowd is gathering to watch the execution."

There was silence for a long moment. Honneure closed her eyes.

So. The end had come at last. It had only been a matter of time. Painfully, Honneure swung her legs over the edge of the bed.

"I'm sorry," Dr. Droulet said softly.

Honneure merely nodded. She couldn't speak.

"I'll leave you to get dressed."

When the door had closed, Honneure pulled the nightdress over her head. She put on clean underlinens and took her best dress from the tiny wardrobe. She washed and carefully arranged her hair. For the first time in many months, she looked at her reflection in the sliver of mirror hanging over her dresser. Satisfied, she left the room.

"Honneure, you look lovely!" Dr. Droulet exclaimed.

"Thank you."

Though the weather was again warm, Honneure took her cloak down from its hook by the door. She threw it over her shoulders and pulled up the hood.

"Honneure!" The doctor stood up as rapidly as he was able. "Where are you going? What are you doing?"

Honneure turned and looked the doctor straight in the eye.

"I think you know," she replied evenly. "I'm going to be with her. She must not be alone at the end."

"Honneure, this is madness! What if you're recognized? They are still looking for you. And you were imprisoned for so long that many know you. And they'll be there, Honneure, mark me. They will be there to gloat. You *can't* go!"

"I have to."

Dr. Droulet crossed the room and grabbed Honneure's arm as she opened the door.

"Honneure! Listen to me. Your service to the Queen is ended...your duty is over!"

A sad smile curved on Honneure's lips. "You are correct," she replied softly. "My duty is indeed over. That is not why I'm going. I have to be there because of love. I love her. I will be with her at the end. I want her to know that she does not die alone."

"Honneure . . ."

"No." She shook her head. "I'm going, you cannot stop me. This is the last thing I will ever do for her. Possibly the last thing I will ever do for myself. But do it I must. For too long, almost all of my life, I put duty first. I did not realize until too late that it's only love that matters. My stubborn refusal to understand that cost me everything I hold dear. Today, no matter what the cost, I must put that right. For *me*."

There was no answer he could give. Miraculously, he had saved her life. Though she had almost bled to death, he had saved her. He had thought the meaning in the miracle was that she might one day be reunited with her family.

But it would be arrogance to try and judge God's purpose. Perhaps he had only saved her so that she might be reunited with her own soul.

"Go with God, dear child," he said at last, and kissed Honneure's brow.

"Thank you," she whispered. "Thank you for everything. If we never meet again, know how I have treasured our friendship."

Leaning on her cane, Honneure left without another word.

* * *

The chamber in which Antoinette had been imprisoned at the end was so small she barely had room to turn around. There were three beds, one for her, one for her attendant, and one for her ever-present guard. She was not even left alone to attend to personal needs and had only a small screen for privacy. She stood behind it now and put on her white piqué dress.

Her last letters, to Fersen, Gabrielle de Polignac, and her sister-in-law, Elisabeth, had been taken by a kindly guard to be posted. She felt better. She wanted them to know that being separated from them and their troubles was one of her greatest regrets in dying.

Antoinette stepped out from behind the screen and turned her back to the attendant so she could fasten the long row of buttons. She winced when the woman accidentally pinched her.

"Oh, I'm sorry, Madame! Did I hurt you?"

"Nothing can hurt me anymore," Antoinette replied calmly. "Nothing, no pain, has been able to touch me since they took me away from my children."

It was not strictly true, however. The memory of it still caused an agonizing pain in her heart. She tried to block the nightmare recollection, but it always returned to her. The knock on the door in the middle of the night. Her son ripped from her arms, screaming . . .

Antoinette shook her head and slipped into her plum-colored high-heeled shoes. At least, in death, the memory could no longer return to torment her.

The attendant handed Antoinette a cup of chocolate, sent for from a nearby cafe, and the former Queen sipped it daintily. Then she set down the cup and put on her white bonnet. She pulled a muslin shawl tightly about her shoulders. At eleven, a tall man entered her cell.

His name was Henri Sanson. His father had executed Louis.

Obligingly, Antoinette put her hands behind her back, and he tied them. With a large pair of scissors he cut her hair, pocketing the tresses in order to burn them later.

Antoinette was led out of her cell.

* * *

It was close to noon when Honneure approached the big town square. It was thronged with people, and she pushed her way the best she could nearer the platform on which the guillotine was mounted. Though the day was warm, she kept the cloak wrapped about her shoulders and pinched the hood closed at her chin. She had already recognized two or three people who had been at the Tuileries during her imprisonment.

Fear rose in her throat, but she pushed it back down. This was no time to think of herself. She remembered instead something the Queen had written to her long ago.

This was the very square where Antoinette had come as a young bride. She had been cheered by the crowd. Men had thrown their hats in the air, and a friend had whispered to her that two hundred thousand people had fallen in love with her.

Now the same people clamored for her death. Honneure shuddered.

A creaking attracted her attention, and she turned. She watched the crowd pull away from something that approached.

It was a tumbril, an open, straw-filled cart. Louis had been driven to his execution in a coach. Yet Antoinette was not only to be murdered, but also totally humiliated first.

Unbeknownst to Honneure, tears streamed down her face. She sat facing backward, hands tied behind her. Her posture was rigid, chin held high. The cart rumbled to a halt.

The former Queen had to be helped from the tumbril. Honneure noticed her pretty plum shoes as she slowly climbed the ladder to the scaffold. Her white piqué dress and bonnet were immaculate.

How like her. How very like her. A sob caught in Honneure's throat.

Though she remained erect, Antoinette began to tremble at last. The executioner seized her roughly and forced her to her knees. He tied her to the plank. The guillotine towered above her, blade glinting in the sun.

"You're not alone," Honneure whispered. It felt as if her heart had, literally, broken.

"Antoinette, dearest friend, you're not alone," she said a little louder. Heads turned in her direction, but she paid them no heed. Pressing closer still to the scaffold, she slipped the hood from her head.

For one brief moment, Antoinette raised her eyes.

There was recognition. Sadness. And grateful love.

"My Queen!" The tortured cry rasped from Honneure's throat. She stretched out her hand, cane clattering to the ground.

The blade fell.

* * *

The white mare danced, prancing sideways with nervousness as her rider guided her through the crowded streets. People were streaming in the direction of the square. They seemed barely to notice horse and rider.

Snow Queen reared slightly as someone bumped into her shoulder. Philippe steadied her with a hand on her neck. But she remained skittish, and he couldn't blame her. He was full of dread and apprehension himself.

For over a year there had been no word of Honneure. He clung to a fragile thread of hope only because her body had never been found after the massacre at the Tuileries.

Had she escaped?

If she had, why hadn't he heard from her?

He knew. Even as he asked himself the question for the thousandth time, he knew.

She would not want to further endanger him. Or their daughter. She was still being sought, and she was in hiding. To protect her family, she had foregone contact with them.

This had become Philippe's prayer. It was all that had kept him going. It was why he left Chenonceau and returned to Paris again and again. To look for her.

Because she couldn't be dead. She couldn't be. Or he was dead as well.

He had almost reached the square. It was where she would come if she was still alive. He was sure of it. She would never let her Queen die alone.

* * *

A great and mighty cheer went up as the Queen's head rolled. The crowd surged forward. All except a few who surrounded Honneure. They had noticed her when she cried out. Now they stared at her.

Though choking on her tears, Honneure quickly pulled her hood up. It was too late.

"It's that woman, from the Tuileries!" a pock-marked woman cried. "It's her!"

"Who? Who is it?" someone asked. A small crowd within the crowd had formed.

Honneure tried to back away, but a hand grasped her skirt.

"The bastard whore!" the scarred woman exclaimed. "The old King's bastard spawn!"

Honneure screamed as another pair of hands tore at her, ripping her bodice.

"No!"

"Get her! Don't let her get away!"

Searing pain shot through Honneure's head as someone pulled her hair. She saw a great handful of it come away.

"Leave me alone!"

Hands dragged at her, pulling her down. She was losing her footing. A fist connected with her nose, and blood splashed.

"No!"

* * *

Snow Queen squealed in terror as a roar went up from the crowd. She tried to whirl and flee, but Philippe held her firmly. He could not give up and turn away. This was his last, and best, hope to find Honneure.

But there were thousands. Thousands. And even though the Queen's head had rolled, they were still filled with blood lust. They were even turning on one another.

Philippe watched, horrified, as the mob surrounded some helpless woman and began to tear her apart. He tried to guide the mare in another direction, and then heard Snow Queen's peculiar little snort and whinny. The one she used whenever she recognized the person she loved most in the world.

"Honneure!"

* * *

She heard him, heard his voice. Philippe! He was calling her!

But she couldn't go to him. They were pulling at her, pummeling her. Blood obscured her vision, blinded her. Pain ripped through her again and again as they pounded her body. She was sinking into the murderous sea, drowning, and she could not get to him.

"Philippe!" Honneure cried as the darkness closed in. No longer able to protect herself from the blows raining on her head, she stretched out her hands in a final supplication.

It was all the advantage Philippe needed.

Snow Queen obeyed at once when her rider jabbed his heels into her sides. She jumped forward, knocking bodies aside, and broke into a gallop. Philippe leaned from the saddle and grasped Honneure's outstretched arms. He pulled her from her feet and onto the saddle in front of him. When he felt her limp body revive and cling to him, he kicked his mare again, and she plunged through the crowd.

Screams rose around them. People fell beneath the flying hooves. Philippe did not care. One arm about his wife, he urged the mare to greater and greater speeds. Within minutes they had cleared the mob and entered a nearly deserted boulevard. Ears flattened to her head, Snow Queen stretched out and ran as if the devil himself pursued her.

Honneure did not open her eyes. She was in a dream.

She was with Philippe once more. He held her in his arms. All her pain went away. All her sorrow and heartache. And if she opened her eyes, the dream would end. She could not bear it.

Greathearted, the mare ran on until they reached the outskirts of the city. Philippe did not pull her to a halt until he was absolutely certain they had not been followed. Then he tugged on the reins, and she stumbled, exhausted, to a walk. At last, trembling, she stopped.

"Honneure? Honneure, my love, open your eyes." Gently, Philippe wiped the blood from her face. "Honneure? You're safe, my darling."

She opened her eyes slowly.

He was there, her beloved. He held her in his arms. It was not a dream.

"Philippe? How did you... how..."

"Sssshhhh." He pressed a finger to her lips. "Don't talk." Tenderly, he kissed her.

"I came because I knew you would go to her if you were able," he said in reply to her unspoken question. "I knew you would go to her out of love, and for your honor. And it is exactly the same for me. I, too, came here...for love of Honneure."

She tried to smile, but it hurt too much. Nevertheless, Philippe knew. He smiled back.

"Hold on to me," he said. "Just hold tight. I'm taking you home."

Honneure laid her head against her husband's chest as he urged Snow Queen into a slow, gentle jog. Her bruised arms crept about his waist.

She was already home.

EPILOGUE

Axel de Fersen lived to become an important political figure in Sweden. Rumored to have been in love with Marie Antionette, he never married but lived quietly with his sister. In 1810, the heir to the Swedish throne suffered a seizure, fell from his horse and died. Political enemies of Fersen accused him of having poisoned the popular prince and, while attending his funeral; Fersen was pulled from his carriage by a mob. He was stoned and beaten to death.

Princess Marie Therese Lamballe was incarcerated in the La Force prison. Shortly before her King went to the guillotine, she was dragged from her cell, raped and beheaded. Her head was impaled on a spike and paraded before the prison where the King and Queen were held.

Gabrielle de Polignac contracted a sudden illness in December, 1793, and within twelve hours was dead.

Madame du Barry followed Marie Antionette to the guillotine.

In 1815 Louis' clever brother Mosieur, Comte de Provence, became King Louis the XVIII on the basis of the principles his older brother had proclaimed. His reign is generally accounted as success.

Louis' youngest brother, Comte d'Artois, followed Mosieur and reigned as Charles X until 1830.

Aunt Adelaide and Aunt Victoire lived to a ripe age in Italy.

The King's youngest sister, Elisabeth, remained in prison following her brother's execution. In May, 1794, she was indicted before the Revolutionary Tribunal and, without witnesses or documentation, was found guilty on several counts of treason. Her headless, naked body was flung into a grave at Monceaux along with twenty-four others. Her clothes had been removed because they were considered a perquisite of the state.

Marie Therese Charlotte remained in prison throughout the Terror. In December, 1795, she was driven to the frontier and exchanged for a prisoner of the Austrians. She eventually married the eldest son of the Comte d'Artois and returned to live in the Tuileries.

Louis Charles, now Louis XVII, eight when his mother was executed, was locked in solitary confinement. For six months his food was pushed under the door. His window was never opened, and his clothing and bed-linens were never changed.

By Honor Bound

His excrement was never removed. No one spoke to him. Suffering from the family's hereditary disease, tuberculosis of the bones, he developed a painful disease and his wrists, elbows and knees swelled. His legs and arms grew disproportionately long and his shoulders rounded. He died in prison on June 8, 1795, and was buried, without prayers, in a common grave in the cemetery of Sainte-Marguerite.

Madame Dupin saved both herself and her beloved Chenonceau by opening her home to 'the people'. The chateau's chapel became a store from which wood was sold.

The Reign of Terror came to an end on July 28, 1794, when Robespierre was finally executed. More than three thousand heads had been lost.

Following the royal family's departure from Versailles, it was never lived in again.